MERRIED

PIPPA GRANT WRITING AS
JAMIE FARRELL

Cover Illustration by Julie Bonart of Qamber Designs
Cover layout & typography by Qamber Designs
Copy Editing by Pauline Nolet
Proofreading by Jessica Snyder

1

Phoebe Moon would never be a normal girl, but sometimes she wished she had a normal uncle.

—Phoebe Moon and the Sneeze Snatcher

While everyone else at the Snow Bride Festival in Bliss, Illinois, watched Santa and Mrs. Claus step onto the stage beneath the massive wedding cake monument, Merry Silver was contemplating theft.

The internet, she decided.

In her next middle-grade novel, Phoebe Moon's diabolical Uncle Sandy would try to steal the internet, which would be housed in a five-story-high wedding cake monument.

No, too obvious. Maybe…a gingerbread house? Yes! A gingerbread house, and—

"Earth to Meredith." Victoria Silver, also known as Mom, tugged on a lock of her hair.

Merry instinctively checked her front pocket beneath her dark blue bubble coat. Phone, ID, and cash were still there. She knew better than to zone out in public places. "Sorry, what?"

Fairy lights twinkled on the bare trees around the illuminated wedding cake monument. Flurries danced through the darkness as though they'd been ordered specially for Bliss's Snow Bride Festival. Patrick Dean, Mom's next victim—er, latest fiancé—winked at her and lifted his paper cup higher, which he'd apparently been dangling for a while. "More hot chocolate for my favorite girls?"

Merry handed her own paper cup to impending stepfather number six. "I'd love some. Thank you, Patrick."

While Patrick trotted off, Mom graced her with an indulgent smile that was thankfully unsuspicious. "Dreaming of your own wedding cake?"

"Wondering if there's a medical billing code for treatment for injuries sustained after becoming trapped beneath the world's largest eyesore." Merry shifted her weight to her left foot, the lie coming easily.

"Hide it all you want, darling. I know you're a romantic at heart."

She humored her mother with a smile, then scanned the crowd around them, subconsciously cataloguing earrings, scarves, and purses. She didn't see Daddy.

Not that she expected him to let her spot him easily. If he were here. He'd only shown up for one of Mom's other weddings—not that Mom had known he was there—but she had a feeling.

A suspicious, tingly, Daddy-had-been-too-quiet-for-too-long feeling.

Especially since she knew there was something else he wanted in Bliss.

Speaking of Daddy and things he wanted, she eyed Mrs. Claus onstage. The blonde woman smiled indulgently and passed a treat to a kid in the crowd, her tiara glittering atop her hair.

Merry sincerely hoped those sparklies in the tiara were rhinestones.

"What's with the skunk?" she asked. The black-and-white creature —large and stuffed, thank goodness—sat behind Santa's magnanimous red velvet throne, its dead, beady eyes trained on the crowd. Oh,

Phoebe Moon's dastardly Uncle Sandy could be training a skunk to help steal the internet. She'd name it—

"Merry." Mom sighed. "It represents the kindly old skunk that showed Felix Blythe the way to Bliss back in 1841 when he founded the town, and then blessed his marriage to his mail-order bride. You haven't been listening at all, have you?"

And reviewers said Phoebe Moon's adventures could never happen in real life. Obviously, they'd never heard of Bliss. Merry fluttered a hand toward the monument. "Sorry. It's distracting."

"I can only imagine the number of calories in a cake that size." Mom shuddered. She'd kept her girlish figure, which she usually showed off with waist-high skinny jeans, heeled boots, fitted silk blouses, and an ivory peacoat. Her once strawberry-blond hair was now intentionally dyed silver and stylishly trimmed. Anything else nature had taken, her ex-husbands' bank accounts had paid to give back.

"Pretty sure concrete calories aren't absorbed well by the human body," Merry said.

Mom sighed again, but then she clapped with all the glee of someone fifty years younger. "I'm so glad we got here in time to see the end of the Snow Bride Festival. I can't wait to see the wedding reenactment. Weddings are fabulous, aren't they?"

Hmm. Phoebe Moon hadn't investigated any reprehensible crimes at a wedding.

She filed that away to consider later. "Amazing," she agreed.

"You should have one someday."

"Um, no."

"Oh, honey, don't grimace. It'll give you wrinkles."

Wrinkles were the least of her worries.

With parents like hers, she was more concerned with ulcers, anxiety, and accidents.

"You can't fool me." Mom's perfectly plump lips spread in a grin, but thanks to Botox, none of the rest of her face smiled. "I know there's a romantic heart in there. Who was it I caught daydreaming over wedding flowers this afternoon?"

"I wasn't daydreaming. I was marveling at the complexities of flower production during the darkest part of the year."

"And swaying to those romantic songs the wedding planner played for us?"

"Must've been my evil twin." Phoebe Moon had an evil twin, but Merry had sometimes thought she might need a morally ambiguous secret triplet too.

Or maybe that would be better for a conversation with a therapist rather than a plot thread to spring on the unsuspecting, mystery-loving tween population of the world.

Not that it would take a therapist to figure out what was wrong with her.

"Can't find a husband if you don't date, sweetheart," Mom said.

"Dating is an activity that typically requires a person to stay in one place for an extended period of time."

Mom's eye twitched. "The right man would move with you for any reason. In the meantime, that's what the internet and all those smart phone appetizers are for."

"Applications, Mom. *Apps* stands for *applications*."

"Regardless, as my only child, it's your duty to give me grandchildren. A woman shouldn't have more ex-husbands than grandbabies. It's not natural."

"Then quit getting remarried."

"Meredith Cordelia Silver, hush your tongue."

Merry burrowed her hands into her jacket pockets. She could feel her phone in her jeans. Overall, Bliss seemed to be a proverbial safe Midwestern town, but she knew firsthand that nowhere was safe.

Daddy had taught her that well. Daddy and karma.

A presence at her back made her jump.

Patrick the winker winked a slow wink that made his right cheek wrinklier than his left. "More hot chocolate for my favorite ladies."

As far as husbands and prospective husbands went, Mom had

done worse. Patrick was in respectable shape for a man in his sixties. His gray hair was thinning, but he didn't drink or smoke to excess. He'd made a fortune by patenting a special type of shoe leather used in military boots, and as such, his shoes always matched. Which couldn't be said for all of Mom's ex-husbands. The rich part, yes. The matching part, no.

"Thank you, Patrick," Merry said.

Mom took her hot chocolate and planted a smacker on his lips.

If Phoebe Moon had had to watch her poor mother kiss a man on the lips, she might have considered suggesting occasionally-heroic-in-his-own-way Uncle Sandy break said man's kneecaps.

But lucky for Phoebe Moon, she was an orphan.

A rumble grew in the crowd.

Merry did a quick sweep, checking her surroundings, subconsciously registering hiding spots, easy marks, and shadows before she let her attention turn to the stage.

"But what do we have here?" Santa said. "Oh, ho, ho, ho! It appears my elf has found a naughty boy."

A massive elf in red-and-white-striped tights, jingle-bell elf shoes, a green tunic, and a floppy elf hat—complete with fake ears—dragged a handsome, well-dressed blond man onto the stage.

But it wasn't the man in black slacks and a wool coat that made Merry's heart twist and her breath flee her lungs in a puff of white mist.

It was the elf.

The thick dark hair beneath his crooked felt hat.

His muscled legs.

His shoulders, broader than Santa's.

Memories swirled thicker than the snowflakes. His hands on her body. His laugh. His sleepy bedroom eyes.

Her favorite memories.

Experiences she'd never have again with a man she never should've dated.

"Someone's been very naughty, Santa," Max Gregory said.

He wasn't hooked into the microphone system, but his voice carried through the night anyway, a resonant sound that sent a jolt through her belly.

She wanted to bottle the sound. To take it with her when she left Bliss for the last time. When she left the country.

When she left behind being Merry Silver.

The crowd laughed, some clapping, some whistling, while a chant slowly grew. "Marry her! Marry her!"

Max grinned, and Merry's heart suddenly felt as though someone had stabbed it with the sharp end of a half-eaten candy cane.

He looked happy.

As he should be.

Was he dating someone? Had he moved on?

Did he hate her?

He had every right.

He delivered his captive to Santa, then stepped aside, blending into the background. A commotion broke out near the stage, and suddenly two older couples and a handful of people around Merry's age joined Santa.

"Ho, ho, ho, ladies and gents," Santa said. "It appears we're parting with tradition this year, and instead of reenacting Felix and Annie Blythe's wedding, we'll be marrying off one of our favorite Bliss daughters."

The cheers were near-deafening. She was jostled from behind and pushed into her mom. She instinctively checked her phone, ID, and cash again, and swept a glance about for any unsavory-looking characters.

Not that unsavory characters ever looked the part. Rule number seven in Phoebe Moon's handbook: You can't detect an evil overlord by his beard alone.

"Oh, Merry, look." Mom pointed behind them.

The crowd parted for a horse-drawn carriage carrying a curly-haired, wide-smiling, visibly pregnant bride. Her white gown draped around her, with a faux-fur shawl on her shoulders and her veil floating behind her. The white steeds pranced up the walk while cameras and camera phones flashed.

"I didn't know you could get married at the Snow Bride Festival," Mom said.

"Most people can't," a nearby woman with pearl drop earrings said, "but Kimmie—that's the bride—she's Felix and Annie's great-great-great-great-great-granddaughter." Pearl Earrings beamed as though Kimmie were her sister or best friend. "Kimmie could've said she wanted to get married while bungee jumping off the wedding cake monument, and there wouldn't have been a soul in Bliss who would've told her no."

"Even her fiancé?" Patrick asked.

"Especially him. He's been begging her to get married for months."

On the stage, the debonair groom helped his bride from the carriage, his smile so broad and uninhibited, Merry's chest ached. And when the groom pulled her in for a pre-wedding kiss, Merry had to physically look away.

She'd been to every one of her mother's weddings. But there was something different—something potent and intimate and real—about this couple.

Something too close to a fairy tale.

And those, Merry knew, weren't real.

She huddled closer into herself and stole another glance at Max.

He was still smiling at the bride and groom.

Odds were good he'd never smile at Merry again.

What were the odds she could avoid him the entire week?

It had been inevitable that Mom would eventually have a wedding in Bliss. But this was exceptionally poor timing.

She forced herself to sip her hot chocolate and act normal. Santa chastised the groom for kissing before marriage. The crowd laughed, everyone jostling closer to the stage, tighter around Merry, pushing her and Mom and Patrick closer to the stage too.

A gust of wind nipped at Merry's cheeks, and the swirl of snowflakes thickened.

So did the knot growing in her throat.

"Patrick, did you notice the lines at the port-a-johns?"

"Now?" Mom's lips turned down, but thanks to Botox, her frown didn't reach the rest of her face. "Honey, you'll miss the wedding."

Merry kissed her smooth cheek. "But I won't miss yours, and that's the important one."

Mom studied her while Santa thanked all the dearly beloved for being gathered here today.

"How often do you get a short line at the ladies' room?" Merry said.

"I suppose that's better than you standing here worrying over pickpockets and jewel thieves," Mom murmured.

Busted. Only partially, thank goodness. "For the record," Merry said, "I didn't say a word about you bringing your purse."

Mom shook her head. "Text me if you head back to the B&B."

"I will."

Merry slipped through the crowd, noting pearls here, opals there, sapphires and diamonds and rubies. Bliss's hometown feel, along with their focus on the joy of bridal events and weddings, gave a false sense of security. There was a police presence, but it was minimal. The private security guard near the edge of the crowd gave her pause until she remembered Mom mentioning some country music superstar having a second home here.

Had Merry been raised by anyone other than Nicholas Raymond, she probably wouldn't have noticed the guard.

Or the jewelry.

Or the nearest escape routes, the easiest-looking mark, or the fact that her mother was not, in fact, in love with her fiancé.

Mom stole hearts.

Daddy stole jewels.

But not tonight. And not here. Not on Merry's watch.

She had just gotten to the street when gasps and shrieks erupted behind her. The private security guard took two steps toward the stage, then stopped, everything about him alert, his attention on the stage. Merry twisted around, panic and purpose colliding in her veins.

"It's an owl!" someone shrieked.

"Mrs. Claus! Is she okay?"

"It got her tiara! That owl stole her tiara!"

Santa grabbed Mrs. Claus and hovered over her while he stared at the sky. Max was suddenly at center stage too, chest broader, his whole body large and intimidating, even in his elf costume. Merry suppressed a shiver. Could any other man pull off that sexy, confident warrior look while in elf tights?

She doubted it. Not like Max could.

He turned a slow circle, scowling at the sky as though he could use sheer willpower to find the beast. The groom was pulling his weeping —no, *laughing* bride off the stage, the wedding party on their heels.

Merry squinted at the bride.

She was.

She was laughing so hard her face glowed. The groom wore a rueful smile, and when the two of them looked at each other—

No. No, Merry didn't have time to contemplate fairy tales.

Because—an *owl*?

"*Dammit*, Daddy," she muttered.

She had to hand it to him.

As far as distractions went, this one was fan-freaking-tabulous. Brilliant.

Something devious Uncle Sandy would do.

Ensuring the safety of the Mrs. Claus diamond engagement ring had been peripherally on Merry's radar when Mom had announced she and Patrick were eloping to Bliss, but now it was front and center. She ducked her head and started toward The Aisle, Bliss's main downtown street, which was lined with bridal shops. The town boasted being the Most Married-est Place on Earth along with being the bridal capital of the Midwest. The shop district left no doubt that the second reputation was well-earned.

She couldn't run without drawing attention to herself. More

shrieks and gasps echoed through the night behind her. Ahead of her, the scattered groups browsing the lighted window displays along The Aisle had all turned their attention to the monument.

Merry cut down a side street and slipped into the darkness. In Phoebe Moon's latest book—released just days ago—she stopped villainous Uncle Sandy from stealing all the sunlight in the world. Merry had struggled with writing the story, because she liked the darkness.

It was an easy place to hide.

She turned and dashed down the alleyway that ran behind With This Ring, Max's family's jewelry store.

She'd dated him for a month before she found out he was from a long line of jewelers. And then he'd dropped the double bomb of not being from just any family of jewelers, but from the family of jewelers who had created the infamous Mrs. Claus diamond.

The engagement ring was relatively new in the world of famous gemstones. Designed to look like a snowflake, it had been commissioned by horror novelist Spencer McGraw in honor of the success of his book about Santa Claus's cursed family diamond that kept killing every Mrs. Claus he chose.

Two weeks after Mr. McGraw had presented the ring to his fiancée, a tragic accident had taken her life, and the ring had been sent back to Bliss for permanent display. Merry had been in her early teens the first time she heard Daddy mention it in passing.

Daddy talked about a lot of famous jewels. Didn't mean he planned to steal them all.

But right now, she knew Daddy had his sights set on the Mrs. Claus diamond ring.

If she'd never dated Max, the ring probably never would've been in danger.

Her steps slowed.

So did her breathing. She studied the darkness, watching for a shadow to shift, listening for a rock to rattle, sniffing for any subtle scent of sin.

Daddy didn't often share his plans with her, but after he'd pulled her into a bungled job in Chicago last year, she'd had to disappear.

It wasn't the first time, but it would be the last. Because last year, she'd left behind a life she'd liked. For the first time in over a decade, she'd been comfortable. Secure. She'd had friends. She'd had a boyfriend.

And because Daddy wouldn't change, she'd had to leave it all behind.

But she could change. So she'd made plans. And in the course of executing her plans two weeks ago, she'd stumbled onto a fake Mrs. Claus diamond in one of her storage units.

Daddy only replicated famous jewels he planned to steal.

He routinely did smaller snatch-and-dash jobs, but those were all done in the name of justice. Of righting wrongs. Of playing Robin Hood.

But the Mrs. Claus diamond?

This one had *personal* and *big score* written all over it.

Merry stood motionless in the alley. Snowflakes drifted lazily in the still air. Santa's voice whispered in the distance, just a tone, no distinct words.

No headlights or flashlights cut the inky darkness.

No one was fiddling with the lock at the back of With This Ring.

She cast a glance at the roof, then studied the buildings on either side. With This Ring shared one wall with As You Wish, the bridal planners Mom had hired to orchestrate her quick wedding, and the other wall with Indulge, Bliss's gourmet chocolate shop. A public parking lot stretched from The Aisle to the street behind it on the other side of Indulge, which was the first place Patrick had insisted on taking Mom this morning.

Mom.

Mom and Patrick were back in the commotion at the festival. Merry whipped out her phone and double-checked her cash and ID. No messages from her mother, so she sent a quick text. *You okay?*

And that was when she smelled it.

Brut.

Her father's favorite cologne.

The hairs on her arms prickled, and her back twitched as though someone had poured diamond dust down her coat. She turned in a slow circle, alert for any change. Atmosphere, scent, temperature, noise, anything. The parking lot was six feet behind her.

"If you love me at all," she said into the stillness, "you will leave. Now. You don't need this score. Go find another mark."

Her scalp tingled and her pulse surged. The scent lingered, but nothing moved. Not a shadow. Even the snowflakes had stopped.

Her phone buzzed. She turned in a slow circle again, watching, waiting. A car engine whined nearby—somewhere within a block, not on The Aisle, but the street behind it—then faded.

"I mean it," Merry whispered. If Phoebe Moon ever got old enough for a phone, she was getting a flip phone. Damn smart phones didn't work for speed dial when silence and alertness were necessary. "Go. Away."

A jingling step approached from the side of the building across the alley. She spun toward the parking lot.

She hadn't seen Daddy in almost a year. And while she'd definitely hug him and hit him, she didn't know which she'd do first.

Maybe she'd yank his ear *while* she was hugging him and see if that would make him listen.

But when the owner of the footsteps came into view, he wasn't Daddy.

Nope.

Not even close.

He was much, much worse.

2

This boy was the kind of boy Sister Mary Elvira at the orphanage had warned Phoebe Moon about. Tall, dark-eyed, and old enough to drive.

He was also Phoebe Moon's last hope.

—Phoebe Moon and the Missing Sunshine

Max Gregory was used to being a man of many hats, though he was looking forward to once again being a man who wore pants. With only a layer of cotton between the winter air and his manhood, he was in danger of freezing his nuts off.

He snagged the tiara off the passenger seat of his sister-in-law's car. The piece was bent and missing several gems, but the crazy-ass, wedding-crashing owl had dropped it back on the stage on its second pass to dive-bomb the festival. Max had rescued the old costume jewelry before the owl could snag it again.

The gems might be fake, but Gramps had designed the tiara for Gran to match the Mrs. Claus diamond engagement ring that had made With This Ring famous. It deserved a place of honor in the store.

Especially now that Gramps and Gran were both gone.

Keys and tiara in hand, Max turned the corner to the rear of the building and stopped dead in his tracks.

Merry Silver—if that was really her name—had her arms crossed over her dark puffy coat, one hip cocked, and a glower that suggested she'd be happy to use her boot to crush his frozen balls to bits.

His heart twisted, adding a kick to the sudden hollow ache in his chest. He tightened his grip on the tiara and mimicked Merry's stance.

Of the two of them, he had more reason for doing the glowering. But instead of lighting up with righteous outrage or fear for his family's jewels, his bones sagged with a relief he didn't want to acknowledge.

Merry's eyes flared wide for a fraction of a second before her glower and her arms dropped.

Had she been expecting someone else?

She had a smart phone in one gloved hand and her other hand balled into a fist.

"What have we here?" Max said softly.

The desire to check the door to his family's jewelry shop warred with an instinct not to take his eyes off her for a microsecond. Not even to blink.

"My mom's getting married," Merry said. "She needs a ring."

"Most people would go to the front door. In the daytime."

Her head cocked, and the ruddy knit hat hiding her ebony hair tilted. She took another step closer to his family's store. "I'm sure most people would."

Max angled toward her and caught a hint of spring flowers. Soft, fragile, feminine. She hadn't changed her shampoo since he'd last known her.

She shifted closer to With This Ring.

Her cheekbones were sharper, her nose more delicate, her body more clothed than when he'd seen her last.

And unlike those two months he'd known her—when, he'd discovered after hours of research into her father, he hadn't actually known her at all—she apparently didn't feel the need to pussyfoot around what she wanted now.

Had she been anyone else, he would've pinned her down while calling the cops.

But Max didn't trust himself to touch her. Because too big a part of him was drinking in the sight of her whole, alive, and seemingly unharmed.

He twisted to follow her, circling instead of stopping her. "Most women want to pick their own wedding ring."

"When you've had seven or eight, the details matter less."

Seven or—*Jesus*. He hadn't looked into her mother.

If she even had one. "She kill the first six or seven?" Max asked.

Her straight dark eyebrows lowered, and he had the distinct impression they'd just put him in his place before she ever opened her mouth. "Only two. And not in any ways punishable by law."

Hot adrenaline surged through his veins, and the heady taste of a challenge sharpened his senses. "Where's your mother now?"

"Gown shopping."

Hell.

Max gripped the tiara tighter. There were three gown shops on The Aisle, and two more within walking distance of downtown.

All owned by his friends and the families of his friends.

"One more thing most people do in the daylight." He reached for his phone, then realized his mistake.

Merry had circled him just right to put herself close enough to the parking lot to make a run for it.

Max lunged. "Stop!" He caught her wrist, but before he could blink, he was flying, flipping upside down, through the air. He landed on his back with a thud, his arm twisted so tight he couldn't move, the air so effectively knocked out of his lungs he momentarily couldn't remember how to inhale.

Merry leaned over him. "Nice tights."

She dropped Gran's tiara on his chest. Max tried to grunt out a coherent response, but she was gone.

ADRENALINE HAD CRAMPED Merry's stomach, and her pulse was still racing fast enough to outpace one of Daddy's getaway cars four minutes later when she stepped into the ornate country club where the festival had been relocated.

Phoebe Moon never broke a sweat.

But then, Phoebe Moon was invincible, and she hadn't yet discovered boys.

Neither of which applied to Merry.

Max probably had cops out hunting for her right now. If handcuffs had to be involved, the Merry of a year ago would've preferred they be handled by Max himself, in his bedroom.

The Merry tonight didn't have the luxury of indulging in lusty fantasies. She had to find her mother.

She followed the ivy-trimmed hallways toward the swell of voices. She turned a corner, and a set of double doors opened before her into a large ballroom. Stately Christmas trees stood in each corner. People milled about, coats unzipped, gloves off, cheeks pink, earrings and necklaces and rings sparkling.

She scanned the room, looking for Patrick or her mother while she plunged into the crowd.

Four steps later, she bumped into a vision in white.

"Oh! Oh, I'm so sorry," the bride said. "I was just—*oh*!"

Her blue eyes went round, her pink lips parted, and she gripped Merry's coat. "You're the one who disappeared."

A shiver danced across Merry's skin. She didn't recognize the blonde woman, but obviously the woman recognized her. Merry plastered a bland smile on her face, gently removed the bride's hand from her arm, and shook it instead. "Congratulations and many happy returns on your wedding. Excuse me—"

"I had this dream about you after you disappeared last year. You were in a jail, except the jail was an elevator without walls, and it swung in the elevator shaft, which was really a disco dance floor. I'm so glad you're not in jail. But it really wasn't nice to disappear like that."

You're busted, Merry Silver, Phoebe Moon said in her head.

The groom stepped up, his crystal-blue gaze sharp and curious while he extended a hand to Merry and slid his other arm around his bride's waist. "Every time I think I've met all of Kimmie's friends, we find another. Josh Kincaid. And you're...?"

"Leaving," Merry said.

"This is Max's last girlfriend," Kimmie said. "Remember, I told you about the one who disappeared?" She tilted her head at Merry. "Are you here to break the curse?"

"Curse?" *Oooh, a curse,* Phoebe Moon whispered. But Merry shook her head and extracted her hand from Josh's. "Never mind. Sorry. I really need to—"

"He found the Golden Bouquet," Kimmie said. "Bliss legend has it that anyone who works on The Aisle who finds the Golden Bouquet is cursed to seven years of bad luck in love, and Max found it during the annual hunt almost five years ago. So when you disappeared, it was like fate. But you're back! The others never came back."

The others?

Merry gagged her jealous side and shook her head at Kimmie. "I think you have me mistaken for—"

"Merry, right? You liked the fruitcake cupcakes. Nobody liked the fruitcake cupcakes, even when I made them, but you tried a sample and bought a half dozen."

She remembered the fruitcake cupcakes. She'd stopped in the bakery on The Aisle on her way to see Max, but she didn't remember this bright, happy girl.

Also, she'd shared the cupcakes with Max's dog. Who loved them even more than Merry did. "Beautiful night for a wedding," Merry said while she shifted a subtle glance around the ballroom. Where were Mom and Patrick? "But how about that owl?"

Kimmie giggled. "It was inevitable. Josh ruined like six of my friends' weddings before ours."

"Two," Josh said.

Kimmie grinned bigger, and Josh gave her a heart-melting, adoring smile that could've made Merry believe in fairy tales.

"Kimmie! There you are." A short, massively pregnant brunette with a giant of a redheaded man and an adorable brown-haired boy in tow descended on the happy couple.

"Congratulations again," Merry murmured, and while the brunette and the bride bumped bellies in a hug, Merry slipped away.

But instead of looking for Mom and Patrick, she put her head down, pulled out her phone, and turned toward the door.

Heading back to the B&B, she texted Mom.

Her phone dinged in response almost immediately. *Sleep well, darling. We'll be out late.*

If anyone else spotted Merry, there was a possibility she'd be out late too.

She just hoped it wouldn't be Max or the police.

By the time Max had regained his dignity, stashed Gran's tiara inside With This Ring, and checked all of the gown shops in Bliss, the festivities were breaking up for the evening.

"Merry Christmas," someone called to him.

He waved back. "Happy New Year." Thanksgiving had been barely over a week ago, but hell if he could bring himself to wish anyone a *merry* anything.

Even if he could still smell her shampoo and had just gotten over the semi he'd had since she laid him out flat.

Who knew getting taken down by a girl could be such a turn-on?

But then, it was Merry.

No matter how furious, how suspicious, or how stupid she made him—both tonight and last year when she'd disappeared—she was also the only woman he'd wished had stayed longer after it was over.

Max limped past the mirror in the lobby of the Rose and Dove and checked a grimace at the sight of his crooked elf hat. He trod through the building to the ballroom where Dan and Rachel were chatting with festival stragglers.

Max's brother and sister-in-law had taken over Santa and Mrs. Claus duties for Gramps and Gran last year, but this year, they were harder to watch.

Not because Dan and Rachel weren't the perfect Santa and Mrs. Claus. Rach had decorated enough candy canes with craft eyes, red fuzzy noses, and pipe cleaners that every kid in Bliss could fully adorn a six-foot Scotch pine with Rudolphs alone. Gramps's old suit fit Dan perfectly, and he had the jolly Santa chuckle down pat.

But Dan and Rachel could never be Gramps and Gran. Max would've sacrificed his frozen nuts to still have them here.

With the festival wrapping up now, Dan had pulled off his Santa hat and let his wiry white beard hang crooked. Rachel glanced at Max and gasped. "What happened?"

"Your car's fine," Max assured her. It had been closer than his, so he'd borrowed her keys for the quick trip to the store.

"Problem with the reindeer?" Santa Dan suggested.

Rachel's features twisted up in sympathy. "Oh, Max. Did the curse strike again?"

"There's no curse." During Knot Fest, the other of Bliss's two annual wedding festivals, a glitzy prize was offered to the tourist who found a hidden gold-painted bouquet. Any local who found it was supposedly cursed. Max had always thought the hex was a story made up to discourage the townsfolk from spoiling the tourists' fun. That a stupid plastic bouquet couldn't actually cause seven years of bad luck in love. But tonight was enough to crack his resolve. "Owl got me," he lied.

"It went after the tiara again?" Rachel reached for Dan's hand. "Is it okay?"

"Tiara's fine. As fine as it was, anyway. I'm fine. But I—"

He what?

He needed to confess that he'd just run into a girl he'd dated who happened to be the daughter of a notorious jewel thief? And that he'd found her lurking behind With This Ring?

And that he'd been irrationally turned on by the idea of playing a real-life chess game with the angel-voiced vixen?

"I've got frostbite places a man shouldn't ever have frostbite, and if I don't get out of these damn tights, loss of circulation is going to kill whatever the cold didn't."

Rachel laughed. "I've always said men should try tights, heels, and bras. When the hex is finally lifted, you'll relate so well to your future bride."

Were she anyone but his sister-in-law, she would've gotten an eyeful of a two-fingered salute. "You guys don't need me?"

Who was he kidding?

He was always extraneous. The second son, the single son, the spare. The spoiled one. The fast one. The party boy.

The one who dated daughters of jewel thieves.

Dan clapped him on the shoulder. "Nah, we got this. You're coming over for dinner tomorrow, right? Rach is practicing the prime rib for Christmas."

"And the chocolate mousse," she said.

It was hard to hate Rachel for being perfect when she made chocolate mousse. "Wouldn't miss it. I'll bring noisemakers and science kits for the brats too. And a camera for when Dan tries on his tights, heels, and bra."

Rachel pecked his cheek. "You're so cute when you act grouchy. But the only thing you need to bring is your hockey stick. Tyler's been practicing. He's convinced he's good enough to score on you now."

"You tell him I eat trash-talking eleven-year-olds for breakfast."

Dan snorted. "Gonna be eating your words when that trash-talking eleven-year-old schools your trash-talking thirty-year-old self."

"Go relax, Max. We'll see you tomorrow."

But relaxing was the last thing on Max's mind when he left the festival.

He had the daughter of a jewel thief to find.

3

Phoebe Moon hadn't ever wanted to return to devilish Uncle Sandy's laboratory, but someone had to stop him from poisoning the water.

—Phoebe Moon and the Sinister Cloud

Since Mom tended to humor Merry's insecurities and paranoia, she had been given the corner turret room of the B&B, with a clear view of all the shady dealings that might occur in the back alley or the side street. But since this was Bliss, there was little movement beyond bare branches swaying in the wind. She sat in the window seat, notebook in hand so she could scribble the occasional Phoebe Moon note while she watched.

Daddy could be out there.

Max could be out there.

The police could be coming for Merry right now.

She'd never ruined one of Mom's weddings before. Or gotten arrested. Not that she was entirely sure what she could be arrested for, but even being questioned by the police would put a damper on

Mom's grand Christmastime wedding plans. And goodness knows they'd both been questioned by the police before.

Not generally because Merry was under suspicion of anything, but there had been a time or two since she'd gotten her driver's license—like last year's incident—when Daddy had pulled her in on something before she realized what was going on.

"Never again," she whispered to herself.

Never ever again. Even for the good causes.

The only thing left for her here in the States was Mom's wedding. And then she was gone.

Shortly after eleven, she heard Mom and Patrick on the stairs outside her room.

She tucked her laptop and notebook into a hidden pocket in her luggage, then stepped out into the wooden hallway of the lovely Victorian house.

Mom hung off Patrick, giggling, her eyes glassy. It had been ten years since Merry had lived with her mother, but they'd done enough weddings that she knew the routine.

Mom picked a groom. Mom set a date. Mom thought about Daddy. Mom got drunk.

And then Mom married an upstanding man who treated her like a queen, but who wasn't Daddy.

"Need any help?" Merry whispered to Patrick.

His wink was longer than usual. "I've got her."

It wasn't a lascivious wink. More like a tired wink. Despite only meeting Patrick a few weeks ago, and despite his unfortunate winking tendencies, Merry trusted he was no more of a scoundrel than any of Mom's other husbands.

If anything, he was the nicest of the princes she'd found so far. He held doors, he didn't leer, and he'd expressed his love and affection for Mom so earnestly before he'd asked Merry's permission to propose, she'd honestly considered warning him away, if she could've figured out how to phrase the idea to make Patrick think it was his own.

Phoebe Moon could've done it.

Merry, however, had no ready tricks up her sleeve to convince a man he didn't love her mother. Nor would her conscience allow her to malign the woman who had sacrificed her own true love to give Merry a series of safe, stable homes—rotating stepfathers notwithstanding—through her teenage years.

Plus, that small part of her that still believed in fairy tales kept hoping one of Mom's marriages would stick.

Patrick slid the key into the lock of the door across the hall, still supporting Mom. "Doesn't he have the most matching-est shoes?" Mom said to Merry.

"They're both a lovely brown," Merry agreed. "And on the right feet even."

Mom giggled.

Patrick swung the door open, and Mom lurched inside.

"Patrick?" Merry said softly.

"Hmm?"

"Gentlemen don't take advantage of their drunk fiancées."

His saggy cheeks went pink. "Oh, no, I—Merry, I promise you, I honor and respect your mother, and I would never—we don't—the bonds of marriage are sacred, and we believe—"

She gave him a slow wink back. "Counting on you, Patrick." She turned back to her own room. "By the way, don't let her eat eggs in the morning. Get her a chocolate chip bagel with peanut butter instead. She'll argue about the calories, but she'll feel better once she eats it."

"Ah—okay, then. Thanks for the tip, Merry."

"If you can't count on family, who can you count on?"

Patrick smiled, the sarcasm completely lost on him. He stepped into the room behind Mom. The door swung shut. Merry waited, but there was no detectable sound of the lock clicking.

Because Patrick was idiotically trusting, or because he was open to the idea of Merry bursting in if she felt the need?

Either way, she wished Mom would let herself be happy with him.

But most likely Patrick was yet another distraction who probably didn't know that Mom's first husband was a jewel thief.

Merry checked out her own bedroom window once more, then stepped lightly into the hallway and softly pulled her door shut.

She'd all but convinced herself she'd imagined the smell of Brut in the alley behind With This Ring. But Daddy had turned her life upside down for the last time last year, and she had no intention of letting her guard down so that he could do it again.

He never meant to.

He simply couldn't help himself. And he always had a solid justification—right or wrong—for any job he pulled.

She tiptoed around the upstairs perimeter, dodging squeaky boards to peek out the lone window over the opposite end of the stairs. Christmas lights twinkled on the houses down the way—blue icicle lights, white lights, candy-cane lights and more hung from eaves and sparkled in bushes and along sidewalks. A giant blow-up Santa in an airplane swayed in the breeze two yards down. The view wasn't too different from the view from her apartment in Toluca, an Illinois farm town about an hour south of Bliss where she'd spent the past year. Cozy older homes, bare maple and oak trees, quiet streets. No black Cadillacs, Audis, or Lexus sedans. The minivans, SUVs, and older-model beaters parked along the street weren't the types of rides her father would stoop to, even in the name of watching his ex-wife and daughter. No cop cars, marked or unmarked.

No classic Ford Mustangs like the one Max drove either. But then, she should've heard that coming in the alley, and she hadn't.

Maybe he'd sold it.

She shook her head. Max wasn't her business.

Making sure Daddy didn't take the Mrs. Claus diamond ring from Max's store, yes. Max himself, no.

Satisfied with this angle, Merry crept down the stairs, guided by the rainbow Christmas lights wrapped with ivy along the banister.

The heater fan whispered through the vents. The yellow glow

from the light above the oven cut the darkness in the empty kitchen. Straight ahead, she paused at the entrance to the B&B's dining room.

There had been a lit Christmas tree in the corner when their hostess showed them around this afternoon, but now inky blackness swallowed the room.

No Christmas lights or streetlamps filtering in through the windows. No nightlight.

She inhaled a slow, deep breath.

Scents of pine, cinnamon, and chocolate chip cookies tickled her nose, but no Brut.

A giggle—Mom's of course—came through the ceiling. When Merry's eyes adjusted to the dark, she navigated around the shadowy figures of chairs and tables to the row of windows overlooking the dormant backyard garden and peered through the wooden slat blinds.

Tension seeped out of her bones, and a saggy, exhausted relief took up residence instead.

Bliss was safe. She was safe. Mom and Patrick were safe.

And as long as Merry had the fake Mrs. Claus diamond secured where only she could get to it, Max's family's jewelry store was safe too. It would take at least a month for Daddy's contact to make a second fake. Even if he realized she'd found it right away, she would have time after the wedding to retrieve the fake ring and mail it to Max. She'd include a warning about Daddy's usual MO when it came to high-value targets, and then she would be gone.

Long, long gone.

She turned to head back to her room.

A massive figure loomed in the doorway, arms and legs spread.

Merry froze. Her heart banged and tried to claw out of her chest. Adrenaline twisted her muscles tight. She'd have to leap four tables to get to the side door to the garden. The windows behind her were locked, and even if they weren't, she'd have to go through the blinds first.

She was trapped. "What do you want?"

"The better questions in this room are about you," Max answered.

Her breath whooshed out, and the subsequent adrenaline crash sent a tingle through her fingers and toes. "How did you get in here?"

"The owners are good friends." He stepped into the room, his movements as graceful as a thief's. The shadow of his arm went out, a switch audibly flipped, and the gentle glow of Christmas lights on the tree cut the harsh darkness.

Max's elf suit was gone, replaced by dark jeans and a black Henley. His silent steps suggested he'd ditched his shoes. She had been fascinated by his eyes during their too-brief relationship. His irises were a unique color between sapphire and emerald, wavering more toward the blue or green end of the spectrum, depending on his clothing. Tonight, they were bright and clear and focused, but the dim light in the room masked the brilliance in the color.

Mom's giggle flowed through the ceiling again.

Max's eyes drifted upward. "That your mother?"

Merry didn't answer.

"I wasn't sure you actually had a mother," Max said.

She almost snorted. More than one well-meaning social worker had said the same to Phoebe Moon when she'd produced stand-ins to keep herself out of the foster care system. "Surprise," she said.

He gestured for her to sit.

"I don't think so."

"I'm not going to hurt you."

She could've snorted again—of the two of them, he was in more physical danger, which he should've remembered—but his honest sentiment soothed her lingering panic at finding herself trapped. "You're adorable. What do you want?"

"To talk. Catch up. Reminisce about the good ol' days. The usual when you run into someone who disappeared out of your life without a word."

She'd known from the moment he stepped into view behind his family's jewelry store that he knew who she was. Not just the Merry he'd dated, but the Merry who was the daughter of Nicholas Raymond, notorious jewel thief.

She'd seen the disgust and the distrust in too many people in her life to miss it in Max.

He curled his fingers around the back of the nearest chair. Casually—no white knuckles, no shoulders up to his chin, no overt anger broadcasting through any of his facial features. "Are you in trouble?" he asked.

Something that felt suspiciously like her heart fluttered. Her acquaintances rarely asked after her well-being, and friends who had been left behind—duped, embarrassed, and often a jewel or two poorer—rarely cared. "Are you wired?"

His brows furrowed. "Wired?"

"Bugged. Taping our conversation. Acting as a snitch to try to catch me doing whatever it is you think I'm here to do. Are you *really* a jeweler, or do you just play one on TV?"

Max stood stupefied.

Either he was honestly shocked at the idea that he'd be wired or he was an exceptional actor.

And that sliver of her soul that was still pure and innocent and unsuspicious hoped it was the former.

She'd liked Max. He'd been both fun and dependable. Not looking to hook up just for sex, but also not dating with the sole intent of finding a bride. Courteous and attentive in public, a shade on the vulnerable side in private, and a tiger in bed.

His jaw tightened. "I'm asking about your well-being out of respect for someone I once considered my friend."

She could've been so much more than just his friend. "You should pick your friends better."

"Are you here to steal something?"

"What do you think?"

His gaze bored into her, hot and hard. A familiar longing pulsed between her thighs, but a far more uncommon feeling pinged under her rib cage.

She'd learned long ago not to get attached, but Max made her want to be stupid.

She'd indulged last year. She'd gotten attached.

She still was, if her quick pulse and the pull in her femininity and the overwhelming need in her soul were any indication.

"Or are you just the lookout?" he murmured.

The budding warm fuzzies in her chest croaked and withered.

But if his suspicions kept him on his toes, then she'd let him believe she was the bad guy. She lifted a single shoulder and stayed silent.

"And now I'm back to wondering if you're in trouble," Max said. "You were in my house. You slept in my bed. You charmed my dog. If you wanted to steal something, if you're helping someone, why now? Why not last year when you had easy access to my house, to my keys, to my life?"

"Maybe I'm honestly only here for a wedding."

"And maybe my fucking curse is real."

If either of them were cursed, it wasn't Max. Although, now that she thought about it, *Phoebe Moon and the Cursed Heart* had a nice ring to it.

Max let go of the chair and turned his back to her. "Your phone was disconnected. Your email bounced. I couldn't call your family to ask if you were okay because I didn't know if you even had family."

The side door called to her. He wasn't looking. She could make it.

But his concern was a salve to the parched, blistered part of her that never expected friends to last long. She didn't want to bolt. She wanted to stand here and soak in his reluctant affection.

But mostly, she wanted not to hurt him. Not to have hurt him last year, and not to hurt him more now.

"My apologies," she whispered. "I'll go away again, but you don't have to worry. I'll be fine."

His head shifted left, then right, and his arms flexed as though he were cracking his knuckles. "You tricked me good."

"I *never* set out to trick you. It wasn't—" She clamped her lips shut.

Whatever their relationship had been, it couldn't be again. Rehashing it wouldn't fix that.

Max twisted back to face her, *gotcha* written in the semi-satisfied twist of his mouth. "What happened?"

Heat prickled over her skin. Who'd tricked who there?

She jabbed a finger in his direction and stalked toward him until she stood a breath from him, heart clanging in her throat. "You grew up in fairy-tale wedding land. My childhood fairy tale was Robin Hood. I was ten before I began to grasp that my father was a criminal, and I was seventeen before I could acknowledge he was wrong. My moral compass doesn't point north. It points to safety. I know my daddy isn't always right, but he's still my daddy. So sometimes I do bad things too. And sometimes that means I have to disappear. But right now? Right now, I want to go dress and cake and flower shopping with my mom like a normal girl, have lunch in a nice restaurant without wondering how valuable the silverware is, and then get my toes done without noticing everyone's jewelry and wondering how well they keep it locked up at night."

He opened his mouth.

Merry covered his lips with her fingers, the firm heat of his mouth and breath making her want to shiver. "Just go, Max. Thank you for a lovely time last year, but we're over. We never should've been at all. As soon as my mom's married, I'll be gone, and I'll never darken the door to your town again."

He eased his arms around her until he had her pinned against a table, his movements slow but unapologetic.

Also incredibly ballsy. He had to know it was a dangerous move, but he did it anyway.

That longing pull between her thighs went deeper.

"Is your father here?" he asked.

"That's a terrible question to ask while you think you have me trapped. I laid you out once. I'll do it again."

He smiled. Not a smirk, no hard edges, but an honest, warm, borderline self-deprecating smile. "If I'd known about your moves last year, we would've spent more time in bed."

An unbidden image of Max beneath her, naked and completely at her mercy, made her feminine parts ache harder. "You're not helping matters."

"Neither are you."

"I'm the daughter of a jewel thief and a heartbreaker. I never help matters."

"You don't have to let yourself be defined by your family."

Her breath caught.

"You told me that yourself last year, Merry. Why would that be true for me but not for you? Are you in the family business? Do you want to be? Or are you something else entirely?"

He was so close, she could feel the sound waves from his words vibrating against her skin. And he was saying all the right things.

You have worth, Merry. Don't let them fence you in. Believe in yourself. I believe in you.

He was seductive.

Intuitive.

Intoxicating.

Max Gregory could've been a con artist in his own right.

She slid her hands up his hard chest, ready to push him away. She wouldn't have to push hard. He'd move. She knew it as well as she knew her own name.

"What are you here for, Merry?" he said again.

"You'll just have to trust me."

"I trusted the woman I knew. But I don't know if you're her."

"No one stays the same. Life happens, and we change."

"That sounds remarkably like the woman who told me family doesn't define us."

"That woman was an idealistic idiot."

"That woman is an intriguing puzzle, and I have half a mind to figure her out."

His heart beat strong and steady under her palm. His eyes wavered from her eyes to her lips, and his breath came quicker.

She wanted to be the daughter of a salesclerk and a teacher, and she wanted him to be the boy next door. She wanted to tell him to give his dog a hug for her and to ask how his grandparents were doing. She wanted to curl her fingers into the soft, warm cotton of his shirt, to lose herself in his clean soap scent, to taste his lips, to entice him to kiss her back.

She wanted to tell him she had a fake Mrs. Claus diamond stashed in a safe location in Toluca.

But she couldn't control what he'd do with the information.

If he knew there was evidence that Daddy was planning to rob his store, he'd get the cops involved. Mom's wedding week would turn into an endless stream of police interviews. The wedding would get canceled, and Merry would miss her flight out of the country on Sunday.

But if she stuck with her original plan—retrieve the ring and mail it to Max on Saturday—then she'd have done what she needed to do. The real ring would be safe, because Daddy wouldn't ever have a chance to get his hands on the fake before she alerted Max to the danger. Mom would be on her honeymoon before the cops got involved. Merry would be in France. And Daddy could take a flying leap for putting Merry in this position.

Max was watching her, looming over her, holding her captive with his steady, questioning, demanding gaze.

"I'm not a convenient distraction for whatever your problems are," she said. "Leave, Max. For both our sakes."

"You can trust me, Merry."

If only. "Why would I trust you when I don't even trust myself?"

"Obviously because we agree I'm the trustworthy one in the room."

She shoved at his chest, a reluctant smile tugging at her lips. "Thank you for being an ass. That'll make it easier for me to make you leave."

"I'm going." He held his hands up. "But make no mistake. If my family's shop is robbed, we'll prosecute to the full extent of the law."

Her heart skipped a beat. "I'd expect nothing less."

His jaw tightened again, and he gave an exasperated head shake. "I don't know what you're planning, or why, but I can't help you if you don't trust me."

"Why would you help me?"

"I missed you."

She pursed her lips and looked down. She'd find another Max one day. A man who intrigued her and inspired her and maybe even loved her. She'd be halfway around the world, living as Amber Finch, and she wouldn't have to worry about her father disrupting her life.

Until then, she'd live with her regrets and try not to make them worse.

Max heaved an audible sigh. Then suddenly his hand was cradling her head, and his lips lingered below her ear. "I'm glad you were okay, Merry." He pressed a hot kiss to her neck, then wrenched away and strode to the door, leaving her feeling as though he'd branded her skin, her heart, and her soul.

The door clicked shut behind him, and Merry's breath all whooshed out of her. "*Dammit,* Daddy."

This was the last time, she vowed.

This was the last time he'd ruin anything of hers.

4

Phoebe Moon crept through the dank, musty underground cavern. This was where diabolical Uncle Sandy had stashed the world's sound. She could feel it in her tiny bones.

—Phoebe Moon and the Stolen Sound

One year ago

Merry loved bookstores, but this particular September afternoon she was well outside her comfort zone.

Because this particular afternoon, reclusive horror novelist Spencer McGraw was here in her Chicago neighborhood on a book tour.

And today, she wanted to sit in the crowd and absorb the vibes. To imagine herself as the reclusive Amber Finch coming out of her private life on a publisher-sponsored thirty-city tour.

As if she wouldn't hire a stunt double should Amber Finch's presence ever be requested for an in-person event.

But still, here she was, sitting in the small coffee shop inside the bookstore, pretending to read, earbuds in her ears while she tried to shift away from a scruffy blond guy with a runner's build, a fake tan, board shorts and a Hawaiian shirt, who was inching closer and closer into her personal space.

She fought the urge to check her pocket for her cash, phone, and ID while she leaned as far as she could to her other side, but a lone, dark-haired, linebacker-looking guy was too close there, reading a car magazine.

"Well, now, what's a pretty thing like you doing at a signing like this?" Surfer Dude said.

Merry started. Glanced around. Was he talking to her?

"A favor for my grandfather," a resonant male voice on her other side answered.

Surfer Dude's lip curled, and she swallowed a surprised laugh.

"I was talking to the lady," he said to Linebacker Guy.

"Ah, she's a lady now," Linebacker Guy said. He didn't look at her, but she was intrigued by the way she couldn't tell what color his eyes were.

Phoebe Moon was too. *Oooh, Merry, they're gonna fight over you.*

Tall, Dark, and Handsome gave Surfer Dude an unfriendly smile. "Where I come from, the ladies are more than just pretty little things."

"Where I come from, the chicks speak for themselves," Surfer Dude replied. "This guy bothering you, honey?"

Oh, swoon, Merry! Phoebe Moon said. *You haven't had a date in two years, and they're both gorgeous.*

Merry pulled her earbuds from her ears. "Could you two keep it down? You're bothering Spike."

Both men peered at her feet, as though looking for a dog or a pet hamster or a stroller.

"Spike?" Linebacker Guy said.

She smiled at him. "My pet dragon? He's very uncomfortable with strangers." She made a show of stroking the air next to her. "It's okay, Spike. Spencer will be here soon, and we'll talk to him about you starring in his next novel, okay?"

Surfer Dude's left eye squinted, and he angled away. "Yeah. Just remembered. I need to go get a book. You, ah…yeah."

But Linebacker Guy's brilliant blue-green eyes seemed to see right through her. The corners of his lips hitched up, and a rare bout of hormones and lust combined to twirl in her belly. He eyed the air where her imaginary pet dragon Spike was hanging out. "Sure it's a good idea to bring a dragon somewhere with this much flammable material?"

"He's had a firebox-ectomy." She frowned at him. "I'm not one of those irresponsible dragon owners."

Can I have a real dragon? Phoebe Moon asked.

No, Merry said sternly.

But what if dastardly Uncle Sandy wants to steal a dinosaur egg. I'd need something bigger than a dinosaur to—

"Enjoy your book," Linebacker Guy said. That secret smile lingered while he turned his attention back to his muscle car magazine.

Merry's belly was still twirling.

Men weren't in her future—ever—so she lifted her book, put her earbuds back in, and continued to watch the crowd.

Linebacker Guy eventually finished his magazine and wandered away. No more men made passes at her. But the twirling in her belly turned to Pop Rocks skittering through her gut the closer it got to the reading.

She rose from her spot at the coffee shop to linger with a clear view of the stage and table where Spencer McGraw would be. Surfer Dude was across the store, chatting with two blondes.

Linebacker Guy was nowhere in sight.

And Spencer McGraw walked right past her.

Not that she noticed.

Neither did any of the close to three hundred other people crammed into the bookstore with her.

Because he looked like a hobo.

A well-dressed, nice-smelling hobo—which should've been a clue—but a hobo nonetheless.

His straggly, straw-colored hair covered his ears. His beard was months past needing a trim. Massive dark sunglasses covered his eyes, and his gait was so stiff, she wondered if he wore leg braces under his designer jeans.

That man is bloody brilliant, Phoebe Moon declared.

Don't say bloody, Merry silently replied.

But she agreed wholeheartedly with the thirteen-year-old protagonist in her head.

Spencer McGraw hadn't been photographed in public since he was twenty-six years old. He was pushing forty now. He could walk into the bathroom, trim his hair, shave, change—including pulling off leg braces?—and walk back out, and no one would know it was him.

Merry's heart sank.

She couldn't do it.

She couldn't pull off a book tour and keep her anonymity. Not like Spencer McGraw could.

"If that man's really Spencer McGraw, I'll eat your imaginary dragon," a voice murmured beside her.

Linebacker Guy was back.

She subconsciously leaned closer to him. "My imaginary dragon doesn't like being eaten," she whispered.

He grinned, flashing a row of straight pearly whites. "So few do."

Before the table laden with copies of McGraw's books, the manager introduced the man of the hour, listing his accomplishments—*The New York Times* list, the Bram Stoker Awards, the starred reviews and praise from all the major literary magazines, the *People Magazine* Man of the Year designation, and the list went on.

McGraw didn't smile.

And Merry realized she couldn't do what she'd come here to do today either.

She couldn't ask this intimidating, anonymous man to sign a book to Amber Finch. Might as well just leave. She wasn't big on reading horror—she'd felt terror enough times in her life—and Phoebe Moon was openly speculating about whether or not Spencer McGraw drew his inspiration from eating people, or if he just looked like that for fun.

"Bet he's got a whole cave full of imaginary dragons who haven't had firebox-ectomies," Linebacker Guy said.

Merry's lips twitched upward. "He has enough money to buy them claw enhancements too."

"Gramps isn't going to believe this."

"The dragons or the man?"

"He'd believe the dragons."

The room burst into applause as the manager finished listing all of McGraw's accomplishments.

Still, the man didn't smile. He gave a single nod, then moved stiffly to take his place behind the table stacked with his books.

Sheesh.

And people were afraid of Daddy.

Daddy smiled. Just last month, he'd stopped by for a visit. An uneventful visit, thank goodness—*Missed my girl. How about some chess?*—and he and Merry had spent a few hours playing board games, talking about his latest legitimate job selling used cars in a little town in northern Illinois, about Mom's most recent divorce, about the summer's blockbuster movie and if it had been better or worse than the book.

She once again hadn't told him she'd quit her online medical billing job because she was writing books that were making her enough money to support herself.

But she'd noticed he was getting older. His distinguished, deep gray hair was threaded with white, the lines around his eyes deeper and crinklier, his bones creakier.

Maybe, she thought, he was getting too old for pulling heists.

Maybe, she thought, he'd finally found his honest calling in selling used cars.

Maybe, she thought, his last jewel heist was behind him.

To the best of her knowledge, he hadn't robbed anyone in at least a year. Maybe two. When Daddy left her apartment, he got straight in his car and drove away. He didn't linger. Nor did he come back.

She knew, because she'd watched.

He didn't have any more tells that suggested he was hanging around for any reason other than to see his daughter.

Because he loved her.

And he knew how badly she'd been rattled by his jobs in the past.

Maybe, she thought, she truly could be settled.

Maybe, she thought, she could consider her own future.

Linebacker guy leaned into her. "Don't suppose you want to get this book signed for me? That guy's scary as hell."

She blinked back at him, then down at his stack of books.

He had a copy of *Phoebe Moon and the Sneeze Snatcher* right on top of his muscle car magazine.

Her lips parted, her eyes bugged, and her pulse surged. "Yeah, I can see where you're having trouble." How she kept her voice steady, she'd never know.

He looked down too, and he laughed. It was rich and deep and intoxicating, with a hint of self-deprecation mixed in. "Ah, that. It's for my niece." An honest smile lingered on his full lips, giving an extra oomph to the effect of his square jaw and thick dark hair. "My sister-in-law gave me an hour-long lecture about girls yesterday when I told Olivia she was wearing a pretty dress." He tugged his ear. "Guess her point stuck, because I spent about thirty minutes trying to find the right smart-girl book."

Merry, he has family, Phoebe Moon squealed. *You've always wanted a family. And he thinks I'm smart!*

She had to duck her head and swallow hard, adding in a few blinks for good measure. "I hope she likes it."

If he noticed the way her tongue choked on the words, he didn't comment. "Me too," he said, and she could hear a warm smile in his voice.

Tell him, Merry! Phoebe Moon crowed. *Tell him you wrote it.*

She could. She could say it right now.

But she'd never said it before. Asking Spencer McGraw to sign a book to Amber Finch was far different from telling this man who held a copy of her book in his hands. Spencer McGraw probably had no clue Amber Finch was a fellow author. Their books were universes apart. But this man—telling him would be like offering him a part of her soul.

The staff at the bookstore was organizing people into rows based on their numbers. Merry checked the wristband she'd been given when she'd arrived for the signing. Ninety-seven.

It would be a while.

Or perhaps she'd simply sneak out. Away from the creepy Spencer McGraw and away from this handsome man with a soft spot for his niece.

"Huh," Linebacker Guy said. He held out his wristband. Number ninety-eight. "Looks like we're stuck together for the next few hours. I'm Max, by the way."

Say it! Phoebe Moon said again. *Tell him you're Amber Finch.*

Not a chance.

But maybe she could stay for a few more minutes. It wasn't like talking to a guy meant she had to marry him. Or confess any of her secrets.

She stuck her hand out. "Merry. And you've met Spike, of course."

Max laughed again, Phoebe Moon swooned again, and Merry —well.

Merry decided that a couple of hours of firsthand research into what Mom found so enticing in men that she kept marrying them couldn't hurt.

Because Daddy was getting older.

Wiser, perhaps.

And for the first time in years, she was intrigued by something other than a plot twist.

MAX STEPPED out of the bookstore, shaking his head at how a fun two hours chatting with an odd but intriguing woman had been ruined by a severe case of the creeps.

He'd met Spencer McGraw once before, when the man had come to With This Ring to pick up the Mrs. Claus diamond, but that man had been far different from the eerie dude signing books today. And now, Max had a ninety-minute drive ahead of him and no funny ladies with imaginary dragons to take his mind off McGraw.

Except—wait. "Merry!" he called.

The raven-haired woman cast a quick glance back at him. Her eyes—like double-chocolate mocha spiced with surprise, wariness, and amusement—scanned him quickly while she shifted until she was facing him, holding her bag of books in front of her. "Hi," she said hesitantly, as though they hadn't spent the last two hours talking.

Max jogged to catch up with her. She'd been motionless in her jeans and long-sleeve brown sweater, as though she couldn't decide which way to go. "I've got a long drive home. Was thinking of getting something to eat." *Join me?* was on the tip of his tongue, but something about the way she held her bag between them stopped him. "Any recommendations?"

She lowered the bag and tucked a lock of hair behind her ear. "Are you looking for normal food, or did staring into the eyes of the devil make you hungry for a human sacrifice?"

"You got me. I'm really looking for a bodyguard," he joked.

She squinted at him for a moment before her lips spread in a full, dimple-popping smile that had Max Jr. sitting up, and not for the first time this afternoon. "Spencer McGraw scared the big linebacker?"

"I think he memorized my face to use as a victim in his next novel." Max probably could've left off mentioning to McGraw that the books were for his grandfather. As soon as Max had said Harvey Gregory, McGraw had tilted his head back to peer up at Max through his sunglasses, and despite the thick beard and mustache, Max was almost positive McGraw smiled.

And not in a comforting way.

Not that he'd share anything about his connection to McGraw with Merry.

No need to ruin the illusion of her being a funny, smart girl who might hang out with him for him rather than because his family was in the jewelry business.

"Do you like cheese?" Merry said.

"Cheese? Sure."

"Because there's this fabulous bistro with the most amazing cheese plate right around the corner. If you need a bodyguard that badly, you can join me. But I'm paying for myself."

"And Spike?" Max said.

"They let me tie him to the bike rack. I'll feed him when we get home."

"Then I'm in."

How could he not be?

She was on the odd side, but he wouldn't have wanted her to be conventionally normal. Her dry delivery when she talked about her imaginary dragon was amusing as hell, and there was something about the shimmer in her eyes when she looked around, her random sideways comments, and the way she fidgeted that intrigued him.

It was as though she saw a completely different world than he did.

And he wanted to know what her world looked like.

Two minutes later, they were on their way to an early dinner.

As new friends.

Not because he would admit to any romantic interest in her.

But, man, when she smiled, he felt as though his engine had been given a tune-up he hadn't realized it had needed. After two years of the increasing demands that came with living with his rapidly declining grandparents, he appreciated the freedom to enjoy an impromptu dinner with a fun woman.

"Did you grow up here?" he asked while they ate.

Her left eye crinkled, but she ducked her head over her French onion soup and pulled out a cheesy spoonful. "I'm Midwestern," she said. "We moved around a lot when I was growing up."

"Military?"

"No, more like chasing better jobs. What about you?"

He twisted a goofy grin at her. "You heard of Bliss? Our welcome-to-town signs tell people we're the Most Married-est Town on Earth because all the bridal shops on our main street have been run by married couples since the dawn of time, but we actually have a few single people and one divorced woman working there now." He took her lifted brows and semi-slack jaw as the usual *You know this is the twenty-first century, right?* that he'd gotten from friends and dates during his college days at the University of Illinois.

"Don't tell anyone," he stage-whispered, "but we're overthrowing our anti-divorce dictator and joining the new millennium."

"You want to get divorced?" Merry said, straight-faced.

He put a hand to his heart. "And most women wait until the third date to pop the question."

She laughed, a twinkling sound that fit her name, and then changed the subject to the Blackhawks' chances this season.

At the end of the meal, she again insisted on paying for herself, and he let her, because it hadn't been a date.

Still, on the way out, his mouth opened, and he asked if she liked baseball. He had two tickets to a late-season Cubs game, and his usual buddies were tied up and couldn't make it.

Taking her to a Cubs game wasn't a date.

It was an afternoon out with a friend.

A friend who happened to be funny, intriguing, and blessed with long legs and perfect breasts.

What could go wrong?

5

"Phoebe Moon, how could you?" Sister Mary Elvira said. "We needed those eggs and that milk to feed all you children."

Phoebe Moon peered at the hungry eyes of her fellow orphans. "But it wasn't me!"

—Phoebe Moon and the Secret Sister

Present Day

Sunday morning, while most of Bliss was still asleep, Max bundled up and took Scout, his golden retriever, for a walk to With This Ring. He hadn't slept so poorly since Merry disappeared last year.

Last year, he'd been up all night, sick to his stomach, combing through his house, through Gran's jewelry box, through With This Ring, making sure nothing had been stolen.

Last night, he'd been up all night, wondering why she came back.

And why he still cared.

Her father's a goddamn abomination, Gramps had said last year when Max had confided in his grandparents. Couldn't bring himself to tell anyone else.

Language, Gran had chided. She'd been fighting a fever, one of many following her broken hip, but despite her grimaces of pain, her wobbly voice, and the way her eyes kept drifting closed, her words had been classic Gran. *Max, if the lady was on a mission from her father, we'd be at least a jewel poorer and a lesson richer. My grandfather was a snake oil salesman, but that doesn't mean my father was too.*

"And none of it means I need to make the same mistake twice," he muttered to Scout as they turned the corner and headed into the alleyway behind With This Ring. "But the woman is a mystery. I'll give her that."

Scout grinned her goofy grin at him, tongue lolling, breath coming out in white puffs in the cold morning.

Goofball pup had missed Merry too.

He needed to put the staff on alert. Beef up security. Again. Mention Merry being in the alley to the cops. He was the friggin' manager at With This Ring. It was his job.

But the Merry he'd known—

He sighed.

She was right. He hadn't known her at all.

Scout bounced alongside him until he stopped in the middle of the alley. She sniffed the ground right about where Merry had flipped Max last night, then sank to her haunches and rolled all over Max's invisible body print.

In the soft light of dawn, the scene in the alley last night almost felt like a dream. But Max had a bruise or two to attest to how real it had been.

He studied the back door of With This Ring.

No scratch marks on the lock or the doorframe. Merry had been wearing gloves. All the better not to leave fingerprints. He'd called the security company, who had reviewed the tapes and confirmed she hadn't done anything more than turn a circle in the alley, and she hadn't returned. But that glower—she'd been expecting someone.

Why here?

The back door of As You Wish opened, and Zoe Scott stepped out. Her family had owned the wedding planning business next door to With This Ring as long as Max could remember. Her short, curly blond hair shone in the morning light and her black skirt twirled below her knees while she headed toward the dumpster between them with a sack of trash.

Scout leapt to her feet and barked a joyful greeting.

"Morning," Zoe said with a bright smile.

Scout lunged for her, but Max tightened his grip on her leash. "Early appointments?"

"All day with an eloper," she confirmed.

"Courthouse at noon?" Most popular place and time for last-minute Sunday weddings.

"Lilac Mills Chapel on Friday."

"Nice." Max ordered Scout to sit, then took Zoe's trash and tossed it up for her. "They need rings?"

"Came in with one from Tiffany's. Sorry." Zoe started to turn, but paused with one of those classic looks women got when they wanted to gossip. "So…how about that owl, huh? Good thing it was Kimmie's wedding. She's already talking about the stories she'll tell her grandchildren. And hey, speaking of Kimmie, I heard this crazy rumor."

"Her mother caught the owl and roasted it as payback for what it did to the wedding and the festival?" Max suggested.

"No, she'd be more likely to put a curse on it. Actually, I give it two days before the Bridal Retailers Association calls for a hunt for the white owl. Don't go looking for that one too, okay? You've got enough hexes already."

Max pinned her with a dark stare. "There is no hex."

"You have to say that since your family keeps a cursed diamond on display."

"There's no such thing as a cursed diamond." But the Mrs. Claus diamond ring was the most notorious, if not the most valuable, item inside With This Ring, which made it the item most likely to have caught Merry's fancy.

If burglary played into her motives in being in the alley last night.

"Speaking of curses," Zoe said.

Max held up a hand. "Nope. Not going there."

"But I heard Kimmie saw your last ex-girlfriend last night." She offered a small smile. "Thought you should know. You know. So you don't run into her without warning."

Twelve hours too late for that.

"Oh! You saw her too!"

He pulled his phone out and hit his photo app, then scrolled back to a selfie he should've deleted months ago. If his hometown had to have a well-oiled gossip machine, he might as well use it to his advantage. He flipped the phone around and held the picture up for Zoe. "You see her, let me know?"

"Oh, boy," she murmured. She flashed him a pained smile. "Merry. I forgot her name was Merry."

And she apparently got around. "You've seen her?"

"I'm planning her mother's wedding. It's Friday. At Lilac Mills." She stomped a foot. "And she seemed so nice."

"She was nice," Max muttered.

"You're not thinking of getting back together with her, are you?"

"Do I look like an idiot?"

The wind picked up, ruffling Scout's fur and sending an errant curl into Zoe's eyes. She brushed it back and glared at him. "Max, she just left. Without a word. I can be professional with her and her mother, but she broke your heart. So yes, I'm going to see her, but no, I'm not going to tell you."

"Thanks for that vote of confidence."

"You still have at least two years left on your curse. It's not your fault."

"There is no curse."

"Bliss has a psychic matchmaker, but curses don't exist?"

"There's no such thing as a psychic matchmaker either."

Zoe huffed. "You men are impossible. I'm calling Rachel."

Max bit back a word inappropriate for Scout's ears. "You don't have to—"

"It's for your own good, Max. If you won't protect yourself from the curse, we'll have to do it for you."

Zoe turned and marched back into As You Wish.

"Women," Max muttered.

Scout huffed at him, then sneezed on his pants.

Max took one last look at the back door of With This Ring.

Zoe was right. He needed to keep his distance from Merry.

But keeping his distance wouldn't get him any answers.

He rubbed Scout's head, then turned around, pulling his dog along with him.

He had a sudden need for some Sunday morning waffles.

MERRY CUT into an out-of-season strawberry on a china plate, almost awake after a half cup of coffee. She was halfheartedly listening to Mom explain to Patrick the necessity of handcrafted ornaments as favors for the small wedding party when her inner Phoebe Moon went on full alert.

She didn't lift her head, but she shifted her gaze to glance about the room, using the ornamental mirrors near the Christmas tree in her subtle surveillance.

And what she saw was a disaster in the making.

If it were possible for a heart to drop to one's toes at the same time it leapt into one's throat, that was exactly what happened to her. That pesky organ just up and stretched like Silly Putty, hitting all the high and low and in-between points at once.

Max in an elf costume in a dark alley was adorably sexy.

Max in clothes of the night, lit by only the glow of a Christmas tree, was dangerously sexy.

Max in faded straight-leg jeans, a leather jacket, and windblown dark hair, in full morning daylight, was potently sexy.

And curious.

He hadn't called the cops on her.

But he apparently had no plans to let her out of sight either.

She gave fleeting thought to shrieking "Owl!" and upending a table as a distraction, but while that would work for Phoebe Moon with charmingly hilarious effects, it would likely result in Merry being put on B&B dish duty at best, and in Mom having hysterics that threatened the likelihood of her impending wedding being as perfect as every one of her other weddings had been.

But then, letting Max any closer to Mom was dangerous in its own right.

She could fake a stomach bug. Or convince Mom she had a stomach bug. Or Patrick.

"Excuse me," Max said, "is this seat taken?"

"Yes," Merry said.

Mom tilted an odd look in her direction.

"By my imaginary friend Raoul. He's a unicorn."

Patrick coughed half-chewed eggs onto the table. His face went the color of the strawberry. Mom's bride-to-be glow dimmed, replaced with a classic Mom frown that actually moved some of the muscles in her upper face.

There had been a time when *my imaginary friend Raoul* was code for *the nice police officers who come around to ask about Daddy every few months*.

Either Mom didn't remember, or she didn't buy it. "Meredith, you'll never attract a man until you quit talking about your imaginary unicorns and pet clowns."

"You must be Merry's mom." Max claimed the fourth seat at their table, reaching across to shake Mom's hand at the same time. "Max Gregory. I had the pleasure of dating your daughter a year ago."

Despite her Botox, the corners of Mom's eyes went tight. "A year ago?"

"A year ago."

"A year ago," Merry agreed. "We had some fun, then it was over. End of story. Excuse us, Max, we have shopping to do."

Max kicked back in his seat and made himself comfortable. "I hear congratulations are in order."

Mom gave him a thin-lipped smile. "Thank you. Tell me, Max, why did you and my daughter break up?"

"I wouldn't actually say we broke up. More like we went our separate ways."

"Mom, we'll be late—"

"You live here in Bliss?" Mom said.

"My family runs one of the jewelry shops."

"And now we all know each other, so we can be on our way." Merry tossed her napkin on her plate.

Mom's eyes had gone harder than diamonds. "Meredith, stay."

Patrick's shoulders hunched in.

Apparently Mom hadn't introduced him to the Displeased and Suspicious Mom Voice yet.

"Mom, I'm not giving you grandchildren with Max," Merry said. "We're incompatible. There's no reason for an inquisition."

"Patrick, dear," Mom said, "I need a second bagel."

Huh. There was an idea.

Let Mom handle Max. She'd have their wedding planned within six minutes. If that didn't scare him, nothing would.

"I'll get it," Merry said.

"You'll stay." Mom took a dainty sip of her coffee, still eyeing Max. "I so rarely get the chance to see what my daughter looks for in a man. She hardly had the best examples growing up."

Max didn't flinch. "So I've gathered."

"Patrick, while you're getting the bagel, could you check the hours on the chocolate shop again too?"

"Noon to six on Sundays," Max said.

"Patrick, be a dear and double-check Matt's information."

Patrick's watery eyes shifted from Mom to Merry to Max, then back again. "Vicky, honey, if you need me here—"

"You sweet, sweet man. I always need you, schmoopsie, but this is one of those things a mother has to handle on her own." Her lashes batted.

Merry again considered faking throwing up.

"All right, but you call me if you need anything." He gave Max a stern finger shake. "I don't tolerate my girls being mistreated."

"Looking forward to the day I can threaten my niece's suitors," Max said. "Don't plan on messing up my chances of living long enough to do it. Your girls are safe with me."

"Merry knows karate," Patrick said.

"Duly noted." Smoky amusement flashed in Max's eyes—a deep aquamarine today—and Merry's feminine parts stirred to life again.

She'd known few men who considered strength and agility as attractive as Max seemed to.

She'd known fewer men she'd let close enough to honestly find her attractive. But for two glorious months, she'd felt it. A reluctant attachment. Both sexual attraction and intellectual attraction. With an underlying affection. From a man who hadn't needed to be generous with physical gifts because he'd satisfied emotional needs she hadn't known she had.

"Tell me, Matt," Mom said, "how did you meet my daughter?"

"Well, Nicky—"

"Victoria. Or Ms. Silver, if you please."

Patrick left the room. Merry's thighs squeezed, ready to bolt. Max stole the last piece of bacon from her plate. "Mrs. Silver," he said, "we met over a shared love of fine literature."

Merry scooted her chair back. "You two are ridiculous. I'm—"

Max's hand clamped around her wrist before she could stand—gentle enough for her to jerk away without having to toss him out of his chair, firm enough to send a message.

Trust me.

"Not likely," she muttered.

"Are you here to win my daughter back?" Mom asked.

"I'm here because I live down the street and I like the waffles." As if on cue, their hostess appeared with a heaping plate for Max. He flashed her a dark-stubbled grin, then finished Merry's bacon.

Mom knit her fingers together and leaned her chin on them. "How long did you date?"

"Not long enough," Max said cheerfully.

"You're just as good at not answering as Meredith is."

"Then maybe we did date long enough. But I'm not a ninja. Yet."

Phoebe Moon would've smashed her strawberry up Max's nose, then conveniently discovered a stray dog with a taste for berries lurking outside the back door who would've been happy to lick the berry out of said orifice. Merry, however, was trying desperately to be a grown-up today.

A grown-up with the superpower of resisting sexy ex-boyfriends who should've called the cops on her once or twice in the past twelve hours, but mysteriously hadn't.

Or had he? "What do you want, Max?"

"To eat my waffles in the company of two lovely ladies."

"Dear God, he's as bad a flirt as your father," Mom said.

"And we're done." Merry stood.

"Have you ever been arrested?" Mom asked him.

"I was a teenage boy once."

"Mom, I have no intention of resuming a relationship with Max. Let's go."

There it was again. A flash of injury that turned his eyes brittle and his lips hard.

"Intention?" he said. "Or interest?"

"Either," she lied.

If they'd been on another continent—or planet—she might've given in to a desire to fantasize about indulging in a relationship with Max again, but not only was she leaving the country soon, she was also the daughter of a man who stole jewels both as sport and to avenge perceived wrongs, especially those done to his family.

Dating a jeweler was inviting Daddy to his own personal playground.

"Tell me, Matt," Mom said, "is your jewelry store known for anything special? Unique settings, original cuts, historically significant clients?"

"My grandfather designed the Mrs. Claus diamond ring," Max said. "We keep it on display."

And once again, Merry was glad she'd made Phoebe Moon an orphan. No mothers to become irrationally suspicious and disappointed.

Or justifiably suspicious and disappointed, for that matter.

"Meredith," Mom said, her voice low and lethal and Mom-like, "is there anything you need to tell me?"

Merry leaned her fists on the table. "Is there anything else you think I should tell you?"

"I don't know, dear. You were the one who left the festival last night just before an owl attacked Mrs. Claus."

"I wasn't feeling well."

"Because of the owl?"

"Weddings make me ill. Except yours, of course."

Mom slid a long side-eye toward Max. "Because you hate weddings, or because you're afraid you'll never have your own?"

Merry thought a word that wasn't fit for Phoebe Moon's ears. "You can take the girl out of the dream, but you can't take the dream out of the girl," she said softly. She pushed herself fully upright. "I'll be ready to go in ten minutes. Max, lovely seeing you this morning. Enjoy your life."

His gaze was too intense. Too all-seeing. Too borderline affectionate. "Why stop the fun? My family's having a practice Christmas dinner this afternoon. Come join us."

"No."

"Meredith."

"No, *thank you,*" Merry said. "Mom, we have appointments all day."

"Hmm..."

"We eat at two," Max said.

"Mom, the cake-tasting—" Merry started.

"Kimmie Cakes or Heaven's Bakery?"

"Heaven's Bakery, of course." Mom smiled. "It sounds so auspicious for a wedding, doesn't it?"

"Go to Kimmie Cakes," Max said. "Best in Bliss. Ask anyone." He flashed a wolfish grin at Merry. "I hear she'll still bake fruitcake cupcakes as special requests."

Merry pinched her lips together.

"Fascinating." Mom batted her lashes at him. "Any other suggestions?"

"None that I know you well enough to suggest. Could change that this afternoon if you come to dinner."

"Hmm," Mom said again. She stood. "So sorry to abandon you to eat alone, Matt, but my daughter's correct. We're in danger of being late."

"*Max*," Merry muttered.

Mom smiled sweetly. "*Max*. My mistake."

He grinned at both of them. "Come hungry." He scribbled an address on a napkin and handed it to Mom.

"You know stalking is a crime, right?" Merry said to Max.

"I come here once a month for the waffles. And it's not stalking if you come to my brother's house. Which you'll apparently be doing this afternoon."

"Neither of us have agreed to that."

"We haven't declined either," Mom said.

"You haven't, but I have."

Max's eyes narrowed, but his lips tipped up at the same time. "All the better to learn your secrets if she comes alone," he murmured.

Crap.

Suspicious was good.

Intrigued was not.

And Merry had a feeling Max was both.

6

"Why are you alone, Phoebe Moon?" Zack Diggory whispered in the darkness.

"I'm not alone. I have Spike. And now I have you."

—Phoebe Moon and the Missing Sunshine

Mom was silent all the way to her silver Cadillac. She'd punched her finger over her phone's screen hard enough that Merry was surprised the glass hadn't shattered. Probably texting Patrick. The bagel shop was on a side street at the other end of The Aisle, and he hadn't returned yet.

But as soon as they were closed inside the chilly car, Mom swung around to face Merry. "When did you see your father?" Her breath flowed visibly in a puff of white, making her look every bit as dangerous as a dragon.

"Would my seeing Daddy change any of your plans?"

"Meredith Cordelia Silver, *when did you see your father?*"

Merry slouched in her seat. "I didn't. I just—I thought I smelled him."

"Is he planning on robbing your former boyfriend's store?"

It was Daddy. Of course he was. Maybe not today, but sometime. "Have you told Patrick about Daddy?"

"What aren't you telling me?"

Merry couldn't tell if Mom was asking because she was worried about Merry or because she desperately wanted to hear something about Daddy. "Would you have divorced him if he hadn't tried to rob the mayor that night?"

Mom gripped the gear shifter. Her face went gray, her voice softer. "Merry, once you came along, our split was inevitable. Your father—he's a good man, but he has an illness. I can't cure him. You can't cure him. I should've left him long before I did, for both our sakes."

"You don't need to protect me anymore."

"I'm your mother. I will always need to protect you." Mom faced forward again and turned the car on. "He's wanted for questioning in four states. If you see him, if you *smell* him, you need to tell the police."

Merry was wrapped in her thick winter coat, gloves and hat and scarf on, but she still felt a chill to her bones. "Could you do it? Could you call the cops on him?"

"You are not me, Merry. You have too many years ahead of you to risk spending them paying for your father's sins. You've done that enough already."

"I was probably just paranoid."

"Healthy talent to have," Mom muttered. "If you can't call the police, call me. Call me anytime. Understand?"

Merry nodded.

"And don't let your father stop you from dating. I need grandchildren to spoil."

"Can we get you married before we work on me?"

"Only if you promise me you will accept a date from a nice young man before this year's over."

"*If* a *nice* man asks me."

"*When* a nice man asks you. Preferably one without any connections to jewelry stores. Promise, Meredith."

"Okay, Mom."

"Pinky swear."

Merry dutifully held out her pinky.

She'd accept a date under those conditions.

But if she told Mom it wouldn't be on American soil, her mother would try to stop her. So as she'd done since the first moment she'd been paid for writing novels as Amber Finch, she let the details slide.

Mom would understand.

Mom would support her.

But Mom would also insist on going with her, and she needed to do this on her own.

BY TWO THIRTY, Max had gotten texts from five different friends that Merry had been spotted shopping with her mother along The Aisle—he'd known telling Zoe would start the gossip mill—but the daughter of the bride and her mother hadn't arrived at Dan and Rachel's comfortable brick home in the Roses on the Lake subdivision, where the most prominent business owners in Bliss lived.

Not that he'd been overly optimistic.

He'd read three chapters of the latest Phoebe Moon book to his seven-year-old niece—pretty neat that Phoebe Moon had a new sidekick with a car almost as cool as his. He'd also let himself get his ass handed to him in a pick-up field hockey game by his oldest nephew, who was gleefully recounting the tale to Dan. "*Six* goals, Dad. I got six goals, and Uncle Max just had *two*."

"That's what happens when you don't practice for ten years, Ty," Dan said. "Gavin, quit hitting your sister with a light saber. Max, you sure your guests are coming?"

"Nope." Max ducked under a flying light saber, then wrestled nine-year-old Gavin under his arm and claimed the light saber for himself.

The bruises he'd gotten last night made holding onto the squirmy stinker harder.

Rachel popped into the room. She was in Grinch slippers, and her Sunday clothes were covered by a spotless lacy apron. Scents of fresh bread and roasting beef wafted into the room with her. "Dinner's on in ten. Olivia, wash your hands and set the table, please. Boys, go wash up and help your sister. Dan, carving time. Max—oh, honey, you really need to let go of this Merry woman. Have you met my friend Alyssa? She works in human resources at the school district over in Willow Glen, and her grandma is a Cajun witch doctor. I could ask if her grandma can help with the—"

"Thanks, Rach, but I'm good." Max released Gavin.

"I don't honestly believe in curses either, but it certainly can't hurt," she said. "And I won't deny being glad they're not here. *Gavin*, we do not steal light sabers from adults, and we certainly don't light-saber Christmas trees if we want Santa Claus to come. Go. Wash. Set the table."

The gangly, dark-haired boy flashed an impish grin, then loped off toward the bathroom, where Olivia was shrieking about something Ty had done. Max paused to look out the window once again—no Merry, no Ms. Victoria Silver, no harried fiancé—then reluctantly shuffled to the recently upgraded kitchen, where Dan was expertly slicing a prime rib on the marble island. Max spied popovers rising in the oven, and steam shot out from beneath the lid of a pan on the stove top.

"Rach tell you she's taking a collection and handpicking a girl to bid on you in the bachelor auction next weekend?" Dan said.

"I was thinking about asking Pepper Blue." Rachel lifted a saucepan and poured its contents into a china gravy boat. "She's supposedly cursed too. That pre-bride thing, you know. Not that we believe in curses."

Dan grinned around his wife and mouthed, *Right,* to Max.

"Pepper's had a longer streak of bad luck in love than you have," Rach added.

Max liked Pepper Blue just fine. She was relatively new to Bliss and pretty enough, but she wasn't...Merry.

He reached into his pocket and discreetly pulled his phone out.

No text messages. No email, no phone calls.

Rachel handed him a bowl of steamed green beans. "Really, there are plenty of other women in the world who won't abandon you without explanation. You can find one, and there are lots of us happy to help. But put this on the table first. And tell Ty to please come here."

Max escaped to the dining room, steaming bowl in hand, and found himself in the midst of a three-way wrestling match. "Whoa, rug rats. What's going on here?"

"Gavin took the small-end spoon!" Olivia shrieked from her position in the middle of the dog pile. "It's my turn for the small-end spoon!"

"Is not!"

"Is too!"

"If you two can't agree, then I'm taking it," Ty said.

Olivia raised her knee up, and Ty grunted and rolled off the other two.

"Uncle Max, make her give it to me," Gavin whined.

This was one of many reasons why Max hadn't been bothered by his supposed Golden Bouquet hex.

He wasn't interested in love. Not the kind that came with being tied down, cancelling poker night because a kid was sick, planning vacations around where it was easy to navigate with strollers, and buying flowers to apologize for something that most likely wasn't his fault.

At least, he hadn't been.

Not when he found the Golden Bouquet.

Not a year later, when he'd moved in and become primary caretaker for his rapidly aging grandparents until they'd gone into a nursing home.

But sometime in the past year or so, he'd begun having occasional weird urges.

"Uncle Max!" Gavin shouted.

Max set the beans on the table, then bent and snagged the scuffed, short, skinny spoon from Olivia. "*I* get the small-end spoon."

"No one gets the small-end spoon." Rachel sailed past him to deposit the gravy boat on the perfect, shimmery green tablecloth. "It doesn't match the silver, and this is practice Christmas dinner. Tyler, pour the milk. Gavin, napkins. Olivia. Wash. Your. Hands." She plucked the small-end spoon from Max's fingers, then marched back out of the Martha Stewart-inspired dining room.

"It's not fair," Gavin grumbled.

"You're a gnarger," Olivia said.

Ty hip-checked her on his way to the kitchen. "Shut up, Olivia. There's no such thing as a gnarger."

"Is too."

"Is not."

"Is too. Phoebe Moon fought them off to save the honey bees when the bastardly Uncle Sandy—"

"*Dastardly*, Olivia." Dan strolled in with a plate of prime rib, lips twitching. "And Phoebe Moon would've had the table set two hours ago before her mother had to yell about it. No popovers for children who don't do their chores."

"Phoebe Moon doesn't have a mother," Olivia grumbled, but she marched herself over to the china cabinet and pulled out the good silver.

"Never dull," Dan said to Max.

No, it wasn't.

And Max was starting to think that Dan always had the best of everything.

7

Phoebe Moon had only been here for one night, but she already understood that the hideaway was special.
It was where people went when the demands of being more than a mere human became too much to bear.
—Phoebe Moon and the Ninja Hideaway

Sunday evening, Merry dragged her weary bones into a bar and grill across town from the B&B, sidled up to the silver semicircle bar beneath an impressive display of purple track lights that were warring with an overabundance of multicolored Christmas lights, and asked the perky redheaded bartender for a shot of vodka.

A cheese plate would've been nice, but cheese goo on fries seemed to be the closest she could get. She scanned the bar, noting bracelets, watches, and earrings, and cringed at the casual way so many women had simply hung their purses on the backs of their chairs or tucked them at their feet, as if that could stop a petty thief.

A familiar voice on the other side of the brunette beside her made her go still.

Zoe Scott.

Mom's wedding planner.

Because today hadn't been awkward enough.

Oh, Zoe had been perfectly polite and pleasant, perky even, and Mom hadn't noticed anything amiss.

But Zoe had had *the look.*

She had figured out who Merry was too. As had half of Bliss, apparently.

"You don't have to do a thing," Zoe was saying in her cheerful way. She was a lively, fashionable blonde with curly hair, red lipstick, and faint freckles dotting her cheeks. "Well, other than show up. Rachel's taking donations, and when word gets out as to why you're bidding on Max, everyone will let you win. Then at least one of your curses will be broken. It's worth a shot, right?"

Another curse, Merry! Phoebe Moon said. *I love this town.*

Merry glanced around the bar again. There was an open seat on the other side of a group of middle-aged men in sports jerseys. She could move.

Not listen to plans for other women with make-believe curses to bid on Max.

"His curse has an expiration date," the brunette said. She sounded familiar too. "But I heard his old girlfriend is in town to win him back."

"I don't think that's going to happen," Zoe answered. "After how she left him, there's no—oh. Ah. Um, hi, Merry."

Merry gave the wedding planner a flat smile. "Zoe. You were a great help today. Thanks."

The brunette turned. Her bright green eyes were set off by her chunky malachite necklace and earrings. She was still in the stylish black silk pantsuit she'd worn at Bliss Bridal this morning, but her friendly, helpful expression of this morning had turned curious and guarded.

Pepper Blue. Merry and Mom had spent two hours with her picking a wedding dress for Mom that would hopefully not be sacrificed on the pyre of broken hearts and shattered dreams in another two years.

Merry's bridesmaid dress would end up donated to a resale shop, as they usually did, regardless of the fate of this marriage.

"Merry," Pepper said, "how's Patrick?"

Currently making Merry very happy that he was Mom's fiancé instead of Merry's, given the man-flu he'd contracted as Mom was paying for their dresses.

Merry didn't do sickbed coverage. Especially when there were bodily fluids involved. "Fairly miserable, but Mom thinks he'll be better tomorrow."

"We hope so," Zoe said quickly. Her fair cheeks had taken on a pink tinge.

More people were looking at them curiously. Thanks to Daddy, she was highly familiar with being the subject of scrutiny based solely on who she was. Or rather, to whom she was related.

But today, she suspected, the scrutiny was all of her own making.

She turned her benign smile to Pepper. "Mom says this dress is her favorite of all her wedding dresses."

Who cares about dresses. Ask her about her curse, Phoebe Moon said.

There's no such thing as curses, Phoebe Moon, Phoebe's newly introduced sidekick, Zack Diggory, replied.

"She'll be a lovely bride," Pepper said.

"Tell Patrick to get better quickly," Zoe said. "You have cake to taste tomorrow."

They'd had to cancel their tasting today after Patrick fell ill. "We can't wait."

The bartender deposited Merry's vodka on the bar, and she turned back to face it. "Anyway, don't let me disturb your evening."

"You're not disturbing us," Zoe said.

Right. Probably a standard Bliss line. Merry reached into her pocket. Phone, ID, cash still there. She had no idea what the shot cost, but a twenty would cover it, and then she could get out of here.

"We were just talking about...um..." Zoe started.

"Our book club," Pepper said.

"Yes! Our happy endings book club." Zoe tugged a ruby stud in her ear. "We don't read anything depressing. Do you like to read?"

"I met Max in a bookstore." Why stop at half-awkward? "But you probably already knew that."

Zoe's eyes went round, but Pepper inched her chin up. "Actually, most of us know very little about you."

"Just that you disappeared without a word to Max," Zoe said softly.

"Which was when half the town found out he was dating anyone at all."

"No one likes to see their friends get hurt." There was both a hint of apology and a prompt for an explanation lingering in Zoe's voice.

As though they meant it. That they didn't know anything about her.

Not who she was. Not what she did. Not who her father was.

All they knew was how her relationship with Max had ended.

Was that even possible?

"It's nice that Max has you watching out for him," she said.

"It's what friends do," Pepper replied.

And they were Max's friends, not Merry's. She got it.

They'd be nice to her because it was their job. They'd make sure Mom got the wedding of her dreams. But they wouldn't stand by if they thought she was planning to hurt Max again.

She grabbed her vodka and tossed it back.

The spirit burned her throat, but it gave her a legit reason for the sting in her eyes.

She slid the twenty onto the bar. "For whatever it's worth, I didn't want it to end the way it did either."

And that was all she could say on the subject without going too far down memory lane. She spun around and collided with a solid mass of heat and strength and leather.

Sure hands gripped her upper arms.

Her wounded heart swelled and leapt into her throat. Without thinking, she arced her arms up and around to break his hold. Before she could finish him off, he jumped back.

"Easy." Max held his hands up, a no-harm gesture. "Just came in for a drink."

Embarrassment and loneliness burned behind her nose. "Last I checked, you couldn't get a drink out of my arms."

His eyes flickered. They were ocean blue tonight, deep and fathomless, telegraphing a seductive combination of irritation, worry, and that dang intrigue again. He didn't physically block her way, but his gaze wouldn't let her go. "Stay. Have a hot chocolate. We're all friendly around here."

Friendly in a suspicious, we-don't-want-you-here kind of way. "Thank you, but no."

He slid a look behind her toward Pepper and Zoe, and his eyes tightened.

"We were talking about our happy endings book club," Pepper said quickly.

"Yeah, somebody picked these kid books for next month," Zoe added. "Phoebe Stars or something."

"Phoebe Moon?" Max said.

Oxygen heaved out of Merry's lungs, and her heart spun as though it had been dropped in a centrifuge.

"Fun books," Max said, one eye still on Merry.

Because he'd figured out her secret?

Or because he'd been buying a Phoebe Moon book for his niece when they met?

"My favorite was *Phoebe Moon and the Ninja Hideaway*," Max said.

Hers too. Or it had been until last week's release of *Phoebe Moon and the Missing Sunshine.*

Probably she shouldn't have given Phoebe Moon a new best friend, the sixteen-year-old, dark-haired, 1970 Dodge Charger-driving Zack Diggory.

There was a possibility Merry had put too much of herself—and Max—in this latest Phoebe Moon book.

"You should come to book club with us, Max," Zoe said. "Pepper will be there."

Merry's lips wobbled.

But it didn't matter.

She was going to France. She didn't need Max's friends' approval. And he had Pepper now. They were going to break each other's curses and live happily ever after.

"Can I walk you to your car?" Max said to Merry.

"Didn't drive."

"Max, actually, we had a question about Saturday," Zoe said.

He ignored her. "How about a lift?"

Merry wavered.

He'd been good to her last year. Trusting. Affectionate. Generous.

But every time she looked at him, all she saw was a jeweler who hadn't known he was sleeping with a jewel thief's daughter. "If I let you drive me back, will you tell them this is strictly platonic and they don't have to worry?"

His wolfish smile set off fireworks in her feminine parts. "Small town. They're gonna think what they're gonna think."

"Then I'll walk."

"Hey, Max," another voice called.

Max waved them off. "C'mon, Merry. It's cold outside. All I'm offering is a ride."

A ride in Trixie. Alone with Max. In the dark. "You'll take me directly to the B&B."

"Heavy traffic this time of night."

"In this small town?"

"Cows claim the roads after eight."

Her lips parted, then clamped shut. If there were cows around Bliss, she hadn't seen them.

"Or maybe ghosts of jilted brides past," he said. "Never know in Bliss."

Max was obviously determined to drive her home. And she

couldn't deny a primal pleasure in letting him when his friends obviously wanted to save him from himself.

She turned toward the door. Max followed. She could tell by the current sparking through the air and casting a figurative shadow over her back.

Max Gregory was dangerous.

But only to Merry's heart.

8

Perhaps devilish Uncle Sandy was right. Perhaps the world was *a better place with silence.*

—Phoebe Moon and the Stolen Sound

The inky sky wrapped itself like an icy cocoon around Max when he followed Merry out the front door of Suckers.

She'd marched out of the bar like a woman on a mission, but her steps slowed, and he swore her ears twitched before she stepped off the sidewalk and into the parking lot.

He hadn't noticed anything unusual about her sense of awareness last year, but then, he hadn't been looking for it. Now, he wondered if she was always on high alert and if she'd noticed something he hadn't.

The Merry he'd known hadn't been on edge. No more than anyone else he knew, anyway. The day they'd met, she'd started out so cautious, he'd wondered if she'd just gotten out of a bad relationship. The last night she'd stayed with him, she'd gone pale and shaky when Scout wouldn't stop barking at something in the backyard.

But every moment between, she'd been more. Perceptive and intelligent with a dry wit one minute, carefree and happy and young the next.

This Merry wasn't that girl. She was still intriguing. Captivating. Fascinating. But she wasn't innocent, and her wit had an edge to it.

He wanted to know how much of her had been real.

He casually scanned the SUVs, sedans, and sports cars in the parking lot, noting she was doing the same, before clearing his throat and tilting his head toward the corner of the building.

Merry fell into step beside him, but she didn't look at him.

She was still scanning their surroundings with sharp eyes.

"You still drive that old Mustang?" she asked.

"Absolutely. Trixie and I are inseparable."

Trixie, the red 1965 Mustang convertible he'd restored during his summers home in college, sat where he'd left her in a nice, spacious spot at the end of the row. He unlocked the passenger door and held it open for Merry.

She sucked her lower lip into her mouth and bit down, and her fingers brushed the top of the door.

"Missed you at dinner this afternoon." His voice came out huskier than he'd intended.

She snatched her hand off the car. "I told you I wouldn't be there."

"Wedding planning going well?"

"As well as it ever does."

Remarkable that he hadn't noticed last year how little Merry talked about herself and her family. Now, her every evasive answer was one more piece of the Merry puzzle.

He had five days to figure her out. To figure out why he wanted to. And the blood surging to his groin right now didn't count as a valid reason. He gestured into the car. "After you."

She scanned their surroundings again, so Max did the same. Small shrubs at the edge of the building rustled in the wind, their Christmas lights swaying. Three men crossed the parking lot, one with a lit cigarette glowing between his fingers.

"Expecting someone?" Max asked.

She didn't answer but instead slid into Trixie's stiff leather seat.

Max closed her in, then crossed around the car. A bell jingled in the distance. Subtle scents of beer and fried food lingered in the chilly air. Nothing seemed out of place here to him.

He stayed silent while he buckled in and cranked the engine. Trixie roared to life, a sound that always put a thrill in his veins. He draped his arm behind Merry's seat while he glanced out the rear window to back out of the parking space.

In his experience, women didn't like silence.

Especially when they were sitting in a car made for speed and sex.

Sure enough, he hadn't even put Trixie in first gear before Merry spoke. "You didn't tell your friends about my father."

"Should I have?"

"I would've if I were you."

"You could've told them. Just now."

"They're not my friends."

Was he imagining the lonely longing in her voice, or was she playing him? "They could be."

"Max." She made a noise in her throat that sent more blood flowing to Max Jr. "I'm here for a wedding. That's *it*. When it's over, I'm gone. *Gone*. Forever."

His gut tightened. "Not many weddings take place in the alley behind my family's jewelry shop."

"I have a paranoia problem, okay? I was just making sure your security was solid last night. Trouble follows me. You were a good friend last year, and I don't want our past to bring you trouble too."

"Was your father the reason you disappeared?"

She didn't answer.

He stopped the car at the edge of the parking lot, looked both ways for traffic, then glanced at Merry.

Her lips were pressed together in a grim line.

He followed her lead and clamped his own jaw shut. For Trixie's sake, he needed to quit provoking the ninja in the passenger seat.

At least until they were safely parked at the B&B.

They'd gone two blocks before Merry spoke again. "How's Scout?"

"Sad that Kimmie quit making fruitcake cupcakes."

Scout had loved Merry to the point of getting herself put in her crate downstairs the nights Merry stayed over, instead of being allowed to sleep on the floor next to Max's bed. If he hadn't kicked Scout out, he'd been more likely to wake up on the floor while his dog snuggled his girl.

And Max had liked that girl.

She was fun. And different. Cool about being casual, and Max hadn't even noticed when they'd passed his usual relationship expiration date.

But a week before Thanksgiving, she'd disappeared.

And Max had started believing in curses.

He steered Trixie onto the side street where Merry's B&B sat prominently in the center of the block. "You remember how Scout wouldn't stop barking?"

He caught a jerky nod out of his peripheral vision.

"Neighbors behind me got flamingoed," Max said.

"Flamingoed?"

"Sixty-eight plastic flamingoes in their yard. Culprits never caught."

"Such awful crime in Bliss."

"Half had wedding veils," Max said. "Actually, two more than half. The paper called it Bliss's first avian lesbian union."

She didn't respond. Max coasted Trixie to a stop in front of the old Victorian house.

Merry unbuckled her seatbelt. "Thank you for the ride."

"Sure."

He killed the engine and unbuckled himself too. He'd agreed to drive her straight home, but he hadn't agreed to leave immediately thereafter.

"You don't have to walk me to the door."

"Afraid I'll talk to your mother again?"

"More afraid she'll talk to you again."

He grinned. "Mothers are impossible when they want grandchildren. I could let you meet mine," he offered. Never mind that his parents were off on a road trip for the week, hunting the best Christmas light displays in the Midwest. "Tell her all about your father. Drop a subtle suggestion or two about our intentions. I know it's a big favor to ask to get her off my back, but—*oomph.*"

She had sharp elbows.

"Goodnight, Max."

Trixie's door opened then slammed shut behind her. He joined Merry on the short walk to the B&B's front door. He kept his hands in his pockets and even tried to keep his breath on his side of the sidewalk.

She walked faster.

He did too.

"Heard we might get snow this week," he said.

She angled a half squint at him, an *are we seriously talking about the weather?* kind of squint. "Tends to happen in winter."

"Technically, it's still fall."

"Because Santa didn't see his shadow?"

That was the Merry he remembered. Dry, funny, and imaginative.

And the closer he could get to the Merry he remembered, the more likely he could get some truth out of her. "You're getting confused with—"

He was cut off by a sudden flurry of white feathers between them.

Something thwacked him in the ear. Merry shrieked and threw her hands in front of her face. The creature hoot-squawked.

Max grunted and blocked it with his arms. "What the—"

Feathers went up his nose. He swung blindly at the bird and took another wing to the face. Merry's body was a blur of motion, dodging and hopping and waving in a sea of feathers.

A hard edge knocked him in the ribs. "*Oomph.*" He stumbled back. "The *bird,* Merry. Go ninja on the effing *owl.*"

"I can't hit an owl!" she shrieked.

Max lunged for it. "It's hitting you!"

"Then you take care of it."

"I'm trying to." Bits of information from the paper's article on last night's dive-bombing owl tickled his brain. *Beak. Talons. Animal control if sighted. Do not engage. Take cover.*

A flapping noise sounded close to Max's ear. Merry lunged toward him—or toward the bird—but the owl lifted itself into the sky, and Merry's shoulder connected with Max's solar plexus.

He grunted again and lost his footing. The world tilted, and suddenly he was falling, fast, hard, until his hip crashed into the frozen yard.

A body landed on top of him, knocking the last of the wind from his lungs.

Above him, the owl's wings gracefully extended. It hovered a moment longer, feathers falling like snow, then it swooped to the side and disappeared into the night.

Merry jerked on top of him, and her head connected with his chin.

Max bit back a curse. The worst hits he'd taken on the football field in high school hadn't hurt like this. But then, he'd had pads on.

And this ninja woman was ten times as dangerous as a high school linebacker.

She put her hands to his chest and pushed herself up, straddling his hips, and despite the pain radiating through his body, Max Jr. stirred to life.

He closed his eyes and forced himself to think of something disgusting. Like kissing his sister-in-law. Or getting puked on by his nephews or nieces. His grandmother naked.

Just when it was starting to work, gentle fingers tugged at his hair.

Sparks exploded all over his scalp, and his stiff shaft pulsed against the warm body straddling him.

Merry froze.

Her fingers were still in his hair. "Sorry," she whispered.

Before she could move, Max gripped her wrist and held it tight. "For being gentle? Much as I enjoy having my ass kicked by you, I might enjoy this more."

She didn't jerk away. No elbows jabbed his gut. No fingers gouged his eyeballs out. No ninja legs squeezed his hips so tight they severed the flow of blood to his legs.

He was almost disappointed at that last one.

"I still miss you," he said.

Her fingers moved in his hair again. And her center moved against him. Slowly, slightly, painfully. But he felt it, and he wanted more.

Her eyes were wide and dark, her breath coming in short bursts. "The owl addled your brain."

"You addle my brain."

"Max—"

"You've changed."

"Everyone changes."

"Are you happy?"

With a quick flick of her wrist, Merry freed herself. "I appreciate the concern, but—"

She started to scoot off him. Max grabbed her by the waist and pulled himself semi-upright. "I always thought you were happy when we were together."

"You need to let me go."

"But what do *you* need?"

He felt a tremble go through her body.

"Who are you, Merry? Who do you want to be?"

She sucked her lower lip into her mouth, and Max's groin pulsed again.

It wasn't smart, it wasn't safe, but he wanted to take her lips in his mouth. He wanted to roll her onto her back and touch her and taste her and devour her. He wanted her to remember who they'd been last year. He wanted her to let him in.

He wanted her to be here for *him*.

Not for her mother.

Not because of her father.

He wanted to strip her down to just *her*, to learn her, to know her, to be able to trust her.

A shaft of light lit up her dark hair. "Merry? Is that—*stop molesting my daughter.*"

"Got this under control, Mom," Merry said dryly.

Max's groin twitched.

"Obviously his fault," her mother said. "This isn't how a nice young man behaves, is it?"

"Depends on how badly you want grandchildren."

Her mother *humph*ed. Merry slid off him, stood, and dusted her hands.

He rolled to sitting with a grunt.

"Have a nice evening, Max," Merry said.

"Be nicer if you came home with me," he replied before he could stop himself.

Not that he wanted to stop himself.

"Max—"

"Would've said goodbye differently if I'd known you were leaving."

She visibly shivered, and her eyes went dark.

Good dark.

"Why didn't you call the police last night?" she murmured.

"Last I checked, being in an alley isn't a crime."

"Meredith? Are you coming in before that questionable young man tries to do unspeakable things to you?"

"I'm coming."

"I wish," Max muttered. He shoved to his feet. "Still live in the same house. I'll be home all night."

She was bundled up in her coat, her back to him, but he could've sworn he felt the current of an intrigued shiver travel through the crisp air.

"Good night, Max," Merry said, more firmly this time.

"Night, Merry." He lifted a hand toward her frowning mother. "Nicky. Nice to see you again."

Her lips twitched, ruining her stern librarian glare. "I'm still debating if it's been nice seeing you again, Matt."

Wasn't hard to smile at the woman, even if she had interrupted the closest thing he'd had to sex in a year. "I'll have to try harder next time."

Merry stepped into the doorway with her mother. Max didn't expect her to look back, but she did.

She turned those mocha soul-suckers on him, and instead of his blood pulsing south, it pooled in his chest, warm and weird as it wrapped around that organ under his ribs.

Merry Silver looked every bit a woman who didn't need anyone to take care of her. She talked tough. She'd physically flattened him twice. Mentally and emotionally once, though he didn't like to admit it.

But something had happened to her in the past year.

Something wrong.

And Max wanted to fix it.

The door shut, closing the two women into the house and Max firmly out.

He'd walked away from closed doors before. He'd walked away from opportunities. He'd walked away from women.

But he didn't know how to walk away from Merry Silver.

THE DOOR HAD BARELY CLOSED when Mom turned and peered out the peephole. "Have all of your ex-boyfriends been this handsome?"

Merry could count on three fingers the number of boyfriends she'd had. "Every last one."

"He's still standing there."

And she could still feel his soft hair between her fingers, the pinging of her pulse, the searing heat of his gaze, the press of his hard length between her thighs. Max Gregory was a difficult man to walk away from. "The owl stole his brain." Ooh, good one. *Phoebe Moon and the Missing Brain.* A Halloween book. Delirious Uncle Sandy could—

"Obviously," Mom said. "I don't know which of you is crazier. A jeweler, Merry?"

Merry caught a glimpse of her feathered dark hair in the mirror over the buffet in the entryway. She picked at the white fluff in her ears and over her upper lip. "I know. Not one of my finer moments."

Was that a wrinkle furrowing her mother's brow? "Such a shame. Too bad he's not a banker. Does he know what happened? Why you left him?"

He'd suffered enough on Merry's behalf. She didn't need to saddle him with more. No matter how broad his shoulders, how solid his chest, how intrigued his eyes were, she had no intention of burdening him with the weight of her father's secrets.

Or her own. "He knows enough."

Trixie's engine roared to life outside.

Merry's heart twisted. "I need a shower." She headed toward the stairs. "How's Patrick?"

"Sleeping. I think the worst is behind us."

"Good."

Mom trailed her up the stairs. "Patrick has a nephew about your age."

"Mother."

"What? He does. I haven't met him, but Patrick tells me Richard is in management for some technical company in Iowa. He sounds lovely. And he'll be here for the wedding."

"I'm not taking Patrick's nephew as a date to your wedding."

Mom heaved a melodramatic sigh. "I can lead you to happiness, but I can't make you drink."

"Pretty sure you've made me drink," Merry muttered.

As had Daddy.

Merry had been eight when she'd first understood they were moving because of Daddy's job, but she'd been eleven before she'd discovered that *Daddy's job* had been stealing a classmate's mother's heirloom pearls after said classmate called Merry white trash.

She'd learned much later that he'd also stolen a ruby-and-diamond set from the mother of a kid who'd given her lice in preschool, and he'd taken a Rolex from her second-grade teacher's husband after Merry had gotten a less-than-stellar grade in storytelling.

Daddy didn't always replace what he took—he generally only bothered with replicas when it was a famous jewel or gem he was hunting for sport. Most of his heists were small-time thefts, vengeance grabs for perceived personal or societal wrongs. He pawned his ill-gotten treasures, and either used the money to put food on his family's table or to help more needy families.

"Sweetheart, I just want to see you happy," Mom said. "Preferably with someone who won't be hurt by your secrets."

She was talking about the secrets about Daddy, but Merry was suddenly back in Suckers, listening to Zoe drop Phoebe Moon's name and wondering how they'd like her if they knew she was Amber Finch.

Mom wrapped her in a hug.

"Are you getting Patrick germs on me?" Merry asked.

"Families share everything, darling."

Family.

Mom would always be her family.

But Merry had recently started contemplating the theory that people were meant to make their own families too. To fall in love. Get married. Have children who would one day give them grandchildren.

However, she couldn't even share her real job with her family, because Daddy always managed to ruin everything.

Everything.

He'd discover she had money. Or he'd hear that Merry and her editor were having a disagreement about something, and said editor could kiss her jewels goodbye. If she had a spat with a publicist or fired her agent or God forbid someone from a national newspaper ripped a Phoebe Moon novel to shreds, Daddy would be there as the avenging angel, making everything worse in his misguided attempts to make everything better.

And if she couldn't tell anyone how she made a living, how could she create a family of her own?

Mom stopped outside Merry's door. "Love you, sweetheart."

"Love you too," Merry choked out.

Mom stepped across the hall to her room. And this time, when the door shut, she wasn't simply alone.

She was lonely.

9

"Wouldn't you like to be me for a day, Phoebe Moon?" her evil twin said.

—Phoebe Moon and the Secret Sister

One year ago

Before Merry met Max, she'd had only two real boyfriends—a failed prom date and the twenty-something college student who'd lived next door to her first apartment. She liked guys. But she'd had precious little experience with normal, healthy relationships. So after a few dates with her neighbor, she'd let him relieve her of her virginity. He'd stuck around until he graduated a few months later, sending her flowers, dropping by to hang out, bringing over a movie, sleeping at her place from time to time, but he had a job lined up somewhere on the East Coast, so one day he left and they amicably agreed to go their own ways.

Fine with her. He'd been fun most of the time, but he talked too much about how much money this company or that company had offered him, and he'd made the occasional snide comments about his professors' love lives, and he'd always taken the last bite of any dessert they shared. In short, he was an experience in dating, but she hadn't been in love with him.

After that, her secret life as Amber Finch had begun to get exciting, with book deals and deadlines and launches. After Mom's wedding to Yo-yo, Merry had made a point to talk to her mother more. Yo-yo hadn't been much of a stepfather—Mom had totally pulled out her cougar stripes when she married him—but he'd been different. Refreshing and interesting and entertaining. By the time Mom had gotten bored with her boy-toy and his love affair with geeky gamer cons, Merry had come to appreciate her mom in a way she hadn't in her teen years, and they'd talked more after that. Gotten close in a way they hadn't been since Mom had divorced Daddy.

Plus, of everyone in the world, Mom understood the complications Daddy presented in her life. So while Merry occasionally wondered what it would've been like to have a real boyfriend, her job, her online friends, an occasional date with an acquaintance, and her relationship with her mom kept her happy enough.

Until Max.

He made her laugh at the Spencer McGraw signing. At dinner afterwards, they talked about nothing at all, really, but she was captivated by his eyes. His hands.

His lips.

Merry Silver had a crush.

Accepting his invitation to the Cubs game was a no-brainer. As in, her brain wasn't involved at all. But they hung out just like buddies at the game. He high-fived her when the Cubs scored. They talked about the players, about Wrigley Field, and Max told her a story about something going on with the Knot Festival committee in Bliss, but he didn't kiss her.

He didn't ask her out again either.

She left the game convinced that Max was simply looking for a buddy.

Heck, she didn't even know what he did for a job. She assumed it involved weddings, but they hadn't talked about it.

Not that she'd told him her job either, and the further they got from the book signing, the easier it was to conveniently forget that he'd bought her first Phoebe Moon book.

Still, when he called and said he had to be in Chicago for a meeting next Thursday and asked if she was free for dinner after, she shouted *yes* so fast she almost embarrassed herself.

When Thursday came, Max's meeting went late. He still had to drive back to Bliss, so Merry met him at a Five Guys near his meeting. As soon as they ordered, Max pulled off his tie and popped the top button on his shirt, and she lost her words.

How had she never realized how potently sexy a disheveled man in a suit was?

She told Phoebe Moon to cover her eyes and ears and indulged in some seriously mature thoughts about the broad-shouldered, five-o'clock-shadowed man across the table from her.

His hair needed a trim, and she itched to run her fingers through it and then help him unbutton the rest of his shirt. To get close enough to sniff him, to feel the heat of his body, to test for herself if his arms and chest were as solid as they appeared to be.

He offered her an apologetic grin. "Sorry about this. Thought we'd be done two hours ago."

"I'll forgive you so long as *Cosmo* says I should." She pulled a magazine from her bag, opened it to a quiz to help determine your perfect color palette, and tortured Max with demanding his answers.

He wanted to be buddies?

She'd show him how women did *buddies*.

"You're neutrals," she declared. "I suppose we can continue dinner. I happen to like gray. Moonrock is my favorite color. Plus, it's compatible enough with my peach palette."

His eyes went from sea-foam green to deep emeralds, and he dropped a fry. "That have any more quizzes about your *peaches*?"

"No, but if you're having any gynecological issues, we should flip to page 167."

"So if I want to know more about your peaches, I'll have to do firsthand research?"

"Unless you want to go to the library and see if any back issues have peach quizzes." She was a terrible flirt.

But Max's full lips curved into a glorious, intrigued smile, and he leaned closer into the table. "I'm more of a hands-on type of guy."

"Are you? So far, I hadn't noticed."

I'm not old enough to listen to this, Phoebe Moon said.

Eyes shut, ears closed, Merry reminded her.

"I'm picky about the peaches I touch," Max said.

"You're trying out multiple peaches?"

He dipped his fingers back into the fry bag with a laugh. "You ask me, there's something wrong with any guy who wants that much drama in his life. One peach is all I can handle at a time. Maybe half a peach."

"Ah. Commitment issues." A mild sting of disappointment pricked something deep inside her. Not that she wanted to consider commitment either. Max probably didn't have any jewelry of his own, but odds were good his mother and grandmother had some, and goodness only knew what Daddy would do if Max broke her heart. Nope, best to keep that little organ out of her love life.

Plus, Mom was queen of commitment issues. But she was happy. And Merry was happy. Why ruin a good thing?

Max shrugged and stared down into the fry bag. "I can commit to anything. Doesn't mean I want to."

The writer in Merry perked up. There was a story there. "Sowing your wild oats, then?"

"My gramps is...was...an artist. Can't see any of it anymore though. He's lost ninety percent of his vision. Gran has balance issues. We just put them in a nursing home, but I moved in with them about two years ago to help out. I was there in the middle of the night if they needed something, at meals, other times. Lot of responsibility, even with everyone in the family pitching in when they could. I'd do it again in a heartbeat—meant the world to them to be able to stay in their own home as long as they did—but for now, I just want to be me."

Phoebe Moon swooned.

So did Merry, if she were being honest.

Max offered her more fries as if he hadn't just confessed to being Grandson of the Year, as if he hadn't made her wish she'd known her own grandparents, and instead of giving in to the urge to hug him, she took a fry and smiled at him. "You tell all your prospective peaches that story?"

He grinned back. "Only if I'm sitting on two tickets to a wine and cheese tasting for Saturday afternoon."

If you don't want him, I'll take him, Phoebe Moon said.

Dream on, brat, Merry replied to the fictional thirteen-year-old in her head. "I can clear my calendar for cheese," she told Max.

When their dinner was over, he didn't kiss her, and she decided taking things slowly was for the best.

But Saturday, after they spent the afternoon walking around downtown Chicago, trying out wines and cheeses in several little shops Merry hadn't discovered yet, she tossed caution to the wind.

She slipped her hand into his and smiled a half-tipsy smile at him when the tour wrapped up. "I cannot in good conscience let you drive home like this. Let's go hang out in the drunk tank for a while."

He laughed, a beautiful, rich sound that tickled her soul. "You never fail to surprise me, Merry Silver."

"You like surprises?"

"I do."

"Then how's this one?" She dropped his hand, grabbed a fistful of his blue button-down, slung her arm around his neck, and pushed up on her tiptoes to capture his lips in hers.

If he kissed her back, she was keeping him.

If he didn't…

At least she'd know he wasn't interested.

But Max didn't hesitate. He pulled her against his hot, solid body, threaded his fingers through her hair, and opened his mouth to her. His tongue touched hers, and a raw hunger ignited in her bones.

She wanted him.

She wanted his body. She wanted his voice. She wanted his laugh. She wanted his affection. She wanted his trust.

She didn't know if she could have it. If she could give it back.

She wanted to stay connected. To lose herself in the drum of his heart under her hand. To bask in the heat of his skin and the lingering taste of wine on his lips and tongue. To give in to the sense of security and safety that came from being in his arms.

She wanted to be his. Freely. Without reservation.

But could she?

"Wow," she whispered when she gradually pulled back from the kiss.

He bent his forehead against hers, his breath coming rapidly against her cheek, his heart still galloping against her hand. "Is there anything you can't do?"

"Pottery," she blurted.

He laughed, then turned them back to the street. She'd forgotten there were people driving and walking by, that they were in front of a giant window looking into the last cheese shop. But he kept an arm firmly around her waist. "You like fondue?"

"I thought you didn't do commitment," she quipped.

"Didn't realize fondue was a marriage proposal."

"Are you kidding? Have we met?"

He laughed again. "You're funny. I like you, Merry Silver."

"And I like the way you talk cheese to me, Max Gregory."

The kiss changed everything.

And yet, it changed very little.

Because while Max was still funny and charming and attentive, he still had his own life in Bliss. And Merry was still happy in her little neighborhood in suburban Chicago and perfectly fulfilled in the parts of her life that she didn't let Max into.

She could do this.

She could have a boyfriend. She could figure out how normal people had relationships. Even slow relationships. With an emphasis on the *friend* part of boyfriend. And if she happened to think about Max every three seconds, that was fine.

Being liked by a guy like Max was new. Exciting. Of course she'd think about him a lot.

And if he turned out to be the one, *her* one, then she'd tell him about Amber Finch and the Daddy problem.

Eventually.

When the time was right.

But for now, she'd enjoy being the Merry he thought she was.

10

"Are we friends or not, Phoebe Moon? Because friends help each other."

"But Uncle Sandy is my problem, Zack Diggory. Not yours."

—Phoebe Moon and the Missing Sunshine

Present Day

Forty-five minutes, one shower, and one harrowing four-block walk with her eyes on the sky after Max had left her at the B&B, Merry banged on the door of a two-story brick colonial decorated with a multicolored line of Christmas lights along the roof in a modest older neighborhood.

A dog woofed inside, but no one answered.

Maybe he'd lied. Maybe he wasn't home all night. Maybe he didn't still live here. Maybe it was a trap.

She stood there, debating with herself.

She could walk away.

Or she could bang on the door again until someone answered. The lamps on either side of the door switched on, and Merry was staring at

Max's tall, dark, broad form backlit from the foyer light. Scout pranced behind him, but he blocked her with his legs.

"Were you going to marry me?" she blurted.

His grip visibly tightened on the edge of the door, making those corded muscles in his forearms bunch and squeeze, but he quickly blinked back the deer-in-the-headlights panic. "Did you think I was?"

"No. Maybe. I—girls with fathers like mine don't get happy endings. But you—never mind."

She turned around. She shouldn't have come.

"Merry."

Streetlamps chased away the darkness, chased away all the good places to hide.

"C'mon in," Max said. "Don't want you blaming me if the owl attacks again."

She knew she shouldn't be here, but she let herself complete a full circle, then refused to let herself think anymore when she stepped into his house.

Max shut the door. Scout leapt for Merry, tongue lolling, tail wagging, nose going straight to her crotch.

And for the second time in two hours, she had to choke back tears.

Someone loved her unconditionally. She went down to her knees. "Hey, sweet girl."

Scout licked her cheek, then put her paws on Merry's shoulders, rear end still wagging, tongue going wild against Merry's ear.

"Scout, down."

The dog ignored her owner, and Merry buried her face and fingers in Scout's fur.

Forget men. Merry was getting a dog. As soon as the plane touched down in France, she was getting a dog. Dogs didn't judge. Dogs didn't steal. Dogs wouldn't tell her secrets to the wrong people.

She squeezed her eyes shut, hugging and petting Scout while she willed the stinging to go away. She swallowed hard until the lump in her throat finally surrendered and she could take a deep breath without worrying that her exhale would come out on a sob.

Before Max, she hadn't known she was lonely. Before Max, she hadn't had dreams of a family of her own. Before Max, she'd never wished her parents were normal.

When she finally looked up, he was gone.

She discreetly sniffled and took a quick swipe at her eyes, then gently helped Scout off her. Muted rock music filtered out from somewhere near the kitchen. She stood, glancing around as she made her way toward the music.

She entered the dining room, where the same regal eight-person mahogany table sat centered and surrounded by matching carved chairs. The china was missing from the hutch.

She froze and stared at it.

The glass wasn't broken or cracked, the hardware was intact, and the shelves weren't splintered.

Of course it hadn't been stolen. More likely Max had asked a female relative to take it. Fine china hardly fit in a bachelor pad, and she'd heard whispers that both his grandparents had passed away early this year.

A real girlfriend would've been here for him. He'd loved them. Even though he'd been pragmatic about death, about how fortunate his grandparents had been to live good long lives and raise a wonderful family, he had to miss them. To grieve for them.

He strolled in the door from the kitchen, a plate of cheese in hand. She shifted her gaze to an early 1990s family portrait on another wall, but he'd seen what she was looking at.

He must've.

Question was, would he think she was simply being curious, or would he think she was casing his joint?

"Havarti?" He tilted the simple white Corelle plate to display mouthwatering temptation.

Her belly grumbled.

Max lifted the plate in the air, far out of her reach. "Gouda on there too. And this ridiculously delicious white cheddar a customer sent from Washington state. Cougar gold something."

And to get any, she suspected she'd have to surrender a few secrets. "You are an evil man."

He jerked his head back toward the kitchen. "All yours if you come out to the garage."

Something else rumbled in her midsection, but this rumble was decidedly lower and not a hunger cheese could fix.

Evil wasn't strong enough. Malicious? Malevolent? Sinful?

Most definitely sinful.

There was something about the sight of Max using tools on an old car that revved her engine as much as riding in Trixie had. And she needed to keep her engine out of it. Still, she trailed him to the garage, Scout on her heels. "I'm running away from home," she said.

"Looking for better cheese?" He set the plate on a vintage kitchen cabinet just inside the garage, then crossed to a dusty powder-blue Dodge sitting next to Trixie.

She propped a hip on the edge of the cabinet and eyed the three cheeses. "Looking for a better life." She took a nibble off a square of Havarti first, and a happy sigh flowed from the depths of her chest.

She wondered if it would've tasted better if she confided in him.

About the ring. About Amber Finch and Phoebe Moon. About —everything.

Max grabbed a wrench and a rag and bent over the Dodge's engine. "Seemed like you had a good life."

"Always does." She had no idea what he was doing under that hood, but his arm muscles flexed again beneath his threadbare gray U of I T-shirt, and her angle gave her a fabulous view of the worn denim hugging his rear end. "You still planning to open a shop for these girls someday?"

He grunted, and the wrench moved. "Never let me forget I said that, will you?"

The way he'd talked about cars reminded her of the way she felt about writing. But either he had his guard up against her now, or he'd given up the idea of pursuing his dream. "Dreams are important," she said.

He shifted a sapphire squint at her. "What's your dream?"

Home. Family. Friends. Roots.

She didn't even have to think about it. She knew. She knew, because he'd nearly given it all to her last year.

She looked away and picked blindly at the cheese plate.

Being here was a mistake. Because being here, eating cheese and watching Max do his manly, macho car thing was reminding her of living her own personal dream with him last year.

She'd thought a hunky, attractive, age-appropriate man being interested in her was the best part about dating Max. But it turned out, *normal* was the part she'd liked best.

He'd shown her normal last year. *This* kind of normal. The normal kind of normal, not the Daddy kind of normal.

After a few weeks of casually dating Max last year, of listening to him talk about his family and his hometown, she'd understood what roots were.

And she'd wanted them.

No, she'd *craved* roots. A home. A forever home, with forever friends.

She'd even indulged in fantasies of her own family.

Of telling Max things she couldn't tell her parents. About how she'd kept imaginary friends well into high school to compensate for how often she'd moved as a child. About how she'd dream Daddy would come home one day and announce he'd been at medical school and was now a doctor instead of a thief. About Phoebe Moon and Amber Finch.

But normal-normal wasn't meant to be for her.

No matter how much she still liked riding in his car or hanging out in his garage, watching him fiddle with a car engine while his dog lay at her feet, she couldn't stay here.

She didn't *want* to stay here. She wanted to go to France. To rent a house somewhere overlooking wine country, to dine on fresh Brie and baguettes and pastries, to write her Phoebe Moon novels in the superior French air.

To disappear somewhere that Daddy and his misguided intentions couldn't take anything from her again. "I'm leaving the country," she said quietly.

Max twisted around and stared at her.

"My mother doesn't know. I don't know how much contact she has with my father, and I don't—I can't—he used to do tea parties with me. He never forgets my birthday. He taught me how to read and how to throw a softball, and he let me have ice cream for dinner long after I'd gotten better when I had my tonsils out. I love my daddy, but he has a way of turning my life upside down, and I can't live like that anymore. I have to go somewhere he can't find me. I need a life of my own."

Max straightened. "What did he do?"

Last year, Max meant. He didn't have to specify.

And the simple truth was, Daddy had called.

That was all it ever took.

Not long after she'd left Max's house after spending a lovely Tuesday night with him last year, Daddy had called. *Hey, Merry-berry. Surprise! Just rolled into Chicago on the bus. Can you pick me up at the station? Got the address right here.*

Except the address had been in a posh neighborhood, and he'd actually just rolled out of a house with Merry didn't want to know how many thousands of dollars' worth of stolen gems and jewels.

Now, baby girl, you don't know what this man did to the people I've been working with, Daddy had said. *Can you drive a little faster? Thought I might've been made back there.*

She'd kicked him out of her car.

A cop had rolled past her, slowly, attentively, at a stoplight two blocks later.

And because it hadn't been her first experience with being a getaway car, she'd known the drill.

Ditch the cell phone. Disconnect the computer. Leave the apartment. Call Mom for help in getting rid of her car.

And start over.

Leaving everything behind.

Including Max.

Especially Max.

She'd given a fleeting thought to turning her father in, but he was her daddy.

She couldn't. He wasn't evil. He didn't hurt people, couldn't use weapons, wouldn't even fire a gun. He just...liked to take things that didn't belong to him, from people who didn't need them, so he could give to people who did.

Prison wouldn't fix what was wrong with him, but being in prison would break him.

"Merry?" Max prompted.

She shook her head.

"Fresh honey goat cheese from a local farm inside," he said.

She shook her head again.

Max grabbed his rag and wiped his hands, his lips set in a grim line. "If he hurt you—"

"Daddy's not dangerous."

"A man doesn't have to use weapons to be dangerous."

"He would never hurt me. He's not that kind of criminal."

"So you learned to be a ninja for the fun of it?"

"Yes." And because it was as healthy an outlet as Mom could find for her preteen and teenage anger over being taken away from her daddy. At least, it had been initially. As Merry had gotten older, she'd begun to process that if her daddy could be a thief, then anyone could.

And then she'd learned firsthand that theft wasn't truly a harmless crime.

Now, she didn't keep all her valuables in a single place. She did her best to ensure her valuables were only of value to her. She practiced self-defense regularly, she had her money split among five different banks, and she kept a constant vigilance about her surroundings.

"Not all wounds are physical," Max said.

Too close to the truth. Merry stared him down while she chewed on a slice of Gouda.

"You ever help him steal anything?"

"Not wittingly."

"Your mother know?"

"Probably."

"You really do that medical billing stuff?"

"I make an honest living."

"Why'd you come here tonight?"

Because she was lonely.

Because she wanted to pretend to be a normal girl for a few minutes.

Because she needed to believe she could find this, and keep it, when she moved to Europe. "Why do you still like me?"

"Who says I do?"

She looked pointedly at his groin, then toasted it with her Gouda.

A slow, sure, suggestive grin grew on Max's lips. "So you're here for a booty call."

"That's all we ever were, wasn't it?"

Thunderclouds overtook the innuendoes in his expression. "Was it?" He tossed his rag aside and took two menacing steps toward her. "You're not like your father at all, are you? You're more like your mother."

"She'll be flattered."

"Tell me one thing, Merry." Two more steps, twenty billion times more dark and dangerous. "Honestly. Tell me you didn't like me last year. Tell me, and mean it."

"Why?"

"So I can justify not kissing you."

Merry sidestepped and stumbled over Scout. "See? That's exactly what I'm talking about. You don't even know me, but you still want to kiss me. What's wrong with you?"

"Must be the curse."

"You don't believe in curses."

He turned and trapped her against the cabinet. "You use your family as an excuse to run away."

"Look at that. A normal dysfunction. Hallelujah."

He was two breaths from getting the kiss he wanted, and she knew what Max's kisses were like. He was the kind of kisser the nuns at that orphanage had warned Phoebe Moon about.

Merry needed to go.

"You ever been the one left behind, Merry? You know what that's like?"

Run, her sense of self-preservation yelled. "Yes," she whispered. Every time Daddy had had to disappear after a botched job, she hadn't known if she'd see him again. She'd catch Mom picking up the phone, then putting it back down. They'd both jump every time someone knocked on the door. Mom had even picked out a burial plot one time.

"Then why," Max said, "did you do it to my dog?"

"I didn't—to your *dog*?" Instinct, injury, and training took over. She snatched his hand and twisted until she had him bent over, elbow in the air like a chicken wing. "I wanted to meet your family. I wanted to come to your stupid Snow Bride Festival. I was going to bid on you in your stupid bachelor auction."

"Easy to say—ow!"

"If it was illegal to design jewelry, but your grandfather did it anyway, would you have loved him any less? Would you have told him to take care of his own damn self when he got sick? Would you have just walked away, without a friend, without any more family, and still been able to live with yourself?"

Scout growled low in her throat.

"Down, Scout," Max said.

Merry shoved him away. Her face was hot, and it felt like someone was trying to suck her heart out of her chest with a Hoover. *Phoebe Moon and the Kink Gone Wrong: Author Amber Finch Arrested For Getting Too Frisky With Former Lover.*

She fumbled toward the door. "You're an idiot."

"You don't have to be alone, Merry."

She stalked through his house without looking back.

Not because he was wrong.

But because she was terrified he was right.

11

"Do you ever wish you could live in the dark forever?" Phoebe Moon whispered to Zack Diggory.
"Never, Phoebe Moon. And you shouldn't either. We should all live in the light."
—Phoebe Moon and the Missing Sunshine

One year ago

Max was vaguely aware that while his brain was fully on board with the idea of Merry as a friend, other parts of him were interested in more. Max Jr., for one. Then there were his hands. His hands wanted to touch her. Not just hold her hand, but caress her skin. Tangle his fingers in her hair. Slide his palm over the curves of her hips, her breasts, her ass. His mouth was fully on board the Merry train, desperate to taste her again, hot and silky and eager.

And then there was his heart.

It hadn't been simultaneously excited and insecure like this about a girl since high school. Every time he had a text, call, or email from Merry, his pulse sped up. But more often than not, her name didn't appear at the top of his list of emails or on the front screen of his text messages or missed calls.

There was a lot he didn't know about her, but he didn't care where she worked, where she lived, who her friends were when she wasn't with him.

Because when she was with him, she was exactly what he wanted. She intrigued him. He wanted to know where this girl came up with the confidence to publicly claim imaginary pet dragons. He wanted to know why her left eye sometimes scrunched. He wanted to know how it was that a girl like her had managed to stay single.

Two weeks after he'd taken her on the cheese and wine tasting, he drove up to Chicago to pick her up for a planned night at a club that had put a massive ball pit for adults in their basement.

He pulled up to the address she'd given him and found her waiting on the front stoop of the apartment building just before sunset. She was in ivory leggings that highlighted her long legs, boots that were more fashionable than functional, and a long-sleeve navy blue sweater thing that showed off her breasts and hugged her hips. Her dark hair was pulled back at her nape, and Max had a sudden vision of himself pulling those silky strands loose, then kissing her until her clothes melted off.

Later.

He'd promised her a night out first.

She eyed Trixie, then glanced down the street. He leaned over and popped Trixie's door before she realized it was him.

Her eyes met his, then went huge. "Is this your car, or did you rent it?" she asked when she slid into the seat.

He grinned and ran his hand over the steering wheel. "Merry, meet Trixie. She's all mine."

"I wouldn't marry you, but I'd marry this car," she declared.

He was okay with that, so long as she was willing to kiss him more tonight. Or more. "I wouldn't marry you either, or let you drive."

"So women can't drive?"

"It's not about you being a woman. It's about you not giving birth to her."

Merry cocked her head at him. "How fast can she go?"

"You like fast cars?"

There went that full, uninhibited smile he'd only seen once or twice. "I don't know."

She had his full attention now. His and Max Jr.'s. "One way to find out."

He revved the engine. Merry's smile faltered, her eyes went black as onyx, and she put a hand on his thigh. "Let's go drive," she said.

"You sure?"

"*Oh*, yes."

He didn't need any more encouragement. He put Trixie in gear and pointed her out of Merry's neighborhood, then out of Chicago, Merry's hand still on his thigh while she peppered him with questions about Trixie.

How old was she? Where did he get her? How long did it take him to restore her? Did he still do all her maintenance? And then mid-sentence, she trailed off. Her eyes went distant as the last of the Chicago suburbs faded and cornfields replaced the cityscape.

Max chuckled, and she made a funny noise.

"Where do you go when you do that?" he asked.

"Do what?"

"Disappear into your head." He took his hand off the gearshift to squeeze her fingers still on his thigh. "It's cute."

"Sorry. It's my job. I, um, work in medical billing. I know it doesn't sound all that exciting, but sometimes there are these cases that could be coded one way or another, and I start to wonder if we shouldn't develop a middle-of-the-road code instead, except I don't know anything at all about computer programming, so I'm just kinda... making things up."

Her smooth round cheeks went a rare pink, her dimple made an appearance, and her left eye scrunched.

"I don't know anything about computer programming either, but I keep a few websites up to date," Max told her.

"Cars and websites, huh?"

"I somehow inherited the job of maintaining the Knot Festival and Bridal Retailers Association's sites."

"Bridal Retailers Association? Oh, jeez, tell me you don't call it the BRA."

"We absolutely do."

She laughed, and with nothing but dusk and cornfields ahead of him, Max opened Trixie up and let her fly. Her engine roared in appreciation of letting loose all those horses, and the rumble vibrated his seat.

Her laughter faded. Her grip tightened on his thigh, and when he looked over at her—*Jesus*.

Her plump lips were parted, her chest angled forward, her eyes glittering. She tilted her head to look at him, and her pink tongue darted out to lick her lips. "Wow," she mouthed.

Max's blood coursed straight to his groin in a tidal wave of lust. "More?"

"*Oh*, yes."

He shifted into third gear.

Merry's hand crept up his thigh.

Max didn't know where this thing with Merry was going, but it was clear as crystal that regardless of the labels they put on their relationship, right now she was his.

His.

They flew through the rapidly darkening early October night until they were decently close to Bliss. But Max didn't want to take her to Bliss.

If he showed up in Bliss with a girl, there would be questions. Whispers. *The curse*.

Instead, he drove her to a secluded little lake and parked near the shore, far from the nearest cabins. Moonlight shimmered off the water's surface.

When he twisted to face her, she was staring at him with an intensity that should've made him uncomfortable, but instead made what little blood he had left in his brain shoot through his heart on its way to his groin. "That was incredible," she whispered.

He didn't know who reached for who first.

How their seatbelts came unbuckled.

Why he didn't spontaneously combust when her cool fingers found the skin under his shirt, or how he ended up sprawled across her, the passenger seat reclined all the way.

He just knew he had to kiss her. Had to keep kissing her.

Tasting her.

Touching her.

Submerging himself in her scent, in her touch, in her pleasured moans and gasps.

Somehow they made it to the backseat. Merry's shirt went flying into the front seat.

Max wasn't one to let a lady be naked by herself, so he tore his own shirt off.

"I'm only doing this to reward good driving," Merry panted.

"I'm only doing this because you're fucking hot," Max replied.

She stuttered out a breathy laugh that hissed into a moan when he licked the spot where her neck met her shoulder. She tasted like sin and speed and sex, and he wanted more.

He wanted all of her.

She pulled him against her while he kissed and nipped and licked at her skin, guiding his head to the tender spot between her breasts. He inhaled her spicy-sweet scent. "Even better than in my dreams," he murmured.

"You've been dreaming about me?"

"Every waking minute."

He trailed a finger along the lacy edge of her bra, feeling her skin pebble beneath his touch. Her breath came out short and uneven, and she shifted beneath him, then wrapped her legs firmly around his back. His shaft strained against the zipper of his jeans, but holy *damn*, when she thrust her hips against his, he thought he might explode.

"I've been dreaming about you too," she whispered.

She tugged his hair. He lifted his head, and she bent forward, lips parted, and brushed her mouth against his. "Make love to me, Max. Just once."

"Just once?" He dipped his thumb into her bra and found the hard tip of her nipple.

She arched back with a strained whimper. "Maybe twice," she gasped. "Oh, God, don't stop."

He lowered his head to her breasts again, licking and teasing and suckling while he lowered her bra straps one at a time. Merry twisted beneath him, and suddenly her bra slid away. She wrapped her arms around his neck and held on. He pulled one nipple into his mouth while he slipped a hand between her legs and stroked, and she tilted her hips into his touch.

Twice?

Hell, they'd do this until the sun came up.

He stroked her again, and her thighs clenched around his hand, her whole back arching. "*Max*," she cried.

He lifted his head and watched the ecstasy skate across her features.

Holy sweet *everything*.

He'd never known a woman could be so sensitive. Had he done that? Or had she?

Her skin glowed in the moonlight, her parted lips full and swollen, her dark lashes touching her cheeks. Her body sagged beneath him, and a soft smile touched her mouth while her chest rose and fell, her rosy-tipped breasts still teasing him.

Max was so hard he was about to bust through his zipper.

"Your turn," she whispered.

"My—"

She gave a lazy push at his shoulders. "Sit up."

He obeyed, shifting in the tight space until he was in the center of the seat with her legs in his lap. She waved a hand at her feet. "Take my boots off."

"So now we're Miss Bossy?" He stroked a line from her knee to the top of her boots.

Her eyes rolled back into her head while her legs twitched beneath his touch. "Thank you, Max," she murmured.

"For taking your boots off?" He stroked her leg again.

She hissed out a breath, and Max Jr. pulsed in his jeans.

"No, you're going to thank me for that," Merry said.

As soon as Max had both her boots off, she pulled herself onto her knees beside him, took his cheeks in her palms, and kissed him.

Slowly.

Soundly.

Deeply.

He popped the button on his jeans.

Merry pushed against his shoulder, and he once more obeyed her simple command, lying back against the opposite window. He held her silky smooth waist, his thumbs inching higher to caress the underside of her breasts again, and she stayed with him, kissing him, her fingers leaving hot trails down his chest and stomach until she reached the waistband of his jeans. She rubbed his pulsing length through the denim of his jeans, and Max groaned.

Suddenly his zipper was down, his boxers too, and he hissed out a relieved breath as Max Jr. sprang free. But Merry took him in her hands, stroking up, then down, then up, then circling the tip of him, and once again, this woman almost made him lose control.

But *God*—her mouth, her hands, her body, her skin—everything about her was perfect. Soft and strong. Silky and hot. Demanding and generous.

"Merry, I can't—"

She released him, cool air wrapping around his rigid length where her hands had been, and he shuddered at the sudden loss of her touch. She slid her hands over his quivering abs, and when she leaned over him, her hair dangled down to tickle his chest. "I want you, Max," she whispered.

I want you.

He wasn't in this for forever, but the simple words touched him to the depths of his soul.

Everyone should be wanted like this.

She kissed him again, then pulled back, tucked her thumbs into her leggings, and slowly, so very slowly, pulled one side down to her hip.

Max's groin pulsed.

He wasn't going to last. Shit, he hadn't come early since high school, but *God.* If she didn't hurry up, he'd be done for. "All. Off. Now."

She inched the other side down, but not nearly far enough. "Like this?"

It took superhuman strength, but he managed to reach up and cup her breasts, his thumbs brushing her tips, all that silky weight of her in his palms, without losing control. "More," he said.

Her eyelids lowered, and her lips parted. "Like this?" Two more inches of flesh appeared on her lower abdomen, along with a hint of dark curls.

He took one sweet bud in his mouth. "More."

"You win," she gasped.

She pulled back, and in one swift motion, her leggings and panties went the way of her shirt.

Max fumbled for a condom, and Merry helped him roll it on.

He almost fell off the seat when she straddled him, one leg between him and the seat, the other perched on the floorboard, but then she lowered herself onto him, and he was lost.

Lost in the sweetest, tightest, most perfect fit he'd ever experienced.

"Merry—"

She shuddered, lifted almost all the way off him, and then slid back down his length.

Max's head dropped back against the window, and he thrust up into her, meeting her stroke for stroke until, too soon, his release overtook him and the moonbeams split into rainbows and stars exploded behind his eyes.

Merry pulsed around him, crying out his name once more, then collapsed onto his chest.

"Okay," she whispered when her breathing had begun to even out, though Max was still lingering somewhere in that heavenly place between reality and utter bliss. "Maybe four times."

Max chuckled. "It's still okay if you don't want to marry me."

And he meant it.

That weird, empty sense of panic in his chest was fear of never getting laid again.

He was sure of it.

12

"Shouldn't you be in school, Phoebe Moon?"
"Some of us have bigger callings, Zack Diggory."
—Phoebe Moon and the Missing Sunshine

Present day

Max spent Monday morning helping customers at With This Ring. Normally, he spent Mondays on admin stuff in his office across from the workroom where Dan repaired and designed engagement rings and other occasional pieces. But today, two of their staff had called in sick with a stomach bug.

Plus, Max had a weird feeling about the Mrs. Claus diamond ring.

Gramps had designed the ring with a nearly flawless three-carat colorless diamond as the centerpiece, surrounded by a pattern of alternated quarter- and half-carat diamonds set in platinum, with decorative platinum touches completing the snowflake look. When Spencer McGraw sent it back, Gramps had set up a locked display case with bulletproof glass in the corner of the store. The ring sat around a black velvet display finger under lights that hit it to maximize the shine effect.

Beautiful piece of jewelry.

Max had seen it for the first time when he stopped in the shop after football practice one November afternoon while he was in high school. Gramps had been "secretly" working on it for months in the workroom, bent over his workbench, his magnifier attached to his glasses, tools scattered about in an order that made sense to only Gramps. "Come on back here, Max. Got something to show you," Gramps had said that afternoon.

Max had been as impressed as most any teenage boy would've been with a ring. Could've bought three old cars for what Spencer McGraw was paying Gramps. Five, if Max bartered right.

But even as a teenage boy, Max had known the ring was about more than the diamonds and the platinum, about more than the design and the time Gramps had put into it.

That ring had made With This Ring famous. Spencer McGraw himself, who had been a ripe old twenty-six—a young literary genius, he'd been called—had come to pick it up with his fiancée. News outlets from all over the country had covered the story of the happy couple leaving With This Ring, that sparkly snowflake-shaped diamond ring sitting on her hand.

And when McGraw's fiancée had died, the reporters had come back to Bliss again, this time looking for the scoop on how Gramps had cursed the Mrs. Claus diamond ring with the same curse McGraw had put in the book.

The fascination had led to the best December the shop had ever had.

Even sixteen-year-old Max had known it was an odd time—celebrating their financial success while the man who had given them fame mourned his lost love—but the family business was their lifeblood. The third generation of Gregory men were poised to join it soon, Dan as the master jeweler in training, Max eventually in management, and business was business.

Today, Max couldn't help but wonder if Nicholas Raymond wanted a piece of the notoriety.

If the ring was part of why Merry had disappeared last year.

Or if she was playing him to help her father get his hands on it.

Not an option he wanted to believe, but his family business demanded he stay suspicious.

"I heard you saw Merry last night," Rachel said beside him.

Max straightened his tie and glanced around at the scattered customers, all either being helped or still just looking. "Just looking for some closure."

"I called my friend Alyssa, the one with the witch doctor grandmother, and she said—"

"No witch doctors. And don't try to fix the bachelor auction. It's for charity, not for breaking a supposed curse."

"Oh, Max, we both know curses aren't real," Rach said. "But getting involved again with a woman who left you—"

"She had her reasons. Be nice to her."

"Max—"

"You ever been the outsider, Rach? Ever been misunderstood? Ever been unpopular for doing the right thing?"

She ran a hand along the corner of the smooth glass countertop. "How can leaving someone without a word ever be the right thing?"

Rach wasn't wrong.

Merry could've left a note.

But watching her get grilled last night by Zoe and Pepper had made him wonder if she'd had a solid reason for not leaving a note.

"I'm over it," Max said. "You can get over it." The doorbell's tone sounded again. *Saved.* "And now we can help this lovely couple pick out an engagement ring."

But when he looked up, Bliss's most famous married couple smiled at him from the doorway.

"Rachel..." he muttered.

His sister-in-law, the devious pain in the ass, plastered a fake surprised smile on her face. "Billy! Lindsey! Welcome to With This Ring. How can we help you today?"

The other customers turned and gawked. It had been nearly a year since Billy Brenton, one of country music's hottest superstars, had gotten himself attached to a Bliss local, but not everyone was entirely used to bumping into him around town yet.

"We need to borrow Max," Lindsey said. Tall, blond, and just showing her belly bump—pregnancy was going around Bliss these days—the former divorce lawyer and current resident matchmaker had too good a poker face.

Max glared at Rachel. "Not interested."

"Shush and go with the nice lady," Rachel hissed.

"And who's going to help the customers here?"

"I don't see anybody needing help.

Max pulled out his phone. "Give me one Tweet about Billy being here and we'll be swarmed."

"We're not here about your love life," Lindsey said. "Put the phone away. Kimmie's saving us a seat for lunch, and Billy's buying. You coming or not?"

Now she had his attention.

"Go on, shoo," Rachel said. "I can sell diamond rings with one arm tied behind my back."

And with the other elbow-deep in some crafty project, a paint-brush between her teeth, while she washed dishes with her feet, if Max knew his sister-in-law.

"Can you do anything about keeping everyone else out of my love life?" Max asked Lindsey.

She smiled. "Probably not."

"I might could," Billy said. "Seem to have some sway round these parts."

"Lunch first though," Lindsey said.

Max handed his display case keys to Rachel. "Call me if you need anything, and lock the front door if you and Dan decide to have a nooner. I'm still scarred from the last time I walked in on that."

Her cheeks went pink. "He's joking," she said to Billy and Lindsey.

"None of our business," Lindsey said cheerfully.

Max grabbed his coat and followed them out the door.

This Monday had just gotten more interesting.

Patrick was on the mend, but he hadn't been up to wedding planning this morning, so it was just Mom and Merry out and about in Bliss with the wedding planner. Shortly before noon, Merry braced herself as they walked in the door of Kimmie Cakes, an adorable cupcake shop just off The Aisle which was apparently owned by Saturday night's bride.

"I can't wait for you to taste Kimmie's cake," Zoe said. She'd been sweet as sugar all morning, the consummate professional, and Merry had gone along with the game for Mom's sake. "It's like eating delicious art."

The bakery was warm and cozy on the inside, with whimsical cupcake flowers in every color painted on the cream walls, round tables with metal-backed chairs bent into the shape of hearts on the black-and-white tile floor, and an upbeat tune Merry couldn't place coming through the speakers. A replica of the wedding cake monument sat atop a display case along the side wall, with a dozen flavors of cupcakes inside the glass case. Three booths lined the back wall, one with a reserved sign on it.

Zoe led them to the only vacant table they could find, which was better suited for two, near the back booths. "You two settle in," she said with a dimpled smile. "I'm sure Kimmie has your samples ready. And I highly recommend the French onion soup and chicken salad sandwich if you want a little lunch with your cake."

She stepped lightly to the counter beside the display case.

"Are you sure the poinsettias are a good choice?" Mom said once Zoe was out of earshot. "I'd really thought violets."

"You had violets when you married Yo-yo," Merry said.

Mom's lip curled, and her nose almost wrinkled. "Hmm. Good point."

"Although I think your error was more in marrying a man named Yo-yo than in having violets at your wedding."

"At least I put myself out there."

Merry wasn't touching that. She still had mortification burns on her soul from last night. She shouldn't have gone to Max's house.

Mom's wedding couldn't be over fast enough. Merry wanted to get to France. Yesterday.

Mom's eyebrows twitched. Must be about time for another round of Botox. "Merry," she hissed. "Merry, *look*."

Merry cast a casual glance over her shoulder.

A pregnant blonde, a scruffy guy in jeans and a ball cap, and Max strolled through the door. Max, in a suit and wool coat, his thick dark hair wind-blown, or possibly mussed as though he'd spent the past twelve hours fisting his hands in it.

Her belly dropped, and she squeezed her thighs together. "Seriously?" she whispered. "I thought we both agreed last night that he's a bad idea."

Mom's lips parted. "Meredith, he's with *Billy Brenton*."

The scruffy guy in jeans winked at Mom, touched the brim of his cap, and continued to the reserved table. Merry refused to look at Max. But the blonde hesitated a moment too long, glancing first at Merry, then at Max.

"Don't," Max muttered to her. "Keep walking."

One more friend he'd told to look out for Merry, apparently.

And Max was done with her.

Good. That was good. Because she was leaving for France as soon as Mom took off on her honeymoon.

"Sweetheart, grinding your teeth isn't an attractive trait," Mom murmured.

"I'm not grinding my teeth."

"Are you feeling constipated? You wear the same look for both."

Max, the blonde, and the country dude were making small talk with a waitress who had appeared with plates of food and cupcakes.

The buzz of conversations around them kept Merry from hearing exactly what they were saying, but she didn't need to hear.

It wasn't her business.

She wasn't interested in Max. She couldn't be interested in Max.

"I have some stool softener in my purse," Mom said. "Wait. You're not coming down with what Patrick had, are you?"

Zoe came back as the waitress departed Max's table. "Sorry, ladies, it'll be a few minutes." She was still smiling her dimpled smile, but it seemed forced. "Little mix-up with the time. But I brought you some sweet tea. It's a Kimmie Cakes specialty. Kimmie got the recipe from Billy's sister a few months ago. If you'd prefer coffee or a soda, I can—

Mom leaned into her. "Can you introduce us to Billy?" she whispered.

"Oh, I wish I could, but we all do our best to respect his privacy when he's here," Zoe whispered back. "It's a delicate balance."

"My daughter used to date the man he's sitting with."

It was Zoe's turn to look constipated. "Did she?"

"She did. He told me so himself."

"They know, Mom," Merry said softly. "Let it go."

There was a slight lull in the conversations around them, which was the only reason Merry heard Billy Brenton's Southern drawl. "Need a car. Lindsey says you might could be able to help."

"Trixie's not for sale," Max said easily.

"That the Mustang?" Billy said. "Was looking for a Charger. Gonna use it for a video shoot here in the spring, then auction it off for charity."

Max's easy smile froze. His spoon paused over his soup bowl. "A Charger, huh?"

The hum of conversation rose around them again. Merry strained to listen in more.

So did Mom and Zoe, she noticed.

"Heard restoring cars is your thing," Billy said.

Max's ears went an adorable pink. "I tinker with them."

"You did the Mustang yourself?"

"Long time ago."

"We all know what's in your garage," the blonde said. The way she waved around the rock on her left hand made Merry feel like she needed Mom's stool softener after all.

The love was thick around here, and the diamonds were the kind that would tempt Daddy like nothing else, especially if he thought his baby girl was getting anything less than the warmest welcome here.

"Yeah, I've got a Charger," Max said, but Merry heard the hesitation. "She's pretty banged up though. Wasn't planning to have her done until summer at the earliest."

"You working on other cars?" Billy said.

"Working my day job."

"Could make it worth your while to take some time off if you could get the car done."

Max's eyes narrowed the way they did when he was thinking. But his jaw ticked like it did when he was thinking something he didn't like.

That he had to say no?

Or that he didn't have an excuse not to say yes?

Either way, it was obvious he wasn't planning to accept Billy's proposition.

"Would you quit thinking so hard and just tell the man you'll do it?" Merry heard herself say.

Max twisted his head to look at her, lips tight, dark brows menacing over those unique blue-green eyes clearly telegraphing the lack of right she had to an opinion about any aspect of his life.

"Don't believe we've met," Billy said to Merry. "You from round here?"

She shrank back in her seat. Her skin was hot, and those bruises on her psyche from last night were pulsing again. "In town for a wedding."

"Friday," Mom said. "We'd be honored to have you attend."

"Mother," Merry hissed. She looked at Zoe. "She's never had a gingerbread wedding cake. Let's just do gingerbread, okay?"

"And my Meredith used to date this lovely young man you're dining with," Mom added to Billy.

So Max was *lovely* today.

Even Phoebe Moon was embarrassed by Merry's mother right now.

And everyone in the bakery was staring.

Max, oddly enough, looked at the blonde again. "You promised—"

"I didn't." Billy grinned. "Meredith, is it? Why don't y'all come over and join us? Got my heart set on getting this car. Could use all the help I can get."

Mom was already up, dragging Merry to Billy's table. "I can't imagine why anyone would turn you down, Billy."

"Max won't do it," Merry said.

"Meredith."

"He won't. He's chicken."

Max Gregory didn't have a chicken bone in his body.

But he did need goading from time to time. And if she'd learned anything in his garage last night, she'd learned he was still holding himself back from going after his dreams. Why, she didn't know. But he was.

"Who's chicken?" Max said pointedly.

"Never denied it," Merry said.

"Fine. Merry Silver, *Victoria* Silver, meet Lindsey and Billy. Lindsey is Bliss's psychic matchmaker."

"I prefer the term *relationship encourager,*" Lindsey said.

"She's eight for eight in Bliss this year, and half of 'em's pregnant now," Billy said.

"Oh, Merry *definitely* needs your help, then." Mom clapped. "I'm ready for grandbabies. But probably not with Matt here."

"Oh, for the love of—we'll leave if you'll do the car," Merry said to Max.

Mom let out an indignant squeak. "Merry, we haven't sampled the cake yet."

Max glowered at Merry.

She glowered right back. "What would your grandfather tell you to do?"

A different muscle ticked in his jaw, and his eyes went Incredible Hulk green. He pulled himself out of the booth, and even though he only had about six inches on her, she felt as though he had eighteen.

Eighteen solid, angry, sexy-as-sin inches.

"Outside," he growled. "Now."

She squared her shoulders. "Your manners suck."

"Merry—"

"I don't like how you're speaking to my daughter," Mom said. "Be nice, or you'll answer to me."

"Frankly, I'm more afraid of her," Max said.

"I raised her well. Meredith, you don't have to talk to him."

She didn't.

But she wanted to.

For his own good, she told herself. "We'll just be a minute." Merry ignored the gawks and stares and put an extra swing in her step, head held high, while she marched outside. The winter wind brushed her cheeks and nipped at her nose, but her blood had passed the boiling point.

The tinkle of the Christmas bells on the bakery door hadn't stopped before she opened her mouth. "I don't care what you think of me, but if you turn down the opportunity to restore an old car for someone because you don't think—*mmph*!"

Max spun her around and pushed her against the bakery's glass window. His fingers pulled at her hair, and his mouth slammed down on hers, hot and hungry and greedy.

She should push him away.

She should break his arm. Maybe use a side-kick to reduce him to a lumpy pile of stubborn Max on the sidewalk.

But the hard scratch of his rough skin around her lips, the scent of soap and the taste of earthy male, and the heady rush of adrenaline that came from deep within her core were impossible to resist.

She parted her lips.

She grabbed the lapels on his suit coat.

And she pushed up on her toes, going all in to his kiss.

His tongue was hot velvet along her lower lip. His hands gripped her hair tighter, almost to the point of pain. The cold of the glass seeped through her coat, but the push of Max's hips into her belly was hot and hard and irresistible.

She arched into him, unable to stop a desperate, moany whimper.

She didn't connect with people. She didn't get close. She didn't let people in.

But she couldn't get Max out.

And right now, with him making love to her mouth on a sidewalk in the dead of winter, she didn't want to.

Their tongues clashed. Their teeth. He thrust a hand against her ass and yanked her against him so she could feel him better.

And Merry let him.

Because she would most likely never kiss Max Gregory again.

When he broke the kiss, her breath hung in short puffs in the space between them. Her swollen heart jackhammered her ribs.

And she wanted more.

Max abruptly stepped back. "Stay the fuck out of my life." He adjusted himself, looked past Merry, made an *I'll call you* gesture to someone inside, and then turned and strolled down the street.

"Hey!" Merry yelled.

He turned around. His mad was fading, but weariness rapidly darkened his expression.

"What the hell was that?" she asked.

Who knew Max Gregory was the king of silence? He stood there, watching her, lips clamped shut, evidence of his woody still poking at his pants, but he didn't say a word.

The vile bite of guilt crept into her throat.

He wanted her to let him in.

How many questions had she evaded from him since Saturday night? Since she'd first met him?

He was a good guy.

Standing on a cold street with a hard-on for her.

He turned again, face down, and walked away.

And when Merry turned, she realized every single person in the nearly full bakery—her mother, the famous country guy, the wedding planner, even Kimmie the baker was there now—had just witnessed Max Gregory all but dry hump her against the bakery window.

13

"Get in," Zack Diggory said. "If we hurry, we can reach the mountain by midnight."

Phoebe Moon hesitated. Never trust a boy with a car. It was rule number three.

—Phoebe Moon and the Missing Sunshine

It was almost nine before Max showed Lindsey and Billy out the door of his house.

He should be on top of the world. Billy Brenton wanted to pay him an ungodly sum of money to fix up the old Dodge Charger he'd picked up on a whim just after Gran and Gramps passed away.

But the car needed a shit-ton of work. An engine rebuild. Complete overhaul of the interior. A paint job, which Max wouldn't pretend he could do himself.

"Don't know if I can get it done in time for your shoot," Max had told Billy. "I can try, but you might want to have your people look around for another car."

To do the job right, on Billy's timeline, Max would need access to a garage with a lift. A few specialized tools. At least four straight weeks off work. And that was assuming no hiccups in the process.

He'd also need faith.

Before he moved in with Gramps and Gran, he'd had a plan. He'd been saving up, and he'd thought living rent-free with his grandparents would help pad his bank account.

He hadn't counted on how many repairs the old house had needed. Nor had he counted on the emotional toll of watching his grandparents grow weaker, more frail, more dependent. And while he knew Gramps and Gran loved him, they'd never thought restoring old cars was a worthwhile job. His dream was the one thing they'd never understood, and by the time they'd moved into the nursing home, his dream had slipped, covered with layers of the realities and responsibilities of life.

He'd bought the Charger to see if he could find the love again.

But he hadn't been able to look at it without remembering Merry with him at the car show. The sparkle and excitement in her expression when he'd confessed his old teenage fantasies. Hell, he'd almost sold Trixie when he realized he'd had sex with a jewel thief's daughter in her.

Fate was calling tonight.

And Max didn't know which fork in the fucking road he was supposed to take.

After an hour of crunching numbers, he grabbed a beer and stalked out onto his back porch. He threw himself into a frigid plastic patio chair and scowled at the sky. Totally open. Completely exposed. Nut-sack freezing.

At the mercy of *fate*. Or possibly that danged owl that still hadn't been caught.

This was Merry's fault.

She should've stayed out of his business.

It had been nine hours since he'd seen her, but about sixteen seconds since he'd thought about her.

Her lips. Her voice. Her legs. Her mysteries.

He'd felt the lingering imprint of her breasts on his chest all afternoon. And then when he'd let Lindsey and Billy in to check out the

Charger, he'd taken one look at his garage and thought about what it would be like to push Merry onto Trixie's hood and kiss the hell out of her right there too.

The sound of distant carolers wafted over on a slight breeze. Christmas lights twinkled on the houses of the street behind him.

Across town, Dan and Rachel were probably settling in to binge-watch some girly-ass TV show. Maybe that British down-town monastery thing. Rachel would undoubtedly be wrapping Christmas presents or assembling packages for a fundraiser or debating the merits of purchasing a cow, a goat, or a llama through one of those farm charities for people in third-world countries. Dan would probably be snoring when he was supposed to be getting caught up with his duties as Knot Festival treasurer—a job inherited from their parents—at least until Rach made him go tell one of the kids to quiet down and go to sleep.

And Max got to sit here, freezing his nuts off, drinking a beer, alone, contemplating if he could afford to take a leap and start his own business.

Just him.

Alone.

No girlfriend. No wife. No kids.

Just him and his curse, devoting the rest of his life to jewels or cars.

"Max?"

He flew out of his plastic chair and upended it, beer sloshing, senses on high alert, ready to go ninja on *her* ass. Not knowing any ninja moves wouldn't stop him either.

Merry stepped out of the shadows of his yard and onto the dimly lit patio, her steps hesitant, her arms tucked awkwardly at her sides. "You didn't answer the door."

"Pretty damn sure that was intentional."

She sucked her lower lip into her mouth, then bowed her head. "I wanted to apologize."

For what she'd done last year? Two nights ago? Yesterday? Today? "We're good."

"You don't sound like we're good."

"What difference does it make?"

She rubbed a hand over her front pocket. "I suppose it doesn't."

Her soft words had enough vulnerability and regret in them to bring even a hardened criminal to his knees.

"Just go," he said.

She hovered at the edge of his patio. "You made me happy." Her voice was a whisper in the bitter air, a ghost, a fragmented memory. "For whatever it's worth, that was real. And I'll never forget it."

"That'll help me sleep at night." He winced. He'd meant to keep that in his head, not let it slip out of his mouth.

"Making someone happy isn't a curse, Max. It's a gift. My mother's about to marry her seventh husband. I moved every two years as a kid, and I quit trying to make friends every time because I knew we'd move, and what was the point? But you made me happy. You made me believe. And if you can make someone like me believe love's possible, then you can do anything. Curse or not."

She stepped back into the shadows.

"Merry, wait."

She didn't answer.

Max set his beer down and followed her. "Merry?"

Still no answer.

He flipped his phone out, turned on the flashlight, and scanned the yard, but she was gone.

She wasn't out front either.

She'd simply vanished into the night, as though she were nothing more than a figment of his imagination.

MERRY HAD one wary eye on the sky, watching for attack owls, and the other scanning her surroundings for Max while she picked her way through backyards on her journey back to the B&B, but so far, she'd seen no hint of either.

Although she put the odds of an owl attack far greater than the odds of Max chasing after her.

Again, she shouldn't have gone to his house.

But she'd hurt him. Again and again. All he'd asked for was the truth. To know if they'd been real or if she'd been playing with him.

And if he'd truly had such a miserable streak of a love life, he deserved to know that he was a good guy and that he could make a woman happy if he let himself.

That he was worthy. That he was desirable. That he was lovable.

Just like she wanted to be.

It's a messed-up life you lead, Merry Silver, Phoebe Moon said.

"No shit, kid," Merry muttered.

Her phone buzzed in her pocket. She checked her surroundings once again, then answered while she stepped onto the sidewalk for the last two blocks. "Hello?"

"Amber! There you are. I've been trying to reach you for days."

Merry's pulse amped up at the sound of her agent's voice. "Janice. Hi."

"Can you do me a favor and keep this number for a few days? I want to be able to get hold of you. Nothing's official, and the lists aren't out yet, but I heard from your editor today, and your numbers last week were good. *Really* good."

"I—yeah. Yes. I'll have this number through the weekend." Her elbows twitched, and the phone trembled against her ear. *Normal* people wouldn't have agents calling to ask how long they'd keep their cell number. But she'd been with Janice through three phone changes, four new email addresses, and more physical addresses than she wanted to count. "When you say 'really good'—"

"Ah-ah. Don't want to jinx it. But have you checked your email? I've been forwarding the best reviews, and, Amber, they're *ah-mazing*. And your ranking everywhere online is unreal. For all six books. I can't even tell you how proud I am. Also, I need a good address. In case anyone wants to send you flowers Thursday. And did I mention at least four movie producers want to talk a deal?"

"Movie?" Merry whispered.

"Mov*ies*," Janice said. "For all six books. Maybe more. I'm waiting until the lists come out to put us in a better position to negotiate. Also, we've exercised your last option on your contract with your publisher, so we're in a fantastic position to negotiate for more on the next one too. This is huge, Amber. All of it. I'm utterly thrilled for you. I hope you have someone to celebrate with. No matter what, this was a fabulous launch."

Celebrate? With *who*? She hadn't even told her mother what her real job was.

"Of course," Merry choked out. "Champagne and caviar. I'm hiring a manservant to rub my feet. Celebrating is a must."

Between the cold air and the pressure growing in her sinuses, her nose dripped. She blinked three times, four—stupid winter wind.

"And you promise this is a good number?" Janice asked.

"Email's better." Merry swiped at her nose with the sleeve of her coat. The pressure wasn't just in her sinuses now. It was growing like a balloon at the base of her throat. "But for this week, yes. This is a good number."

"Merry Christmas, Amber. I'll be in touch soon. Call if you need anything, okay?"

"Yeah. Thanks, Janice."

Merry disconnected and shoved her phone in her pocket.

She'd come to a complete standstill across the street from Once Upon a Page. With barely a thought, she crossed to the closed bookstore.

A street lamp glowed overhead, giving just enough light for her to see the Phoebe Moon display in one window.

Phoebe Moon and the Ninja Hideaway. Phoebe Moon and the Sneeze Snatcher. Phoebe Moon and the Sinister Cloud. They were all there, artfully displayed with random tokens that were important in each book. A stopwatch. A skeleton key. A diary.

An announcement about Amber Finch being the featured author for this month's book club sponsored by the store.

Merry swiped at the moisture on her cheeks.

She'd invented Phoebe Moon as an imaginary friend shortly after Mom divorced Daddy. She'd been too old for imaginary friends by then, but she'd wanted someone she could count on. Someone she could take with her. Someone who wouldn't judge her for loving her daddy even though he was a common criminal, or for hating her mom for taking her away from her daddy.

And while Merry had aged, Phoebe Moon had stayed the same. A thirteen-year-old girl who could do things Merry couldn't.

She could stop Uncle Sandy from accidentally hurting someone in his misguided plans to take over the world. She could convince people to believe things that weren't true, but made the world a better place. She longed for more friends, but she took solace in knowing that her mission was bigger than herself, since she was the only person in the world who knew fiendish Uncle Sandy well enough to foil his plans.

But Merry wasn't like Phoebe Moon.

Merry couldn't stop Daddy.

She was too afraid he'd give her up if she tried.

She pressed her fingers to the window. There was something of her father in every Phoebe Moon book she'd written. Uncle Sandy's love of oysters. His soft spot for daddy longlegs. His insistence on driving black luxury cars.

And if Phoebe Moon didn't battle Uncle Sandy, she'd have no stories to tell.

Admitting where her inspiration came from would've been akin to endorsing Daddy's crimes, to justifying what he did. Even if his heart was mostly in the right place, his methods were still wrong, and she couldn't condone his thieving. She couldn't even tell her mother for fear the secret would get back to Daddy, even accidentally.

Phoebe Moon was everything she had that was just hers. The only thing no one could take from her.

And now, she was on the brink of an amazing milestone, and she had no one to share it with.

A sob came out on a hiccup. Then another.

She gulped in air, and—

Brut.

On the wind.

She tasted Brut.

"No," she whispered.

Daddy couldn't be here. She tried to sniff harder, to detect it again, but her nose was running too hard. Her vision was blurred, and she couldn't catch her breath.

A rumble grew behind her. She spun toward the street, the familiar engine both comforting and terror-inspiring. The red car drew to a stop beside her in the darkness, and the passenger door opened for her. "I'm going to regret this, aren't I?" Max called from across the seat.

Merry sniffed once more, trying to detect Daddy's signature scent, but it was useless.

She flung herself into the car. "Just drive."

Max hesitated. She buckled herself in, then dropped her head into her hands.

She had to pull herself together. There was movie interest in Phoebe Moon, even if the books didn't top the bestseller lists. She could see her stories on the big screen. And if she *did* hit the bestseller lists—*The New York Times* list. The mother of all lists. And her name —*Amber's* name—could be on it.

For the first time ever. Hopefully for the first of many times.

This was *good* news.

"Look, I'm sorry—" Max started.

She waved him off. "Not you. It's good. *Please* drive." Patrick was feeling well enough to take Mom out for dinner and get caught up on the wedding plans, so Merry wasn't expected or needed anywhere until tomorrow.

Trixie slowly moved forward, her engine sending a rumble

through Merry's body. She shuddered and sank lower in the seat, wanting to absorb the vibrations, to lock this moment away and take it with her forever.

"This is...good?" Max said.

"Faster." She hiccupped. She shivered, then hugged herself. The leather was cold, but warm air was flowing through the car, mingling with a subtle scent of pine and cinnamon and Max.

If Mom's weakness was love, and Daddy's weakness was jewels, Merry's was fast cars.

"I sort of got a promotion," she said into the darkness.

She didn't have to look at him.

His suspicions and disbelief and questions hung in the air, palpable like summer humidity.

"Do you really work in medical billing?"

She shook her head.

"What do you do?"

"I can't tell you."

"Are you in law enforcement?"

An honest laugh caught her off guard. "Even my mother would disown me."

"Are you in the family business?"

That was decidedly less funny. "Can you—will you go faster?"

He slanted a glance at her, then shifted into fourth gear as they hit the town limits. Trixie roared—she apparently loved this as much as Merry did—and suddenly the world was flying by, a swirl of darkness with Christmas lights fading into the distance, nothing but pavement illuminated ahead.

Merry sucked in a deep breath, closed her eyes, and gripped her armrest on the door.

"I was barely seventeen the first time my dad pulled me into a job," she said. "This guy—he'd asked me to prom, but he found out what Daddy did a week before the dance, and he told everybody. My friends. Teachers. A school board member. *Everyone*. Mom went in and had a conference with the principal, and she came home and told me no one would take my junior prom from me. So I—I went. And it was miserable. I ended up leaving after an hour because no one would talk to me, but I felt like everyone was talking *about* me, and every time I went on the dance floor, all the other kids cleared out. I couldn't even hide in the bathroom, because they were whispering. All of them."

Max rested his hand on her thigh and squeezed, and her tears threatened to erupt all over again. She willed them back and continued.

"When I got to the parking lot, Daddy was there. I don't know how he heard—I never know how he hears anything—but he knew. He had a big bouquet of carnations, and he said he wanted to take me out for ice cream. We were halfway there when he told me to pull over quick, that he saw something. And because I was an idiot, I didn't catch on until the house alarm went off."

"He pulled a job on your prom night and used you as his getaway car?"

"The kid who dumped me. Daddy cleaned out his mother's jewelry box. He came flying out of the house, jumped in with his pockets jangling, and told me it was just a dog, but I should probably floor it."

Max rubbed a hand over his five o'clock shadow. "That's…not something I can say I'll ever do for my niece."

She had put Phoebe Moon on paper for the first time that night. She'd been mortified, confused, and scared. She hadn't told Mom—though the policemen who had come around asking if she'd seen Daddy was probably a clue—but Merry had announced the following Monday she wasn't going back to school.

Ever.

"I dropped out," she said. "I had my GED by the end of the summer. Mom got divorced—that one lasted like three months—and we moved to this little town in Wisconsin. I took a few classes at a community college and waitressed for a while, and two years later, Mom found me a medical billing job. I got my own apartment, Mom married stepfather number three, and life went on."

Max didn't say anything.

She glanced at him and found his jaw clenched and his fingers tight on Trixie's wheel.

"When I was in grade school, before Mom divorced him, he used to listen to me tell knock-knock jokes for hours. *Hours*. He'd sing me the *Full House* theme song anytime I got in a mood. He told me my drawings and Play-Doh sculptures were the best he'd ever seen. He sat by my bed and read me books for four days straight while I was recovering from an appendectomy when I was seven. He made me feel like I was important. Like I mattered, no matter what. I thought when he told me that life didn't do handouts, that you have to take what you want, that he was telling me to be tough and work hard to get what I wanted. I thought when he said that he stood up for the little guy, that he was a crusader. He was a good dad. I adored him. And I thought we were normal."

Max whipped Trixie around a corner. Gravel spewed and the road crunched under her tires. Merry followed the momentum of the car, leaning into him, riding the wave of adrenaline that came from the sharp curve.

"I can hate what he does but still love him," she said.

He stayed silent. He turned deeper into the grove of trees until the night sky broke through the canopy of spindled branches and the town's lake appeared before them. The wedding cake monument glowed in the night across the way, and Christmas lights sparkled around town beyond it. He pulled Trixie's brake, then angled himself to face her straight-on. "You're not responsible for him."

"Being an adult doesn't always mean being independent. How long did you live with your grandparents to help take care of them?"

"They couldn't help getting old. Your father? He chooses to be a criminal. And you choose to let his life rule yours."

"I don't—"

"Don't sit there and tell me you disappeared because it was easier than telling me you wanted to break up. Don't sit there and tell me you disappeared because your job demanded it unless you're going to tell me what your job is. And don't sit there and make excuses for a man who *wasn't* the perfect father. Are you going to live your life, or are you going to let him run it for you?"

"Why the hell do you think I'm leaving the country?"

"Why don't you just tell him you're driving him straight to the cops if he ever fucks with your life again? Why are *you* the one who has to leave?"

"You—you're—*argh*."

He rolled his hands over the steering wheel. "Didn't come here to fight."

She rubbed her fingernail. She kept them cut short to make typing easier, but Mom had insisted on manicures this afternoon. Merry had picked silver polish in honor of Phoebe Moon, and the smooth texture was still foreign. "The second time I remember moving, I asked Daddy if we could move to Australia. I'd just seen *The Princess Bride*, and that line—the one about criminals in Australia?—I thought that sounded cool. Mom used to laugh and tell Daddy he was such a criminal, like that was a good thing."

"Merry." Max sighed.

"I know. Stupid. I was a kid. But every time we moved, we ended up in the same place. Somewhere we didn't know anyone, somewhere to start over, somewhere that was different, but not. I've never seen the mountains. I've never seen the ocean. But I want to. I'm not just running away so I can have a life. I *want* to go. I want to see someplace different. I want—I want to go find out who I can be."

All this honesty was killer. But Max deserved to know as much as she could tell him.

"I missed you," he said quietly.

Tension loosened in her neck, and a foreign warmth swelled in her chest. "I'm sorry."

His hand settled on her thigh again, warm and solid and real. He rubbed his thumb over her jeans. She put a shaky hand over his, soaked in the heat radiating from his skin, and gave in to the urge to scoot closer to him.

"When I guessed why you were gone, I spent hours looking into your father. And then my grandparents passed, and—" He cut himself off with a long sigh. "I didn't know how much I liked you until you were gone."

"I knew how much I liked you before I left."

"But you still left."

"You wouldn't have asked me to stay."

"I—no, you're right. I wouldn't have."

She dropped her head to his shoulder and squeezed her eyes shut. She hadn't expected him to deny it, but she'd still hoped he would. "We should go back. You have to work tomorrow, and Mom's planning a tour of the winery, which means we'll all be drunk before two."

But Max didn't move.

Not to put the car back in gear, anyway.

Instead, he pressed his face into Merry's hair. The roots of her hair tingled when he inhaled, then his fingers curled around her neck. "I've been thinking about you all fucking day."

More than just the roots of her hair tingled at the suggestions in his raspy voice. "That's what you get for kissing me."

"I want to kiss you again."

Oh, yeah. Her core pulsed, and her nipples perked up. "Maybe *your* mother can watch this time."

"She's out of town. Maybe next time." His tongue flicked her earlobe.

Her breath hitched, and her bra was suddenly painfully tight. "Who says there'll be a next time?"

"You smell amazing." He nuzzled her neck, his scruff igniting her nerve endings everywhere. "Like if fried chicken and engine grease got together and had flowers."

She choked on another surprised laugh. "That's disgusting."

"I missed your laugh, Merry." He reached across her, his arm and chest brushing her breasts, and she whimpered.

Then her seat went back, her seatbelt disappeared, and Max lifted a wolfish, tempting grin. "For old times' sake?"

"You just want to watch my ass when I climb back there."

He shifted his position, one hand sliding up her inner thigh, the other tangling in her hair. "Actually, I was wondering if you could use your ninja moves to throw me back there."

She laughed, but his teasing grin faded.

"Merry—"

"I'm leaving again."

"Not gone yet."

"Max—"

"I haven't wanted another woman since you left. Not like I want you." He caught her lips in his again, aggressive, possessive, demanding, while his fingers brushed her sensitive places.

Merry groaned into his mouth, grabbed him by the jacket, and yanked him against her. She leaned back in the seat, pulling him toward her with his lower lip caught between her teeth. He slid across the center console. Something banged against the door, then the car shook. He landed on her with a grunt.

She giggled.

She hadn't giggled in over a year, but there it was—a girly, free-spirited giggle. "You're still not very good at that."

He swore, then buried his head in her shoulder. His words were muffled, but they were perfect. "I missed you," he said again.

The idea that he'd say it until she believed it made her eyes sting again.

He knew she had secrets, he knew who her father was, but he still wanted her. The *her* she wanted to be. She swallowed. "Okay. I guess I can let you see my ass."

"And touch it?"

"And touch it."

"Watching your ass crawl into the backseat would've been easier before you used your ninja strength to pull me on top of you."

She tilted her hips up to his, and he sucked in a breath. "Am I not worth the trouble?" she whispered.

"Merry." He brushed his thumbs over her cheeks. "You're not trouble."

"I am."

His lips followed his thumbs, hot kisses against her cool face. "You're strong. You're sexy. You're smart. That's not trouble."

He was *so* getting laid. "You're a very dangerous man, Max Gregory."

"Are you still ticklish inside your elbow?" His fingers fiddled with the zipper on her coat.

She thrust her hands through his hair. "Danger," she said against his mouth.

He chuckled. "I love danger."

She apparently did too.

She made quick work of unzipping his coat, then thrust her fingers under his shirt while he treated her to a long, slow, *everything* kiss. His stomach was hot and rigid, the wiry hairs on his chest tickling her fingers, his nipples hard.

She'd missed being wanted. Being appreciated. Being bold.

But she'd also missed Max to the point that she physically hurt, and not just in her heart. She'd hurt in her legs when she'd had to walk away. She'd hurt in her fingers when she'd typed Zack Diggory's scenes. She'd hurt in her memories.

She'd probably hurt again.

But this time, she was moving on to make a new life.

This time, she'd get to say goodbye.

She tweaked his nipples, smiling into his kiss at his surprised gasp. "C'mon, speedy."

"Speedy? You're asking for it, you little minx."

"What? I was talking about your driving." She scurried from beneath him and crawled into the backseat, taking her time in letting him have as good a view of her backside as the light would afford.

The car rocked, and before she'd scooted across the backseat, Max was with her. He gripped her knees, then slid his hands up her thighs while his dark eyes telegraphed exactly what he wanted to do to her.

His thumbs brushed the denim covering her center, and she had to bite down on her lip to keep from moaning.

She yanked her jacket off and tossed it into the front seat. Her shirt was harder to get off—she banged her elbow against the window, and the air was cooler than she expected, but Max dipped his head and pressed a kiss to her collarbone, then made a path from her bra strap to the edge of one cup and across to the other while his fingers continued to flick at her center.

"This isn't real," she whispered.

"But it feels damn good," he replied.

It did.

And so she shut her mind off, sealed up her heart, and let herself simply feel. Max's thumbs on her nipples. The stiff leather bench seat beneath her. His tongue on the underside of her breasts. The slide of her pants when he stripped them off her. His sandpaper cheeks and chin on her inner thigh. His thick, remarkably soft hair between her fingers. The heady, salty taste of his skin on her tongue. The sound of his voice dancing through the air. The hard steel of the muscles in his arms and chest. The perfect fit of his erection inside her. The rocking of the car. The stars behind her eyes—and the sun and the moon and a few planets too—when Max hit that perfect spot inside her and sent her into oblivion.

She fell apart, into a thousand shards of rainbow light, and floated through the winter night, wishing she never, ever had to come back down.

His weight was solid and heavy, his head cradled between her breasts, his breath quick but steady. She squeezed her eyes shut, pretended moisture wasn't leaking out the corners, and let her hand rest in his hair.

"I missed you, Merry," he whispered once more in the dark.

"I'll miss you too."

It was well after midnight when Max dropped Merry at the B&B. He'd wanted to invite her home with him, but he knew where that would lead.

Danger.

To his brain, to his heart, possibly even to his family's business.

Had Merry meant to tell him her daddy liked to take things from people who hurt her? To warn him?

Or had she simply been telling an old story about her father's misguided intentions?

Max should've told Dan about her. Probably needed to put in a call to Spencer McGraw's people as well, just as a heads-up. See if McGraw wanted to put a temporary halt on displaying the diamond.

He pulled into the driveway of his grandparents' old house and hit the button on the garage.

The lights came on as the door lifted. No owl sightings tonight. No angry fathers waiting for him inside.

Just the old Dodge Charger and all of Max's tools.

What would your grandfather tell you to do?

Max sat in Trixie, her engine chugging, and stared at the other old hunk of metal.

Fixin' cars is a working man's job, Gramps had said when Max was nineteen. *You got the privilege of brains and an education. Be a sin to waste it.*

The same man had been beside Ma and Pops at every one of Max's football games in high school. He'd taught Max how to spot a fake diamond and how to charm the ladies to make a sale. Max had used that charm for other advantages through his teen years and his twenties, which Gramps had most likely known. Whenever Max had swung by to see Gran for cookies after school, if Gramps was home, they'd sit and talk sports, the family business, grades, and how much money Gramps would've won if he'd been playing on *Wheel of Fortune* last night.

The *Wheel* was sacred in the elderly Gregory household.

When Max had moved in to help out after both Gran and Gramps started having mobility issues three years back, he'd gotten addicted to the damn show too.

But Max's obsession with cars was the one thing Gramps had never understood.

Dan or Pops either.

But Max had a solid job offer on fixing an old car now. He had all the parts. He knew who he'd call for a paint job. He could find a way to make the time.

He didn't want to believe Merry was right, that he was a chicken for not jumping at the chance, but was he?

Was he holding back because he didn't want to lose the love he'd barely begun to rediscover of working on old cars?

Was he worried that he didn't have a good enough business model, the right connections to form a client base, that he'd fail and have to go back to With This Ring with his tail tucked between his legs?

Or had his dream simply died when Merry walked out of his life?

He stroked a hand over Trixie's wheel.

No, his dream hadn't died.

But life had given him too many losses in the past year for him to want to face another one.

14

Phoebe Moon felt the pressure behind her dainty nose, but no sneeze would come. Just like the grown-ups, she'd had her sneezer stolen from her. "That dastardly Uncle Sandy!" she cried.
—Phoebe Moon and the Sneeze Snatcher

One year ago

On a late-October Saturday, one week after Max had had his mind—and possibly his heart—blown by Merry in Trixie's backseat, he took her to a car show in Willow Glen. He hadn't expected her to want to go, but he'd tossed out the offer so she wouldn't think his only intention was having her come down to spend the night.

Which was his real intention.

He liked hanging out with Merry, sure, but Merry in bed?

Yeah.

He wanted more of that.

And since the only place they'd had sex was in Trixie's backseat, the car show turned out to be an exceptionally bad idea.

Every backseat he saw made him picture Merry's skin, her breasts, her legs, her head thrown back, her face in utter ecstasy. For the first time in his life, Max didn't want to linger over muscle cars.

He wanted to take a woman home.

Now.

But she was either oblivious, or she was enjoying torturing him. She was in jeans that showed off her amazing ass, a purple-gray vest over a white shirt, with a light scarf looped around her neck and her long dark hair loose so she kept having to tuck it behind her ears. They'd been at the show for an hour, and now she was eating a hot dog—yeah, watching her wrap her lips around that wasn't a problem at all—and pointing to a black 1970 Charger with chrome rims and a bench seat up front that had Max Jr. getting ideas again.

"I like this one, but I'd want it in blue," she said. "Does it have all that power-torque V-whatever stuff too?"

"Yes."

She tilted her head at him, took another bite of her hot dog, and waited.

The last time Max had taken anyone with him to a car show, his companion had been yawning and obviously feigning interest within the first fifteen minutes. Merry, though, was bright-eyed, inquisitive, and, Max suspected, soaking in every word he said.

As if she liked cars as much as he did.

He pointed to the sign next to the Dodge. "This one's a beast. Three-ninety horsepower with a V8. If I ever give Trixie a sister, it'll be one like her."

"A nineteen-seventy model?"

"Or a sixty-nine. Like the General Lee."

"Does it come in red too?"

"Bright red."

"You know a lot about cars."

Unlike his family, she seemed impressed. "It's a hobby."

"Trixie's much prettier than that Mustang behind you."

And more powerful. Max had checked. "You have excellent taste."

"So what's keeping you from giving Trixie a sister?" She shoved her last bite of hot dog in her mouth and lifted her brows at him.

She was always doing that—changing the subject back to him. Different from what he was used to with women.

Also uncomfortable right now.

"Haven't had the time to take on a second car," he said.

She was still chewing, still staring at him.

"My grandparents needed more help than we realized when I moved in with them. I got home from work one night, and Gran was sitting on the floor in the kitchen, having a dizzy spell, trying to tell Gramps where to step to avoid broken glass. He could navigate the house pretty well, but Gran would put cans behind glass jars in the cabinets, so when she asked him to get out a can of soup, he'd dropped a full jar of spaghetti sauce on the floor." And that had been one of the easier situations.

With Gramps's eyesight going, he'd known he'd never see Dan's newest pieces or his own favorites again. He'd quit going to the shop, quit talking about it unless someone else brought it up. Another time, Gran had had a dizzy spell while baking cookies and burned her arm on the open oven door. Gramps had wanted to go to the emergency room with her, but wasn't confident in letting anyone help him navigate the hospital, nor would he consider using a wheelchair.

The emotional wounds, watching his grandparents cope with knowing they would never get better, had been more than Max had been prepared to deal with when he moved in.

"Your family must've been grateful you could be there for them."

"My parents did a lot too. Getting them to doctor appointments, hiring house cleaners, visiting. My sister-in-law was always dropping off meals and audiobooks. I just mowed the grass and made sure they were safe overnight."

And worried he'd sleep through one of them needing something, had the occasional fling with the wrong women, and wondered how he'd handle himself when his time was just as imminent as Gramps's and Gran's was.

"Do you miss seeing them every day?"

"I still see them almost every day."

She smiled a faraway kind of smile, and before he could ask if she ever saw her own grandparents—or her parents, come to think of it—she went up on tiptoe, slung her arm behind his neck, and brushed her lips over his.

He hooked his thumbs through her belt loops, and she sucked his lower lip into her mouth.

When she'd kissed him in Trixie's backseat last weekend, primal lust had taken over.

Today, he wanted her in his bed again, but he wanted her to stay.

To talk. To listen. To simply *be*.

Someone jostled them, and Merry pulled back with a grin. "You should be ashamed of yourself for being so irresistible in public. Look what you made me do."

"My apologies, your highness."

She laughed and took his hand. They turned to the next car, a sixty-seven Camaro. "Trixie could run this one over with both hands tied behind her back," Max told her.

"You really love this, don't you?"

More than he'd ever admit to his family. "I'm a guy. Motor oil is in my blood."

"You like your day job as much as you like cars?"

"Old cars don't put food on the table and a roof over my dog's head the way With This Ring does."

She froze, then tilted an odd look at him. "With This Ring?" she said in a voice he'd never heard before.

"My family's shop."

She didn't say anything else, but just stood there watching him as if he'd sprouted a third leg and a second set of elbows.

"My parents are retiring, so I'm taking over as manager," Max said into the vacant space of the conversation. "Dan, my brother—he's the creative genius. Took over from Gramps. Even helped Gramps design the Mrs. Claus diamond ring, and—"

Merry squeaked, then seemed to choke on air.

"Ah. Right." Max tossed her a grin he didn't feel. He liked her. They had a good thing. She wasn't going to get weird about his family working in the jewelry business now, was she? "Forgot to mention that's why Gramps sent me to the signing, didn't I?"

"Uh, *yeah*."

"Would it have made a difference?"

"Obviously."

He laughed, relief seeping into his bones. That was Merry—funny and sarcastic. "You seem surprised."

Her complexion was too pale. She shrugged, then gestured to the cars around them. "Between this and Trixie, I guessed you were into custom bridal getaway cars or something. But it's not like our day jobs define who we are."

And there she went, surprising him again. "Not many people make a living with their dreams," he said.

She didn't reply, but she gave him a look he was coming to think of as the *Merry's got an idea* look, with a touch of a blush on top of it.

It made his pulse kick up the same time a rush of *never gonna happen* hit his gut.

He was a jeweler, born into a long line of jewelers, destined to maybe one day add a kid or two to the family legacy.

But it would be damn fun to spend his days covered in grease.

And she was watching him as if she knew it. "I guess it's good to keep it just a hobby," she said. "I mean, if you had to do it all the time, you might hate it, right?"

Hate cars? Never.

She smiled, and even though telepathy was impossible, he could almost hear her saying, *That's what I thought.*

Possibly with a side of *So do it.*

"These cars are fascinating," she said. "I could spend hours here."

Max didn't detect a hint of sarcasm.

But for once, the cars weren't the most interesting thing at the show. "Wanna blow this Popsicle stand and head back to my place?"

She blinked once, then smiled, even if it didn't feel entirely Merry-ish. But when her fingers brushed his thigh, he didn't care what kind of smile she gave him.

"Does your place have cheese?" she whispered.

"White cheddar, Brie, and muenster. And if you're nice, Scout might share it."

She arched a mock haughty brow at him. "Or I could go home and eat my own cheese."

He slipped his arm around her shoulders and steered her toward the exit. "But I wouldn't be there to feed it to you."

Her eyes went cloudy, and her lips drew down.

Almost as though she were considering going home.

His ticker hammered.

Shouldn't have. This was just for fun. Not serious. He wasn't ready for serious.

Maybe it's the curse, an ugly voice whispered.

But then Merry smiled again. "I suppose I can give up my independent eating ways for one night."

He blew out a breath.

One night.

Yeah, this was just about one night.

And he wouldn't have traded his left nut to have his family's support for the idea of him quitting at With This Ring and restoring muscle cars for the rest of his life.

If he had to lie to himself, he might as well lie about everything.

MERRY'S excellent secret-keeping skill was the only thing keeping her from hyperventilating while she followed Max from the car show to his house in Bliss.

She was dating a jeweler.

A freaking *jeweler.*

If Daddy found out—

No.

No, Daddy would *never* find out. Merry hadn't mentioned anything about Max to Mom. She was all tied up in post-divorce drama right now. So Merry would keep Max to herself, and she'd break up with him.

Her heart twisted.

"Why?" she whispered to the sky.

It didn't have any answers for her, so she focused on Trixie's taillights and kept driving.

She liked Max.

She liked Max more than she'd ever liked any man. Yes, she'd kept her secrets from him, but everyone had secrets. And it wasn't like she and Max were serious. They were just having fun.

Which was all the more reason for her to break up with him sooner rather than later.

But she was twenty-seven years old. If she told her father to stay out of her dating life, he would.

Wouldn't he?

And what about Daddy seeming to have settled down? He had a good job. He'd been in the same place for almost two years now. He was getting older, and he seemed to be acknowledging his limitations.

Dammit.

She needed to break up with Max.

But...if nothing went *wrong*, Daddy wouldn't have need for any vengeance, right?

And even Daddy couldn't argue that anyone in Bliss needed to be taught a lesson. The whole town was devoted to love and weddings. There was even—she squinted into the distance—holy *crap*. Was that a gigantic wedding cake?

Why had Mom never gotten married here?

Merry shook her head. Not the point.

The point was, she couldn't date a jeweler.

But maybe if she told Max that she was Amber Finch, if she showed him it *was* possible to make a living from following your dream, then maybe he'd leave the jewelry business and instead take a job restoring old cars, and—

And if Daddy was still thieving, and if something ever went wrong with her relationship with Max, and if Daddy found out about it, Max's family would still be in trouble.

She switched on her blinker and followed Max as he took a side street just inside Bliss.

That was a long list of things that had to go wrong before she would actually be putting Max or his family's business in danger by dating him.

She was already in this deep.

One more afternoon wouldn't hurt anything.

Would it?

A few minutes later, Max pulled into the garage of a two-story brick colonial house in a comfortable older neighborhood.

A place where children had grown up in the same house from birth through high school. Where families stayed put for a full generation, sometimes more. Where grandmas made cookies for the grandkids they watched after school, like Max had told her his grandmother used to do for him and his brother.

A yearning hit Merry so deep in the pit of her gut that she almost couldn't breathe.

It was too idyllic to be real, yet it was Max's life.

His life that he was sharing with her, one little piece at a time.

Max waved her into the garage too, so she took the empty stall beside Trixie. She slowly climbed out of her car and followed him to the door. As soon as he opened it, a mass of golden fur shot out into the garage, nose going straight to Merry's crotch.

"Scout! Down, girl," Max said. He gave Merry a sheepish grin. "Sorry about that. She's friendly, I promise."

An eager nose flicked at Merry's hand and followed it with a lick, and before she knew what she was doing, she had sunk to her knees to hug the dog. "Hi, you sweet thing," she crooned.

This was what a home was supposed to feel like.

Normal. Stable. Forever.

It was entirely too good to give up just yet.

15

"Spike, you stay here," Phoebe Moon said to her clumsy but well-intentioned iguana. "And if I don't come back, run to the nunnery. They always took such good care of you."
—Phoebe Moon and the Ninja Hideaway

Present day

Having sex with Max last night might've made the chilly blue sky brighter, the Christmas decorations around Bliss more charming, and the task of planning Mom's wedding more enjoyable, but it had also made the guilt hang thicker.

Merry had been as honest as she could with him. She'd given him more of herself than she gave anyone.

But she still felt as though she'd stolen something she couldn't return.

So when she saw no hint of him all day Tuesday—not at breakfast at the B&B, not at the wedding planner next door to his family's store, not at the winery where she'd told him they would be half the day—she started to relax.

Maybe last night had been his goodbye. Or she'd been overly full of herself in thinking that she meant something to him. Or he'd gotten her out of his system.

I'm only thirteen, and even I know that's a load of crap, Phoebe Moon said.

Merry put imaginary duct tape on Phoebe Moon's mouth and forced herself to focus on Mom and Patrick and the dinner menu at Suckers.

The bar wasn't Mom's usual joint, but she insisted Patrick have a bachelor party when his brother and nephew arrived in Bliss, and Zoe had said Suckers was the best place in town.

Unfortunately, Merry recognized several of the other patrons from her trip here the other night.

There was Zoe. Pepper. And a vaguely familiar blonde wearing a pair of amethyst drop earrings and matching necklace, a Cartier watch, and a diamond wedding ring that rivaled some of Mom's. The blonde was clearly running the show at their table.

Mom hadn't noticed them because she'd been too busy trying to accidentally catch Billy Brenton's eye. He was in the back corner booth with his wife, along with two other men—one tall, broad, and redheaded, the other tall, slender, and bald—and two more pregnant women.

"Mom, stop," Merry whispered. "You're going to give Patrick a complex. Besides, Billy's married. And he's half your age."

"Not quite, Meredith, and I'm simply marveling at the wonder of so many beautiful pregnant women. Make sure you drink the water, dear. It's obviously effective here."

"Now, now, Vicky, Merry's a career woman." Patrick winked at her. "With so many young people failing to find their places in this world, we should celebrate what she's accomplished instead of worrying over what she hasn't."

He's almost as good as your mother, and he doesn't even know I might be on a bestseller list this week, Phoebe Moon said.

"Ah...thank you, Patrick," Merry said.

He patted her shoulder awkwardly. "Of course, Merry. I'm

honored to be getting such a smart, independent stepdaughter. You're a testament to your mother's raising."

"Oh, Patrick, you're such a dear." Mom pecked him on the cheek.

Their waitress stopped to take their order, and when she left, Mom leaned her elbows on the table. "Merry, I heard the most interesting tidbit while you were exploring the gift shop at the winery."

"Seems there's a lot interesting in Bliss these days."

"You remember that sweet Pepper who helped us at the bridal gown shop? Apparently every last one of her boyfriends has married the woman he's dated directly after her. They're saying she carries the pre-bride curse."

"Mom, there's no such thing as a curse," Merry said.

"*And* I heard that Matt boy who keeps sniffing around has his own curse. Obviously this town isn't the best place for the poor residents to find their happily ever afters."

"Billy seems happy. So do all those pregnant women."

"Still, it's a good thing we're all leaving on Saturday."

"Ms. Silver." The blonde materialized at the edge of their table. She extended a hand to Mom. "Rachel Vaughn-Gregory. We haven't met, but Zoe Scott tells me you're an absolute dear, so I wanted to say hello. May I?"

Mom stiffened, but Rachel sat at the empty seat at their table before anyone could object.

Rachel's smile oozed *troublemaker*, with a side of *take no prisoners*. "I hear your wedding plans are coming along beautifully."

"I'm sorry, who are you?" Mom said.

Rachel laughed, a tinkling sound that inspired thoughts of Phoebe Moon stopping dancing Uncle Sandy from ruining a debutante ball. "I'm sorry, I should've mentioned. I'm the president of the Bridal Retailers Association, and my husband, Dan, and I play Santa and Mrs. Claus at all the local events now. Of course I volunteer at the kids' school every week, and there's Girl Scouts and Cub Scouts—my oldest crosses over to Boy Scouts this spring—and I help Dan at With This Ring from time to time. He discovered his passion for following in his grandfather's footsteps when dear Gramps was designing the Mrs. Claus diamond ring, and now he's the head jeweler." She thrust her hand out. "He designed my wedding set too."

Merry's stomach dipped.

It was a lovely set—the diamond engagement ring was at least a carat and a half, set in platinum, with the wedding band a wrap with three lines of diamond chips swirling about the engagement rock.

And if Daddy were here, and if Daddy thought anything about this woman was obnoxious, he'd relieve her of the ring in a heartbeat.

"Beautiful," Mom murmured with a slanted glance at Merry.

Patrick made an approving, "Mmm."

Poor oblivious man.

"Anyway, we take weddings very seriously here in Bliss, and we just want to know that you're happy with yours," Rachel finished.

"Well. Thank you very much," Mom said.

"It's our pleasure, Ms. Silver. I trust you enjoyed the Snow Bride Festival?"

Mom cast one more glance at Merry, but then nodded at Rachel. "Charming festival."

"Officially, it's over for the year, but we locals don't really call it closed until after our annual bachelor auction for charity. It's this weekend."

"Pretty sure Mom doesn't need a bachelor," Merry interjected.

Patrick chuckled.

"Nor does Merry," Mom said.

"Yep. One too many ex-boyfriends in Bliss already," Merry agreed cheerfully.

"Between you and me, I'm honestly worried about my brother-in-law," Rachel stage-whispered, as though everyone except possibly Patrick hadn't figured out who her brother-in-law was. "He's had a horrible string of bad luck in love lately, so we're taking up a collection to help my friend Pepper bid on him."

What an excellent way to shove Merry out of the way and make Max forget all about her. With a woman who belonged in Bliss. Who knew the town's history. Who loved the town for it. And who had never abandoned one of their beloved sons.

"Pepper the pre-bride?" Mom said.

Rachel nodded ominously.

"Not that I care one way or another, but whose curse do you think will be lifted first?" Mom asked.

"Hard to say, but we can hope both. Not that any of us actually believe in curses."

"Of course not, of course not," Mom agreed. "But the notion is fascinating."

It totally is, Phoebe Moon agreed. *But they're stealing your man, Merry.*

He's not mine, Merry fired back.

Merry Silver, you know you want him, Phoebe Moon chided.

Shut up, you little brat. I want to go to France.

"What does a bachelor typically go for at your auction?" Mom asked.

Merry stifled an indignant squeak. Polite interest was one thing, but Mom was taking it too far.

I thought you wanted to go to France, Phoebe Moon taunted.

"We have about two hundred dollars in our fund for Pepper, but we've had bachelors go for as much as seven hundred before," Rachel said.

Mom looked over at the table where Pepper and Zoe had their heads together, then back at Rachel. "What charity does your cause support?"

"Other than the worthy cause of breaking curses against love?"

"Knock it off, Rach," Max said.

Hooray! Phoebe Moon cheered.

But Merry's tongue went sideways, her biceps clenched on their own, and her legs tensed for flight.

A warm, solid, terrifyingly comforting hand settled on her shoulder. "How about I save us both and take you to dinner. We can plot our revenge against my dastardly sister-in-law and her unsuspecting accomplices."

Something even more terrifying caught in her throat and threatened to choke her.

He said dastardly, Phoebe Moon crowed. *And unsuspecting accomplices!*

Rachel beamed at him. "Olivia will be so thrilled."

"At vengeance?" Merry forced out.

"No, that her favorite uncle Max is quoting her favorite books. Pepper," Rachel called, "do your nieces read Phoebe Moon?"

Merry needed air.

Now.

She shoved out of her chair without waiting to hear Pepper's answer.

Max steadied her, questions she would never answer springing up in the blue-green depths of his eyes. "You okay?"

"Just great," she lied. She flashed her phone at Mom, then grabbed her coat. "My boss is calling. Gotta go."

Mom frowned, obviously seeing right through the lie. "Meredith, we need your help picking Patrick's bachelor party menu."

"Patrick's a big boy, Mom. He can read the menu himself and everything."

"Pleasure as always, Nicky," Max said behind her.

"It's obviously all yours, Matt," Mom replied. "And Meredith doesn't need your help with a phone call from her boss."

"No, but I just remembered I need to be somewhere."

He caught up with Merry in the parking lot. The icy air stung her lungs, and her eyes weren't adjusting to the dark fast enough.

Also, she couldn't find the other sleeve of her coat.

Max held the offending article still and helped pull it up to her shoulders. "Sorry about that. Rach can be a little driven when she has a goal."

"It wasn't—" Merry caught herself.

Rachel was sort of like another Mom. Pushier, but hardly anything Merry couldn't handle.

It was the idea of Max still reading Phoebe Moon that had sent her over the edge.

Had he started *Phoebe Moon and the Missing Sunshine* yet?

Had he noticed Zack Diggory's car?

For that matter, had he noticed he *was* Zack Diggory?

"Thanks for the rescue," she said. "You can get back to your... whatever, and I'll tell Mom you took me back to your place, stuffed me full of cheese, ravaged me, and then drove me home like a gentleman. She'll love that."

"Or we could go back to my place, have some cheese, and I can ravage you and then drive you home like a gentleman."

Merry sniffed the winter air, but all she smelled was cold with hints of beer and French fries. "Max—"

"You're leaving in a few days, I have a couple years left on my curse, and you have legitimate reasons to worry about our family businesses. Got it." He slipped his hand in hers, his fingers warm and strong, and he tugged. "But you turn me on, Merry Silver."

"You're a shameless flirt."

"Oh, you want shameless flirting?" He angled his body to align with hers and put a hand to the small of her back, drawing her closer. "What's a pretty girl like you doing in a place like this?"

"What would your sister-in-law say if she heard you say that?"

"Probably that I should use my charms on a different woman. But is it working?"

"No."

"Liar."

She absolutely was.

Max nudged her toward Trixie, who was angled across two spaces right outside the door. "C'mon. Let's get you in the car before the owl gets you. Too bad Spike can't take care of him." He looked down again, his brow furrowed, and Phoebe Moon blew a loud, blaring panic alarm in Merry's head.

Had he just connected Phoebe Moon's accidental pet iguana, Spike, to Merry's imaginary dragon? "Yes, well, I had to give Spike up when I left Chicago last year," she said. "My new apartment had a no-dragons clause. Even dragons with firebox-ectomies."

He opened Trixie's door for her, and because she liked Max, and because she'd miss him, and because she could almost be all of herself with him, she didn't argue, but instead settled into Trixie's seat. No Brut on the wind tonight. No sign of the owl.

Just the lingering tension of knowing that they were so wrong for one another even Merry's mom was interested in who else might buy Max at a bachelor auction.

I'd buy him, Phoebe Moon said.

Hush, or I'll write Phoebe Moon and the Time Reverser *and take all your hormones away,* Merry snapped back.

Max crossed around the car, climbed in, and cranked the engine. "Where'd you go when you left last year?"

Ah, her disappearance. An oddly safe topic. "St. Louis with Mom for a little bit, and then this little town called Toluca. It's about halfway between here and Springfield. Around a thousand people. And The Cheese House, which is what sealed the deal. They serve great pizza and ice cream too."

He grinned at her. "You have the cheese plate at Cupid Creek today?"

"Um, duh."

"Try all thirty-four cheeses?"

"Alas, even my cheese tooth couldn't accomplish all thirty-four." Mom had sampled all thirteen wines in Cupid Creek's tasting room, and Merry had sampled eight cheeses in the winery's bistro. Mom had stayed just this side of tipsy, and Merry had had to pop the button on her pants.

"Want to go back?" Max asked.

"Max Gregory, are you going to ply me with cheese and wine and try to get back in my pants?"

"Yes."

"Do we have to talk?"

"No."

"Okay. I'm in."

He smiled at her again, a soft smile, an understanding smile, possibly an *I like you even if you want to pretend not to like me* smile, and something more than the Brie she intended to sample again tonight went warm and gooey in her center.

"Do you like Pepper?" she asked.

"On steak. Sometimes in soup."

"*Pepper Blue.* From Bliss Bridal. The Pepper who's going to bid on you on Saturday."

"Thought we weren't talking."

"We don't *have* to. That doesn't mean we won't. Obligation versus desire."

He was grinning again, and she had to squelch an overwhelming urge to lean over and kiss him.

He was a big, strong, sexy linebacker, and he was absolutely adorable when he grinned.

"You don't have a clue what you want, do you?" he said.

"Do you want to get laid again tonight or not?"

He grinned bigger. "I would never deny a lady in need."

"That Stilton better be fantastic," Merry grumbled.

"It is. But I'm better."

There was a rapidly increasing chance that she might sic devious Uncle Sandy on Zack Diggory. Except then Phoebe Moon would have to save him. Although Janice's email this morning had indicated Zack Diggory was a huge hit with fans. *Phoebe Moon and the Best Friend Rescue?* No. Not enough ring. She'd have to think on it a while longer.

Max navigated through Bliss, then opened Trixie up and let her fly down the rural back roads to Cupid Creek Winery. Multicolored Christmas lights twinkled from the slanted roof over the central entry of the building, which housed the gift shop, tasting bar, and bistro. Inside, matching Christmas trees on either side of the massive double maple doors were hung with Victorian Santa ornaments, white lights, and gilded bows.

The bistro's hostess greeted Max by name, then quickly showed them to a private two-person table at a red velvet-draped window with a view of the wedding cake monument in the distance.

Merry didn't bother with the menu. "You know everyone here."

"Small town."

"Not *that* small." There was a civic center on the other side of town. They had their own minor league baseball team. She'd heard their annual Knot Festival could draw as many as thirty thousand tourists—brides, grooms, and weirdos who simply dug all the wedding stuff. And while The Aisle was quaint and adorable and had a total small-town feel, the town itself was larger than the blocks around The Aisle suggested.

"Small enough," Max said. "Your mom ready for her wedding?"

"Oh, sure. She's done this so many times, she could get married in her sleep."

"You like her fiancé?"

"Mmm-hmm."

"Really?"

"Of all the men she's married, I've only disliked two." Blunt honesty wasn't one of Merry's more practiced skills, but she was falling into the easy old rhythm of trusting Max. Not enough to tell him everything, but more than she'd been willing to trust someone new in years. "I hated my first stepfather. He wasn't my daddy. And he never would be. I probably didn't give him a fair shot, but I was fourteen, I had to change schools again because we moved when Mom married him, and he wasn't my daddy."

"And the other one?"

"Mr. Frocklestein." She shuddered. "Stepfather number four. He was seventy-one. Former high school principal who'd won fourteen million in the lottery. He smelled like boiled cabbage and had a handshake like limp spaghetti. Turned out, he and Mom had a business marriage. When he died, three cousins appeared out of nowhere and contested his will. Mom invited them over for dinner one night with Mr. Frocklestein's lawyer, and I never heard another word about them. She donated eighty percent of his estate to charity, and then she married the lawyer six months later."

"How old were you?"

"Oh, this was only a few years ago. She was getting over that divorce when we—when we met last year."

They paused to order—a steak and the house pinot noir for Max, a plate of apricot Stilton, a seven-year farmhouse cheddar, triple-cream Brie, and fresh mozzarella along with a glass of Syrah and a salad for Merry. When Max handed the waitress his menu, he leaned on his forearms and peered at her as though he had all night to unlock her secrets. "Have a favorite?"

"Cheese?"

"Stepfather."

Well. That was a new thought. "None were my daddy."

"They're still in your life. If Dan had six ex-wives, I'd have a favorite."

"I imagine you would."

"Might even be Rachel. She makes a killer chocolate mousse."

Nope, that wasn't jealousy surging like a green-eyed dragon through Merry's veins.

Or maybe it was. Rachel was stunning, could carry a conversation, and, Merry suspected, was organized enough to manage three husbands, fourteen children, and an orphanage in Phoebe Moon's world. In short, the perfect woman.

But Merry had France coming.

She eyed Max's unashamed smile, the warmth in his expression, the corded muscles of his forearms, and sighed.

France would be lovely.

And she had no business indulging in fantasies about Max going with her. His life was here. With his family. With Rachel's mousse.

"Yo-yo," she ground out.

"Pardon?"

"Yo-yo. He's my favorite of my mother's ex-husbands."

"Circus performer? Punk rapper? Did he live with his mother?"

"He lived with his aunt Topanga in a treehouse and made a fortune modeling for romance book covers."

Max not-so-discreetly flexed his muscles. "I could do that."

And then millions of women would ogle his washboard abs, he'd have tribal tattoos Photoshopped onto his waxed chest, and Merry would take up licking book covers.

Where was her wine?

"Actually, Yo-yo was a victim of the dot-com bust. He helped write some key software that saved a company I'm not allowed to publicly mention from breaking when Y2K happened, then was let go a couple years later. His brother's a financial advisor and had insisted Yo-yo diversify when he was raking in millions, so now Yo-yo pretty much plays RPGs and goes to cons all the time. I guess one of his screen names is semi-famous."

"RPGs?"

"Role-playing games."

Max's eyes went dark. "I could do that too. Do you have a ninja costume?"

She nudged his shin with her foot. "Knock it off."

"Just making sure you know what you're worth and that your standards in men are set high before you leave the country."

After the waitress delivered their wine and a complimentary bread basket, Max lifted his glass. "To adventures," he said softly.

Merry clinked.

Not because she wasn't looking forward to her own adventure. Not because she didn't love giving Phoebe Moon adventures.

But because right now, she wished she could live the adventure of Bliss for just a little longer.

16

"Ah, Phoebe Moon, we meet again," devious Uncle Sandy said. "No hug for your dear uncle?"

Phoebe Moon stood as tall as her short bones would allow. "I'm not here to hug you, Uncle Sandy. I'm here to stop you."

—Phoebe Moon and the Sneeze Snatcher

By dessert, Max was simultaneously wondering at his chances of getting Merry in his bed tonight and how popular muscle cars were in...what country had she said she was going to?

Maybe he'd visit her someday. Wherever it was had to have something to check out other than Merry.

Not that Merry by herself wasn't a decent reason to go. "Hey, you've read those Phoebe Moon books, right?"

Her spoon hung suspended in midair, a peak of hardened caramelized sugar sticking out of the crème brûlée. "Yes." Her voice was higher, and the rosy circles the wine had given her cheeks spread wider.

"That where Spike came from?"

She slipped the spoon into her mouth, wary eyes searching his face, and Max Jr. sat up.

"Don't meet girls who fend off bad pickup lines with imaginary dragons every day," Max said.

She swallowed, her delicate throat working, and Max Jr. pulsed again.

Max dug into his chocolate lava cake.

"Well, how did you name Scout?" she said.

"Shelter named her."

Her nose wrinkled. "Oh."

"But I've read *To Kill A Mockingbird* enough to like the name."

"You haven't told Trixie you're reading kids' books now, have you?"

"She loves *Harry Potter*. I used to read it to her at bedtime. But I'm holding out on starting *Percy Jackson* until her carburetor behaves better."

"Do the other cars know?" Merry whispered. "That's kinda...nerdy."

This was what he'd missed about her. The teasing. Her quick wit. The way her voice was like silk against sandpaper when she whispered.

"You think any other car's stupid enough to mock Trixie?" he said.

"Maybe they're jealous."

"Did you get picked on when you were little?"

And there went the blank Merry mask. She set her spoon in her half-eaten dessert and stretched back in her chair. "That was delicious, but I am stuffed with a capital *S*."

Of course she'd been teased as a kid. She'd moved a lot. Always the new kid, compounded by being the new kid with a criminal father. He gestured to her dessert. "Want it to go?"

"I have to fit into a bridesmaid dress on Friday."

Max wiggled his brows at her. "I wouldn't mind if you—"

An alarm suddenly shattered the peaceful conversations in the room, slicing through the muted sounds of other patrons.

Merry leapt out of her chair and it tipped over. Her face went an ashen gray, eyes wide and panicked. She fumbled for her front pocket.

Everyone else had simply paused and were darting curious looks about the room.

Smoke wafted from the door to the kitchen. Two waitstaff stumbled out, both pointing everyone outside, while the manager flew toward the trouble.

Max stood and reached for Merry. "Hey—"

"We have to pay!" she shrieked.

Her phone tumbled to the ground, then her driver's license. Max scooped both up, then snatched her hand. "We have to leave."

"But—"

"Fire, Merry. March." He grabbed her coat with his other hand and tugged her toward the door.

She walked stiffly, as if her joints had been screwed straight, lips parted, chest heaving. They followed their fellow diners out into the parking lot and gathered in a cluster between the cars and the frozen man-made pond at the entrance to the winery's grounds.

"Do we need to stick around?" one guy asked.

"We didn't get our check yet," another one said.

Red lights flashed in the night, sirens growing closer.

The alarm still blared inside.

Merry twisted and turned, peering into the darkness as though she were looking for someone, making Max wonder if her father routinely started kitchen fires as distractions when he was on a job.

She held a death grip on Max's hand.

"Hey. Here. Put your coat on."

"This wasn't Daddy," she whispered. "He's not here. Not his style. He wouldn't have—"

"Merry, it was a kitchen fire." He pulled her close and kissed her crown, letting his nose linger in her flowery scent.

She trembled.

"Hey, it's okay."

Had this happened often when she was growing up? Had she been there when security alarms had gone off?

"My phone," she said suddenly. "I don't have—"

"Right here."

She snatched it faster than Scout lunging for a piece of chicken. Then she felt in her front pockets again, pulling out two twenties, but nothing else. "My—"

Max held her driver's license between his first two fingers.

Her body sagged. "Thank you."

The winery's staff trickled out of the building. Some were friends, some familiar by name or face only. The bistro's manager trotted over to them. "Sorry, folks," he called. "Had a little kitchen fire. It's contained, but I expect you won't be able to finish your meals. Dinner's on the house, so you can—"

The approaching sirens drowned out whatever else he was saying. A fire truck barreled up the curved drive leading to the building, followed by a police cruiser, an ambulance, and two more fire trucks.

She trembled harder against him, then pushed herself upright and pinched her lips and clenched her fists, as though she were willing herself to calm down.

And to do it on her own.

The manager held up a finger for the crowd, then crossed to talk to the firemen. The sirens flipped off, and Max could suddenly hear Merry's ragged breathing. "Can we go?" she said.

"If I say no, are you going to go ninja on me?"

She didn't answer.

Not good.

"Fire trucks are blocking the road," Max said.

She shuddered again. He touched her shoulder, but she jerked away. "I'm fine."

Other people were taking refuge from the wind in their cars, so Max led Merry to Trixie. He prompted her into the backseat and slid in after her. Red lights pulsed through Trixie's interior. Suited-up firemen jogged through the night and into the winery. But here in Trixie's backseat, they were alone.

Max Jr. wasn't the only part of him happy when she curled into his body and let him wrap an arm around her. That flower scent tickled his nose, but something more tickled behind his breastbone.

"Been through this before?" he asked.

Wasn't hard to assume she and authority figures weren't buddy-buddy. He could make a semi-confident leap that alarms reminded her of some not-great times too.

But her ashen complexion, the shudders, the quick breaths—this was like when his neighbors' yard got flamingoed last winter. When she'd seemed on the verge of a panic attack.

"Won't tell a soul, Merry," Max murmured into her hair. "It was a long time ago."

He guessed.

He hoped.

"I'm just using your hot body for warmth," she said.

He sighed, and she pulled away to stare out the window, her breath a foggy circle on the glass.

"I was robbed," she said quietly.

His hands curled into fists.

"A long time ago," she confirmed. "It was my first apartment after I moved out of Mom's house, in a place I thought I was safe. I went to the grocery store, and when I came home, the door was open, and everything was trashed. My favorite books were ripped apart, like they were looking for cash shoved between the pages. And my upstairs neighbor's fire alarm was going off the whole time. I didn't have much jewelry—why tempt my father, right?—but what I had was gone. It seemed inevitable though, you know? Karma or something."

"*You* don't have to pay for your father's sins."

"Don't I? Never mind. I just—alarms get to me. They make me remember. Daddy doesn't use weapons. He works alone, in the dark. No one gets hurt." She visibly shivered. "But that was the first time I understood what it was like to feel violated. Even when I quit school so I wouldn't have to face the guy who dumped me before prom, I didn't feel like I'd lost anything. Like I'd had anything taken from me. And that's what my daddy did. *Does*. He takes things. He might not physically hurt people, and he always uses his scores for good, but he leaves scars all the same."

Merry, he suspected, had more scars than she realized. "You ever think about just telling people about him?"

"What, like, 'Hi, I'm Merry, and my father's a jewel thief'?"

"Yeah. Something like that."

She snorted.

"At least they'll know why you disappear."

"Do you have to keep bringing that up?"

"Have you met Kimmie yet? Her mother's a real piece of work. She doesn't steal jewelry, but she does steal souls. Pretty sure she eats them with caramel sauce."

She twisted back to face him. "Kimmie, the pregnant bakery girl?"

"Yep."

"Her mother—"

"Is the formidable beast who runs Heaven's Bakery."

Merry shuddered.

"Ah, so you've had the pleasure," Max murmured. "And she's actually nice at Heaven's Bakery."

"But Kimmie's so—so—"

"Not her mother? Like you aren't your father?"

Merry stuck out a petulant lip, and Max had half a mind to bite it.

"Try it," he said. "Next time you see Zoe or Pepper, mention your dad's a jailbird. Tell them that's why you disappeared. See what they say."

"He's not a *jailbird*, and I'm not here to make friends."

"You could use the practice before you go to...where was it you're going?"

That raised eyebrow told him he was wasting his breath asking. "Are you enjoying yourself?" she said.

"More like torturing myself."

Because she was leaving.

And with every passing minute, he didn't want her to.

"Looks like they're letting us go," she said.

Sure enough, cars were moving past the emergency vehicles in the parking lot.

"We should go pay," she added. "We finished our meal."

"I'll text the manager and let him know I'll swing by tomorrow."

Her eyes went squinty and displeased.

Max stifled a sigh. "Get strapped in. I'll be right back."

She shoved her two twenties at him.

He ignored her money and climbed out of the car.

When he returned five minutes later, having been chastised for suggesting he'd be paying for a dinner interrupted by a kitchen fire, he found her suspiciously quiet and serene, strapped into the passenger seat just like he'd told her to do.

He pulled Trixie's door shut and eyed her. The Merry he knew—both last year and today—didn't do quiet, obedient, and serene.

"Can we go back to your place?" she whispered.

How could a guy say no to that?

If Merry were to list her top three favorite places on earth, Max's bedroom might be on the list.

Might, because putting it on a list would be admitting how much she liked it.

It had changed since last year. He'd moved from a front room on the second story to the back master bedroom. A flat-screen TV hung over the fireplace, and the room smelled faintly of fresh paint, but otherwise, little was different. His gray plaid bedspread still covered flannel sheets on his low platform bed. The black wood chest of drawers was simple and utilitarian with his four scale-model Mustangs displayed in the glass case on top.

She lay in the dark beside him, waiting, his arm a comforting weight across her belly, his breath steady and hot against her shoulder, his leg wrapped in hers.

Max was a ridiculously light sleeper.

But she wouldn't stay here tonight.

Mom needed her first thing in the morning for their final dress fittings. Merry's dress had needed to be hemmed, and if she didn't quit eating all this cheese, it would need to be let out too.

But more—she'd given Max enough of herself already tonight. And last night. And last year.

Not even Phoebe Moon was awake when Merry finally slid out of Max's grasp. She had an overwhelming urge to press a kiss to his forehead, to thank him for—for being a friend, for being a lover, for being *Max*—but instead, she slowly lowered her feet to the wooden floor, gathered her clothes, and avoided making the floor creak as best she could.

Scout pawed at her leg and whined. Merry put a finger to her lips, then hugged the dog tight.

She couldn't say *I'll see you again soon.* No telling if it would be true.

But she buried her nose in the dog's fur, then snapped and pointed to the bed. "Lie down," she whispered.

Scout snorted, but her nails clicked against the floor as she obediently went back to her doggy bed on the floor.

Merry dashed down the stairs and let herself out into the night.

Max hadn't set the alarm when they'd gotten to his place. Sure, he'd been occupied with getting his hand up her shirt and his tongue in her mouth, but she suspected it was a conscious decision.

So she could leave if she wanted without setting off the sirens.

The wind had picked up, and the moon was nowhere in sight. She pulled on her knit hat and her gloves, and she started the half-mile trek back to the B&B, straining for any hints of the owl—last she'd heard, it hadn't been caught—or other nefarious forces.

It was late, and all but the most die-hard Christmas fans had turned off their decorations for the night.

Did the French decorate for Christmas? She hoped her French-English dictionary would be good enough to help her ask someone where to find a *bûche de noël,* the French log cakes, but there would always be next year.

Merry was two blocks from the B&B when she heard an engine approaching from behind. Headlights sliced the darkness.

It wasn't Trixie. The roar of the engine was too catlike. Too modern. Too sophisticated.

The hairs on the back of her neck stood at attention.

And her hyperawareness was rewarded thirty seconds later when a black Audi sedan pulled up beside her.

Of course.

Of course he was here.

She was too old to roll her eyes, but Phoebe Moon wasn't, so Merry indulged her inner Phoebe Moon while she yanked the door open and peered inside.

New car smell, Brut, and jazz music danced into the night and enveloped her.

He couldn't let her have one easy week, could he? Not that this week had been easy, but it was supposed to be her last week in the States.

"Ah, there's my angel." Daddy's whiskey voice rolled into her ears, soothing and monotonous and strong. His eyes crinkled in the corners. His prominent chin was stubbled, and his hair—a rapidly whitening salt-and-gray—was freshly cut and combed to the side. "Miss me, sweetheart?"

She missed the man who'd read her *The Monster At The End Of This Book* when she was five. She missed the man who'd kept her stocked with coloring books and crayons. The man who had gone to school plays and dance recitals and award assemblies.

But this man?

"Carrying anything hot?" she said.

He had the grace to flick his eyes downward. "No."

She didn't entirely believe him, but she still climbed into the car and socked him on the arm. "What are you doing here?"

He didn't flinch but instead pulled away from the curb with a pleasant smile. "Merry-berry, what's all this? You want your old dad to retire, don't you?"

Right. *One more score, Merry-berry, and your old dad can afford to retire*. She'd fallen for that line six years ago. Last year, at least, he hadn't bothered lying. "So go after the Star of Knight. Or the Gator Tooth. Or—or, I don't know, the Hope Diamond."

Daddy chuckled. "Ah, my little jewel. You always did believe I could do anything." He steered the car toward the B&B. "Have faith, Merry. Your daddy's doing the right thing. Now, you know I don't like to ask you for help, but—"

"Mom's getting married again."

"Good, good. Your mother deserves to be happy."

He was as good at conning people as he was at stealing jewels, but she knew him well enough to notice the hardening of his lips and the subtle tightening of his grip on the steering wheel.

"You remember Horace, her fourth after you?" she said. "He left Mom a few mil. *And* a nearly flawless two-carat yellow diamond." Mentioning Mom's ex-husbands to Daddy was low, but Daddy was crossing a line in being here. Not the first line he'd crossed, but it would be the last.

"Horace was a tool," Daddy said. "And his Viagra didn't work."

Probably true, given their legal arrangement. Still, nothing like a chat with Daddy to make Merry glad, once again, that she'd made Phoebe Moon an orphan. "That's not what Mom told me."

Daddy pulled up to the B&B and put the car in park. He turned toward her, casually draping his left arm over the steering wheel. "Merry-berry, I need the fake."

Oh, *hell* no. "The fake...?"

He angled his head, gave a slight thrust of his chin, eyes twinkling warmly. "*The* fake."

Ooh, Merry, a crime-stopping spree of your own! Phoebe Moon squealed.

Merry shushed her, then lifted her brows and treated Daddy to his own classic *I have no idea what you're talking about* face.

Dad answered with a closed-lip movie-star smirk that could've earned him as many ex-wives as Mom had ex-husbands.

If he'd been a drunk or violent or a deadbeat, it would've been so easy to hate him.

But despite his criminal day job, when he was home, and when Mom would let him visit after she divorced him, he'd made her feel as though she and Mom were his world. He'd danced and sung along to all of her favorite boy band music. He'd made sure both *his girls* had Valentine's Day presents every year, even if he hadn't been physically present. He'd inspired Merry's love of books, which he'd always insisted on buying instead of stealing. *Authors aren't rich, Merry-berry. We don't take from the poor. Besides,* he'd always added with his signature eye-twinkle, *books aren't jewels.*

He was wrong.

About so much.

She leaned into his space. "You stole from my friends. You disappeared for weeks or months at a time, and for all we knew you were dead. Mom had to change our names because of you. I thought I was settled last year. I had a home and friends and this—this *peace,* like I'd finally found where I fit, like maybe I could have a normal future, but once again, you waltzed into my life with all your chaos and you took it away from me. Again. I love you, Daddy, but I'm twenty-eight years old. I deserve the life *I* want. If you don't leave Bliss right now, I will turn you in to the police myself, and then I'll give them everything I have on you. I'm done being the daughter of a jewel thief, Daddy. *Done.*"

Once again, he managed to exude charming embarrassment. "Merry, I need the fake to destroy it."

She froze, fingers clutched around the door handle. "You're going to destroy it," she repeated flatly.

"Swear on the Hope Diamond." He squeezed her shoulder. "You changed your number before I could apologize for what happened last year. I miss you, Merry-berry. Miss my family. Had a good run, but there comes a time when a man realizes what's important. I'm going straight. Just cleaning up loose ends. The fake's a loose end."

He didn't blink. Didn't fidget. One eye crinkled with his intentionally lopsided grin. "Gonna melt down the setting. Get rid of the stones. Last thing I have to do before I'm a free man."

He'd never be free. The jewels called to him, just as Merry's stories called to her.

"And what do you intend to do in retirement, Daddy?"

"Get a little plot of land. Grow some grapes, try my hand at making wine."

"Wine?"

"I hear it's a big thing."

She didn't believe it. She knew him too well. And it was too convenient an excuse mere hours after she'd had dinner with Max at the winery and spent half the day there with Mom. "So you're going into selling fakes instead of stealing the real thing first?" she guessed.

"Meredith—"

"No. No, Daddy. Don't lie to me. If you were done, you'd ask me to destroy what you think I have. If you were done, you'd retire and buy your winery and invite me to come visit. If you were done, you wouldn't be here asking me for something you hid in my storage unit. If you were done, you wouldn't have gone back to retrieve it."

"I—"

"Don't. Lie. To. Me. The manager called. He told me my unit had been broken into after I was there the last time."

"Merry, retiring from a life of procurement isn't as easy as—"

"Yes, Daddy. It is. You walk away." Merry flung the door open. "Walk away, Daddy. Just walk away."

She thrust herself out of his car before he could answer.

Daddy wasn't dangerous. But he had an insatiable desire to continuously take what didn't belong to him and a misplaced, overblown pride at getting away with it.

And he was remarkably creative when it came to removing obstacles in his way.

She had never been that obstacle. She'd never stood in his way.

She'd also never asked him to love her as much as he loved the high of a big score.

Merry didn't bother checking her cash and ID. Cash had no emotional value to her father, and IDs were only beneficial to him if they allowed him easy access to something otherwise off-limits.

Daddy loved her in his own way. And in his own way, he did what he did out of the good of his own heart.

But he loved the thrill of getting away with a big score more. And that, as much as anything, put a lump back in her throat.

She hadn't just lost a home and budding friendships when Daddy had flung himself into her car this time last year, carrying hot goods, and asked her to floor it away from the scene of his last crime.

She'd lost Max too.

And when she'd lost Max, she'd severed her final thread of hope that she could ever have a normal future so long as Daddy was in her life.

Behind her, the Audi pulled away.

She bent her head over the keypad and punched the first number on the code for the door lock. The wind swirled up. She felt a presence, turned, and found herself nose-first in a mass of white wings and feathers.

Again.

She shrieked and threw her arms out, fending off the bird. Feathers flew up her nose and stuck to her lips. The thing lifted, and cool air rushed around her head.

The owl had stolen her knit hat.

"Bloody thief," she yelled as the white figure disappeared into the sky.

She swiped at the feathers in the air.

Dastardly Uncle Sandy needed a hench-owl. And Merry needed Phoebe Moon to feed both of them their fictional nut sacks.

It might not be publishable—Merry was thinking too many foul words for her middle-grade audience—but writing a bad guy's demise would soothe her soul.

Not long now.

She'd chase Daddy out of Bliss, get Mom married off, send the fake Mrs. Claus diamond to Max and suggest he display it instead of the real thing for a few months—or years—and then Merry would be free.

Free to escape her family, to start a new life in France, and to finally simply be herself.

Whoever she discovered that might be.

17

The underbrush scraped Phoebe Moon's hands and knees, but she stayed on her path. There was only one way to stop defiant Uncle Sandy now.

—Phoebe Moon and the Ninja Hideaway

Max was bleary-eyed and irrationally grumpy when he met Dan at the back door of With This Ring Wednesday morning. No reason to be—he hadn't tried to stop Merry while he'd listened to her put her clothes on, whisper goodbye to his dog, and creak down the stairs and out of his house last night—but he couldn't shake his foul mood.

He was basking in it, honestly.

"If that's how you feel after a night with her, maybe she's not the best thing for you," Dan mused, eyes on the back door.

Merry was good for him.

Her family wasn't. Not for Max, and not for Merry either.

Not a conversation he'd be having with Dan today though. Not when everyone in his life was already determined not to like her.

They slipped into their usual pattern—check up and down the alley, listen for anything weird, note anything out of the ordinary—

then Dan slid his key into the back door, hit the security code, and the two of them went into the shop.

Crime was rare in Bliss, but even without the daughter of a prominent jewel thief in town, one of the first lessons Max had learned about the family business was not to let your guard down.

It was a lesson he'd forgotten too much recently.

Dan flipped on the lights to his workroom and did his usual visual sweep. Max stepped across the hall to his own small office and did the same, then the two of them wandered out front to check the floor.

If Max wasn't in the family business, would Merry stay?

He paused in front of the Mrs. Claus diamond. "Rach have big plans in January?"

"Aside from figuring out a new way to break your curse?"

"Curse isn't real."

Correct, but you're having doubts, aren't you? replied a pompous voice that sounded how he imagined Zack Diggory from that Phoebe Moon novel talked. Max had meant to wait and finish the book with Olivia this weekend, but when Merry left last night, he'd needed a distraction.

He liked the new character. Kid had a cool car.

"Yeah, Rach doesn't believe in curses either," Dan said with a smothered grin.

"Think she'd fill in for me for a month?"

Dan looked up from inspecting the jeweler's microscope they kept out for customers to use, his attention fully on Max. "A month?"

"Thinking of taking January off."

Dan's frown was too similar to Gramps's old frown. "This about that car Billy asked you to work on?"

"Thought you left the gossiping to your wife."

"A month's a long time to take off."

"Got the time saved up." If Max put in weekends and sacrificed sleep for the Charger, he was almost positive he'd have it in good enough shape that he could finish it by Billy's deadline.

And that month would be enough time to see if he could find his dream again. To work out the numbers, come up with a business plan, put out feelers for more customers.

"What happens when one of Billy's friends wants a car too?" Dan asked.

Max shrugged. "Dunno."

Dan leaned back against the counter and blew out a breath. "You know we'll always be here for you," he started.

"So when I fail, I can come crawling back to the family."

"I didn't say that."

"Didn't say *Great opportunity, Max, have fun in January* either."

"You're an important part of what happens here in this store. We depend on you."

"Store won't fall apart if I leave. I'm management. I'm replaceable. You're the art. You love it. You're where you belong. And I'm—"

He was here because it was convenient and easy. Because he'd been using his job with his family to save money until he moved in with Gramps and Gran. Somewhere in the past three years, all the family commitments, then Merry, then losing his grandparents so close together, Max had fallen into the easy daily routine of coming to work here because it was stable and steady and dependable when so much else was in upheaval.

But it was time to move on.

It was time to find out if he was supposed to be management in his family's jewelry shop, or if it was time for him to take a chance and fall back in love with old cars.

Merry had been right last year.

He hadn't held out on telling her about his family's business because he honestly believed she'd be a gold digger. He'd held out because he didn't want to admit to her that his life was boring.

"You belong here, Max. It's not about the building. It's not about the jewelry. It's not about the job. It's about family. You're an integral part of our family."

And there was the subtle guilt that Gramps had dished out for so many years too. "You get that out of a fortune cookie? We supposed to add *in bed* to the end?"

Dan's mouth hitched into a grin, and Max turned back to unlock the cabinets beneath the glass display counters. "I'll get the rubies out. Can you grab the diamonds?

They went back to more mundane everyday conversations, the subject of Max and cars and vacation dropped.

But it was still on Max's mind. Everything Dan and Rachel didn't understand.

Cars.

Merry.

And an unbidden image of him driving through some foreign countryside in an old Ford convertible, past vineyards and through quaint towns while a brown-eyed, dimpled girl laughed in the passenger seat.

Max still had dreams.

He just didn't know how he'd get all of them.

For a woman who'd had sex with a hot guy two nights in a row, Merry was very much out of sorts.

Maybe because she hadn't seen him today. Not that she'd expected to. Unlike her, Max had regular work hours. But he hadn't called either. Not that she'd given him her number, but he knew where she was staying.

Zack Diggory is such a stick in the mud, Phoebe Moon whispered.

Keep thinking that, kid, Merry silently answered. The Zack Diggorys of the world grew into the Max Gregorys, and Max Gregory was anything but a stick in the mud.

Not that she needed to be thinking about Max.

Because he wasn't honestly her problem today. He couldn't be, because they were simply old friends exploring short-term benefits.

She had snuck out of *his* place last night. Of course he wouldn't call.

So she'd convinced herself that her mood had nothing to do with Max. Instead, she was suffering a healthy dose of pins and needles from knowing *The New York Times* list would be available to Janice sometime today. Or, possibly, her mood was a direct result of the bridezilla mother effect.

Despite what Merry had told Max last night, Mom couldn't get married in her sleep.

And it was starting to show.

"Can you believe the *nerve* of some people?" she pronounced after waking Merry from a post-florist-disaster nap late Wednesday afternoon.

Merry squashed the desire to check her phone for a message from Janice and instead looked at Mom.

This new problem couldn't have been the dresses. Those were safely tucked in the B&B's laundry room behind a locked door. Probably wasn't the groom either. Mom rarely got upset with her grooms, which, Merry was beginning to realize, was probably a sign of unhealthy relationships. She hoped it wasn't the cake, because Kimmie had been a total sweetheart at lunch every day this week. "Caterers, minister, or photographer?" she asked.

"The bachelorette party!" Mom shrieked.

Merry rubbed her eyes and sat up. "We're human. Someone has to have nerves." She hadn't mentioned Daddy to Mom. No need to worry the bride with news that her ex-husband was possibly planning to steal the most famous diamond in town on the eve of her seventh—or was it eighth?—wedding. Eighth, Merry decided. The one where Mom left her groom at the altar counted because they'd had to do all of the planning. "Now, what have the bachelorettes done to ruin your special day?"

That stress line almost appeared between Mom's eyes. "Don't get smart with me, missy. I've never had a karaoke bachelorette party, and by God, some *special event* won't stop me from having one now."

Behind her, Patrick winked a sad wink. "Melodie's is closed to the public tomorrow night."

"Ah. The horrors."

"Watch your tone, young lady. They might be closed tomorrow night, but they're open tonight, and that's close enough. Meredith, get dressed. We're going karaoke-ing."

"We're wha…?"

"Karaoke-ing. For the bachelorette party," Mom said. "Tonight. I hear Billy Brenton himself shows up sometimes. Such a nice gentleman. Too bad he's married."

"Too bad for you, or too bad for me?"

"*Meredith*. Such a question. But I do hear some of his band members are single." She flicked her wrist. "Anyway. I've already started our set list."

"Awesome." On second thought, thank God Max hadn't called. If Merry had to suffer utter humiliation, she preferred it not to happen in front of sexy quasi-ex-boyfriends. Or was he a sexy ex-quasi-boyfriend?

Who cares? He's hot, Phoebe Moon said.

That girl really needed to remember she was only thirteen.

"Are we doing this drunk or sober?" Merry asked.

"You have a lovely singing voice, sweetheart," Mom said.

"You do." Patrick lingered in her doorway and nodded vehemently. "You shouldn't hide your talents."

The man was adorable, if still a touch on the pale side. "Thank you, Patrick. Will you be joining us?"

"Oh, no, a groom isn't allowed at the bachelorette party. Besides, my brother and nephew are getting to town tonight." He winked. "I think your mother might've mentioned that Richard is about your age."

Merry would miss Mom, she was beginning to realize, but she wouldn't miss the romantic meddling. "Great."

Mom sighed. "I'm afraid she's hopeless."

"Cheer up. I could be hopeless, unemployed, and dealing Beanie Babies out of your basement."

"At least I'd see you more often than every Christmas, wedding, and Talk Like A Pirate Day."

Oh, Phoebe Moon and the Pirate Wedding. That had a ring to it. "I see you at least every other month. And you'll never let me live down my freshman year of high school, will you?"

"Any child who can convince her gym teacher she's a time-traveling victim of gender reversal and is actually Blackbeard come forth to plunder cafeteria food is a genius worth celebrating. Don't hide your light, Merry. Never hide your light. Now, let's go sing."

An hour later, with no more sightings of either Max or Daddy, and no phone calls or emails from Janice, Merry followed Mom into a barn in the middle of town.

And by barn, she meant karaoke bar with a straw problem. Straw bales decorated every surface. They were beside the karaoke stage, lined beneath the wooden bar, in the rafters. A few bales had red noses and reindeer antlers attached, and Merry half-expected to see a Santa Cow or Elf Sheep waddle out from the swinging doors to the kitchen.

Mom's linen pants and silk blouse didn't exactly fit in, but then, neither did Merry's wool skirt and Mom-approved Christmas sweater.

"Oh, isn't this quaint," Mom exclaimed over the country twang coming from the speakers in the barn's—er, bar's rafters. "Look, Merry, we can be the American Gothic couple! You be the farmer. I always wanted to be the farmer's wife."

The hostess grinned at them. Her freckles were painted on, but her straw hat, braids, and overalls seemed real enough. "Aww, you two are just too cute. Here, I'll get your picture."

Merry dutifully stood behind the six-foot-tall wooden board with the old farmer and his wife painted on it and stuck her head through the higher cutout while the hostess snapped a few pictures on Mom's phone.

"Just the two of you tonight?" she said.

"It's my bachelorette party."

"Well, yee-haw. We'll get you a veil, hon, and you just let us know what songs you want to sing."

They were seated at a wobbly table near the doorway to the bathrooms. Merry spotted some familiar faces amid the hay bales, but no one she'd spent enough time with to recognize immediately by name.

"Smile, Merry," Mom called over the sounds of three middle-aged men on stage doing an out-of-sync version of Vanilla Ice's "Ice Ice Baby." "I know my weddings can be trying for you. But I'm so grateful for how good a sport you always are."

An unexpected lump knocked on Merry's throat, asking permission to come in and take up residence. "Patrick's a good guy," Merry called back. "You should keep him."

Patrick would keep Mom safe. He'd help her every time the bursitis flared up in her hip. He'd assist with redecorating the house, plant flowers in the garden, and listen to her worries over whether the maids had done an adequate job or if she should hire someone new.

He'd load the Christmas tree with presents, and he'd assure her she was loved, even if Merry couldn't be there for next year's Talk Like A Pirate Day, Fourth of July fireworks, or other regular visits.

"I always plan to keep them," Mom said. "They don't always want to be kept though. But I'll always have you."

She shoots, and she scores! Phoebe Moon crowed. *Straight hit to the guilt bull's-eye.*

A perky blonde in the same straw hat, red plaid shirt, and painted-on freckles bounced up to their table. Unlike their hostess, this one had a single braid and a jean skirt. "Hey, ladies. I hear this here's a bachelorette hoedown!"

"No bachelorette hos here," Merry said.

The blonde's brow crinkled.

Mom kicked Merry under the table. "Two tequilas, please."

"Mom, I'm driving."

"Those are both for me, honey."

Phoebe Moon sounded the alarm gong.

Had Mom seen Daddy? She wasn't usually a heavy drinker. Not even when she married Yo-yo at the Bellagio in Vegas.

"Iced tea," Merry said to the waitress. "And what do you have with cheese?"

But she'd need something more than even Stilton Gold to handle her mother if Daddy had paid a visit to her too.

"Not much give in that dress," Mom warned.

The best the barn had was cheese goo on nachos, so Merry went with a burger and a salad and promised to walk it off tomorrow. Mom asked for a side of coleslaw to soak up her tequila.

Mom watched her figure, but coleslaw and tequila for dinner?

First, gross. Second—"Everything okay with you and Patrick?"

"Oh, you know the trouble never starts until the third month of marriage. Do you remember when we used to sing 'Tiny Bubbles' at bath time? We should sing that tonight."

"Mom—"

"Don't let me be your example. Or your father. You're such a good girl. You could be so happy. You could have forever. You deserve forever. All you have to do is believe, sweetheart. Just believe."

Merry struggled to find a normal smile. "You *really* want grandchildren."

"I want to know that I haven't screwed you up forever."

Never let it be said Mom didn't know how to throw a memorable bachelorette party. "Mom, you saved me."

"You should've gone away to college. You should've had spring break. You should've been able to get a normal job around people and dated whomever you wanted. If I'd taken you away sooner—"

"I might've run away from home and joined the circus." Merry blinked back the unwelcome intruders in her eyeballs threatening to betray her emotions. If she let the first little boogers through, she'd start thinking about getting on a plane on Sunday, and then she'd be lost. "It was my secret dream when I was ten."

Mom's eyes went shiny. "I'm so proud of you. You know that, right?"

This was what she should have if she hit the bestseller lists. Celebrating. Happy crying. *Being* somebody.

But she couldn't even celebrate her successes without worrying she would be celebrating Daddy as inspiration. "You say that to all of your kids."

Mom's lips spread in a thin smile. "Not often enough."

Merry squeezed her hand. "Love you, Mom."

"You didn't when you were fourteen."

"I couldn't. It's in the fourteen-year-old's rule book. You just don't remember because you're ancient."

Mom *humphed,* dashed her fingers under her eyes, then grabbed the song list from the wire rack holding the salt, pepper, and ketchup. "Just for that, we're singing 'Bohemian Rhapsody' tonight."

"Ooh, can we follow it with 'American Pie'?"

"Maybe I raised you right after all."

Between Mom's tequila and Merry's secret love of belting out karaoke songs, she almost forgot about Daddy and about waiting for Janice's call.

But she didn't forget about Max.

They reclaimed their seats after a rousing rendition of Aretha Franklin's "Respect" when Merry noticed Zoe and Pepper at the next table.

Mom noticed too.

But unlike Merry, she seemed completely oblivious to the weird tension. Or perhaps having so many ex-husbands now qualified Mom to feel completely at ease with tension. "Zoe! Pepper! It's my bachelorette party. Won't you join us?"

The two women shared a glance. "Oh, we shouldn't—"

"We wouldn't want to intrude—"

"Nonsense. Parties are more fun with more people, aren't they, Merry?"

"Absolutely," Merry agreed.

She couldn't blame Zoe and Pepper for not wanting to be her best friend. She'd hurt Max, and there was a very real possibility she'd do it again.

Still, Merry could put on the all's-fine-here show for the sake of her mother's wedding week.

Zoe and Pepper shared one more look, then scooted over to Mom and Merry's table. "I thought we'd set up your bachelorette party at the bowling alley tomorrow night," Zoe said.

"I changed my mind."

Zoe flashed a sweet dimpled smile. "As is a bride's right."

"Pepper, how's the fund coming for your mission on Saturday?" Mom asked.

Pepper flinched. "Very nicely, thank you. I just realized I never asked how you met Patrick."

Zoe blew out what looked to be a relieved breath, then clapped her hands. "I love how-we-met stories."

And that was all the nudging Mom needed. "It was quite romantic. My tire went flat right outside his house, and he came out and put on the spare for me, then insisted on following me to the nearest tire store to make sure I was safe."

Merry tipped her glass up to avoid suggesting how Mom's tire had conveniently gone flat in front of a millionaire's home.

She'd met two other ex-husbands the same way.

"Oh, what a sweet man," Pepper said.

"I hear that's a good way to meet serial killers too," Zoe offered. "But good on you! I haven't managed to do love right once. You're so brave to try it twice."

"Oh, honey, men are like shoes," Mom said. "You keep trying them on until you get it right. Patrick will be my sixth...no, seventh husband." Her lips curved in a not-so-funny smile that she aimed at Merry. "I always forget about your father."

"If only it were that easy."

Pepper lifted a glass. "To lucky number seven."

"He's a good guy." Merry lifted her own glass. "I like him."

"And healthy again," Zoe said.

"So very healthy," Mom agreed.

They clinked and drank, and Mom convinced Zoe and Pepper to join them, along with a random waitress, for the Spice Girls' "Wannabe."

And because Pepper had ten sisters—*ten!*—she insisted they do "We Are Family" too. Except when she sang that she had all her *bitches* with her, Merry snorted so hard in the microphone that the sound system screeched. The next chorus, Mom squealed like a pig after Pepper sang about her bitches, and soon none of them could sing anymore for laughing.

The deejay ordered them to take a ten-song time-out, so they returned to their table, laughing. Almost as though the tension had never been there at all.

Pepper told stories about her sisters. Zoe added her own stories about karaoke nights gone bad. Mom shared a story or two about her ex-husbands that Merry had never heard, and Merry was smiling so big her cheeks hurt.

Had she *ever* smiled that hard?

"You two are party animals," Pepper declared.

"It's too bad Patrick and I are so far away in St. Louis, or we'd come back often," Mom said. "But Merry's close. Aren't you, sweetheart?"

Close enough to hop over and boink Max regularly if you weren't flying off to France, Phoebe Moon said.

Merry needed to get that girl a muzzle.

Possibly Mom too, since Zoe and Pepper were both eyeing Merry with those daggers labeled *Max Defenders*. "It wouldn't be the same without you, Mom," Merry said.

"Aww, that's so sweet," Zoe said. "Do you ever karaoke with your mom, Pepper?"

"Maybe? I can't remember. There are too many of us to tell if she's on stage with us when my family gets together to do this."

Ten sisters. And two brothers. Merry couldn't even imagine what that was like.

"Hate to leave this lovely party, but I have to work tomorrow," Pepper said.

Zoe agreed, saying she'd see Mom and Merry bright and early. Mom hugged both of them.

No one hugged Merry.

They did offer her honest smiles, though, which was more than she'd expected when she'd spotted them.

And when Mom and Merry stumbled out into the darkness not long after the other two women left, Merry was smiling too. Despite the weirdness, it had been a fun night.

She and Mom had needed this.

Still, she sniffed the air, trying to detect any hint of Brut while she scanned the parking lot for Audi sedans and morally compromised fathers.

Satisfied that they were alone, Merry loaded Mom into her Cadillac. Her veil got stuck in the door, and Merry had to open the door back up, push the veil in, and try again. "Your friend Matt should've come out," Mom slurred.

"Oh, so you like him better after a few shots of tequila?"

"I don't dislike him. His job's simply all wrong for all of us. But I got his number from that sweet Scoey Zott."

"You mean Zoe Scott?"

"You say avocado, I say armadillo." Mom hiccupped. "Maybe we'll crash the private party tomorrow night and do it all again. Girlfriends are good for your soul. And they were huggers! I love huggers. We should both get some."

They should.

But Merry's girlfriends would be in France. "Mom?"

Mom's lips grinned, and her lids slid half-shut. "Hmm?"

"This was your best bachelorette party ever."

She hiccupped again. "Almost as good as the time your father stole Grace Kelly's engagement ring for me."

Merry closed Mom in the car and suppressed the shiver in her bones. She should've been grateful that one parent had been willing to go completely straight for her. Mom and Daddy—they'd been the Bonnie and Clyde of jewel thieves. Without the guns. Or the public notoriety.

Still, they'd been quite the criminal pair. Mom had given up riding along with Daddy on heists when Merry was born, though she hadn't been able to quit Daddy until many years later.

Merry still wondered where her genes had failed her.

If she could've been as comfortable as Daddy was with a life of thievery, she would've fit better into her own family. She could've found a conscienceless biker boy to be her getaway ride, and they could've had six leather-clad children whom they would train to be internet thieves as well as pickpockets so that the family business could continue into the next generation. And Mom and Daddy could've gotten back together years ago.

Except neither was as nimble as they'd been in their heydays, and they'd probably be separated by iron bars now instead of by their own insurmountable flaws. And Merry would probably have plenty of girlfriends. Prison girlfriends, with names like Tinkerbelle and Spike and Lucky, and instead of doing karaoke, they'd have a secret code for communicating their plans for their next prison break.

There's my girl, Phoebe Moon said. *We've missed your crazy imagination, haven't we, Zack Diggory?*

Merry's imagination will make it difficult should she ever need to pass a polygraph, boring Zack Diggory replied. *She should stick to dreaming about things she has the guts to follow through on. Which eliminates me getting another look at that Mustang.*

Merry wrenched open the driver's side door and flung herself in beside Mom.

If she kept up this kind of thought process, she'd have to get Phoebe Moon a new author. One who still specialized in semi-innocent adolescence and outlandish but lovable-in-his-own-way villains.

One who would use a time machine to make Zack Diggory too young to drive. Or have teenage boy thoughts.

A thump on Merry's window shook the car.

She instinctively knife-handed the glass, and the car rocked again. Mom hiccup-shrieked.

Pain radiated from Merry's hand down to her elbow. Outside, the snowy white owl picked itself off the ground and fluttered into the night, leaving a trail of downy feathers in its wake.

"Dammit, Titus." Every good hench-owl needed a name.

"Am I owl, or did that car just attack my drunk?" Mom giggled. "Take me home to my lover, Merry-berry. I'm skunk as a drunk. And you need a girlfriend."

"Won't get any grandbabies that way."

"Modern miracles are medicinous. I just want you to not be alone."

Merry put the car in gear, backed out of their parking spot, and scanned the lot for Daddy's car once more. "I'll never be alone, Mom. I have you." And Phoebe Moon, and Zack Diggory, and dastardly Uncle Sandy, and her online peeps Bubbles53 and BikerWriter.

She was pathetic.

And, despite having spent two hours hanging out with Mom and Zoe and Pepper, she was once again lonely.

Get used to it, kid, Zack Diggory said. *The best heroes always are.*

Except Merry wasn't a hero.

She was simply a girl who liked to tell stories.

And even in France, that was all she'd ever be.

18

Men and women hurried past Phoebe Moon on the crowded street, panic in their faces, their mouths open but their voices silent. Diabolical Uncle Sandy! He was behind this, no doubt.

—Phoebe Moon and the Stolen Sound

Janice called just after Merry tucked Mom in for the night.

Merry had hit *The New York Times* list. And she hadn't just hit it. She'd nearly topped it, with her first and her latest books hanging out at number four and number five on the list, respectively.

And she had no one she could tell.

So for the third night in a row, she found herself at Max's house.

She didn't have to knock. Scout announced her presence for her. A moment later, the door opened, and there was Max.

A scowling linebacker standing between her and her own personal heaven-hell haven. He was in low-slung camo pants and a black T-shirt, his feet bare, his hair standing up at the crown as though he'd just rolled out of bed, his complexion pale in the night.

Hell-oo, sexy man, Phoebe Moon said.

That girl needed a sock in her mouth.

Scout twisted around Max, her entire back end wriggling, nosing Merry's crotch. Merry repositioned the dog and scratched between her ears.

"Looking for round three?" Max said.

She flinched at his flat, not-amused tone.

Also because round three sounded like a great way of celebrating news she couldn't bring herself to say out loud.

"If I hadn't been back at the B&B when my mother woke up this morning—"

One dark brow arched over his tired eyes and silenced her meager excuse. "I was seventeen the last time a woman snuck out of my bed without saying goodbye."

There went that green-scaled dragon roaring its envious displeasure in her ears. "We're just friends. I didn't want you feeling any obligation if I was still there this morning."

"Obviously you staying would've meant you were planning to skip moving to Canada and wanted to stay here and live with Scout and Trixie and me forever."

"I'm not moving to Canada. And see? This is exactly why I couldn't stay."

"Saying goodbye would've been so difficult? For all I knew, the owl got you on your way home."

"You know what? Never mind. I thought we were friends, and I thought—"

"Friends worry, Merry. Friends argue. But friends stick around and work it out." He pushed the door wide. "You want to come in? Or you want to be owl food?"

"The owl's at the karaoke bar."

Even half-strength, his smile could've been the eighth wonder of the world. "You sounded good."

"You were there?"

"Video went up on Facebook half an hour ago, and my phone exploded."

Probably a video of her snorting in the microphone. Had she joined Pepper in singing about her bitches? The parents of her fans would love that.

Not that Amber Finch would ever become non-anonymous. "You're welcome for the entertainment."

He waited, watching her with wary, tired eyes. She should step inside. All the warm air from his house was leaking into the winter night.

"It was fun," she said. "I don't ever just hang out with people. In real life. All my…coworkers are online. But it turns out I like people. And I don't think your people will ever like me."

Max crossed his arms. He had to be getting cold, but he kept standing there, his attention fixed on her.

Not on his dog wrapping herself around her feet. Not looking for the owl. Not checking his watch, even though there were bluish smudges beneath his eyes and a general weariness about him tonight.

Just focusing straight on her.

"You want my friends to like you," he finally said.

Yes. "I didn't mean that," she said quickly. "I'm leaving Bliss Saturday. You're staying. They *should* pick you over me. And they've all been really nice."

She swallowed before she could push forward with her list of *buts*.

He tilted a know-it-all brow at her. "People are inherently good, Merry. Especially my friends. Tell them why you left. They'll get it."

"You'll tell them once I'm gone."

"I told them to be nice to you. The rest of it isn't my business. We're not serious, remember?"

As if she could ever forget. She rubbed her hand over the throbbing behind her breastbone. "Thank you for asking them to be nice to me. I don't think my mom's even noticed how weird this is. Bride stuff, you know?"

"Bridezilla stuff," he corrected with a half-smile. A tired, worn half-smile, with heavy-lidded eyes still trained on her. "I noticed."

Merry fisted her hands to keep from reaching for him. Because he deserved a woman who would still be there in the morning, and she couldn't. "Sorry," she mumbled. "It's late. You have to work tomorrow, and I have to—"

A distant bell whispered over the wind.

Every molecule in her body went tense. Max's eyes snapped to attention.

"No," she whispered.

His phone rang. A police siren wailed in the distance.

"*No,*" she said again. She tripped over Scout while she backed down the stairs. "No."

All the blood had drained from Max's face, but he hadn't answered his phone. "Merry—"

"You don't deserve *this.*" She'd made him a target. The minute she'd agreed to go to dinner with Max after the Spencer McGraw signing, she'd made his family and their business a target. This was her fault.

And she didn't know how to fix it. "I have to go."

Far away. To France.

The sooner, the better.

MAX DIDN'T TRY to stop Merry.

Because it was all he could do to get to the bathroom.

The roiling in his gut had been building all evening. Indigestion from the hamburger he'd had at Suckers for lunch, he'd thought. Maybe guilt from not telling Dan that Merry's dad was a jewel thief after Dan pissed him off over the idea of fixing the Charger.

Scout whimpered on his heels. His phone kept ringing. A cold sweat broke out at his hairline and under his arms, his chest and stomach burned, and his legs trembled.

Shit.

He hadn't had a stomach bug since he was a kid.

Max wobbled into the bathroom, slammed the door, and slid to the floor. He managed to get a text to Dan, and then he surrendered to the enemy inside his body.

AFTER RUNNING ALL the way back to the B&B, Merry dashed up the stairs to her room.

This had to end.

Now.

She banged on Mom's door, and a moment later it opened. Mom's eyes were bloodshot, her lips turned down. Her hair was clipped back over her ears, and she was in her silk pajamas and robe. "That tequila was a terrible idea. Why didn't you—Merry? What's going on?"

"Can I borrow your car?"

Daddy undoubtedly knew what it looked like, but Merry had let Mom pick her up in Toluca on her way to Bliss, since it was on the way.

She hadn't mentioned she'd sold her car in preparation for her trip overseas or that she only needed to go back to Toluca for one last thing before boarding a bus to the airport in Chicago Saturday evening.

Mom folded her arms.

"Please?" Merry's voice cracked. "It's important."

She had been twelve the morning she woke up alone for the first time. They'd been living just outside Pittsburgh in a comfortable, slightly shabby older neighborhood. She remembered the daffodils blooming on either side of the front stoop when she'd stepped outside and peered at the driveway, looking for either of her parents' cars.

She remembered the chill of the concrete under her bare feet.

The thick swelling in her chest, the acid in her stomach.

She'd never been alone before.

Never.

And then Mom's old teal Chevy had whipped around the corner and screeched to a halt. "Meredith, get in."

She hadn't gone to school that day.

She'd worn her pajamas for two straight days, sneaking into bathrooms behind gas stations to pee along the way, sleeping off and on in the backseat, until Mom had finally stopped the car for good at a little bungalow in Nebraska.

"I'm divorcing your father," Mom had said the next morning.

She hadn't cried then, but Merry had heard her later.

Every night.

For weeks.

Mom had gotten a job as a waitress. She'd left Merry at home with textbooks she'd picked up here and there—Merry hadn't asked—and Merry had started school in Nebraska that fall.

And she'd hated her mother.

Because Mom had taken her away from Daddy.

"You can hate me all you want, Meredith. Honestly, I hate myself right now. But I'm your mother. It's my job to protect you. And right now, I need to protect you from him. I know you don't understand, but I love you, and I will *always* stand between you and the poor choices he makes."

And she had.

For years.

But tonight, Mom couldn't protect Merry or fix this for her.

Someone had tried to break into With This Ring. "You have to trust me," Merry whispered.

"That's what your father always said."

"I am *not* Daddy."

Mom pursed her lips. But she stepped back into the bedroom and returned with her keys. "Call me if you need *anything*."

Merry pecked her mother's smooth cheek, and five minutes later Bliss was disappearing in the Cadillac's rearview mirror.

MERRY'S DRIVE took barely over an hour, and she couldn't even summon Phoebe Moon to keep her company. By the time she pulled up to the post office in Toluca, she felt like two weeks had passed.

She hadn't hit *The New York Times* list. She hadn't spent a few fun hours at a karaoke bar. She hadn't slept with Max.

That girl was someone else. This girl?

This girl was once again in the midst of her daddy's mistakes.

She hadn't been followed to Toluca, and the streets were silent outside. Unintentionally phallic-shaped Christmas decorations hung from every street lamp along Main Street, but otherwise, the blow-up yard decorations had been deflated and most of the lights on the houses and businesses in the sleepy little town had been turned off.

Merry slid out of Mom's car. She held her head high and carried herself with purpose as she entered the twenty-four-hour post office lobby.

Phoebe Moon, if you don't want people to be suspicious of you, you shouldn't do things that look suspicious.

Merry scowled at Zack Diggory. *Go away. I want Phoebe Moon.*

She squatted before the post office box she'd rented, turned the key in the lock, and blew out a short, relieved breath at the sight of the small brown package in the narrow box.

A strand of her hair was visible under the clear packing tape on each of the six sides, and the address label had the purple smiley face in the corner, just as she'd put it.

If Daddy had figured out where she'd stored the ring, he hadn't been able to get to it. And no one else had touched it either.

She left the keys in the post office box, tucked the small brown package into her purse, and forced herself to walk normally back to Mom's car.

No police officers cruised by. No sirens sounded in the distance. No rabid owls swooped down to steal her treasure.

Obnoxious treasure that it was.

If she were caught with it—

No. Having a replica of a famous ring wasn't a crime. Possession didn't prove intent.

She wasn't going to steal the real thing.

She was going to give the fake to Max.

Tomorrow.

First thing.

She'd go tonight, but who knew how late Max would be at the store with the police?

She'd just pulled out of the parking lot, firmly ordering herself not to drive past either the Cheese House or her old apartment, when her phone rang with a number she didn't recognize.

Her pulse pinged.

You should've told the police where to find it, Amber Finch. You can't write my stories from jail.

Zack Diggory was a terrible influence on Phoebe Moon.

Merry answered her phone and put it on speaker, eyes scanning the horizon and her mirrors for any sign of a tail or movement. "Hello?"

"Merry-berry, I didn't do it."

She tightened her grip on the steering wheel, and the car whined. "What didn't you do, Daddy?"

He hadn't stowed away in the trunk of Mom's car—she'd checked before she left Bliss.

"I didn't try to break into your boyfriend's jewelry store. Sweetheart, you need to take your mother and get out of Bliss."

"First of all, he's not my *boyfriend*. You screwed that up just fine a year ago, and I learned my lesson. No dating. Second of all, I'm not leaving Bliss. *You* are."

"Meredith—"

"Don't, Daddy. Don't lie to me."

"I need the ring, Merry. You give me the ring, and I'll end this all."

"I don't have the ring."

Daddy's sigh filled the dark cabin. She checked her mirrors again, then slowed the car.

No reason to get pulled over for a stress-induced lead foot.

Plus you're setting a bad example for impressionable me, Phoebe Moon's voice chided.

"The cops aren't going to look for the real perpetrator. They're going to assume it was me. I didn't do this, Merry. Even if I wanted the ring, you know it's not my style to take it without giving something back."

She turned down a dark country road just outside of town and pulled over. The car's lights illuminated darkened, barren cornfields around her. Her palms were slick on the wheel, and her leg muscles trembled. "Did someone *actually* steal something?"

Daddy paused.

Merry Silver and the Hot Diamond. Phoebe Moon could write it, because Merry would be in jail. What if the ring she had *wasn't* the fake?

"Tonight," she said. "Did someone steal something *tonight?*"

"I don't know."

"Daddy—"

"Merry-berry, we're going to get out of this. Got a plot of land all picked out in Oregon—"

"Heard that before." But she still desperately wanted to believe him.

You're my pride and joy, Merry-berry. Worth more than any jewel. Come over here and play chess with your ol' Dad.

"Where do you want me to settle? You tell me where you'll come visit, and I'll go there."

"I want you to go back to 1983, and I want you to go somewhere with no diamonds, no rubies, no emeralds. I want you to go somewhere you could have just been my daddy, and I could've been your Merry-berry, and Mom could've been happy."

"It doesn't work like that, angel."

"Then go anywhere but Bliss."

She disconnected, tossed her phone into the cup holder, and dug into her purse.

Her fingers shook while she ripped the package open.

If she had the real Mrs. Claus diamond in here, she was dead.

She'd kept six different storage lockers, putting her childhood memories in them, scattered about so that if one was robbed, she wouldn't lose everything. Her mismatched furniture. Pictures. Her books.

The rhinestones she'd worn to her junior prom just before the only time she'd been Daddy's willing accomplice.

She'd still been in her prom dress.

And she'd kept the dress too.

Locked away.

Daddy knew about two of her storage lockers, but not the rest. And she'd been cleaning them out the past few months, one by one, consolidating what she absolutely couldn't part with in preparation for her move.

Had she not, there was no telling if she would've discovered Daddy had been using the one in Peoria to store his replica Mrs. Claus diamond ring.

She'd found it inside her old Caboodles case, nestled between the locket her grandparents had supposedly given her when she was born and her favorite rainbow-colored scrunchie from her teen years.

And she hadn't looked closely.

She'd just found a box, wrapped up the ring, and she'd found a place to stash the fake Mrs. Claus diamond. Somewhere ridiculously safe despite being ridiculously public.

Barely a week ago, she'd gotten the call that her unit had been broken into and ransacked.

Not Daddy's usual style.

Until now, it wouldn't have occurred to her that Daddy might've already pulled his heist.

The box popped open, and the ring went flying through Mom's car. *"Dammit!"*

Language, Phoebe Moon chided.

"Shut *up*."

That's not how we make friends, Merry Silver.

"You too, Zack Diggory, or I swear to God, I'll feed you to the giant alligators in Sandalico."

She crawled onto the floorboard, using her phone's flashlight until she saw the sparkle. Hunched over with the gear shifter poking her leg, she shone the light straight on the center diamond of the setting.

Rainbows sparkled in the depths of the gem.

Merry's body sagged in relief.

She had a fake.

Just to be certain, she did a quick fog test. Her breath lingered on the stones until she wiped it away, and her throat clogged.

Daddy hadn't screwed up. Yet.

The Mrs. Claus diamond ring was beautiful. With a nearly flawless three-carat round-cut diamond surrounded by diamond chips in a setting shaped like a snowflake, and decorative strings of platinum adding depth to the arrangement, the real thing was a work of art.

Even the fake was gorgeous. The setting made the ring, not the diamonds inside it.

Someone rapped on the car's window.

Merry dropped the ring, said a word Phoebe Moon wasn't allowed to repeat, and untangled herself from the passenger wheel well, heart in her throat.

A Marshall County sheriff's deputy stood beside her window.

And there went another word Phoebe Moon wasn't supposed to know.

She rolled down the window. "Evening, Officer."

"Everything okay, ma'am?" He flashed his light into the depths of the car, to the passenger wheel well, where the Mrs. Claus diamond sparkled.

Her stomach bounced to her toes. "My contact was giving me trouble," she lied, gesturing to her eye.

She winced as his light aimed right into her pupils.

"Ah. Sorry, ma'am. Don't see cars parked on the side of the road around these parts often. Especially this time of night. You sure you're okay?"

Having a mild panic attack, but otherwise… "Very much so. Thank you."

"Where you headed?"

"Bliss." *Always tell 'em as much of the truth as you can, Merry-berry. Makes it more believable when you have to do the stretching.* "My mom's getting married. Stressful, you know? I just needed some breathing room for a while."

"Ah. Completely understand, ma'am. My niece got married up there a few weeks ago. You need directions? Pointed the wrong way there to get back."

"No, I've got it. Can I do a U-turn here?"

He looked up and down the road. "Just this once." He gave her an easy smile. "Drive careful. Lots of deer this time of year, especially at night."

"I will. Thank you, Officer."

He left, and Merry sagged back into the seat.

But only for a moment.

She had a ring to deliver to Bliss.

If the real one wasn't already missing.

19

Phoebe Moon stared in wonder at her own wide eyes, her own bow-shaped lips, her own chin-length dark hair. "But who are you?" she said to the girl.

"I am all of the best parts of you, Phoebe Moon," the girl replied in Phoebe Moon's voice. "The parts that secretly want sweet Uncle Sandy to succeed."

—Phoebe Moon and the Secret Sister

Merry had survived Mom's other half-dozen weddings, but she was fairly certain this one in Bliss would kill her.

Not because of the wedding.

Because of it being in Bliss.

And maybe partly because Patrick's family had arrived, and she'd been roped into breakfast when she would've preferred to be heading to Max's house. Or to With This Ring.

Anywhere to get rid of the jewel currently guarded by her shampoo bottle.

"You've been married how many times before?" Patrick's brother said to Mom over breakfast.

"Oh, honey, once you've had three ex-husbands, you stop counting." She smiled at Patrick, who appeared to have a case of indigestion. "The point is that Patrick is the last one I want."

"Or maybe the point is that you want his money."

Where Patrick was a winker, his brother John was a boomer. John's inside voice was loud enough to make small children cry from half a mile away, and his comb-over was the stuff of legends.

Had Merry had four more cups of coffee this morning—and no fake diamond sitting upstairs in her room—she might've been tempted to touch it.

For research. Maybe devilish Uncle Sandy needed a new hairdo.

"The point is that *I* want to marry this woman because she makes me happier than I've ever been in my life." Patrick covered Mom's hand, then grabbed Merry's hand as well. "And I'm getting the world's best stepdaughter to boot."

Way to find your gonads, Patrick, Phoebe Moon cheered.

Coffee.

Merry needed coffee.

But her stomach had been twisted more ways than a mutant pretzel since those alarms went off at With This Ring last night, and she couldn't even handle the thought of toast without getting nauseous.

She should've gone straight to Max's house last night, but she'd been terrified Daddy would be expecting that.

So instead she'd called Mom, claimed to be afraid of walking through the B&B's parking lot with the owl on the loose, and used her rapidly sobering mother as a security guard against her father.

"So we'll be stepcousins, Merry," John's son, Richard, said. Unlike his uncle, Richard's winks were leery and lecherous.

"I'm a lesbian," Merry said.

"Meredith."

"Um, I *wish* I was a lesbian?"

Richard's wink suggested he'd be down with some role-playing.

"Mom, didn't you say you need to get your ring checked out today?" Merry said abruptly.

Mom's knuckles went white around her china coffee cup, and her forehead almost wrinkled. She hadn't asked any questions last night, but the attempted break-in at With This Ring had been the topic of conversation all over the dining room.

And Mom wasn't stupid.

"I do," Mom said tightly.

"What's wrong with your ring, sweetheart?"

"I thought the stone felt loose last night at the bachelorette party." Mom kissed Patrick's cheek. "You boys run along and make sure your tuxes fit. Merry and I will meet you at the bridal planner's. John, Richard, so lovely to have you here for our wedding. I know it means the world to Patrick, so it means the world to me."

Merry forced a smile at both men. "So lovely to have more family. Excuse me, please, I need to brush my teeth before we leave."

The fake Mrs. Claus diamond was still safe and sound in her empty shampoo bottle. She shook it out, then wiped it down until it sparkled.

She hadn't seen the real thing—she made a point of avoiding jewelry stores—but Daddy's contact seemed to have done an impressive job with the replica.

She'd just thrust her arms into her coat and pulled on her gloves when Mom knocked on the door. "Ready, sweetheart?"

Merry wiped the ring one last time in case the ring was big enough to hold an incriminatingly sized sliver of her fingerprint, then gripped it in her left hand and shoved it in her pocket. "Yes."

She opened the door, and Mom scrutinized her whole body with that classic Mom X-ray vision. "I was thinking With This Ring," she said flatly.

"Perfect," Merry answered.

Mom squeezed her eyes shut and sighed.

"I'm doing the right thing," Merry whispered.

She was.

She was taking away Daddy's opportunity to steal the real Mrs. Claus diamond. And she was doing it in broad daylight. On chilly winter streets that might not have been bustling with shoppers, but with enough witnesses that Daddy wouldn't try anything.

"Shall we drive?" Mom said.

"I love the smell of new car in the morning."

"Merry..."

"It's for Max."

Mom popped the trunk and peered into the empty space. "I think I left my scarf—oh, I guess I didn't."

Merry bent over to peer under the Caddy's carriage. "Did you drop it on the ground?" No odd wires under the car, no unusual bulges, no footprints in the fresh dusting of powdery snow. No fluid leaks on the ground either.

"Maybe it's in the backseat," Mom said. "Oh, nope, not there either. Damn. I loved that scarf."

At Merry's subtle nod, Mom unlocked the car. They both slid in, and Mom locked the doors and cranked the engine. Nothing exploded, nothing pinged. She backed out slowly.

Daddy wasn't dangerous.

He wasn't.

But Merry had never intentionally stood in his way before either. And the fact that she and her mother could silently agree to check the working condition of her car before getting into it was a very bad sign.

The drive to With This Ring wasn't far, but she felt as though they'd gone halfway around the world before Mom pulled into the parking lot beside the chocolate shop.

Merry's arms ached from holding them so tense.

So did her jaw. And her thighs.

She placed herself to Mom's right, keeping her gloved hand wrapped around the fake ring in her pocket while she huddled as close to her mother as she could. When Mom flung open the door to the jewelry store, Merry's body nearly sagged in relief.

So close.

This was almost done.

A few customers were being assisted over various display cases, but Merry didn't spot Max immediately.

"Welcome to With This—oh! Vicky. Merry. So lovely to see you." Rachel smiled brightly from behind the far back counter. "What brings you in today?"

"I—" Merry started.

"I want to make a donation to Pepper's bachelor auction fund," Mom said. "So she can bid on your brother-in-law."

Merry's eye twitched, and her stomach dropped into a crater.

Rachel glanced at Merry, then gave Mom a hesitant smile. "That's remarkably sweet of you."

Remarkably *evil* of her.

"Love is important," Mom said. "Merry and I just wanted to let Max know we're behind him. Is he here?"

"He's not in today. He came down with that nasty stomach virus that's been going around."

Well, isn't this craptastic? Phoebe Moon said.

Merry's hand wobbled so hard, her elbow shook. "He's—"

"Sick as a dog," Rachel said.

"I hope he'll be well enough to participate Saturday night," Mom said.

Wow, she's good with torture, Phoebe Moon said.

Merry couldn't help but agree. Perhaps perfidious Uncle Sandy needed to take a bride. Merry had a good idea who she'd force on him, though she wasn't sure who'd be getting the better end of that marriage.

"We're optimistic he'll be feeling better soon," Rachel said. "If not, I'm sure Max will insist we auction him as a mystery bachelor. He's always so supportive of Bliss's causes."

"In that case, is a check for three hundred enough?"

Mom pulled out her checkbook, and Rachel's eyes bulged.

Merry's might've too. And there was a possibility she'd just squeezed the fake ring in her pocket tight enough to puncture her leather gloves and leave a permanent imprint in her palm. "Three hundred?"

"You're right, sweetheart. Let's make it five."

"Ms. Silver, that's so…wow. Thank you." Rachel tilted her head toward a door behind her while Mom scribbled a check. "Dan? Honey, that lovely woman I was telling you about last night is here."

"We heard about the alarms," Mom said. "That must've been terrifying."

Merry kept her mouth shut.

She needed to see Max.

"Oh, it happens more than you might think." Rachel smiled the innocent smile of someone who was either an exceptional actress or who had no clue there was a jewel thief in town. "The police think that crazy owl probably ran into the window."

"That owl tried to attack my car last night too," Mom said.

A tall, heavier-set man with Max's eyes strolled through from the back. His hair was thinner and threaded lightly with gray, but it was impossible to miss the family resemblance. He smiled at Merry and Mom, but it looked forced. "Ms. Silver, is it?" He held out a hand. "I'm Dan. What can we do for you ladies today?"

"They're making a donation to my fund for Pepper to bid on Max on Saturday," Rachel said. "A *large* donation."

"Oh." Dan looked at Merry, then back at Mom. "Thank you. That's…incredibly generous."

"We believe in no hard feelings," Mom said.

Mom glanced at Merry, but when Merry didn't move, Mom slid the check to Rachel, then thrust her hand out to display her teardrop-cut Tiffany diamond. "Also, we were out last night, and I thought I felt the stone slip."

"Hmm." Dan took her finger. "Lovely setting. May I?"

"Oh, honey, I wish you would."

Merry forced the sigh to play her part. "Sorry," she muttered. "This is why she's had seventeen ex-husbands."

"Six, Meredith."

"Well, who can blame her for wanting to flirt with this guy?" Rachel put a slender manicured hand on Dan's chest and laughed.

"He is a catch," Mom said.

"And young enough to be your grandson," Merry said.

Mom slid her a look that dastardly Uncle Sandy probably used often.

So maybe that was taking it too far.

But she had a freaking fake Mrs. Claus diamond ring in her pocket, Mom had just practically bought another woman for her favorite ex-boyfriend, and they were wasting time. She needed to go see Max.

Dan took a little tool to the ring, pushing and poking at the jewel, then inspected the setting with his loupe. "Seems solid," he said. "But I can take it in back and look more closely if you'd like."

"Oh, *could* you?" Mom gushed before Merry could stop her. "That would be wonderful. We're getting married tomorrow, and I'd be beside myself if something happened to the diamond. *Such* a bad omen."

"A terrible omen," Rachel agreed. "Not that we believe in superstitions."

Dan smiled at his wife. "Of course not. Be right back, ladies."

He disappeared into the back room, and Mom slid two paces to her right. "Is this the Mrs. Claus diamond?" she asked Rachel.

Merry's stomach clawed its way into her chest.

"The one and only." Rachel mirrored Mom's movements, both of them leaning into the display glass to peer at the cursed ring on a black velvet finger.

"It's a true work of art." Mom laughed her tinkling society laugh. "And I've had enough diamonds to know."

"Dan helped design it when he was barely out of college," Rachel said. "It's been an honor for the family to display it for so many years. Spencer McGraw himself came here and shook Dan's hand when it was done."

"Just amazing," Mom said.

"Would you like to try it on?" Rachel whispered.

Merry's belly turned into a fish out of water, flipping and flopping and gasping for air.

"Me? Try on the Mrs. Claus diamond?" The fake awe in Mom's voice was enough to make Merry nauseous.

"As a matter of protocol, we always let Spencer know when there's been a security issue, and last night, he told Dan he was thinking of selling it," Rachel continued in her whisper. "Plus, for such a generous donation toward a cause near and dear to Bliss's heart, it's the least I can do."

Mom glanced at Merry.

Max wasn't here.

Merry had to walk out this door with the fake Mrs. Claus diamond and take it to his house and ask him to keep it safe.

Rachel didn't know who Daddy was, or she never would've suggested letting Mom try on the infamous diamond, donation to Pepper's bachelor auction fund or not.

"I would be honored, Rachel," Mom breathed.

Merry's lungs shrank to the size of a thimble.

Was *Mom* in on it with Dad?

Before she could squeak out a protest, Rachel had the display case unlocked and open. The Mrs. Claus snowflake ring sparkled.

Merry had to go.

She had to take the fake to Max.

Right. Now.

But her feet were cemented to the floor, her knees not just locked, but dead-bolted.

"Your engagement ring is about three carats?" Rachel said. "The center diamond here is three-point-two."

"Just beautiful," Mom breathed.

A muted doorbell tone sounded. Merry jumped as though it were gunfire. A slender woman darted out from behind the counter. "Hi,

Mrs. Mosely. Looking for that perfect gift for us to suggest to Mr. Mosely?"

"The man couldn't find his own nose in a snowstorm," a grumpy female voice answered.

Mom had the Mrs. Claus ring, holding it between her thumb and forefinger.

The real ring.

The one Daddy wanted to get his hands on.

"*So* beautiful," Mom said. "May I try it on?"

"Of course." Rachel smiled brightly.

Mom slid it onto her ring finger on her right hand and held it up for all of them to admire.

If this were my book, Uncle Sandy would have one of his minions drop from the ceiling right now and pluck that thing clean off, Phoebe Moon said.

Merry forced herself to breathe and not look at the ceiling.

Mom shifted beside her. "Here, Merry. You've had your share of bad luck in love. Maybe if you try on the ring, its curse and your string of misfortunes will—oops!"

Before Merry could move, the diamond slipped through Mom's fingers and fell, tumbling in a circle to the flat gray carpet.

"Mom!"

Rachel gasped.

Merry's knees unlocked. Her hips too. And before she could think, she dropped into a squat, the fake Mrs. Claus diamond held against her palm with her thumb while she extended her left hand to grab the real ring.

When she stood, real ring clenched under her last three fingers, fake ring extended between her thumb and forefinger, her heart was pounding so hard the people walking by should've seen it bouncing out her back, through her spine, cartoon-style. Her pulse rushed so loud in her ears that the sound hurt her eyeballs. "Here." She thrust the fake at Rachel. "Please put this back before my mother breaks it and has to buy it."

Rachel frowned at her gloves. "Are you cold? That's how the stomach bug starts. You feel really cold until—"

"This ring is making me very nervous," Merry blurted.

"Oh, of course, of course." Rachel quickly took the ring, gave it an efficient dusting with a cloth, and locked it back up, a slight flush in her cheeks. "If Mr. McGraw decides to sell it, you'll be the first people we'll call."

Merry's knees wobbled like a dam about to give way.

Dan stepped through the door again. "Beautiful diamond, Vicky. It's in there snug and perfect."

Mom smiled too brightly at him. "You are *such* a dear to check for me. I must've had a wee bit too much tequila last night."

"I'm sure they saw the video, Mom." Merry's voice wobbled, and she was nearly certain she would sweat through her leather gloves before they got out of this store.

Maybe she should tell Dan.

Max trusted Dan, right?

Max's voice echoed in her head. *He's the perfect oldest child. We got along well enough, but he can be annoying. Always does the right thing.*

Nope.

Wouldn't be telling Dan. Because *the right thing* would be to demand what Merry was doing with a fake, and why she thought she'd get away with walking out the front door with the real diamond ring, and what if this was just the opportunity Daddy was waiting for?

What if she had already done what Daddy was waiting for?

Dan and Rachel and Mom were laughing. Merry was probably supposed to know about what, but she didn't.

"Mom?" Merry interrupted. "I'm not feeling well."

"Oh, dear." Rachel took a giant step back.

Dan angled away too.

Merry was going to puke.

Not because she had a stomach virus.

But because she was about to walk out of a jewelry store with Max's family's most famous diamond.

Mom put her hand to Merry's shoulders. "Oopsie-daisy, let's go," she said cheerfully.

Merry put one foot in front of the other, then did it again and again until she was crossing the threshold of With This Ring with a priceless diamond clutched in her gloved hand inside her pocket.

So this was what a million or two bucks felt like.

Nope.

She didn't get the thrill.

Outside, the winter air slapped her in the face.

"You really don't look well, dear," Mom said.

"I need to lie down." And possibly breathe into a paper bag.

But most of all, she needed to get this diamond to safety.

You are truly a wuss, Merry Silver, Phoebe Moon said. *You did the right thing. Max is the only person you can trust, and you* will *make it to his house safe and sound. You got ninja moves, babe. You can do this. Make me proud, author-mama.*

Were prisoners allowed to write books when they were behind bars?

Because Merry would miss Phoebe Moon. And Zack Diggory.

And even dastardly Uncle Sandy and his hench owl, Titus, who hadn't even made it into a book yet.

Mom and Merry forgot to check the trunk. The backseat was empty, which Merry knew because Mom insisted she lie down on it.

She didn't ask if Merry had switched the diamond.

And Merry hadn't asked if Mom was in on it with Daddy.

Two blocks later, Merry sat straight up. "I feel better. Can I get out here?"

Mom didn't know where Max lived. Daddy probably did, but Mom didn't.

Or did she?

Mom eyed her in the rearview mirror. "Merry? Sweetheart—"

"Please, Mom. I'll meet you at the cupcake place for lunch. Cross my heart. I just—I just get nauseated in jewelry stores. I need some fresh air. Or—or I'll go to the bookstore. I love bookstores."

Mom scanned their surroundings. They were still on The Aisle, about four blocks from Max's neighborhood south of downtown.

"We need a movie night," Mom said.

Code for *we need to talk somewhere we won't be overheard.*

Daddy wasn't dangerous. He wasn't the type to bug Mom's car. He wouldn't attack to get what Merry had.

Or did she really know her daddy at all?

Why *did* Mom and Merry need to use code words in supposed private?

"Can we watch *Terminator*?" Merry forced out.

"You and your movies." Mom's lips twitched in an affectionate smile. "Where's this bookstore?"

Merry directed her around the corner, and thirty seconds later, Merry unlocked the door and slid out into the frigid morning, senses on full alert, and began her quest to reach Max's house.

MAX WAS HAVING one hell of a dream.

There was a purple tree in his living room, except he was tucked safely away in his attic, listening to Phoebe Moon explain how dastardly Uncle Sandy planned to steal all the cheese from the moon so Merry couldn't have any more.

He tried to reach for Merry, sitting atop her gilded snowflake throne on Bliss's wedding cake monument, but the cake floated away on a cotton-candy breeze.

Also, his arms and legs were locked, and he was in his bedroom with Scout stretched beside his body.

He could see his bedroom.

Daylight filtered through the blinds. His door—newly repainted white—was half-open to the hallway, and he could see the cream-colored wall across the way.

But he could also still see Merry on her throne.

"Max," she said. "*Max*, I know this is Bliss, but you have *got* to lock your doors. Do you understand?"

She reached down from her throne and tapped her fingers against his cheekbones. "Max? Max, can you hear me?"

Why was she wearing a coat? It was bloody hot in here.

Because you're sick as a dog, Phoebe Moon's irritating high-pitched voice answered him.

Dogs don't get sick, Phoebe Moon, that Zack Diggory voice answered.

"Max."

Merry was so real. As if she were actually right there. He smiled at her.

"I stole the Mrs. Claus diamond," she said. "My daddy made a fake. I switched them."

Max blinked. He was in his room. Scout beside him. Real sunlight streaming through the windows. And—he wasn't alone. "Merry."

She sank to the edge of his bed, rattling words and phrases he couldn't hear over the roar of indignation pulling him out of the pudding that was his brain. Finally, she came into focus again.

And she was still here.

Right here. With him.

"Max, please don't hate me." Pleading dark mocha eyes drilled into his while guilt slammed his chest, and he clawed his way out of the pudding of his muddled brain.

How many times had he told her this week that he trusted her? How many times had he told her she could trust him?

And here he was, dreaming that she'd do something as horrible as help her father steal Gramps's pinnacle work of art.

When Merry had come back to him. After all the times she'd run away from him this week, she'd come back to him, and his dumbass dreams were trying to convince him she was the same as her father.

Fucking fever.

"Merry." He sat and reached for her, and there she was. Solid and too hot against his clammy skin, but *there*. Real.

She'd come back.

Cool fingers pressed onto his forehead. "Oh, Max. You're burning up." She pulled back, peering down at him with worry lines he wanted to wipe away. "Are you okay?"

"Perfect. You're here."

Her lips wobbled up, and her eyes went watery. "So we...we're okay?"

"Always," he rasped out.

"You heard me?"

He nodded. She could've told him anything—*anything*—and he'd trust her. Whatever it took to make her stay.

Her light fingertips brushed his forehead again. "When's the last time you had anything to drink?"

He couldn't remember. Hell, he didn't even know what day it was.

"Lie down," she whispered. "I'll take care of you.

Scout's tail thumped his leg. Merry pushed gently on his shoulders, and Max obeyed.

And before she was out the door, he was drifting back into a dream, this time with a smile on his face.

20

Phoebe Moon should've left Zack Diggory behind. Now, not only did she have to steal the sunshine back from dastardly Uncle Sandy, but she also had to save her new best friend.

—Phoebe Moon and the Missing Sunshine

One year ago

Merry was living a lie.

It was an occasional lie—she probably only saw Max once a week, though they did email and text decently regularly—and she was beginning to wonder if this lie could honestly become her truth.

Daddy was still behaving himself in Wisconsin. She'd talked to him over the weekend, and he'd sounded tired but good.

She hadn't told him she was dating someone.

He hadn't asked.

Nor had she mentioned Max to Mom at any point in the past two months.

She had lots of practice with keeping secrets, and she was beginning to wonder how long she could keep this up before she'd have to tell someone something.

But she could honestly admit to herself that she missed Max during their first weekend apart after that night in Trixie's backseat. So when he dropped a text late Tuesday night and asked if she'd consider teleworking from his place tomorrow since he had a fridge full of cheese he couldn't eat by himself, going to Bliss had been a no-brainer.

Late morning, she let herself into his house with his garage and alarm codes, then sat on his low leather couch before the fireplace, feeding Scout fruitcake cupcakes and working on Phoebe Moon's next story.

Shortly before five, she packed up her laptop. She was digging through his cheese selections when he got home. He walked in through the garage, tugging off his tie, swept a glance over Merry and the mess she was making of his kitchen, and treated her to a smile that made her heart stop.

"Missing your pearls and an apron," he teased. He stopped behind her and slid his arms around her waist, pressing a kiss to her neck below her ear. "Not that you'd be wearing them for long," he added.

This.

This was why she hadn't told him about Daddy yet.

And why she hadn't left him yet.

She was wanted. She was appreciated. Other than the few little omissions about her life, she was stepping into the shoes of a Merry she wanted to be. Of the life she wanted to live.

She twisted in his arms to face him, put her palms to his ears, and pulled him in for a kiss that ended with a string of discarded clothing and a very satisfied, very naked Merry on his couch.

They lay there whispering to each other until Max's stomach growled. She pushed him off and shrugged into his dress shirt, then retrieved the cheese plate and a sleeve of crackers from the kitchen.

They sat there eating, talking, teasing and flirting and laughing. So normal. So *right.*

Until Scout exploded in barking and dashed to the back windows.

Daddy.

"No," she whispered.

"Scout. Down, girl." Max stood and went to peek outside. "She's crazy," he said to Merry, but she must've given something away, because he frowned. "Merry? You okay?"

She tried to nod.

But Scout wouldn't quit barking.

Merry had never heard anything like it.

"Hey, it's okay." Max leaned over the back of the couch and rubbed her shoulders. "Probably just some kids."

"Your…alarm?" she gulped out.

He gave her a fuzzy frown, but stepped to the front door and hit his alarm code. "All set."

But it wasn't.

It wasn't set at all.

Daddy wouldn't—surely he wouldn't do anything to Max? Max was a good guy. Merry was happy here. She was safe. Her life was stable.

Daddy wouldn't come to Bliss just to mess with one of Merry's boyfriends.

He waited until they'd hurt her first. It was how he worked.

But she'd never been involved like this before.

And Max had been pretty clear that he wasn't looking for serious commitment.

So why couldn't she breathe? Why did it feel like her life was on the verge of imploding again?

Scout's barking had slowed, but she was still growling low in her throat.

Max pulled Merry into his lap. She should resist, but she didn't want to. "Somebody hurt you?" he murmured softly.

Not Daddy. At least, not on purpose. Never on purpose. "No. It's…" She dropped her head to his shoulder. She shouldn't be here. She shouldn't be letting him stroke her back, shouldn't let him pepper her head with kisses, shouldn't lean on his inherent strength and steadiness.

Because she couldn't offer him the same promises he was silently making her.

I'll take care of you.

I'll protect you.

I won't hurt you.

Scout stopped growling. She slunk to Max's feet and collapsed with a grunt, one wary eye still on the back windows.

"See?" Max murmured. "All better."

It wasn't, but she stroked a hand over his rough cheek, then up through his hair, and pulled him in for a kiss.

A desperate, hungry plea of a kiss.

Whether he understood or not, he kissed her back.

And then he picked her up, and he carried her upstairs, and he used his mouth, his body, and his whole heart to soothe her lingering panic until she finally fell asleep.

21

"Stop, Uncle Sandy!" Phoebe Moon cried. "The world needs its sneezes!"

Duplicitous Uncle Sandy laughed his maniacal laugh. "Ah, my impressionable little niece, you have so much to learn."

—Phoebe Moon and the Sneeze Snatcher

Present day

Merry tore through Max's cabinets, digging for soup and crackers. Scout had followed her into the kitchen, whimpering. Her food bowl was empty, but the dog practically had worry wrinkles around her eyes. "I know, sweetie. We'll get some liquid back in him, and he'll be okay.

She'd done it. She'd gotten here.

She'd about hit the roof when she realized Max's front door was unlocked, a situation she'd quickly rectified. She'd made a thorough sweep of his house, then changed the code on his alarm—who didn't change the code on their alarm when they found out their vanished girlfriend's father was a jewel thief?—and left a sticky note to that effect on the back of his front door, where only Max could see. She'd also texted it to him.

But then she'd found him feverish and restless upstairs, and every bit of fear and adrenaline she'd felt since leaving With This Ring had swung back around like a boomerang, except bigger.

But he'd listened to her, irritation popping up in his beautiful sea-green eyes when she confessed to stealing the Mrs. Claus diamond, then disappearing as she explained about Daddy being in town and that the real diamond was safe in the passenger seat of his scale-model Mustang.

And then he'd held her.

Forgiven her.

Understood her.

And now nothing was more important than helping him get better. Not what any of Bliss's citizens thought of her being here, not Daddy suspecting she'd hidden his precious ring here, not even knowing that every moment she spent with Max would make it that much harder to leave.

And she was leaving in forty-eight hours.

She called Kimmie Cakes and ordered chicken noodle soup, which Kimmie's dashing husband delivered without an ounce of judgment. "Take care of him," Josh said. "We need him healthy for the bachelor auction this weekend."

When Merry walked back into Max's bedroom half an hour later with a bowl of soup and a soda that wasn't quite flat yet, he lifted his head. "Phoebe Moon?" he croaked.

The bowl wobbled, and warm soup sloshed over her hand.

She caught herself and drew in a deep breath.

Max didn't know. Of course he didn't. But she knew he'd been reading to his niece, so maybe Phoebe Moon was on his mind.

Duh. I'm unforgettable, Phoebe Moon said.

"You be a good boy and drink something, and I'll read you a bedtime story," Merry said to Max.

He blinked at her once, twice, three times, those dark lashes fluttering. "You're still here."

Guilt and regret rolled in her belly. "I'm taking care of you today."

He grunted.

She lowered herself to the edge of the bed, put the soup beside his alarm clock on the small wooden bedside table, then held the soda cup for him. She nudged it against his lips until he took a small sip.

"You remember?" she said.

"Yeah."

"Are we still good?" she whispered.

"You're my Merry."

Her hand wobbled again, but her heart cut the strings tying it down and swelled.

"Drink some more," she forced out around the watery lump in her throat.

He obliged, his hot fingers covering her shaky hand around the cup.

After two small sips, he dropped his head back to his pillow.

But his hand stayed on hers around the cup.

"Your belly okay?" Merry asked.

"Stay," he said.

She touched his feverish skin.

Taking care of people was usually Mom's domain. But Merry couldn't be anywhere else today.

Not if Max needed her.

"Read," he mumbled.

Phoebe Moon and The Sneeze Snatcher was on his dresser. "This is so weird," she whispered to herself.

But she grabbed the book, then climbed onto Max's bed. "I'm only doing this because you're dying," she said.

He turned his head and buried his face in her thigh, and it was the most natural thing in the world to let her fingers comb through his deceptively soft dark hair. Scout leapt onto the bed and snuggled against her other side, and for the first time in her life, Merry opened a print copy of her own book and began to read aloud.

"'On a day when most children were in school, at a time when most children were at recess, in a place where most children dared never go, Phoebe Moon and her iguana, Spike, whom she liked to pretend was a dragon, set out on a doomed mission to save the world…'" There was that surprise watery lump again, this time with the added bonus of pressure behind her nose and a sting behind her eyeballs.

She hadn't visited Phoebe Moon's beginning in at least four years. Four years in which Phoebe Moon had grown and changed, battled real and imaginary enemies, and grown into a strong, capable, mature superhero.

Four years in which Phoebe Moon's audience had grown and changed until they'd put her on the biggest bestseller list in the world.

While Merry herself had stayed the same.

Max grunted, his breath hot against her thigh.

No, check that. Merry wasn't the same.

But she wasn't done yet either.

A POUNDING on the house pulled Max out of a deep sleep.

His stomach was so hollow it was swollen, his tongue glued to the roof of his mouth, and something sticky was sealing his lips shut.

There was also a body pressed against his, a hand in his hair, and a warm, flowery scent tickling his nose.

The pounding came again.

Max pried his rusted eyelids open, and the body beside him jolted.

"Oh, crap! The rehearsal dinner!" Merry said.

"Mmmerrr."

"Liquid. Here, sweetie. Drink." A cup was thrust at his lips, and more of the sickly sweet stuff dribbled down his cheek. "Max?" Cool fingers brushed his forehead. "You feeling any better?"

He smiled. Merry called him *sweetie*.

An annoying *click, click, click* echoed over the sounds of his dog snoring. "Can I take your picture?" she said. "You look like hell, and that's really the only thing that'll get me out of trouble with my mother for missing her rehearsal dinner. And the only thing that'll keep her from banging through your door down there, because if she thinks you'll give her the plague right before her wedding, she won't want to come in."

Max steadied the cup at his lips and sipped. The soda hit his stomach like a rock, but it didn't threaten to come right back up.

Good sign.

"Thank you," Max rasped.

She'd stayed.

She'd read to him. And fed him soup.

"You stayed."

"I was afraid if I didn't, Rachel would come over, and I couldn't bear to sic her on you like this."

Max flung a wooden arm over her leg. "You're a good friend, Merry Silver."

"No one should die alone."

He wasn't dying.

Not yet, anyway. The next time she left? Distinct possibility.

And the fact that she was joking about him being sick enough to die was evidence she was probably leaving soon. "More soup?" he asked.

"It's cold. Want me to go warm up a new bowl?" Her fingers threaded through his hair, the simple gesture enough to bring him to his knees if he hadn't already been on his stomach.

Merry was a firecracker in bed. She was a spitfire when she was riled. Cheeky as a general rule.

But Merry as his nursemaid—maybe he'd already died.

This was what he wanted. His best friend. Here. *Home*. Always. For everything.

"Max?" she whispered.

"Stay."

Her fingers hesitated, but they didn't retreat. "We're really still good?" Her voice was so soft, it almost wasn't there at all. "With—with the *thing*?"

Women and their *things*. "We're always good."

A suspicious sniffle sounded above him. Max pried his rusty eyelid open again. "Merry?"

"Don't pretend to die on me ever again, you big lump."

He felt his lips turn up. Wasn't that what what's-her-name said to Zack Diggory? "Yes, Phoebe Moon."

"And *stop that*." She slid off the bed, and his arm thumped to the mattress. "Nothing's changed. Nothing's settled. I still have secrets. My daddy's still my daddy, and he's still a jewel thief, and you're still the Mrs. Claus diamond jeweler, and I'm going to France on Sunday. *Sunday*, Max. I shouldn't be here at all, except I—I couldn't—I couldn't leave you to die. And...you know. And soup. You need warm soup so Pepper can bid on you in the bachelor auction on Saturday."

She disappeared out the bedroom door.

Scout nosed Max's elbow.

"Women," Max muttered. He buried his hand in Scout's fur and rubbed her side while she licked the soda off his face. "Think she's coming back, girl?"

"Did you not hear me say I wouldn't leave you to die alone?" Merry called up the stairs.

"Pretty sure she's madly in love with me, Scout," he said.

Or that was delirium talking.

Yep, probably delirium.

But if it wasn't—then she needed to know a few things before she left for fucking *France*.

He rolled over, his limbs and back stiff, his belly grumbling, and reached for his phone.

Sixteen missed texts.

Most asking if he'd be better before the bachelor auction.

Crazy town.

He scrolled until he found a message from Dan and then punched out a reply. *Need to talk. Come by tonight. Wear a hazmat suit.*

Merry appeared in his doorway, cheeks flushed, wearing her tough-girl walk while she stalked into his room with one of Gran's old green-flowered Corelle bowls. "Patrick's nephew wants to have a step-cousin romance with me."

Max tossed his phone aside and forced his achy body into a sitting position. "I suddenly have an overwhelming urge to go to your mother's wedding."

"There's no punching at my mother's weddings." She sat before him and stirred the soup. "Well, there was the time she married Roscoe, but that's why she has the rule now."

"If he touched your butt, would you go ninja on him? I want to watch."

"Have I told you you're adorable?"

"Not today."

She held out a spoonful of soup, and he dutifully swallowed it. "Really good," he said.

"Secret family recipe."

He stared at her.

"From Kimmie's family," she grumbled. "Or maybe her husband's. It wasn't entirely clear."

He tucked a strand of her dark hair behind her ear, and she raised wary mocha eyes to him. "You realize all of Bliss knows you ordered me chicken noodle soup by now, right?"

"And where was all of Bliss fighting over who'd get to read the eulogy at your funeral and bringing flowers and casseroles to console your absent family in your final hours on earth?"

"Lot easier to just say, 'I was worried about you today, Max.'"

She huffed. Closed her eyes.

Her shoulders slumped funny, one lower than the other.

Max put a hand to her thigh, and Max Jr. stirred. Apparently *he* wasn't feeling any ill effects from the past day or so.

"You get to me, Max Gregory," Merry whispered.

He took the bowl from her hands and set it aside, then looped his arms around her back and pulled her close. "You get to me too, Merry Silver."

"I should let you get your sleep."

"Slept all afternoon."

"And you still look like reheated liver and onions."

Max buried a smile in her hair. "All right, all right, quit begging. I'll go to your mother's wedding with you. But only if you promise to defend my honor if Patrick's nephew grabs my ass."

"You're impossible."

"I'm cursed, Merry. And nearly dead. Give a corpse-in-waiting one last thrill on this earth."

She laughed into his shoulder. "I'll miss you, Max."

Her voice cracked, and Max's stiff limbs tightened around her.

He couldn't fix her father, but he could fix how she saw herself. He could fix her misconceptions about her situation, about what made family, about acceptance.

And he'd start with his own family.

22

Phoebe Moon watched the young orphans dance at their new parents' feet. How she would've loved parents. But her family gave her a greater mission in life.
—Phoebe Moon and the Secret Sister

Merry left Max's house after getting some soup and water in him, then reading him more Phoebe Moon until he fell asleep again. She rushed to the B&B, changed into her wool skirt, a comfortable silver sweater, and heeled black boots, then headed out into the frigid evening.

Mom and Patrick were having their rehearsal dinner at a private dining room in the chapel off The Aisle, where they would say their vows tomorrow. By Merry's calculations, she'd arrive just before the cheesecake dessert.

In other words, right on time.

But when she hit the parking lot of Lilac Mills Chapel, a gorgeous renovated paper factory with wood pine beams and antique glass windows, she barreled headfirst into a cloud of a familiar scent.

"Merry," Daddy said from his perch between his Audi and a big black SUV.

Her heart clawed her throat while her belly dove for cover.

You're a ninja, Merry Silver. You got this, Phoebe Moon said.

Merry folded her arms, but they shook. "Go. Away."

He flashed his warm Daddy-smile and held a hand out to her. "Not here to make trouble. Just miss my girl."

"You could've told me that at the B&B."

"You weren't at the B&B."

"Or maybe I didn't want to see you."

"Sweetheart—"

"You know what I miss, Daddy? I miss playing Scrabble. I miss tea parties. I miss believing you were safe. That I was safe from *you*."

"Merry—"

"But you won't change. You didn't love Mom enough to change. Why would you love me enough to change?"

"If you'll listen—"

"Leave. Leave me alone. Leave Mom alone. You know when I needed to talk? About ten years ago, when I was a brokenhearted kid running away from my prom. But you don't talk, Daddy. You pretend to be Robin Hood when you're really no better than King John."

"Meredith," he called, but she turned her back on him and marched into the chapel.

He didn't follow.

Inside, in the elegantly rustic lobby, she ran into Patrick, who was leaving the men's room. "Merry! You made it." He pulled her into a loose, squishy hug. "How's Max?"

"On the mend." And having Patrick ask easily, without judgment, made her ache for both herself and Mom.

They would both one day lose really great men, though Merry's would be gone long before Mom's would.

"Do you have a minute?" Patrick asked.

"Sure." And then she'd text Max and remind him to keep all his doors and windows locked.

Patrick tugged at the knot of his red holiday tie, and she realized he had a light sheen of sweat along his receding hairline.

Uh-oh, Phoebe Moon said.

Don't jump to conclusions, Phoebe Moon, Zack Diggory answered.

Merry shushed them both.

"I know I'm not your mother's first husband," Patrick said, "or even her third, but I'd honestly like to be her last."

Oh, swoon! Phoebe Moon said.

Oh, crapadoodle, Merry answered. This wasn't awkward at all.

"She makes me feel like I'm a better man," Patrick rushed on into the uncomfortable silence. "She makes me believe I can do things I've never done before. And I—I want to do that for her. But she's so competent, and so lovely, and so perfect, I don't want to suggest she could be improved, because she can't, but I think if she could feel how much of a difference she's made in my life and let me fill whatever holes her other husbands couldn't, then I—then I—" He shook out a handkerchief and mopped his forehead. "Your mom—I just adore her, Merry. I don't want to mess up and lose her."

"Have you told her that?" she said.

"I tried, but she—well, you know your mom. She told me I was special and perfect, and I believe her, I do, but—"

He stopped with a sigh, and a ruddy hue crept up his neck.

"None of her other husbands have ever been that astute, Patrick." She squeezed his hand. "You've already got a head start."

But he'll still never be your father, Zack Diggory wisely pointed out.

"Thanks, Merry." Patrick's smile didn't quite reach his pure blue eyes. "I hope I can be everything you need in a stepfather too. I know you don't need one, but I'm here for you."

I'd give up orphanhood for a dad like that, Phoebe Moon said.

"Surprise her," Merry said. "Keep her on her toes. Treat her to an afternoon playing paintball. Go bungee jumping. Or—I don't know—blindfold her and take her to dinner at the top of the Sears Tower."

"Merry, we're practically senior citizens."

"But Mom likes *fun.*"

You mean adrenaline, Zack Diggory intoned.

Avocado, armadillo, Phoebe Moon chanted.

Patrick rubbed his index finger over his lower lip. "You sure?"

"Think of the makeup sex if I'm wrong."

His mottled ruddy hue went more purplish. "I don't think we're supposed to discuss that."

"I'm rooting for you, Patrick." Merry patted his arm, then stepped around him. "I probably need to get in there."

"Me too, me too."

He gestured her ahead—*Such a nice gentleman*, Phoebe Moon said on a sigh—and she typed a quick text to Max while she walked down the romantically lit wooden hallway, reminding him to keep his doors and windows locked and that she'd changed his security code on his house's alarm system.

If she had to have accidentally fallen into uber-friendship with a jeweler, at least he was semi-equipped to battle her father.

Hopefully he had a safe hidden behind a picture somewhere in his house too. She hadn't thought to check, because she wasn't *actually* a criminal.

Usually.

She stepped into the austere private dining room, where servers were clearing dinner plates of mostly eaten chicken from the linen tablecloth. Poinsettias decorated the sideboard. The windows overlooked the wedding cake monument. A tray of individual servings of cheesecake—*yes!*—sat near a door she assumed led to the kitchen. Mom stopped mid-conversation with John, who was the color of a man who'd just been put in his place by his future sister-in-law, though Mom appeared cool as an early spring daffodil.

"Sorry I'm late." Merry headed toward the empty seat between John and Richard.

John nodded.

Richard ogled Merry's chest.

And Mom smiled, but her eyes were brown puddles of anxiety. "Merry, darling. How's poor Max?"

"*Poor* pretty much sums it up, but he'll pull through."

"So nice of you to tend to a friend in need." *And have you seen your father and disposed of the Mrs. Claus diamond?* Mom's expression seemed to add.

I have no idea what you're talking about on either account, Merry attempted to telegraph back.

Merry, you just told your mother you'd rather eat frogs than touch that diamond again, Phoebe Moon chastised. *You need to work on silent communication.*

Telepathy is impossible, Phoebe Moon, Zack Diggory said.

Obviously you've never had a mother.

Neither have you.

Touché.

Merry told the two teenagers in her head to hush, and concentrated on her mother. Mom was a master at running formal dinners, and putting on *everything's good* here acts, and tonight seemed no different.

"Glad you could make it in time for the toasts," Mom was saying. "And the cheesecake, of course."

"Cheesecake can go in a box, but the toast can't," Merry said.

Mom's smile spread wider. "Isn't she the best daughter?"

"She's wonderful," Patrick said with a wink.

"Don't know her well yet," John boomed.

Richard merely continued to stare at Merry's boobs.

Merry shook out her red cloth napkin and put it in her lap. "I invited Max to your wedding."

Close enough to the truth.

Not even Botox could disguise Mom's obviously conflicted feelings about Max though. "You've never brought a *date* to any of my weddings before."

"If he's feeling up to it," she added quickly.

Richard smirked.

"I've promised to defend his honor if anyone tries to feel him up while he's under the weather," Merry said. Pointedly.

"Merry's a ninja," Patrick said.

"Kinky," Richard purred over his wineglass.

"I thought ninjas were invisible," John boomed.

"Common misconception." Merry eyed her fork. If it were to accidentally slip and land in Richard's eyeball, that would probably only half-qualify as a wedding disaster in Mom's mind. But Merry had probably committed enough crimes already today. "Oh, is that strawberry sauce on the cheesecake? My favorite."

"Merry once ate an entire cheesecake while hiding under my bed," Mom announced. Her forehead shifted, a good sign she was ready to be done with Richard and John.

Merry could sympathize, and she'd only been here three minutes. "I didn't eat it by myself. I shared it with my imaginary best friend, Clarence the Clown."

"You were so adorable at twenty-three," Mom said.

That finally got Richard's eyes off Merry's chest.

"Can I have Terry's cheesecake too?" Merry winked at Richard. "He's my imaginary taxidermist friend."

Max would've been stifling a grin, but Richard angled closer to Patrick on his other side.

John's lips puffed out in a frown. "Patrick, you know the girl has issues?"

"But at least she's not ogling your son's testicles, John, dear," Mom said with a sweet smile.

It's a really good thing Patrick loves your mom so much, Phoebe Moon whispered.

"I miss Jim the Juggler," Patrick announced. "Remember him, Merry?"

Mom's brows almost wiggled higher on her face, and Merry felt another surge of affection for impending stepfather number six. "My imaginary friend last month," she explained to John and Richard. "He kept breaking things and blaming it on me."

"I'll never get that Ming vase back, but he was such a good friend to you," Mom said.

"They're all touched, Patrick," John boomed. "They've made *you* touched."

Patrick put his arm around Mom. "John, I've waited my whole life for love. Living with Merry's imaginary friends is a small sacrifice to pay for the privilege of having these two lovely ladies in my life every day."

Something got stuck in Merry's eye. A feather, maybe, or a speck of strawberry sauce.

Or possibly, it was a doomed wish that this time Mom's husband would stick.

IT WAS dark the next time Max opened his eyes. No Merry. No Scout.

But someone was downstairs.

Max rolled to his back with a grunt, his gaze landing on the dark shadow of his display case.

He'd had some fucked-up dreams today, and the guilt was still lingering.

"Max?" Dan called. "You up?"

"Yeah," Max grunted.

"What's up with your girlfriend's paranoia?"

The click of the front door locking echoed up the stairs, then the beep of Dan entering the security code.

A minute later, he appeared in Max's doorway and flipped on the lights. "No Christmas tree yet? You still have all of Gran's ornaments, don't you?"

Max squinted. Scout wagged her tail and followed Dan into the room. Dan dropped into a spare kitchen chair that Max kept in the corner, but Scout made herself at home on Max's bed.

Right where Merry had spent half the day.

He thought.

"Today Thursday?"

"For a few more hours. You tell Merry to change your alarm code?"

"Her dad's a jewel thief."

Smooth, dumbass, Zack Diggory intoned.

After a slack-jawed moment, Dan folded his hands over his gut and laughed. "Rachel said she was funny, even if she did leave you last year. Rubbing off, is it?"

Max felt around for his phone.

Two missed texts from Merry, one telling him she'd changed his alarm code, the other reminding him to lock his doors and windows.

A little extreme, even for Merry.

His thumbs hovered over his phone, but he stopped himself before he asked if her dad was in town.

She would've told him.

Wouldn't she?

"Nicholas Raymond," Max said to Dan. He pulled up a browser on his phone and entered the thief's name in the search bar, then held it out for his brother.

Dan didn't move to take it. "The dude who made off with Grace Kelly's engagement ring," he said, more a statement than a question.

"He's Merry's dad."

"You're serious."

"I'm cursed, man." Max tried to smile.

Dan didn't. "You're dating the daughter of a jewel thief."

"Not actually dating—"

"She disappeared. *Last year.*"

"I didn't know until she left."

"Does Pops know?"

After years of being assistant manager, Max had taken over full duties from their father, who was now happily retired, planning to spend his summers on the golf course and his winters in the bowling alley whenever Ma wasn't taking him out on road trips. "Gramps did."

"Jesus, Max."

"She's not her father."

"Where *is* her father?"

Good question, considering Merry's sudden paranoia. "Would you love Rachel any less if her father was a jewel thief?"

"You think you're in love with a jewel thief's daughter."

"She. Is. Not. Her. Father." Which was the entire point of telling Dan.

Because if his whole family could understand why Merry left, why she thought she'd had to leave last year, why she was catching a plane to fucking *France,* then they'd back him up.

They'd help him convince her to stay. They'd all show her she could belong.

Dan dropped his head to one hand and rubbed his brow. "Okay. She's not her father. But you still should've mentioned this sooner."

"Did you know Gran's grandfather was a snake oil salesman?"

"Why don't we save this until you've held down some food for more than four hours?"

There, there, widdle Maxy-waxy. Let Daddy Dan take care of you. Daddy Dan knows best. "I told you," Max growled, "because I trust you to help me show Merry the people in this town don't give a damn who she's related to."

Dan suddenly looked older than his thirty-seven years. "The dressmakers don't have to care. The photographers don't have to care. The bakers and caterers and florists don't have to care. But we're *jewelers.* We have to care."

"That's what Gramps said."

"Gramps was a wise old man."

"Gran chewed his ass up one side and down the other for it."

"Max—"

"Get out."

Dan's brows shot up. "Max," he started again, this time like he was placating a three-year-old, "leaving aside the fact that she abandoned you last year, I could potentially like Merry. But—"

Max's stomach twisted and grumbled, and his face flushed. "But her father might try to rob the store one day, so I need to move on?"

Scout whined.

"I didn't say that," Dan said.

"Then what the hell is the issue?"

"If you won't tell me when you're dating the daughter of a jewel thief, what else won't you tell me? Was that really Merry's mother with her today in my store? Are they really here for a wedding? Who *is* she? What does she do? Where does she live?"

Wasn't just Max's stomach bug making his face hot now.

Because he couldn't answer half of those. "It's *our* store, and as manager, I took appropriate actions to increase security as soon as I knew. You want to know why she left last year? She left to protect *me*. To protect our family. She knows he's wrong. She's suffered for him more in her life than you can even begin to imagine. But you still won't give her a chance." A giant ball of conflicted, gassy, emotional slime roiled in his gut.

Dan stood. "Rach sent some soup over. I'll lock the door on my way out. We can talk about this tomorrow."

In other words, *You'll still be wrong when I lecture you tomorrow.*

Scout scooted closer to Max, her tail swishing against his covers, big brown eyes worried.

Downstairs, Dan hit the code, then slammed the door.

"So that's how you fuck up a relationship and make sure the girl flees to France as scheduled," Max muttered to Scout.

His dog didn't answer.

And even though the lights were still on in his bedroom, Max flipped onto his stomach, tossed an arm around Scout, and closed his eyes again.

If he couldn't be right and if he couldn't have the girl he wanted, at least he could be unconscious.

23

Phoebe Moon might be tiny in stature, but she wasn't afraid of Uncle Sandy. Nor was she afraid of spiders, snakes, or quicksand. She was, however, afraid the grown-ups would one day make her be a kid again.

—Phoebe Moon and the Secret Sister

"One of my more memorable rehearsal dinners, wasn't it?" Mom said to Merry after they returned to the B&B. Patrick was out at Suckers for his bachelor party with John and Richard, and Merry was itching to go check on Max one more time tonight.

"Sorry to have missed so much of it."

"Sweetheart, when's the last time you missed any part of one of my weddings?"

"Um, never?"

"Exactly. You're due." Mom sighed. "I'm sorry you can't keep him. You seem quite smitten."

"Maybe we'll stay friends."

Mom studied her for a minute, then reached for Merry's hand. "Have I ever told you how much I admire your independence? I'm not sure I've had a day in my life when I was as strong as you are."

"Yes, you have."

They were propped on a comfy plaid couch in the B&B's sitting room, a Christmas tree twinkling merrily in the corner while the TV played *It's A Wonderful Life*. Mom was still in her rehearsal dinner pantsuit, complete with a poinsettia pinned at her heart and her feet snug in her fur-lined boots.

Merry opened her mouth to change the subject and say what she almost always said the night before her mother's weddings—"You got a really good guy this time, Mom"—but it wasn't right.

Mom *always* went for the good guys. Stable men with solid careers, good relationships with their mothers, and no criminal backgrounds.

But they never stuck.

"Would you take Daddy back?"

Mom's head turned slowly, like it was on a crank with gears too small. "What happened to you last night?"

What she'd done last night and this morning was filed away in her brain under *Speak Of This To No One. Ever.* And she'd already broken the rule by telling Max as much as he needed to know.

"Do you ever just want to go far, far away?" Merry whispered.

Mom got her. Mom sat at fancy dinners and had the right amount of fun with Merry's fake imaginary friends. She texted Merry every time she went shopping, asking which dress or pants or shoes looked better, and Merry did the same.

But Merry still didn't know how much Mom might speak with Daddy. And she didn't know how much Mom might confide in Daddy.

All she knew was that Mom had never gotten over Daddy.

"I can't run from who I am and what I've done," Mom said. "They say your past catches up with you, but they're wrong. It doesn't catch up, because it never leaves. You learn to live with what you've done and how it's molded you into the person you are today. To accept that you're imperfect, that you're fallible, that you're human. And, ultimately, how to forgive yourself."

Merry didn't feel human. Well, maybe a small part human.

Like the heel part.

She stole a freaking *diamond* today. And shoved it inside a toy car.

"I want to be someone else sometimes," she confessed to Jimmy Stewart's George Bailey.

George Bailey wouldn't have stolen a famous diamond ring today.

But I would've, Phoebe Moon said.

See what you've done now? Zack Diggory chastised.

Mom pulled Merry into a warm, vanilla-scented Mom-hug. "You can be someone else for a while," she whispered into Merry's hair. "But promise me you'll come back to being you soon. Because you're perfect just the way you are."

There were moments when Merry wondered if her mother knew more than she gave her credit for.

This was one of them. "You have to say that because you're my mother."

"I have to say that because I happen to very much enjoy the woman you've become, and I would hate to see the world deprived of what only you can offer it."

Did she know?

About France? About Phoebe Moon?

About what Merry had done with the Mrs. Claus diamond? "Wow. I forgot how mushy we get the night before you get married."

"I was actually thinking how lovely it is that you're talking to me before this wedding. Such an improvement over my first three."

"So is your choice in grooms."

"Now we simply have to find you a nice man who's not a jeweler."

"I thought you admired my independence."

"I do, but you're depriving me of beautiful grandbabies."

"How could I possibly raise a baby when I can't even raise my parents?"

"For that, I'm taking away your maid-of-honor gift."

"Hey! I let Richard ogle my rack for that cheese basket."

Mom snuffled out a laugh. "That poor boy. You can do some of your ninja moves on him after the wedding tomorrow."

Max would love watching that.

And the idea of his eyes going smoky and intrigued by her self-defense moves made Merry warm and tingly in all the right places.

She had a ticket to Paris on Sunday. She had an apartment booked just outside Lyon for the next two months. She'd been reading the French-English dictionary on her phone. Her new life was waiting.

But her new life didn't have a Max.

"Meredith, you are not seriously considering doing any ninja moves on Richard at my wedding tomorrow. Promise me."

Merry smiled. "It wouldn't be one of your weddings if it wasn't memorable."

MAX WOKE up late that night to a room with its lights still on, a snoring dog, and a weird feeling about his scale-model Mustangs.

He was also starving.

But stumbling downstairs in the dark to heat up a bowl of soup zapped most of his energy. Halfway through the bowl, he collapsed onto his couch. Scout padded in and curled up on the braided rug beside him. He let his hand drop into her fur, and she nuzzled his arm.

"Good dog," he murmured.

His limbs were heavy, his stomach still sore, and his head oddly empty, but something was missing.

And not just sleep.

Max lay on the sofa and watched the dim shadow of the fireplace grate until his eyes crossed, but he couldn't fall asleep. He'd bought this sofa specifically because he *could* fall asleep on it, but not tonight.

He lifted a wooden arm and fumbled for the phone in his pocket.

She was leaving again.

But she was here *now*, and he wanted to hear her voice. So he dialed her number and listened to it ring on the other end.

"Hello?" Merry answered on a whisper.

What time was it? "Did I wake you?" the frogs in his throat croaked.

"No, I was just wri—working. Catching up on some work."

Max opened his mouth and waited for a brilliant response to come out. "Huh."

"Max?"

"Mmm?"

"You okay?"

"Yeah." He was great. Obviously a charming flirt and masterful conversationalist.

Merry was smart. She deserved a masterful conversationalist. Was that her day job? Her real job? Being smart and witty? She'd be rich if it were.

"Do you need help?" Merry asked.

"No," he said quickly.

Masterful conversationalist? Master of the one-word answer, maybe. Some chicks dug that. Smile and nod and let them talk.

But Merry had never been that girl.

"Are you sure?" she asked.

"Don't want you to get sick." There. Fourteen words. Or…more than three.

Her laughter sparkled and shimmered, and he saw colors flash through his dark living room.

"I have my mother's iron immune system," she said. "Plus, I'm already exposed."

"Mmm."

"Who usually sits with you when you're sick?"

"Don't get sick."

There was that rainbow laugh again. "All right, tough guy. You don't get sick. So who sits with you when you need soup and crackers?"

His mom.

Not that he'd admit that to anyone. "You."

She didn't laugh this time. He shivered in the dark.

Something was wrong.

"I shouldn't be at your house right now," she said softly.

Because she was leaving. Because she only wanted him for his body. Because her father was a jewel thief. "Right."

"Are we…okay?"

For a few glorious hours this afternoon, they'd been perfect. "Yeah."

"You should get your rest. I hear you're still expected at the auction Saturday night."

They'd auction him off even if he wasn't there. "Bid on me?"

He felt her weary sigh as if it had come from the depths of his own bones. "It'll never be that simple."

No, it probably wouldn't. "Read to me?" he said.

She laughed again, and flowers bloomed in his chest.

You got it bad, dude, Zack Diggory's voice said.

"Which book?" Merry asked.

He opened his mouth, ready to say *Phoebe Moon and the Sneeze Snatcher,* but first, it was the most ridiculously unmanly suggestion he could've made, and second, Merry probably didn't have a copy with her. "Anything," he mumbled.

"You want more Phoebe Moon?"

His lips tipped up at the way her words tumbled out. As though she were embarrassed to ask.

"You steal my copy?" he murmured.

"I have an e-reader."

"Yes, please," he said.

"Hold on a sec. Where were we? Oh, right. Phoebe Moon and Spike had just discovered all the grown-ups were going to the hospital for swollen noses since their sneezes were stuck."

Max put her on speaker, dropped his phone to the floor, and rubbed Scout's head once more. He closed his eyes and let her voice carry him off to sleep.

But just before he drifted unconscious, Max had one last lingering thought.

Merry and Phoebe Moon were a lot alike.

No wonder he liked the kids' books so much.

24

Phoebe Moon had crossed mountains and deserts, and now one last obstacle stood in her way:
herself.
—Phoebe Moon and the Secret Sister

A banging ruckus startled Merry out of a dream that dissipated and hung like a mist just out of reach in the fog of her brain. She blinked at the door of her bedroom in the B&B and then at her computer with the cursor still blinking on the original *Phoebe Moon and the Sneeze Snatcher* document. "What?" she called to the door while she rolled out of bed and slammed the laptop shut.

"The wedding's in an hour, Merry!"

Oh, *crapadoodle*. "An *hour*?"

"No, silly, our hair appointment is in an hour." Mom cackled. "But you've still overslept. I saved you a breakfast burrito. Get up, chickadee. Today's my big day!"

Merry shoved her laptop into her luggage, then opened the door.

Mom's pearly whites could've been used to send a distress signal to the International Space Station, and her giddiness could've powered half the town of Bliss.

"I just love wedding days," Mom said.

Wedding days were Mom's Christmases. Unfortunately, she tended to never get exactly what she wanted and always ended up in the return line before the warranty was up.

Merry took the fragile china plate with the breakfast burrito. She needed to call Max, see how he was doing this morning. See if he'd taken care of the Mrs. Claus diamond. "Are you sure you want to do this?" she asked Mom.

Mom kissed her cheek. "Have you ever met a more lovely man?"

Never was the usual answer in their pre-wedding Merry-plays-the-mom routine. "I'd love to someday marry a man who adores me as much as Patrick adores you," she said instead.

Mom's eyes went misty. "My baby's turning soft. Listen to you. It's Matt, isn't it?"

"Max."

"Oh, honey. It breaks my heart to know you can't have the man you love."

"I don't love him. I just happen to know his name."

But you could love him if you let yourself, Phoebe Moon interjected.

Merry waved her burrito at Mom. "I'll be down in twenty, okay?"

"Don't wash your hair. Angelina specifically said no hair-washing."

"Shall I wash my face and brush my teeth?"

"*Meredith.*"

"Just checking. Where's Patrick?"

"At the hotel, coming down with temporary hearing loss after listening to his brother all night." Mom's smile dimmed for a brief moment. "It's too bad all families can't be as lovely as you and I are. No matter, I suppose, since we'll still be on our honeymoon over Christmas. Are you sure you don't want to join us?"

No, she didn't want to join them. She wanted them all to join her in France instead.

Except Daddy.

Unless he honestly, truly, really could give up his misguided ways. "Keep inviting me on your honeymoon and I'll wash my hair."

Mom gasped. "Don't you dare." She flicked her hands toward the bedroom. "Get ready, young lady."

"Yes, Princess Bride Mom."

Mom pranced across the hall into her bedroom, and Merry shut herself into her room once more. She dug into the burrito and sent Max a text.

Everything okay today?

She was pulling clean underwear out of her luggage when her phone rang.

An honest smile crept over her lips, even if the leap in her pulse at Max's name on the readout wasn't entirely welcome. "I have two minutes," she said.

"You make an excellent nursemaid, Merry Silver." His voice was gravelly with sleep, but still stronger than it had been yesterday. "Ever thought of changing careers?"

"So you're feeling better."

"Much."

"The auction committee must be relieved."

"I told them you'd be putting in a four-figure bid."

"You did not."

"Highest Dan ever went for was a hundred and eighty-seven dollars."

"Rachel has at least seven hundred in her fund for Pepper to bid on you." The words tasted like a rancid lemon.

"I heard your mother donated."

Merry saw green, and it wasn't the money, and it wasn't the Christmas decorations. "She likes you enough to hope this lifts your curse."

"Not cursed. Just waiting for the right girl to decide to stick around."

Did he mean her? Or was he speaking hypothetically? She

slammed her luggage shut and moved toward her bathroom. "It'll happen one day. You're a good guy."

"Merry—"

"I'm glad you're feeling better today. I need to run. Hair appointments, then makeup, then flowers and pictures and—well. You know. Wedding stuff."

"Right."

He likes you. Like him back, Phoebe Moon said.

"It's at four," Merry blurted. "Not that I can invite you, though you already invited yourself yesterday. Mom has everything planned out for just the five of us. Plus, how would that look? It's bad enough everyone's going to talk about you again after I leave town. You shouldn't have to—"

Shut up, Merry, Phoebe Moon said.

"Anyway." She blew out a sigh. "Thank you for a lovely time in Bliss. I hope you have a wonderful Christmas."

Silence rang in her ear.

Probably just as well. She was leaving Bliss this time tomorrow, and the country this time on Sunday.

"You too, Merry Silver," Max said softly. "Call me anytime. From anywhere."

He doesn't want her either, Phoebe Moon, Zack Diggory said solemnly.

They're both idiots, Phoebe Moon snapped back.

"I—" *I love you.*

A horrified squeak slipped out of her mouth.

How had that happened?

"Gotta go." She pounded on the screen of her phone to disconnect the call, then dropped her head against the plaster wall.

Phoebe Moon was right.

She was an idiot.

DESPITE THE MASSIVE *Dan's Pissed Off* signals bouncing up and down The Aisle, and despite Max's strength still being in hiding, he pushed into With This Ring shortly after noon on Friday.

They'd been short staffed at the store all week, so Max figured it was his familial duty to get in there and take care of anything he could.

Like appeasing his older brother.

He stopped in the doorway to Dan's workroom and let the doorframe support him. "Busy day?"

Santa wouldn't have scowled at his elves like that, but then, Dan only played Santa a few times a year.

And, unfortunately, that was a Gramps-approved scowl.

"Been sitting here all morning wondering why I'm being just as big a dumbass as you," Dan said.

Max pulled the door shut and propped himself beside the microscope. Not what he expected his big brother to say.

Dan glowered from his perch at the center table. "We need to fix this."

That was more like it. "Fix what?"

Dan set his tools aside and wiped his forehead with his apron. "You need to tell the staff."

"She's leaving in two days. Let her mom get married in peace."

"If her father's in town—"

"She would've told me." Wouldn't she? Something tickled Max's brain. *Had* she told him that yesterday?

Dan looked more constipated than convinced.

"I wouldn't put the store at risk," Max said quietly. "Our staff is well-trained. Security is top-notch. You want me to call McGraw and tell him, see if he wants us to pull the ring off display, I'll do it. But Merry puts us no more at risk than we were already for having the Mrs. Claus diamond here in the first place."

"He's thinking about selling it," Dan said.

Max gripped the table. "You told him."

"Talked to him after the alarms went off the other night." Dan sliced another *you should've told me* glare Max's way. "I haven't told anyone about your Merry problem."

"She's not—did you say *anyone*? You didn't even tell Rachel?"

"Olivia has an earache, Ty has his Christmas program tonight, and Rach volunteered to organize a toy drive in Gavin's class. Not to mention the time she's put into raising funds for Pepper's pity bid for you tomorrow night."

Because Merry wouldn't be here to bid on him. And he was a fool for wishing she'd stay. "McGraw say why he wants to sell it?"

"New woman? Midlife crisis? Who knows. He sounded more unhinged than you are."

"Thanks."

"He wants it to stay on display for now." Dan snorted. "Probably hoping it *does* get stolen."

"More notoriety, higher sale price," Max muttered.

"Or insurance money. Either way, we look like the idiots."

"We can take it off display for a few days. Tell folks it's being cleaned or inspected."

"You want to pull the Mrs. Claus diamond three weeks before Christmas?"

Considering the traffic the ring brought in during the holiday season, it was a dumb move. "No, but if you're going to be hung up on who Merry's father is, then maybe you need to."

Dan turned back to the emerald necklace on the table before him. "Go home, Max. Still look like shit. I'll handle the ring."

Max didn't want to go home. He wanted—

He wanted Merry to have a different father.

So she could stay.

So she *would* stay.

Max pushed off his perch and opened the door. "Fucking curse," he muttered.

"Curses aren't real," Dan intoned behind him, copying Zack Diggory in his head word-for-word.

Curses might not be real, but it sure as hell felt like bastardly Uncle Sandy was out to steal Max's love life.

BY QUARTER TO FOUR, Merry's hair was shellacked in place, her makeup flawless enough to emulate Mom's Botox, and her red halter-top maid-of-honor dress was expertly displaying her boobs, which thankfully drew attention from the tightness in the waist.

Mom was in a gorgeous green gown, her short silver hair tucked into a wreath, her makeup more flawless than Merry's, her heels sparkly red. Her poinsettia bouquet matched the velvet ribbon tied around her waist, and she was wearing a perfume that smelled like Christmas cookies. She peered at herself in an oval mirror in the corner while Degas ballerinas watched her from their spot on the ivory-papered walls.

The only thing missing today was the serenity Mom had worn to all her other weddings.

"Mom? You nervous?"

"I've had six perfect weddings, Merry. Am I really lucky enough to have the seventh go off without a hitch?"

Who was this woman, and what had she done with Merry's mother?

Or had Mom seen Daddy?

Come to think of it, where *was* Daddy today?

"Aw, look at you." Merry squeezed Mom's hand, since hugging would risk compromising their flowers or dresses or makeup or hair. "I think being nervous is actually normal."

Mom huffed. "Don't be ridiculous. I'm not nervous."

"In any case, you're beautiful, and your wedding will be perfect. And if not, at least it'll be memorable."

The pine wreath on the door to the elegant bride's room jiggled when the door opened. Zoe stepped inside. "You ladies ready for the photographer? She wants to get some mother-daughter shots before the ceremony."

Some shots turned out to be closer to a hundred, but the Lilac Mills Chapel was gorgeous with Mom's poinsettias accenting its exposed beams and soft light, the photographer was a fun woman barely out of college, and she had an infectious enthusiasm that reminded Merry of Phoebe Moon.

That's Phoebe Moon, The New York Times *bestselling character, to you, missy,* Phoebe Moon said.

Maybe Merry would tell Mom once she was settled in France.

Or once Mom got over the shock of Merry moving to France.

When the photographer was done, Zoe ushered them back to the bride's quarters. "The justice of the peace is on his way. I'm so sorry for the delay. He had a...personal issue."

Mom stood stiffly beside the carved wood love seat and fanned herself with a wedding program. "A personal issue?"

Hope it's not your daddy, Merry, Phoebe Moon said.

Zoe's cheeks went scarlet. "He had to stop by the ER for stitches after lunch."

"This is a bad omen," Mom whispered.

"Oh, no. It's a *good* omen." Zoe tried to smile. "He, ah, had an accident with his zipper after his, ah, noon appointment. With his wife. And what's Bliss about if it's not about rolling with the punches in the name of marital bliss?"

Huh. Even Daddy couldn't have planned that.

"I need to sit down," Mom said.

"He's coming," Zoe said. "Right now."

"So soon again?" Mom murmured.

Zoe's cheeks went from scarlet to maroon. "I mean, I spoke with him a minute ago, and he's almost here. It won't be long now. And your groom is dying to see you. You're a lucky woman, Vicky. Sit tight. Can I get you a glass of water?"

Mom nodded, and Zoe slipped out of the room.

"Deep breath, Mom," Merry said. "Remember Kimmie? The

cupcake girl? That crazy owl interrupted her wedding, but she's happily married now."

"Yes, well, she still has a few decades to try getting a perfect wedding again."

"Mom."

"Do not take that tone with me, missy. You are not my mother."

"If you don't want to marry Patrick..."

"Of course I want to get married."

"Because it's what you always do? Or because you want to marry Patrick?"

The door swung open, and Zoe hustled in with a bottle of water. The label had been replaced by Mom and Patrick's engagement photo. "Two minutes, Vicky. Everyone's in place. Wait until you see Patrick. He's so dashing in his tux."

Mom took a hit off the water bottle, then stood. "I'm ready."

And two minutes later, Merry stood at the entrance to the chapel with her small bouquet of poinsettias while "Carol of the Bells" played over the room's speakers. Two wooden church pews sat on either side of the aisle, and Patrick, handsome if a little flushed in his tux, beamed at her from his place beside the justice of the peace.

John stood behind him, looking as happy to be here as a crocodile would be in Antarctica. Richard twisted from his spot on the front bench to peer at her legs.

But it was the dark-haired linebacker in a suit on the other bench that made her knees nearly buckle.

Max was still pale, his movements slow when he turned to smile at her, but when his aquamarine gaze landed on her, firecrackers lit up in her heart.

She couldn't have stopped smiling if she'd wanted to.

She held his gaze for the short walk up the red carpet that had been rolled over the wood aisle, only breaking eye contact when the music changed to Mom's favorite song, "Canon in D."

Max stood and looked to the back of the room. Mom stepped into the arched doorway, lifted her chin, and spread her lips in her bridal smile.

Patrick breathed out a small gasp.

And Merry said a silent prayer that Mom would make it all the way up the aisle.

That she'd let Patrick love her.

That she'd love him back, heart, mind, and soul.

Merry slid a glance at Max.

In his profile, she could see his lips were turned up, his eyes soft. She wasn't used to seeing Max still, or even in his suit often, and suddenly she wanted to see him in a tux.

Standing where Patrick stood.

Losing his breath at the sight of his bride.

Merry losing her own breath at the idea of him being hers.

She blinked quickly, steadying her breath.

Mom stopped beside Patrick. Merry dutifully took her bouquet, and her mother turned and gripped Patrick's hands.

"Vicky, you look—" Patrick's voice broke.

Max smiled softly at Merry.

And for that moment, she was the girl she'd been a year ago. Happy. Optimistic. Brave.

Except this time, Max knew her worst secrets. He knew about her father. He knew about the fake Mrs. Claus diamond ring. He knew her mother was a serial bride and that Merry herself had done some fairly reprehensible things in her life.

Yet he was still here.

Smiling at her.

Believing in her.

France would still be there next week. Or the week after. Or—

The door to the chapel banged open, and six uniformed police officers burst in. "Meredith and Victoria Silver," the first one said, "you're under arrest for the theft of the Mrs. Claus diamond ring."

25

The rain fell in sheets, battering the old tin shed where Phoebe Moon huddled beneath her threadbare blanket. This rain didn't smell like rain.

It smelled like Uncle Sandy's laboratory.

—Phoebe Moon and the Sinister Cloud

Time went into slow motion. The police moving through the room at the speed of snails. Max's neck twisting, bringing his head to face Merry, his lips parting, surprise and denial battling betrayal in his beautiful eyes. Mom's arm reaching out, a barrier between Merry and the cops.

Even Phoebe Moon spoke in slow motion. *Oooooh noooooooo.*

"What?" Patrick said.

"*What?*" Mom said.

Patrick straightened and stepped between Mom and the police. "Gentlemen, there's been a mistake."

Zoe hustled after them down the aisle. "A big mistake," she echoed.

"No mistake," the lead cop said.

"Excuse me, but we're getting married," Patrick said.

Another cop snorted. "Wouldn't do that if I were you."

Max was still gaping at Merry with disbelief and a total lack of comprehension. "The Mrs. Claus diamond?"

Something metal clinked around Merry's wrist. Then her other wrist. She vaguely realized she was shaking her head. "No," she said. "But I—"

"*Quiet*, Meredith," Mom commanded.

"Officers, *stop*," Patrick said. "Vicky, Merry, don't say a word. Not a word. I'm calling my lawyer right now. *Quit manhandling my bride.*"

"Max—" Merry said.

But he seemed just as bewildered as she was.

"I told you they were trouble," John boomed.

"I could go for some jailbird action," Richard said with a wag of his brows.

Matching bright red spots appeared high on Max's cheeks. "Merry?"

"Max, it's a mistake. Tell them. Tell them what I told you."

"Meredith, *be quiet*," Mom ordered again.

Max gaped at Merry as though he had no idea what she was talking about.

This wasn't happening. She hadn't stolen the diamond. She'd *saved* the diamond.

"Did you set your alarm?" she gasped.

"Did I…?"

"Set. Your. Alarm."

"*Merry*," Patrick said.

The cop behind her was talking, something about her rights, being silent, attorneys, courts of law.

"Max, set your—"

"Merry." Patrick stepped between her and Max. "Please, honey. Please be quiet until we figure out what's going on." He touched Mom's cheek. "We'll get this straightened out, Vicky."

Merry blinked back at Max, but all she saw was his retreating back.

The policeman gave her a firm shove, and while her instincts shrieked for her to fight, to shake him off, to run, instead she followed Mom's lead and let herself be pushed out of Mom's wedding in handcuffs.

ADRENALINE WAS the only thing keeping Max upright when he stormed through the crowd gathered on the sidewalk outside With This Ring. He banged on the locked door.

Dan looked up sharply from a conversation with a cop beside the Mrs. Claus diamond display case. He sent Max a withering glare, then turned his back.

Fuck.

Max hadn't eaten a full meal in almost two days, and he was sweating unnaturally beneath his suit. Despite the frigid December temperatures, a coat was too hot.

But he still marched around to the rear door of With This Ring and let himself in.

A tear-streaked Rachel met him at the back door. "I didn't know," she whispered. "God, Max, I didn't know."

"Why the *fuck* did my girlfriend just get arrested at her mother's wedding?" Max snarled.

"Because she switched the Mrs. Claus diamond for a fake," Dan said.

He stepped into the short hallway between the offices, wearing his pissed off with a righteous indignation that made Max want to punch him.

"The hell she did." No. No. That had been a dream. A hallucination. She hadn't. She wouldn't have—

"We have it on video, Max."

"I'm so sorry, Dan," Rachel said.

Dan grunted. "Once again, it's not your fault we didn't know who we were dealing with."

"There's no way—" Max started.

"The real ring was there yesterday morning. But today? Today, I find *this*." Dan thrust the Mrs. Claus diamond at Max.

Max didn't touch it.

He didn't have to.

Even without taking it, he could see that the setting wasn't the work of art Gramps had designed. It was an impressive replica, but the platinum didn't bend right and the snowflake tips weren't perfectly symmetrical.

And the diamonds—they weren't diamonds at all.

"Merry didn't do it."

"Her mother dropped the real ring," Rachel whispered. "Merry picked it up. It was my fault. She wrote a big check for Pepper's bidding fund, so I let her try it on. And I—I didn't look closely when I put it away."

"No."

"You need to leave," Dan said.

"*No*." She wouldn't have. Merry wouldn't have switched the Mrs. Claus diamond.

She wasn't her father. She was running away to France to get away from her father. She'd been robbed herself, and she'd accepted it as punishment for the way she was raised.

Or had she told him everything he'd wanted to hear so he would believe her?

She wasn't a psychopath.

Was she?

"The cops have a few questions for you when you're feeling up to it," Dan said. "We told them you'd been sick. But you won't have long, Max. This is a fucking disaster. For all of us."

Max turned on his heel and banged out the back door.

A disaster?

Nope.

This was worse.

THIS WASN'T REAL. If Merry didn't open her eyes, she couldn't wake up, and then this couldn't be real.

She was sleeping at the B&B. Mom's wedding was still hours away. The Mrs. Claus diamond was safe at Max's house. No, check that. Daddy had never made a fake Mrs. Claus diamond, and Merry hadn't switched them yesterday. And she had just broken through that plot complication that had backed Phoebe Moon and Zack Diggory into a corner.

It's okay, Merry, Phoebe Moon said. *Max will save us. How swoony will that be? Saved by your hunky boyfriend?*

He's not coming to save us, Phoebe Moon, Zack Diggory replied. *He should've stopped the cops back at the wedding. Merry's screwed.*

Merry grunted and squeezed her eyes tighter.

She should've saved herself. She should've refused to come to Bliss. She should've explained the situation herself to the cops, but who would believe the daughter of a jewel thief? And where was Patrick's lawyer, and why hadn't the police tried to question them yet?

Dastardly Uncle Sandy laughed his evil laugh, and Merry pressed her hands to her ears to shut him up.

It didn't work.

"Merry? Sweetheart, it's going to be okay," Mom said. "Patrick's lawyer will have us out of here in no time."

Would he?

Because she had done it.

She'd stolen the Mrs. Claus diamond.

She was guilty.

"I'm sorry about your wedding," she whispered.

She still couldn't open her eyes. Couldn't look at Mom, still in her beautiful green wedding gown, sitting in the next cell over, steel bars separating them.

"I'm…simply sorry," Mom whispered back.

Merry couldn't hide forever. She forced her eyelids to move, even if she refused to acknowledge the gray ceiling, the fluorescent lights, and the cobwebs in the corner. Her feet hit the concrete floor, and she faced her mother. "Did you see…?"

Mom's hesitation was answer enough.

She'd seen Daddy too.

"I didn't say anything about your trip," Mom said.

"My…trip?"

"Were you going to say goodbye?"

She *knew*? Merry peered around the jail, looking for listening devices or peeping LEOs listening in and taking notes. Being overheard talking about fleeing the country wouldn't help her case here. "Mom…"

"I've always known you'd go one day. But I kept hoping you'd tell me. And then you seemed so taken with that handsome young man, even though we both know he'd be a horrible temptation for your father, I thought maybe you'd change your mind and stay."

If only Daddy had been a plumber. "There will never be a way for us to have a happy ending."

"Once this is behind us—"

"*No*. No, Mom. What happens the first time Daddy hears we had a fight? What happens when Max hurts me, even accidentally? What would happen if we broke up? *Daddy* would happen. Daddy's *always* waiting to happen. I don't work in medical billing anymore. I have a good job. A *very* good job that I'm amazingly good at. Did you know *that*?"

Mom's lips parted, and she blinked.

"You don't know, because I can't tell you. What happens if I have a professional spat with someone?" Merry hissed. "What would Daddy do then?"

"Oh, Merry…"

"So what choice do I have if I'm ever going to give you grandchildren?" She didn't mean to let her voice crack. But she couldn't go ninja on her vocal cords to keep them in check. "I want to be normal, Mom. And I can't do that here."

Not that she'd get a chance to be normal anywhere now.

What was the penalty for stealing a famous diamond ring?

And why hadn't Max said anything when the cops showed up?

"Merry, we could talk to your father—"

"He won't change. You know it and I know it. Mom, you could've married Patrick. He's normal. He's mentally and emotionally healthy. He's dependable. He's head over heels for you. *Why* don't you let yourself love him back?"

Mom picked at the velvet ribbon around her waist. "Are you asking me that about Patrick, or yourself that about your Max?"

Her Max.

You're not your father, he'd said. *You're my Merry*, he'd said.

He'd forgiven her. He'd made love to her. He'd let her back in, time and time again this week. But he'd still walked away at the very moment she needed him the most. "If he were my Max, we wouldn't be here."

"Oh, Merry." Mom sighed again. "Come here, my sweet girl." She reached through the bars separating their cells.

And because Mom was everything she had in the world, Merry went to the bars and hugged her back.

26

"But would you have come if I'd told you he was my uncle?"
"I guess we'll never know, will we, Phoebe Moon?"
—Phoebe Moon and the Missing Sunshine

One year ago

Max pulled up to his house Thursday night, half hoping Merry would still be there after she'd come down to Bliss last night.

And a good night it had been.

All she needed was an internet connection to work, right? Since she hadn't called, texted, or emailed to say she was home yet, maybe she'd decided to hang out one more night. Eat some more cheese, watch him tinker with Trixie to figure out where that odd noise was coming from, make love to him all night long…

But his garage was empty.

So was his house.

Huh.

Maybe she'd left late and got stuck in traffic. Her apartment in Chicago was only ninety minutes away.

Errands, then? She might've been low on groceries.

He grinned to himself.

Or cheese.

He dialed her number, then waited for the phone to ring while he filled Scout's food bowl.

After half a ring, the tinny recording of the phone woman came on the line. "We're sorry, but the number you have dialed is not in service. Please check the number and try again."

Max pulled his phone down and peered at it for a moment, then hit Merry's picture to dial her again.

Same message.

Odd.

He tried a text.

It bounced back.

Had she forgotten to pay her phone bill?

Her car was an old beater—had Max missed the signs she was having money trouble?

Was that why she always paid in cash?

He opened his email and typed out a message.

Just checking that you made it home safely. Give me a call.

He shut his email down and changed his clothes, then headed out to see Gran and Gramps for a few minutes before dinner. Rach had invited him over for steak, and Olivia was itching to start that next Phoebe Moon book.

On his way into Dan's house, he pulled up his email.

His message to Merry had bounced back.

Undeliverable.

He tried her number once more—computers could be glitchy—but it was still disconnected.

Hell, maybe it was his phone. He dialed Dan's house phone while he walked into their house.

Three kids darted past him to lunge for the phone while he listened to it ring through his cell phone, then he heard the echo of their argument bounce in his ear.

So it wasn't his phone.

Rachel appeared in the doorway. "Max? Everything okay?"

He hadn't said much about Merry—too many people were always waiting for the other shoe to drop in his relationships, thanks to the ridiculous Golden Bouquet hex he supposedly had—but Dan and Rach had figured out he was seeing someone. "Nope. All good," he lied.

His pulse had sat firmly in the worried zone all through dinner.

After dinner, he read the first two chapters of *Phoebe Moon and the Stolen Sound* to Olivia, bought two more bags of Cub Scout popcorn from Ty and Gavin, then headed home.

Max still couldn't get a call through to Merry.

Two more emails to her bounced back.

Scout whimpered by his bedside all night long while Max lay there, telling himself he'd be able to reach her tomorrow.

He wasn't worried because he was in love with her or anything. This was a normal worry for a friend.

A friend he liked.

A friend he missed.

A friend who was completely and totally out of reach.

He would've called one of her other friends to check in on her, but he didn't know who her other friends were.

Did she have family? She'd mentioned moving around as a kid, but she hadn't said if her parents were still alive. And she was an only child.

Wasn't she?

He still couldn't reach her on Friday.

By Saturday morning, he'd had enough. So he hopped in Trixie and headed up to Chicago.

When she didn't answer her door, he went to the police. Heart in his throat, his hands shaking so badly he almost couldn't shift.

Something bad had happened.

He pushed through the double doors of the local precinct closest to Merry's house and approached the desk.

A uniformed guy with a mustache and round cheeks looked up. "Morning. How can we help you?"

"I haven't been able to get in touch with my girlfriend since she left my house two days ago," Max said.

The older guy's dark eyes said he'd heard this story before.

"Her phone's disconnected, her email's bouncing, and if she's home, she's not answering her door."

Wasn't often Max felt like a creep, but this guy's flat stare made quick work of questioning everything from his sexuality to his capability of hurting a woman enough to make her want to disappear. "You sure she wants to talk to you?" the cop said.

"She's not sending me to voicemail. Her phone's disconnected." Max held up his own phone and hit Merry's picture, then turned on the speaker so the cop could hear the phone lady's recorded message himself.

The guy squinted and held out his hand, twitching his fingers. "That her picture?"

"Yes. Merry. Merry Silver. Short for Meredith. I think."

He hadn't paid that much attention.

They hadn't been serious.

But Max got a punch in the gut every time he thought of never seeing her again.

He rattled off her address for the cop, but the guy was busy typing something into his computer. Two grunts later, he twisted the screen so Max could see it.

"This girl?"

It was a grainy picture, more than a few years old, but those were definitely Merry's eyes. "Yes."

"Wouldn't want to be found either if Nicholas Raymond was my father," the cop said.

Every molecule in Max's body turned to ice.

"Nicholas Raymond?" he repeated.

"Suspected jewel thief. Heard of him?"

Everything narrowed until Max's entire life was one little pinprick of light at the end of a long dark tunnel. "No. No, that can't be right."

"Son, you missing anything valuable?"

Other than his heart?

Max gripped the edge of the desk.

He didn't know.

Merry wouldn't have—she couldn't—not *his* Merry.

"Haven't been able to reach her in two days, you say?" the cop said. "Suppose that warrants a look. Got an address?"

And suddenly an address wasn't all he had.

He also had questions.

Doubts.

Fears.

And a sudden all-too-real belief in curses.

27

"You were supposed to be the good guys," Phoebe Moon cried. The two ninja shared a glance. "Good and right are not always the same."

—Phoebe Moon and the Ninja Hideaway

Present day

The first thing that struck Max when he banged into his house was that he'd forgotten to set the alarm.

The second was that Scout didn't come running.

Set your alarm, Max. I changed the code.

He softly latched the door, then set the alarm code. It beeped, echoing over the wooden floors in most of the house. "Scout?" Max called. He whistled.

Her joyful bark answered from the backyard.

Max made his way slowly to the back door. Nothing seemed out of place, but then nothing about the past two days was right. Too many weird dreams, too much Phoebe Moon, and then watching Merry get arrested—nope. Nothing was right.

He flipped on the back lights. Dusk was settling, and there were too many shadows. "Forgot I let you out, girl," Max murmured to Scout.

She happily trotted inside and went straight for her food bowl.

His dog was fine. He was fine.

But Merry wasn't fine.

He fed Scout, then considered feeding himself, but decided his stomach wasn't up to the kind of liquid diet he had in mind to close the day out.

That dream yesterday—it *had* been a dream. Hadn't it?

An itchy, unreasonable suspicion pulled his shoulder blades back. He made his way to the stairs, his stiff legs protesting each step, then climbed to his bedroom.

The sheets were still rumpled from where he'd tossed and turned most of the past two days. He worked his tie with shaky hands. Eating was probably a good idea.

But what was Merry eating in jail tonight?

Not her mother's reception dinner. Or the wedding cupcakes.

He eyed his model cars.

She'd said something about his cars. While he was beating himself up for dreaming that she'd steal the Mrs. Claus diamond, she'd been talking. About his cars.

He tossed his tie on the bed. Let his suit jacket follow. His stomach grumbled a protest, but Max bent over the wood and Plexiglas case housing his model Mustangs.

The trunk on the '72 model wasn't flush.

Max wiped his palms on his shirt, then reached behind the case to unlatch the hinged top. He lifted the cobalt blue '72 Cobra and opened her back hatch.

Empty.

But the movement made something rattle in the passenger cabin.

"Holy shit, Merry," Max muttered.

What the hell had she been thinking?

He finagled the ring out of the passenger seat. Hadn't held it in his hand since Merry disappeared, because he hadn't wanted to. The metal band was cool in his fingers, the diamonds real, the setting smooth, polished art.

Merry wasn't Phoebe Moon, but she'd pulled a trick straight out of the teenager's handbook.

What else had she said? After she told him she stole the ring, what else had she said?

The paranoia over the alarm made sense now. And changing the code—*had* she told him that her father was in town?

He had to call Dan. Get the ring back to the store. Talk to Merry. Talk to the police.

"Don't usually like to do things this way, but my daughter didn't leave me much choice. I'll take that now."

Max's fingers curled around the ring while he turned to face his intruder.

An older man stood in the doorway in a tan suit with a black dress shirt beneath it. His hands hung at his sides, a smirk playing on his lips, a farce of a gentlemanly apology lingering in the eyes he shared with his daughter.

He carried no visible weapons, and he was a head shorter than Max, but if Merry had taught him anything, it was never to underestimate anyone.

Was she in on this?

Or had she truly been trying to keep the ring safe?

"How'd you get past my dog?"

"Sweet girl. She likes chicken."

Motherf—"You have to the count of three to get out of my house, and I'm calling the cops."

"You mean *or*?" Nicholas Raymond said.

"No, I mean *and*. But if you'd rather have a seat and talk about how a father's not supposed to fuck up his daughter's life while we wait, we can do that too." Damn hard to dial a smart phone while keeping one eye on the danger in the room though.

Raymond took a seat in the corner chair and crossed his ankle over his knee. "I staged the robbery I pulled her into last year so she'd disappear. I have enemies. They threatened her."

Max thumbed the nine on his screen. "Nice story. You still belong behind bars. Which is where your daughter currently is, if you hadn't heard."

"Good. She's safe there. Her mother with her?"

Max grunted and double-tapped the one.

"Merry gets on that plane to France on Sunday, Whitey Burgess is going to follow her, and I can't do a damn thing to protect her after that. So you can give me the ring so I can take it to him, he'll call off his owl, I'll turn myself in, and Merry goes free. Or you call the cops now, try to get that ring back to safety yourself, and if we're lucky, you'll wake up in a hospital bed instead of the morgue. You feeling lucky?"

No, Max was more on the nauseous side of the spectrum. "Whitey Burgess is in a maximum security prison for killing an armored truck guard."

"Whitey Burgess Junior. Bloodthirsty gnarger."

It pains me when common criminals use Phoebe Moon's words, Zack Diggory intoned in Max's head. "Haven't heard of him," Max said.

"You wouldn't. How he gets away with it. And he's ten times as mean as his father."

"Enough." Max hit Dial and put his phone to his ear.

Raymond's foot dropped to the floor. He leaned forward, forearms on his thighs. "I know Merry thinks I'm the bad guy, but I've been clean for three years. I wouldn't be here if I didn't have to do it. For her. I'm asking nice. Give me the diamond, she doesn't get hurt."

If Merry were truly in danger, Max would've surrendered the ring without hesitation.

But Nicholas Raymond was a thief. A liar. He'd broken into Max's house—his grandparents' house—and now he was spouting stories so he could make off with Gramps's most prized engagement ring. "Merry's damn good at taking care of herself."

"Phone's not ringing, is it?"

A chill prickled Max's neck. Raymond was right. His phone wasn't ringing. "It's ringing."

"You're a bad liar. Whitey's getting impatient. Hand over the diamond."

Max's fingers tightened around the ring until the setting pressed into his skin. This was all a game. A setup. A ruse.

But what if it wasn't?

Max was getting Merry out of jail as soon as her father was gone. He'd talk to Spencer McGraw and make Dan drop the charges. He'd make this right for her.

But what if she was honestly in danger?

"I know you did your research, Mr. Gregory. So I know you know I play a harmless game. Things are just *things*. Not worth getting hurt over. I also know you know I don't make a habit of visiting with people whose wealth I'm redistributing. Would've preferred to find what you found for me before you got here, but I didn't, and I can't wait any longer." He stood. "If I'm not walking out of here with that diamond, they can wheel me out on a stretcher."

"You gonna hit me?"

"If I have to." His steps were steady, but while the lines at the corners of his lips and eyes hinted at a lifetime of laughing—probably at his victims' expense—his body seemed weighted down, his cheeks too weathered, his intentions reluctant. "My little girl—she's not like her mother. Not like me. Did too much wrong by her over the years, and I'm paying for it now. Likely lost her forever. But I'll be damned before I let my sins hurt her again."

"Like she's hurting by being tossed in jail for trying to keep you from doing this?"

"Would've kept her there all week if it'd been an option. She'll get out. Live a good life. Might not ever forgive me, but she'll bounce back. Heard you're good for her. So are you going to be the man she needs you to be and hand over that ring, or are you going to put both of you in danger? That ring what her life is worth? Couple million dollars? You willing to risk it?"

Max didn't stand down when the old man stopped inches from him. He still had the ring in one hand and his phone in the other. It beeped—call failed. No service.

"He's coming for all of us," Nicholas Raymond said.

Max couldn't stomach the thought of *this* man near Merry, much less some faceless, lurking enemy. She was strong. She was smart.

But she was still only human. Could she battle a man coming at her with a knife? With a gun?

If Max didn't give her father the Mrs. Claus diamond, was he putting her in danger? What if Max gave Nicholas Raymond the ring, and then the bad dudes wanted something else? "When does it stop?"

"Tonight." Raymond dragged a knuckle over his brow. "That bastard threatened my daughter. His reign ends tonight. But I can't get to him without the ring."

Max's fist clenched around the diamond. Downstairs, Scout growled, then barked.

Of everything Gramps had done in his life, he'd been most proud of this ring. The shop as a whole. The family.

And Max was about to betray them all.

"So help me, if Merry gets hurt, I'll hunt you to the ends of the earth and make you pay." He shoved the ring at Merry's father. "Go," he snarled.

Raymond tucked the ring in a pocket, and before Max could blink, he was gone. Out of the room, down the steps, banging through the front door.

"Scout!" Max yelled.

His dog bounded up the stairs.

Moments later, the house alarm went off.

And Max had full bars on his cell signal once again.

"*Dammit.*"

Whitey Burgess Junior hadn't been here with a cell signal blocker.

Merry's father had.

And Max had fallen for it.

Two hours later, Max was politely shown out of the Bliss Police Department after giving his statement. He was almost back to Trixie when he heard his name.

"Max! Max, wait."

Did it count as being jilted if a guy's bride was arrested at the altar? Even Bliss didn't have guidelines on exactly what to call that. Either way, Patrick wasn't enjoying the wedding night he should've. Max turned and nodded to him.

Patrick huffed to a stop. "They're saying Vicky's first husband is a jewel thief. It's not true, is it?"

"It's true."

"But—" Patrick slumped against Trixie's door. "You knew?"

Max was too drained to worry about the bro code on this one. Too drained and too worried about Merry. She should be out. Max had given his statement. He'd told the story to Spencer McGraw, to Dan, to the cops again. McGraw had said he didn't want to press charges. Even Dan had given up his arguments for her incarceration.

"I knew," Max said to Patrick. "Take it you didn't."

Patrick's breath huffed out in abbreviated white puffs. "Vicky didn't—she didn't say much about any of them. I guess it didn't matter. It shouldn't matter."

Max clapped the older man on the shoulder. "Been there, man."

"You knew, and you still..."

He nodded. He knew, and he *still.*

And he probably would forever.

Merry was smart. She was funny. She was pretty. But she was so much more.

Sexy. Intriguing. Compassionate.

All despite the way she'd been raised. Or maybe because of how she'd been raised.

"I still would too," Patrick said to the dark sky.

Max clamped his jaw shut. Vicky had had how many husbands? Patrick was facing insurmountable odds for a long and happy marriage if she was still his choice in brides.

"Might make me as big a fool as my brother says I am," Patrick continued, "and I know she probably has more secrets, but I love her. She makes me feel alive. What kind of man offers a lady his hand and then abandons her when she needs him the most?"

"Not the kind of man I want to be," Max said quietly. And so he'd be here as long as it took. He didn't know exactly why she took the ring. He didn't know if she was still planning to go to France. He didn't even know what her real job was. But he understood why she had trust issues, and she wouldn't ever let him in if he didn't prove he was worth it.

"You love her?" Patrick asked.

An owl hooted nearby. Max's whole body went rigid. He scanned the sky, but no white winged creatures swooped in. "Never loved a woman before," he said to the stars. "I'm furious with her one minute, worried sick about her the next, and then I wish it was still yesterday, stomach bug and all, just so she'd be there feeding me soup and reading me stories. Is that love?"

"Pretty good case of it, I think."

Max was starting to think so too. "You staying till they're out?"

Patrick nodded. "You?"

"Damn right."

Headlights cut the darkness, and the soft sound of a hybrid engine whirred to a stop behind them. Rachel and Olivia climbed out. "Max, I'm so sorry," Rach said.

Again.

Wasn't her fault though. Max should've told them about Merry's dad sooner. Or he shouldn't have told them at all. If Dan hadn't known, would he have looked closer at the Mrs. Claus diamond display? Would Merry have mentioned the ring again to him?

She wouldn't have let it sit there in his display case forever.

Would she?

"I brought you food," Rachel said. "The kids love applesauce sandwiches when they start feeling better after having the sickies."

"Applesauce sandwiches are gross," Olivia muttered.

"They're delicious."

Max was leaning toward siding with his niece here. "Thanks, Rach." He pulled Olivia in for a hug, because she was seven, and seven-year-old girls were incapable of judging their uncles for falling in love with daughters of jewel thieves.

He hoped. "Shouldn't you be in bed?"

"Ty's play went long, and then Gavin said Amber Finch is really a computer because no one has ever seen her and the newspaper people can't find her. Amber Finch isn't a computer, Uncle Max. She's my favorite author in the whole wide world, and she's real, and she's going to write me back a letter and sign it with a real pen and probably give me lots of books for telling Gavin he's a gnarger."

"Olivia, we don't call people gnargers," Rachel said.

"Phoebe Moon does."

"Yes, and Phoebe Moon is thirteen, and she has to deal with evil Uncle Sandy and his nefarious plans all the time. You are seven, and you live a very comfortable life."

Unlike Merry, who grew up in a constant state of flux and whose father was definitely a gnarger.

Whoa.

Wait.

Merry, whose father had called a fellow thief a gnarger tonight.

Merry loved to read, and she said her father inspired that, but would Nicholas Raymond read kid books?

Was—no. No, that was crazy.

But Zack Diggory drove a sixty-nine Charger. Bright red.

The exact car Max had told Merry he'd buy to give Trixie a sister.

"Olivia, Uncle Max is right. It's past your bedtime." Rachel handed Max a brown bag. "There's a banana and Pedialyte in there too. Call me if you need anything else. Dan said your parents should be home tomorrow too. I'm so sorry, Max."

A lone siren rang out in the distance, and a chill slithered down Max's spine.

Too much drama tonight.

"Thanks for the sandwich," Max said to Rach.

"I hope it helps." She kissed his cheek, a guilty smile making a rare appearance. "We want you healthy as you can be tomorrow night. If you're still willing to participate."

"Wouldn't miss it." His heart wouldn't be there, but the rest of him would be.

Rachel and Olivia climbed back into the car, and Max was once again alone with Patrick. "Applesauce sandwich?" Max offered.

Patrick shook his head.

"Me neither. Think they'll let us wait inside?"

"Worth a try."

And if he were lucky, they'd let him mooch off their Wi-Fi while they waited. Because Max had his phone, and he had an outlandish idea playing out in his head.

If he couldn't talk to Merry, he could Google his suspicions to death while he waited.

28

The gorge loomed deep before Phoebe Moon and Spike, with dastardly Uncle Sandy's minion monkeys bearing down behind them.

They were in serious trouble now.

—Phoebe Moon and the Stolen Sound

The clink of metal and the swoosh of a door pulled Merry out of a fitful sleep. "Ladies," a young officer said, "you're free to go."

She sat up on the thin mattress and blinked at the harsh lights. Free? They were free? But she hadn't even been questioned yet. Neither had Mom.

They'd been fingerprinted and had their mugshots taken. They'd had to surrender their personal belongings and jewelry. But they hadn't been questioned.

Patrick must have some amazing lawyers, because Merry was guilty.

She'd taken the ring.

Or maybe Max had straightened everything out.

Heat flooded her face.

She'd stolen from his family. Done what she thought was best for everyone, without regard to the law or to the implications for Max.

She was no better than Daddy.

It didn't matter where she went in the world, she would never be normal.

Mom hustled out of her cell, dress swishing, heels clicking, and snapped her fingers. "Let's go, sweetheart."

Merry didn't deserve to go. She was a nuisance.

Still, she trudged behind Mom and the cop, her dress swishing, her feet oddly achy for how much she hadn't been on them this afternoon. They gathered their personal items, then silently followed their escort to the front of the station.

Max sprang to his feet from the ugly cushioned couch beside the front door. Like Patrick, he was still in his suit from the wedding. His complexion was ragged, his suit rumpled, his eyes a soft blue, stark against his pallid cheeks and haunted with questions. *Why? How? What next?*

Merry ducked her head and continued toward the door.

"Vicky! Vicky, honey, are you okay?"

"Oh, Patrick, it was awful. Just *awful.*" Mom collapsed against him. "I'm so sorry, darling. And on our wedding day. I'm never getting married in Bliss again, that's for certain."

Merry's fingers curled into her palms and more heat flushed her neck. Mom and Patrick would've been married by now if it weren't for her.

But if they were being set free, the Mrs. Claus diamond must be safe now.

"Merry?"

More questions in Max's voice.

And what was she supposed to say? *Had a lovely time in jail. Thanks for sticking up for me back there. Have to run—I'm not fit to exist in this society.* She shook her head and pushed out the door.

"Merry." Max kept pace with her. "Stop a minute."

"No." But she drew to a standstill in the chilly black night.

She had no car. No coat. No idea how much of her stuff was left at the B&B. How much the cops might've gathered as evidence.

Oh, *no*.

What if they'd taken her computer? Oh, jeez, the search history on that should've kept her in jail for another month. Thank God they probably hadn't cracked her password yet.

Or was this a setup? Had they let her go so she could lead them to Daddy?

"You brought me the ring yesterday," Max said. "I thought it was a dream."

"Stop talking."

"Merry—"

"Stop. Talking." She was stupid. She got it. Life wasn't a Phoebe Moon novel. And whatever Daddy's job was, it wasn't over yet.

Her bones never lied about Daddy's jobs.

It wouldn't have mattered if she had told Max the truth. If she'd given him the ring a week ago. If she'd given it to Dan and Rachel yesterday. If she'd burned the damn thing, or if she'd mailed it to Max next year.

Daddy had a job, and he wouldn't quit until it was done.

"I saw your father."

She whipped around to face Max.

Headlights passed over his face, illuminating his solemn eyes, his downturned lips, his still-pallid cheeks. He dangled his suit jacket from two fingers, offering it for her bare shoulders.

But not touching her. Because he knew she'd lay him out flat if he tried, or because he didn't want to touch a woman who deserved to be behind bars? A woman whose father was a menace to the world?

"I gave him the diamond," Max said.

A tremor rumbled in her core. "No."

Max was one of the good guys. The law-abiding, *normal* guys.

"He told me you were in danger. That if he didn't get the ring—"

"No."

"Merry—"

She held a hand up and backed away.

"Merry, I love you."

No. *No*. This wasn't happening. "Love can't fix this, Max. You don't even know me. And now you're helping my father?"

"I'm not so sure he's the bad guy here."

No, she was the bad guy. Because she was the one who'd freaking stolen the Mrs. Claus diamond. "He wasn't the good guy either. And you're still a jeweler, and I'm still the daughter of a jewel thief."

"He wasn't stealing it for himself. I *gave* him the ring."

"And now you're an accomplice in the theft of the most important diamond in your family's history. I don't want you to steal things for me. I want you to be safe. I want you to be the upstanding, right-side-of-the-law guy you were before you ever met me. Before you knew who I was. You can't go back. You can never go back. But you can at least not make it worse."

Mom and Patrick stepped out of the police station, Mom in theatrics, Patrick wide-eyed but *there*.

Being a good guy.

A guy who hadn't been tempted to aid and abet a petty jewel thief. Who hadn't fallen for a stupid story her father had made up in desperation to get his hands on one more score.

"Go live your life, Max," Merry said. "Call the cops on jewel thieves. Date normal women with normal families. And don't ever talk to me again."

"Merry—"

She turned around and walked away.

"Amber!"

Every cell in her body seized. Her breath whooshed out, and the mouthful of frigid air she tried to suck back in hit her lungs like a sucker punch. She ordered her legs to move, but her feet wouldn't lift and her knees wouldn't bend.

He knew.

He knew her biggest secret.

Phoebe Moon and Zack Diggory and even dastardly Uncle Sandy were *hers*. Amber Finch was the one thing Daddy couldn't destroy.

But only because he didn't know about her.

Max had seen Daddy. If he told—

"Do not *ever* call me that," she breathed.

She shot a look back at the doorway where Mom was still moaning to Patrick about their jail time. Max had crept up on Merry. She glared at him, her voice low. "You have no idea how hard I've worked to make sure no one can take this from me. Daddy can't steal Amber's jewels. He can't take Amber's friends. He can't destroy Amber's life. I swear to God, if you ruin her for me, you'll wish stealing the Mrs. Claus diamond was the worst thing I ever did to you."

"Does Amber have friends? Does she have jewels? Does she have a life?"

"Shut. Up."

"Why can't you trust me?"

She could turn around, close her eyes, lean back, and he would catch her.

But Merry didn't need anyone to catch her.

She caught herself.

And if she fell, she'd fall by herself. She wouldn't take anyone down the way Daddy always did. She wouldn't be Mom, so hung up on needing someone to fall on that she kept falling for the wrong men. Merry would catch herself.

She was the only person she could rely on.

And look how well you did that today, Phoebe Moon said.

"Shut up," Merry muttered again.

"Stay," Max said. "Trust me. Give me a chance. Give *us* a chance."

She couldn't catch her breath. Her whole body trembled.

She trusted her father would forever be a jewel thief. She trusted her mother would forever be stuck in a cycle of marriage and divorce. She trusted she could take care of herself.

But she'd never trusted another soul with her deepest secrets. And she didn't know if she could be trusted with anyone else's.

She also didn't trust she could be the woman Max deserved.

She couldn't be the woman *any* man deserved. She didn't know how to do anything beyond protect herself.

Why prolong the inevitable?

"I'm going to the airport," she said. "I'm not going to France. I don't know where I'm going. But it's not here."

"I'll go with you."

"No."

"I can—"

"No. *No*, Max. No means no. And I mean no. Leave me alone. I don't want you in my life. Not now, not ever." She shoved his chest, the contact sending electric sparks down her arms and short-circuiting her heart. "How many times do I have to say it?"

She didn't want to go.

She wanted to stay. With him.

But how could she? She was a morally ambiguous middle-grade novelist with a messed-up family. If people here liked her, they'd like her for Amber Finch and Phoebe Moon. If people here never learned to like her, Max would lose all his friends. Probably his family too.

God. What would his family think of him giving Daddy the Mrs. Claus diamond? What would *everyone* think of him dating the daughter of a jewel thief?

"Phoebe Moon must be so disappointed in you," Max murmured.

Pretty much, the teenager in her head said.

Merry's teeth clenched, but she still forced two more words out. "Go. Away."

Max watched her a moment longer. She stared him down.

And when his shoulders slumped, she almost slumped too.

Fucking curse, the wind whispered.

He cast his eyes downward and turned away, his head shaking slowly. "I'll miss you, Merry Silver. Take care of yourself."

She sucked her lips into her mouth and forced the tears back behind her eyeballs.

This was for the best. She'd made the right call. For both of them.

Mom had apparently finished her tirade to Patrick. She stepped to Merry, swinging a look between her and Max's retreating backside. "Where's Matt going?"

"I stole his family's pride and joy, Mom. Where do you think he's going?"

Patrick gasped.

"Meredith, not in front of the police station."

"Ms. Silver and Ms. Silver?" A guy in a dark suit, a five o'clock shadow, and doom in his eyes slid out of a black SUV and approached them. "A minute, please."

"We've been held prisoner in this godforsaken place long enough." Mom marched past him. "If you want to talk, you can call my lawyer. Patrick, take us home."

"You're Nicholas Raymond's daughter?" the man said to Merry.

She put her head down and limped on her heels to follow Mom, lips once again clamped tight.

A badge flashed in her vision, but not a police badge. "Special Agent Cafferty, FBI. Mr. Raymond was assisting us with a case tonight when he was shot. He's in surgery now."

Merry's face whipped up. "*What?*"

"I have a car waiting to take you to the hospital."

No. First of all, Daddy wouldn't work with the FBI. And on the off chance this guy was telling the truth, Daddy certainly wouldn't be able to keep it a secret. Secondly, he didn't do guns, and he valued his own hide too much to put himself in a position to come face-to-face with a weapon. "I think you have us confused with another family."

"Ms. Silver, your father approached us approximately fifteen months ago when one of his colleagues made a threat to your well-being."

Mom stopped moving. Her complexion went gray. "Merry's father was injured in the line of duty?" she whispered.

"Yes, ma'am."

"Is he—how serious is it?"

"We're waiting for word from the doctors, ma'am."

Merry's palms itched. Her legs were heavy as dried concrete, and she couldn't swallow past the rocks in her throat.

Trixie's engine roared to life on the other side of the parking lot. The pit of Merry's stomach hit the pavement.

Either Daddy had fooled the FBI too, or he'd been telling Max the truth.

And if he'd been telling Max the truth, Max had probably been in danger too.

And now Daddy could—he might—Merry wrapped her arms around herself and stifled a sob.

"If you'll come with me, ladies, I can take you to the hospital."

Patrick looked down at her, then reached a hand out to Merry. "Which hospital? I'll drive them."

"Sir—"

"With all due respect, Agent Cafferty, law enforcement hasn't exactly been kind to my ladies today. *I'm* driving them."

"Thank you, Patrick," Mom whispered.

"Did you get the bad guy?" Merry said.

Agent Cafferty lifted a brow. "Both him and his owl. You'd still be in jail if we hadn't. Safest place in town since we couldn't fit you in a PO box." The agent nodded to Patrick. "Stay on my tail and don't stop for lights."

Merry's feet moved, and moments later, they were on their way to hold vigil for Daddy and wait for news.

29

"Why do you do it, Uncle Sandy?" Phoebe Moon cried. "Why can't you just be good?"

"My dear, there's no reward in being good."

—Phoebe Moon and the Secret Sister

The winter sun was too bright and happy for Max's mood, but since he couldn't stop the sunshine—he wasn't bastardly Uncle Sandy—he put on a scowl and his darkest sunglasses, made two quick phone calls, then loaded Scout up in the car.

Thirty minutes later, Lindsey showed him into a brightly lit living room in an old farmhouse tucked up out of the way a few miles outside of Bliss while Scout happily played outside with Lindsey and Billy's dog.

"Heard you've had quite a week," Lindsey said.

Max grunted and handed her a bag. "For the baby."

She lifted out a copy of *Phoebe Moon and the Secret Sister,* one of the six books in the series Max had picked up at the bookstore on his way. "Olivia loves 'em," Max added. "So do my nephews, but they won't admit it in public. Guess it'll be a few years before your baby's old enough to understand, but…"

But every kid needed a copy of Merry's books.

She studied him curiously. "That's so sweet. Thank you."

"Ask you something?"

"Sure."

"You believe in curses?"

She was supposedly a psychic matchmaker. If *she* didn't believe in curses, then Max would give them up too.

Her blond hair tilted, and she put a hand to her baby bump. "I believe in love."

"Love trumps curses any day, you ask me." Billy strolled into the living room with a brown hat on backwards and his flannel shirt open over a T-shirt with one of his album covers on it. He shook Max's hand. "How you holdin' up, man? Sit on down. Get you anything to drink?"

Max shook his head. "Just stopped by to tell you I'll do the car."

"Yeah?"

Max nodded. "Looking forward to it. Been a dream for a long time to restore old cars."

Billy grinned. "Know a thing or two about dreams."

So did Merry, apparently.

She was fucking *Amber Finch*. That whirlwind mind of hers had crafted vibrant characters and incredible stories. *Art*. Bestselling, critically acclaimed art. Max would never again be able to read Phoebe Moon to Olivia without hearing Merry's voice. She put herself, her life on every page for the world to see and judge. She'd gotten some amazing reviews, but also some pretty horrific ones that made him want to throat-punch someone.

But she kept writing. Kept telling her stories. Kept putting herself out there until a huge national newspaper suggested she was a computer instead of a flesh-and-blood person, since all her books were copyrighted to a company owned by another company in the Caymans, the owner of which even *The New York Times* hadn't been able to uncover.

If she could succeed and make a life of her own in a difficult profession without any support from her family, without anyone knowing it was her, while intentionally hiding that it was her, then what excuse did Max have not to take this opportunity to restore the old Charger for Billy?

"Got most of the parts," Max told Billy, "but if you want anything custom, we'll need to get on that now."

"Nah, not for the Charger. But I'm getting this idea—"

"Oh, no, you're not," Lindsey interrupted.

He flashed her a smile that made Max's heart hurt. "Shoot, lawyer lady, I can afford two cars."

There went Max's butterflies. One car was a hobby. Two was getting close to career material, especially with a big name like Billy Brenton behind him. Billy wasn't known for his love of cars, but he had several million fans and followers on social media. Three words from Billy could have Max in business for two years.

At least.

"Afford two cars for yourself?" Lindsey said. "Yes. Scare your wife half to death driving like Max does? No."

Billy wrapped his arms around her and rested his hands on her belly, and the butterflies in Max's stomach turned into something closer to rancid milk.

No means no, Max. I don't want you in my life.

He'd offered her everything despite her father, and she still didn't want him.

"I'll drive safe," Billy said. "Promise." He glanced at Max. "Can you get one of them latch systems for car seats in an old car?"

"Probably. Have to look into it."

"Thanks, man."

"Max?" Lindsey said. "Everything okay?"

No. He was lonely and tired and slightly lost. "Yeah. Long week."

"Heard about your excitement last night," Billy said. "Merry doing okay? And her dad?"

Max didn't give a jewel thief's ass about Nicholas Raymond. And he didn't want to talk about Merry. "Wouldn't know."

The lovebirds shared a look, and Max's jaw clenched shut.

"Seemed like you liked her," Billy said.

Liked her didn't touch it.

But he'd proven to her time and time again that she could trust him. He'd listened to her. He'd let her back in his house, in his life, in his heart. He'd told her he loved her. He'd guessed her biggest secret. He'd surrendered his family's most prized possession for her.

If that wasn't enough, then he'd just go back to enjoying the luxury of having a cursed love life.

Far better than having a broken heart.

"Your family giving you shit?" Billy asked.

"They're leaving me alone," Max replied pointedly.

At least, he was ignoring them since the texts had started flowing in this morning with speculation about his going price in the bachelor auction tonight going way up, thanks to him being a hero.

The FBI's official and unofficial statements on the arrest of Whitey Burgess Jr. and his attack owl had mentioned the younger son of a prominent family connected to the Mrs. Claus diamond ring finding the stolen article and providing it to the authorities to assist in their sting. It hadn't mentioned Merry and her mother being arrested at the wedding or that her father had been involved or that he'd been shot.

But no one could remember a time when there had been a crime in Bliss worse than someone's yard getting flamingoed. Since the Bliss gossip express was decked out and running in all its Christmas glory, everyone knew Max was the *younger son* mentioned in the paper.

"You're still in the bachelor auction tonight?" Lindsey asked.

"It's for a good cause."

Rachel had over seven hundred in donations for Pepper to bid on him. Maybe going out with someone equally cursed was a good idea.

Lindsey reached out to touch his hand, seeming on the verge of saying something, but then she shook her head. "Hang in there, Max," she finally said.

Billy nodded. "It'll work out. 'Sides, can't appreciate the good if you don't go through the bad."

True enough.

But Max was about done with the bad.

At least he had a car to look forward to.

PATRICK WAS some kind of superhero.

He'd been in the waiting room down the hall from Daddy's room most of the night, occasionally stopping in to ask if Mom or Merry needed food or coffee or tissues, then making himself scarce while they continued to sit by Daddy's bedside, waiting for him to wake up.

Daddy's shoulder was bandaged and his arm immobilized in a fancy sling contraption. An oxygen line was taped beneath his nose, and Merry could count the veins in his eyelids.

He was so pale.

So very, very pale.

The doctors said he'd lost a good deal of blood and a part of his shoulder blade, but the bullet had missed his vital organs and made a clean exit. He'd been lucky, they said.

He'd live. Probably with minimal long-term effects.

"I always feared this day would come," Mom whispered shortly after Patrick had delivered a fast-food breakfast of egg muffins and yogurt cups.

"That he'd be hurt, or that he'd be caught?" Merry asked.

"Both."

In going to the authorities, Daddy had put himself in a position of having to answer for his own crimes. According to the FBI agent, Daddy's job with Whitey Burgess Jr. initially had had nothing to do with the Mrs. Claus diamond. But when the bastard had spotted her with Max last year, he'd decided to go for it too. Daddy had stalled him, working smaller jobs for Whitey to try to get enough evidence to get him tossed in jail with his father, but it hadn't been enough, and Whitey had given Daddy a deadline.

And now Daddy was strapped into a hospital bed, recovering from a wound he'd gotten to protect her.

Mom hadn't sat still since they'd arrived. She stood, she sat, she stood again. She looked out the window, and she went pale when she eyed the police guarding Daddy's room.

But she kept looking toward the door.

"Patrick would come in and sit with us if you asked him," Merry said.

A blush crept into Mom's smooth cheeks. "That would be awkward."

"Your entire love life is awkward."

The blush went deeper. "Remind me again why you sent that nice Matt away last night?"

Oh, she zinged you good! Phoebe Moon crowed.

Forget being a crazy cat lady. Merry was a crazy lady with voices in her head. And when she died, the voices would go with her. Unlike the cats.

You're so morbid, Phoebe Moon chided.

"Mom, I'm not built for relationships."

"Meredith—"

"I don't have Cinderella dreams. I don't need a man to make me feel fulfilled. Not that there's anything wrong with that. But having a man isn't for me. I like taking care of me. I like not sharing. Maybe someday I'll change my mind, but right now, I want to be alone."

Liar, Phoebe Moon said.

Yes. Yes, she was.

"You always were so strong," Mom said. "But, sweetheart—"

Daddy grunted. His head rolled to the side and a grimace crossed his features. His eyes slowly blinked open.

"Nicholas? Sweet—Nick, are you awake? Merry, call the doctor. Your father's waking up."

Daddy lifted his head, then his shoulders. He winced. His brown eyes slid from Mom to Merry, and a weak but classic Daddy smile spread over his lips. "So a guy has to get shot to see both his girls at once?"

"Not funny," Merry said.

"And I'm not your girl." Mom blinked as though she were surprised with herself, then glanced at the door again. "I'd slug you for what you put us through, but I'm not your girl, Nicholas Raymond. I'm…I'm my own girl. Just like my daughter."

"Merry-berry, your mother's adorable."

"And you're jacked up on morphine." Mom went to the door and said something to one of the guards, then crossed her arms and took up a position looking out the window.

"Safe now, my little girl," Daddy said. "So sorry I put you in danger. Did that owl hurt you? Never wanted to strangle an animal like I wanted to strangle that one. Damn FBI's planning on retraining it to help them."

"I'm fine, Daddy."

"I'm sorry I got between you and the Mrs. Claus boy too. Seems like a decent fellow."

The sting was back behind Merry's eyelids. "Hush. You need to get better."

A nurse came in, and Merry and Mom stepped outside while she took Daddy's vitals.

Patrick stopped his pacing at the end of the hallway and looked at them.

"He's a good one, Mom," Merry whispered.

Mom dashed a finger at her eyes. "He is, isn't he?"

"Daddy's not good for either one of us."

"Oh, Merry, your father always loved you more than he loved anything."

Merry cast a wary glance at the two guards outside her father's room. "Not more than he loved his job."

"That's a sickness, sweetheart. And he's beating it."

Maybe today. But what about tomorrow? "You should take time to be yourself, Mom. But don't cut Patrick out. There's not another Patrick in the whole world."

"Nor another Max," Mom murmured.

"Shush. We're having a Merry-as-Mom moment, not a Mom-as-Mom moment." And Argentina sounded like an interesting country. Her Spanish was almost as good as her French. She could count to ten and say *please, thank you,* and *where's the bathroom* in both languages.

And it was far, far away from here.

Mom wrapped her arms around Merry. "I'm going to lose you, aren't I?"

Merry's throat clogged. "I'll call."

"I'd rather you just stay."

Before they'd been arrested, Merry would've given in to wishing the same.

But today, all she wanted was to go away and pretend Bliss didn't exist.

Pretend Max didn't exist.

Someday he'd make a nice, normal, trusting woman very happy.

But that woman wasn't Merry.

She didn't know how to trust, and she didn't want to be normal.

30

"Would you do it again, Phoebe Moon?" Zack Diggory said. "Even knowing what you know now?"

—Phoebe Moon and the Missing Sunshine

After a three-hour nap at the B&B Saturday afternoon, Merry showered, changed into jeans and a soft gray sweater, then started packing.

Her computer was safe. Her notebook was safe. Daddy was recovering. Mom was—

Mom was good, actually.

She'd asked Patrick if they could date a while longer before planning their next wedding.

Merry had expected Mom to cut him loose and throw herself into planning Daddy's future if the FBI got him a deal, or into planning Daddy's defense if they didn't. Instead, when they'd left him at the hospital to get his rest, Mom had wished him well and told him to stay out of trouble, because his daughter still loved him, much as he didn't deserve it.

No histrionics. No drama. No hints—thinly veiled or obvious—that she had another man in her life or that she needed to make Daddy jealous or herself feel better for having a man who worshipped her despite what he did or didn't know about her.

"You're keeping Patrick?" Merry had asked Mom when they returned to the B&B for some rest.

"You were right," Mom replied. "He's still here. Despite everything, he's still here. Perhaps we'll try to get married again one day, but for now, we're going to see if I can find who I am outside of being a girlfriend, fiancée, or wife. And Patrick...he's okay with waiting." Mom shook her head, a wondrous sort of bafflement in her smile and an odd glow in her eyes. "I'm an expert at getting married, but I've forgotten how to simply love."

Was that Merry's problem?

That she didn't know how to love? That her love was inferior? Or insufficient against the extra challenges and baggage she carried in her life? Was she afraid that one day, she would do the same as Mom and move on to the next new and exciting thing, leaving a stunned, perfectly adequate man behind?

Or was she terrified she'd be the one left behind when he got tired of the complications of her life?

Life would be so much easier if she could go back to that time when she'd been happy being on her own.

Except her heart hurt at the thought of never knowing Max.

So she made herself think about Phoebe Moon and the sometimes misunderstood Uncle Sandy—but not Zack Diggory—and folded her clothes, cleaned her toiletries from the bathroom, and zipped up her luggage.

She had her passport. She had all her earthly belongings that she cared to take. She had her ticket to Paris and a credit card to pay the fees to change her ticket to wherever she wanted to go when she got to the airport. Australia, maybe. That was good and far away. Or maybe Japan.

Maybe she'd stay long. Maybe she wouldn't.

But she couldn't stay here.

She'd stay a town or two over until Daddy was released from the hospital and his fate was decided, but she didn't want to stay in Bliss, where everyone knew her. Where everyone knew what her father did.

Where everyone would soon know about Amber Finch?

She opened her door and came face-to-face with the older, softer version of the man she was running away from.

"I won't take long," Dan said. "Spencer McGraw asked me to pass along his thanks for your handling of his ring."

Merry blinked. "Seriously?"

"Good publicity, apparently."

Ah. That made sense. Sales of his Mrs. Claus diamond ring book would probably skyrocket, thanks to renewed interest and scandal surrounding the piece. "He's welcome," she said dryly.

Dan's lips twitched, and her belly flipped.

She'd miss Max's smile. "If that's all, I need to—"

"Who are you?"

Her heart stuttered. Had Max told his family? Did they know she was Amber Finch? Was her secret out? "I'm sorry?"

"Max told me who your father is, and I reacted...as you might expect. But he's rather enamored with you. He's never been a bad judge of character, and my wife has suggested that it must be difficult to make friends when people react to your relatives the way I did. So. Who are you?"

She slowly closed her mouth.

Who *was* she? Not the daughter of a jewel thief. Not Amber Finch. Not the daughter of a serial marrier. Who was Merry Silver?

"I'm a woman about to miss a flight."

Merry Silver is a chicken, Phoebe Moon said.

Don't insult chickens, Zack Diggory chided.

"I hope you're not leaving because of anything we've done here in Bliss," Dan said.

"No, you've all been very nice. I just..." She trailed off, realizing *I just have to run away from myself* wasn't something she wanted to admit to anyone.

Max knew about her father's thievery. He knew about her mother's list of ex-husbands. He knew her darkest secret and her biggest secret.

But he'd stayed by her side until she ordered him to leave.

"I've never seen my brother tied up over a woman before," Dan said. "I won't deny I would've wished better in-laws for him, but I also don't want to stand between him and his happiness."

She felt as though carbonated water was fizzling beneath her skin. "I stole from your family."

"As my wife has pointed out—repeatedly—you moved an endangered piece to what you believed to be a safer location with the intention of foiling a known threat. Never mind that we have safes and top-notch security in the store and a trustworthy, upstanding police force at our beck and call. However, as my wife has also repeatedly pointed out, you were in a tough spot, and we were virtual strangers."

Not entirely an apology, but then she hardly merited one.

Dan shook his head. "I don't care if Max gets married or has kids or works at With This Ring, but I care that he's happy. And right now, he's not happy. If that matters to you." He looked as though he wanted to say more but instead he turned away. "Best of luck to you, Merry."

The stairs creaked when he walked away. When the door to the B&B opened a minute later, Mom peeked out of her room. "He seems like a nice man."

Merry shrugged. "It's like a law or something to be nice in Bliss. Unless you're the police and you're arresting someone."

"It would be a nice place to live." Mom's eyebrow almost twitched. "If you're not on the receiving end of being arrested here. Again."

And that was all that needed to be said on the subject.

"If your father and I weren't here, what would you do?" Mom asked.

"You and Daddy are here. Both of you. For which I'm infinitely grateful, though I appreciate you each in your own individual ways."

"Meredith, I don't want us to be a hindrance to your life. If you want to stay, *stay*. I want to learn who I am, but if I haven't figured it out in my thirty-six years on this earth, I may never learn."

"Mom, you're fifty-eight."

"Hush. It's far more important to me that you get one chance to be happy than for me to work on it one more time. So if you need me to keep obstacles out of your way so that you can stay here, I will."

Merry narrowed her eyes. "Are you suggesting you'd get back together with Daddy?"

Mom's shudder was instantaneous and actually caused a real wrinkle in her forehead. "Dear God, no. It's taken thirty of my thirty-six years on this planet, but I think I've finally outgrown him." She sagged onto her wood-paneled door. "I think I'm actually falling in love with Patrick," she whispered. "It's so odd—he's not really my type at all."

Crapadoodle. Merry couldn't go to Australia. Mom couldn't handle being single by herself. "Maybe the last thirty years have finally been good for you," she whispered back.

"And maybe the next thirty could be really good for you. You were such a sweet, happy girl once. I wish I could wave a magic wand and give that back to you."

"Magic isn't real."

"Just something to think about." She gestured to Merry's luggage. "You're not leaving yet, are you?"

"The B&B needs my room. I'll be close though. For a little bit."

Mom smothered her in a hug. "Be brave, my little Merry," she whispered. "Be brave, and be happy."

Could she?

What if Max got hurt? What if his family got hurt because of her?

But what if they didn't?

An odd sensation prickled her belly and spread through her chest, a blood-pumping adrenaline rush coupled with something else that had always been just out of reach.

Hope.

She'd already stolen Max's family's most prized possession. She'd been arrested at her mother's wedding and tossed in jail. She'd sat at her father's bedside, waiting for him to wake up after being shot.

Could life get any more difficult?

And if it did, did she want to face it alone when she could have Max holding her hand to face it with her?

And what about Max?

Who would be there with him to hold *his* hand the next time he faced a disaster?

Life isn't always a disaster, Merry Silver, Zack Diggory intoned.

And your pessimism is a real drag, Phoebe Moon agreed. *Can you please just go take a leap of faith already?*

Maybe. Just maybe, she could.

Despite Rachel's suggestion—echoed by the entire bachelor auction committee—that Max wear board shorts, his sash, and a Santa hat when it was his turn to be bid on, he strolled onto the stage on stiff legs in a suit and his elf hat. He wanted to go back to bed. He had to suppress a yawn as the emcee, CJ Blue, read his stats. And when CJ jerked a *show your wares* look at him, Max's left knee cracked and his stomach gurgled. But he stepped up dutifully, flexing his arms beneath his suit jacket and twisting so the ladies could check out his ass.

CJ snickered. "Let's start the bidding at—"

"One hundred dollars!" cried one of the women who'd asked Max about his role in capturing the dastardly jewel thief and his attack owl during the social hour before the bidding.

"Sure, we can start with a hundred," CJ said.

The crowd laughed, and he called for one fifty, which came easily.

Rachel hovered next to Pepper Blue—no conflict of interest there with Pepper's brother acting as auctioneer—and nudged Pepper to bid. "Three hundred," Pepper called.

Pepper was nice enough. Solid job, good reputation in Bliss, relatively new in town. She busted her ass for the Knot Fest committee, volunteered at the pet shelter, and had an abnormally large number of sisters, but they were normal sisters with normal occupations and normal parents.

She probably had a sense of humor, and she was probably adequate in bed, and she probably also had an eccentricity or quirk or two that would drive him crazy, but he was cursed.

He was bound to never find the perfect woman.

"Five hundred!"

Jeez. The blonde from—where was she from? He forgot. But she'd been too giggly during social hour, and she'd kept eyeing his crotch like that was all she wanted from him.

All Merry had ever asked of him was that he go away and not die.

"Seven hundred," Pepper countered.

Rachel was starting to sweat. She signaled someone at the edge of the ballroom. Max caught sight of Kimmie Kincaid and Pepper's sister-in-law combing through their purses.

"Seven fifty," the blonde yelled.

"Seven fifty…two?" Pepper said.

"Seven seventy-five," Rachel hissed.

"Eight hundred," the blonde said.

Max Jr. went into hiding.

It was one night. One night of his life to pretend to enjoy a woman's company. All the money was going to a scholarship fund for kids who had lost a military parent.

He could do this.

"Eight twenty-five." Rachel was holding Pepper's bidding card now, squeaking and sweating, and, if Max wasn't mistaken, looking around to make sure Dan didn't know how much she was bidding.

But Max hadn't seen Dan tonight.

"Nine hundred," the blonde said.

Probably her daddy's money, Zack Diggory's voice helpfully suggested.

Rachel shrugged helplessly.

"We have nine hundred," CJ said. "Going once…"

The blonde smiled at Max, then licked her lips.

Oh, hell no. Max wasn't going home with that woman.

She wasn't Merry.

None of these women were Merry.

Max lifted an aching arm. "One thousand dollars!" he yelled.

The room went silent.

After a long pause, CJ spoke. "Dude, I don't think you can bid on yourself."

If Merry wouldn't, then Max would. And since Merry wasn't here, he didn't have a choice.

He didn't want a night with the blonde. He didn't want a night with Pepper. He didn't even want a sympathy prime rib with a side of chocolate mousse from Rachel.

He wanted to watch Merry try to use chopsticks. He wanted to spoon-feed her cheesecake. He wanted to make love to her, then listen to her read him to sleep.

"Why can't I?" he said to CJ. "It's for charity."

CJ covered the mic. "Are you sure you're worth a grand?"

"He's worth far more," a feminine voice in the back called. "But since the woman who thinks so apparently isn't here, I'll put him out of his misery. Five thousand."

Heads swiveled. Another blonde waved a bidding card, this one visibly pregnant and breaking her promise to stay out of Max's love life.

"Ah, Lindsey, does Billy know you're bidding on a bachelor?" CJ said.

"Habit," she called back. "I can't help myself."

"Ten grand," Billy drawled from the doorway. "She can have him, but danged if I'll let her pay for him herself."

Laughter erupted, along with hoots and cheers.

"Ten grand," CJ said. "Going once, going twice—"

"Fifteen thousand!"

The new voice sliced through the room and threw it into surprised gasps that faded to an eerie silence.

Merry.

His Merry was right next to Billy at the door.

Max's knees wobbled.

A murmur stole through the quiet crowd. Heads twisted to stare at her, and the whispers got louder.

Her mocha eyes connected with his, telegraphing sheer terror.

"Does she have fifteen grand?" CJ murmured to Max.

"And how did she get it?" someone else whispered.

"Shut up and close this thing," Max ordered.

Merry was here. Taking one step, then another, and still another, straight toward him.

Whispers of "It's Merry," and "The jewel thief" and "The one who disappeared" swirled about the room beneath CJ banging the gavel to close the bidding.

"Sold, for fifteen thousand dollars, to Miss Merry Silver," he said.

Merry faltered, but Max's legs moved, his feet barely skimming the floor the closer he got to her.

She opened her arms, her eyes watery, her chin wobbling. "I love you," she whispered.

And then he had her, holding her tight, while she gripped him back with all her strength. "I love you," he told her hair. Then her ears. Then her cheek. Then her lips. "I love you. You're my home. You challenge me and you frustrate me and you make me work for it. And I admire you, Merry. I respect you. Look what you've done with your life. With everything you have going against you, look how much you've succeeded. You're amazing. Worth more than any gem in the world. I want to be a man worthy of a woman like you. Give me a chance. Stay. Please stay and let me love you."

"You better love me, because this is freaking terrifying."

"You can do it, Merry. *We* can do it. We're bigger than the fear."

Her breath came out on a hiccup. "I love you, Max."

The crowd was squealing. Max smoothed Merry's dark hair back. "I love you too. And look. They like you too."

She blinked at him, then slowly looked over at their audience.

Every last one of the two hundred women here tonight were on their feet, cheering and clapping and beaming at them. The few men scattered around the room—mostly married—wore rueful, sympathetic, *this is the end of you* man grins.

Merry wrinkled her nose at Max, and a tremor shook her body. "You told them?"

"Told them—" *Oh*. About Amber Finch. "No. *No*. Merry, sweetheart, they like *you*."

A pink flush crept into her cheeks, and tears welled in her eyes. "Oh," she whispered.

"But not as much as I do." He didn't know why she was here, or why she'd changed her mind, but he didn't care.

She was everything he needed. Everything he wanted.

She'd put the *Merry* back in his life.

MERRY WOKE up alone Christmas morning. The spot beside her was still warm, so she knew her favorite Christmas present couldn't have gone far. She rolled out of bed, grabbed her robe, and tucked her feet into the ridiculously adorable bunny slippers Max had insisted any writer living in his house had to have.

In the weeks since the bachelor auction, she'd had moments of panic over staying, but fewer and farther between. Patrick's lawyer was close to sealing a deal for Daddy so he could avoid jail time in exchange for a guilty plea to several lesser charges from his days of crime. He'd have to go to court-ordered counseling as well, though he had his pick of which state he'd seek it in. He was leaning toward Wisconsin.

Mom had threatened Daddy to within an inch of his life if he interfered with Merry's love life.

So had Max.

And Patrick, for that matter.

Patrick had sent Mom on their honeymoon alone, but he'd been waiting when she got back, and now they were taking their relationship slow. Mom was giving up her Botox.

And Merry was working hard on believing good things would continue to come.

Max's belief in her helped.

She crept down the stairs and turned the corner to find Santa Claus putting a present under the tree, with blankets and pillows spread in a makeshift bed between the tree and the roaring fireplace in the living room.

A surprised laugh slipped from her lips. Santa Max quirked a grin over his shoulder at her. "There's a punishment for young ladies who sneak out of bed and catch Santa in action, you know."

"Are you threatening a ninja, Santa?"

"Depends. If I am, will you have to teach me a lesson?"

"Is that what Santa wants for Christmas?" She padded to his side and pressed a kiss to his cheek above the fake beard. "I think I like you as an elf better. There's something sexy about those tights."

"Elves don't have coffee. Or cheesecake for breakfast."

"Now you're really talking dirty." She pulled at his fake beard to give her easy access to his mouth, still thrilled at the combination of smooth lips and rough stubble in his kiss.

"Merry Christmas, love," he said.

Love.

One simple word, now her whole world. She loved Max. She loved Scout. She loved his house. She loved waking up with him every morning. She loved watching him in the garage. She loved arguing with him over dinner. She loved going to bed with him every night.

And she loved letting herself love him.

He guided her to the blankets on the floor, still touching, still kissing. Her feminine parts tingled. "I like this Christmas present," she said.

He treated her to a slow grin the real Santa Claus would've probably found scandalous. "Me too."

She flicked the buttons open on his red fur jacket and ran her hands over the warm, white T-shirt hiding solid muscle beneath. "But I also got you something else."

"Funny. I got you something else too."

He lowered her to the floor. His lips landed hot on her neck, and Merry leaned into the pillows, tilting her head to give him better access. He hovered over her, kissing, sucking, and she rubbed at the bulge in his Santa pants. "You did get me something, didn't you?"

"Another something else." He started to chuckle, but she stroked him again, and he hissed out a breath against her skin. "Upstairs," he gasped.

"I like here." She slipped her hand into his pants.

"Oh, God, Merry."

His beautiful blue-green eyes drifted shut, and his neck arched back while she gripped him and slowly stroked. He was hot and solid and silky, and touching him was making her ache in all the best ways.

"Merry Christmas, Max," she whispered.

"Office," he grunted.

She giggled. "You want to move this to an office?"

"Giving…you…an office."

Her hand stilled.

"Upstairs. Merry, don't stop."

She rolled and pushed him to his back, then slung a leg over him and settled on him with his erection nestled between her legs, her robe gaping open. "You're giving me an office upstairs?"

"Cleaned out the front room." He tugged at the tie on her robe. It parted, and his eyes went a smoky green. He palmed her breasts, rubbing his thumb over her nipples. Sparks exploded all over her skin.

"I'll paint it," he murmured. "Move furniture. Blow up your book covers and have them framed. Whatever you want."

He thrust his hips up into her, and she stifled a moan. "Sugar mama," she whispered.

"You want a sugar mama?"

She arched into his touch and slid against his length. "I'll *be* your sugar mama."

Max laughed. "You're already my sugar."

"Amber wants to buy you a garage."

His hands stilled.

"She has a movie deal in the works," Merry whispered. "And a new three-book contract pending with a significant pay raise."

Apparently sitting on a major bestseller list for three weeks and counting came with other perks besides having her boyfriend lick celebratory champagne out of her belly button.

Max was staring at her.

"But only if you want it," she said quickly. "You can do whatever makes you happy, I just thought—"

"Have I ever told you that you're perfect?" Max caressed her cheeks with his thumbs, then pulled her down for a kiss. "I love you, Merry Silver," Max whispered.

And as Max proceeded to show her just how much he loved her, it occurred to Merry she had accomplished the biggest heist of all.

She'd stolen his heart, and given him hers in return.

EPILOGUE

As soon as Max led Merry to the back door of Bliss's local bookstore on the last Saturday in January, she turned around. "Nope. Can't do it."

"Yes, you can." He gripped her by the shoulders and pointed her to the store.

"Don't push it, Max Gregory. I've laid you out in an alley once before, and I'll do it again."

Her complexion was white as snow except for the bright pink spots high on her cheeks. Her dark hair whipped around her head in the crisp wind. And he felt the tremors in her body even through her coat.

"No white cheddar for you if you don't," Max threatened.

"You're such a gnarger," she muttered.

Voices swelled on the wind from the packed parking lot, and she huddled closer to him. He wrapped her tight and pressed a kiss to her hair. "They already love you," he whispered. "But if you're not ready—"

The back door banged open, and Charlotte, the bookstore's owner, stuck her head out. "Hi, Am—oh. It's you. What are you doing here? Use the front door before you scare her away."

Max checked a snort.

If Merry was bailing, he had to keep her secret a while longer.

But she lifted her head and leaned closer to the door. And Max felt the moment excitement overtook her fears. "Janice?" she said.

A willowy brunette who looked to be about forty-five swiveled to face them. "Amber?"

"No, this is Max and Merry," Charlotte said.

"Rule number eight," Merry said. "You also can't judge a villain by his mustache."

The secret code she had told her agent she'd use when she arrived at the signing today.

"Amber!" The brunette charged the alley, arms held out to grab Merry from Max. "Oh, Amber, it's so lovely to meet you. Come in, come in. Before someone sees you."

"But that's Merry," Charlotte squeaked.

Max grinned at her.

Realization dawned, and Charlotte hauled off and punched him in the arm. They'd grown up together, and Max had a feeling she was the first of many people today who'd be punching him or wishing they could. "*You knew?*" she said.

"Hurt my boyfriend and I'm leaving," Merry called from the doorway.

"Does Olivia know?" Charlotte demanded.

Max shook his head. "Nobody else knows."

"Nobody?"

"Merry, me, and now you. And her agent."

If Max thought it was fun watching one person realize the secret Merry had been keeping, that was nothing compared to the gasps and squeals and then the thunderous applause when Merry was introduced to the crowd packing the bookstore.

Olivia was there, right up front, and she looked on the verge of crying happy tears. Rachel wiped her eyes while she laughed, and she wagged a finger at Max while he stood back and watched.

Locals who had come in just to check things out picked up complete sets of Amber Finch's novels. Merry laughed with her fans.

She smiled. She got excited over everyone's favorite book, favorite scene, favorite character.

She blushed.

Repeatedly.

His Merry, blushing like the girl she'd been when he first met her, but more.

And just when Max thought the day couldn't get any better for her, the best moment of the signing was interrupted by a woman Max had come to know all too well the past two months. She burst into the door and shouldered and elbowed her way to the front of the line. "*Meredith?*"

Merry paused in the middle of signing a book for one of Olivia's friends, and her smile faltered. "Hi, Mom."

"You—you're—this—" Vicky put a knuckle in her mouth, and her eyes welled. "Meredith Cordelia Silver, I am so proud of you."

While Vicky reached across the table, Merry stood and hugged her mom back. "Surprise," she said. Her voice was watery and just loud enough for Max to hear. "I was going to call you later."

"You still are, missy. You have some explaining to do."

Patrick joined Vicky, bewildered amusement twitching his mouth. He nodded to Max. "You knew?"

"Since…that day."

"Remarkably good day," Patrick mused.

It had been a hellacious day, but all had turned out perfectly afterwards.

"I want six of every book," Vicky declared. "One set for me. Sign the rest to any teacher who ever told me you wouldn't amount to anything."

"None of my teachers ever said that."

"Hush, Meredith. Mine did. Let me have my moment."

Max stepped forward to sling an arm around Merry's mom's shoulders. "Vicky, you can have her later. How about you let the little kids have a turn? Come meet Merry's agent. She loves Merry almost as much as you do."

"I discovered her," Janice said with an agreeable nod.

"I gave birth to her," Vicky sniffed.

"Well, thank God for you then. Where would any of us be without you?" Janice steered Vicky and Patrick toward the office. "Cheese? Let me tell you about the movie option Amber just signed."

It was another few hours before Max had Merry to himself again. Back home, he squeezed her once more and pressed a kiss to her cheek. "Have I mentioned you were amazing today?"

Her face lit up when she smiled. "I feel amazing. *Not* hiding is—it's strange, but good."

"So you're glad you went?"

"It's the second best decision I've made in my life."

"Yeah?"

"Yeah."

"What's the first?" He knew, but he wanted to hear her say it.

And she did. "You."

If this was a cursed love life, then Max would take it.

ABOUT THE AUTHOR

Jamie Farrell is the alter ego for *USA Today* Bestselling romantic comedy author Pippa Grant. She believes love, laughter, and bacon are the most powerful forces in the universe. When she's not writing, she's raising her three hilariously unpredictable children with her real-life hero.

Visit Jamie's website at:
www.JamieFarrellBooks.com

THE COMPLETE JAMIE FARRELL BOOK LIST

The Misfit Brides Series

Blissed

Matched

Smittened

Sugared

Merried

Spiced

Unhitched

The Officers' Ex-Wives Club Series

Her Rebel Heart

Southern Fried Blues

Jamie Farrell's Pippa Grant Titles:

The Girl Band Series

Mister McHottie

Stud in the Stacks

Rockaway Bride

The Hero and the Hacktivist

The Thrusters Hockey Series

The Pilot and the Puck-Up

Royally Pucked

Beauty and the Beefcake

Charming as Puck

I Pucking Love You

The Bro Code Series

Flirting with the Frenemy

America's Geekheart

Liar, Liar, Hearts on Fire

The Hot Mess and the Heartthrob

Copper Valley Fireballs Series

Jock Blocked

Real Fake Love

The Grumpy Player Next Door

Standalones

Master Baker *(Bro Code Spin-Off)*

Hot Heir *(Royally Pucked Spin-Off)*

Exes and Ho Ho Hos

The Bluewater Billionaires Series

The Price of Scandal by Lucy Score

The Mogul and the Muscle by Claire Kingsley

Wild Open Hearts by Kathryn Nolan

Crazy for Loving You by Pippa Grant

Co-Written with Lili Valente

Hosed

Hammered

Hitched

Humbugged

Printed in the USA
CPSIA information can be obtained
at www.ICGtesting.com
LVHW050501210624
783560LV00007B/750

9 781955 930055